The Last Scientist

Cassandra Morphy

Chapter One
The Briefcase

Eric

It was raining like there was no tomorrow. The dark skies hid the sun, making it seem like the night had fallen early. The streets, poorly maintained over the past few decades, did little to stop the water from forming a torrent as it flowed down the hill. The city had been sinking even before the world changed, and the expansion south wouldn't save it from being swallowed whole by the lake to the north. The streams that flowed down the roads was just a hint of the flood to come. But this was little concern to the lone figure as he walked along the sidewalk.

The man was tall, easily six feet, though he was hunched in on himself against the bitter cold of the day. His long overcoat was old, ragged, and did little to protect him from the cold winds as they blew in from the north. The coat was grey, though oddly speckled in places as the coloring was uneven. This was due to the coat being bleached with an unskilled hand so that it wouldn't look black. The suit underneath it, pressed and sharp, was a more proper grey, matching the man's hair and eyes. Despite the grey hair, Eric didn't look that old, barely showing his fifty years.

Like many his age, Eric held his rain rod close to his chest, as if it were one of those old umbrellas that no one used anymore. He huddled close to it, trying to stay within the small space that it kept dry. His feet were already soaked, as the rod's radius didn't extend that far down. This was largely due to the fact that it was supposed to be held just above the waste. If he had just strapped the rod to his belt, or kept it in a pocket, it would have been enough to protect him from all but the deepest puddles, or the road itself.

The buildings around him were already crumbling down in some places, though the neighborhood was one of the last to be built with technology. The rain and wind wore away at the stone, making the once vibrant city look like little more than a ruin. Not many came into the city anymore, into any city anymore; fewer still walked the streets. If anyone had bothered to look out the windows, down at the lonely man walking there, he would have stuck out like a sore thumb. They would all know immediately what he was. A normal. A pure blood. A remnant of an old age that no longer existed. Despite this, despite an immense amount of luck that kept him from being discovered, he had been trying to keep a low profile. His mission relied on no one stopping him.

Eric jumped as he saw something flash out of the corner of his eye. He stumbled backwards, away from the buildings, his foot almost falling into the river that the street had become. There was suddenly a poster hanging on the building he was standing next to, one depicting the face of a man, old, his eyes hollow, ashen. Beneath the photo was the man's name, Mark Zecker, and the words "Missing. Last Seen Friday, October 29, 2066." Once he got over the initial shock of seeing something appear out of nowhere like that, he continued down the road to the end of the block.

Eric stopped outside of the building at the corner, staring up at it and the similarly made one across the street. Neither had numbers on them, and the sheet of paper that he had written the address on had long been washed away by the storm. With the river that ran down the road too deep to cross, he hoped that he had the right building. He hoped that he wouldn't need to go swimming in the rain just to get where he was going. The last thing he needed was more stares when entering the bar than he was already going to get coming in from the street.

He took a deep breath, sending out a silent prayer, before entering the building on his side of the street. The door was stiff, solid in its frame, and he thought for one terrifying moment that they hadn't bothered to unlock it. After one last heavy tug, the door swung open. Eric went tumbling backwards a few steps, his left foot sinking deep into the river. Its current threatened to pull him in further, but he managed to keep a hold of the door and used it to pull himself out. He could just barely hear the voices from inside over the cacophonous sounds of the river. As he went through the door, he hoped that it was a good sign. He hoped that there was enough of a crowd inside that his arrival would go unnoticed. Once he entered the hallway, the door slammed shut of its own volition. The sound of it echoed into the hall and the voices went silent for a gut wrenching second before resuming its old volume.

A tall woman was leaning against a desk off to the left, in a small depression in the wall. Her fiery red hair danced in a breeze that didn't exist. She was wearing what would have previously been called a bikini, though the orange outfit was much more common for day to day wear. Despite the chill coming in through the door behind him, she didn't seem bothered by the lack of clothes. Behind her were several rows of racks that were reminiscent of a simpler time. There were only three coats hanging from them, though they all seemed to have been there a while. The moths had gotten to them and they looked like they would fall apart in a strong breeze. An odd smell of cinnamon hit his nose as he started down the hall.

Eric nodded at the woman as he moved to walk past her, but she flicked out a finger. She curled it towards herself in a classic come hither flick, one that had a lot more than the usual power behind it. Eric could already feel it, as ignorant as he was to the ways of the world. He could feel the power behind that finger, and what that power could do to him. He knew better than to ignore that signal.

The woman reached out through the gap above the desk, grabbing onto Eric's tie and pulling him closer. The instant her hand touched him, he could feel heat coursing through his entire body. Steam started up around his legs, flowing upward and warming him up faster than the heat that was coming off of the woman. He could hear his waterlogged shoes start to bubble, though the old leather kept its form and coloring. In mere moments, his soaked suit was dry once more and the sniffles that were just settling into his chest went away.

"Can't have you mess up my perfectly cleaned floors," the woman said. "Care to check the... coat?" She looked Eric up and down, staring at his old suit and tie, the remnant of a lost era, his era. The hot air that surrounded him had flipped open his overcoat, revealing his aged look for her perusal.

Despite the heat of the hall, and looks he was already getting just from the one woman, Eric kept his overcoat in place. He didn't trust it, or the information contained within, to the woman, to anyone. He just shook his head at the woman as he started to head down the hall. As he passed the edge of her area, she gave him a look. It was one of those looks that he had been getting a lot since he came to town. The look that said they didn't think he had any right to be in their world anymore.

Once he passed the entry area, darkness surrounded him. It was only then that he realized there were no lights near the door. The light that had bathed the area just inside the door had come from the woman herself. She still shined in the distance as she stuck her head out from behind the desk, watching him as he headed down the hall. Before he could wonder at that, three people popped out of thin air into the space that he had been standing in. The woman's fiery hair blew out behind her as the displaced air tried to find a home. The cold breeze hit Eric in the back, carrying with it the cinnamon scent of the woman.

The hallway was dark, with just the low glow behind him and a much brighter one ahead. The sounds of the bar flowed down the hall towards him, drawing him further, a siren call towards the light ahead. The walls of the hall, hidden from view, played with his imagination, making the darkness more mysterious and fear inducing than it needed to be. Yet, with the way the world worked those days, danger could be just as hidden in the bright light of day.

When Eric came out of the hall into the bar, he paused there, trying to get his bearings. The three that entered behind him bumped into him as they passed, not even giving a word of apology or outrage as they did so. They laughed, taking no notice of him, as they went over to the bar on his left. There were several patrons all standing by the bar, trying to get the attention of an overworked bartender behind it. Several glasses and bottles were already floating in the air, trying desperately to keep up with the demands being thrown towards them. One bottle got confused and started pouring its contents into several drinks at once, ruining them. It had been an old scotch from the old world, expensive in its own right. The glasses seemed to scream at the bottle, dumping their contents into the large sink in the back before starting over again.

Eric shuddered at the sight of those floating glasses, at the bartender that was barely paying attention to them. He averted his eyes from that scene as he scanned across the tables that filled much of the rest of the room. Against the far wall was a small stage, a lone mic stand positioned in the center, though there was no mic in it. A man was standing on the stage, bowing to the crowd, though none of them were paying much attention to him, let alone clapping. After a moment, he seemed to realize this and departed the stage, letting the next act replace him. Eric paid little notice to the short, blonde woman that started to make her way up the stairs.

Hanging down from the ceiling at regular intervals were chandeliers. Actually, they weren't really hanging down so much as hovering there in the air. They were no longer connected to the ceiling, though the supports for them were still in place. Held in the chandeliers were various light sources, candles, torches, and oil lamps. They seemed to be randomly positioned, with just the lamps around the center. Though the candles would have been burning for hours, there was no sign of any wax dripping down. From what Eric could see of one of the lamps, he would swear that there was no oil in it.

In the far corner, hidden behind the stage, was a man, sitting with his back to the walls. His bright blue coat called to Eric from across the room. As Eric started to make his way across to him, he eyed the other patrons in the place, making sure there were no other bright blue coats. Almost everyone there wore darker colors, mostly blues and greens, with oranges and yellows mixed in. There were a few black coats and one very bright white in there as well. The woman heading onto stage wore a bright blue dress, though Eric knew that she wouldn't be his contact. No, he knew he was supposed to look for a man in a bright blue coat.

Just before Eric came to the table in the far corner, music started to play from the stage. The tune was familiar, though it took him some time to recognize it. The song was reminiscent of the old days, the days of his youth, back before the world had gone so wrong. It wasn't until the woman started to sing the words that he recognized it as "Let it Go", specifically the version from the movie. She was singing into the mic stand, which amplified her voice as if there was an actual microphone in it. As she got to the refrain, she started to flick her hands, much like Elsa had in the movie, sending icicles into the air in pretty patterns. Eric didn't like being so close to the stage, especially with magic being thrown about, but it wasn't his choice.

Eric sat down in the empty chair across from the man in the blue coat. As he did, his foot kicked something heavy under the table. The metal briefcase slid out into the open and the man hastily pushed it back under, hiding it from view. Eric leaned forward, trying to be heard over the music without needing to raise his voice. "Apophis flies beautifully tonight," he said. It was the code phrase that had been agreed upon earlier.

"A bright orange ball that has plagued the sky for far too long," the man said. "You must be Eric."

"Yes," Eric said. "Is that it?" He kicked the briefcase again, pushing it pointedly towards the man.

The man's answer was drowned out by the music as it crescendoed once more. The woman stomped her foot onto the stage, making a huge pillar of ice pop up from beneath her. Despite the extensive show of magical talent, no one in the crowd took much notice of her. No one, that is, except for Eric, who was just a few feet away from the stage. As the ice stretched dangerously close to him, he shrank away from it. The room was already getting colder, though no one seemed to mind much.

"Why did you pick this place?" Eric asked. He scooched his chair around the table, trying to get further away from the mage on stage and closer to his contact. The briefcase slid out once more while he maneuvered himself, though Eric was already blocking it from the view of the rest of the room. The Contact didn't bother moving it back again.

"You're going to need their help to get it where it's going," The Contact said.

"No shit, Sherlock," Eric said. "I already have a lead on one that will help me, for a small enough fee. It's not going to be cheap, this thing we're doing."

"Of course not," The Contact said. "Revolutions rarely are. You're going to have to get used to these people, though, if you're going to stop them."

"Get used to them? Why? When we're done... No, I won't be getting used to anything in this strange world."

"Nothing strange about this world, just the people in it. If you or I were born with the gene, we wouldn't be here."

"Speak for yourself. I'd be doing this either way. It needs to be done to restore order to the world. No need to mix words."

"The world already has an order to it, it's just that it doesn't work for us. Look around you. Look at these people collected here. The world's order works for them. It's always worked for one group better than others. The only difference is that we can actually do something about it this time; something that doesn't involve killing innocent people. Well... at least, I hope it doesn't. If it does... just don't tell me that part, okay? This thing... I've heard it used to be dangerous."

"Very," Eric said. "And with the proper protection, it still is. It is still protected, isn't it? You didn't open the case?"

"Don't worry," The Contact said. "The merchandise is still intact. Check it if you'd like."

"That would defeat the purpose of the protection. I'll just have to take your word for it."

Eric reached down to pick up the case, standing up in the same motion. While he was sitting near the stage, the mage had built an ice tower around it, almost as thick and solid as the ones in DC. The song was over and she was bowing from inside the tower, barely visible through the ice. Again, no one in the crowd took much notice of her, with just a couple of pity claps coming from over at the bar. Eric looked towards the bar, towards the claps, and shuddered once more when he noticed that the clapping was coming from the glasses themselves. They smashed into each other several times, loudly, spilling their contents onto the floor.

The bartender eyed the glasses menacingly as he fumbled around behind the bar.

The Contact's hand grabbed hold of the case before Eric could go far. "My payment?" he said, his free hand extending towards Eric.

"Payment?" Eric asked. He hadn't heard anything about any payments.

"The rod." He pointed towards the rain rod, which Eric had tucked into the inside pocket of his coat when he came in from the storm.

"What about it?" Eric asked. He pulled the rod out of his pocket, placing it on the table. The metal thumped heavily on the wood. "It's just a rain rod, isn't it?"

"It's not just any rain rod. It's the rain rod. The first one, the prototype, the first enchanted device this world has seen in millennia. That thing is worth a fortune."

"Seriously?" Eric asked. His hand left the metal faster than if it had burned him as he stared down at the unassuming object. It didn't seem all that different, just a long metal rod, shining in the lights from above. "Well, I guess I'll have to take your word for it."

"No, you don't have to take my word for it. No one would... You have the certificate, too, right?"

"Certificate?"

"You should have gotten a piece of paper when you got the rod, something with writing and a seal on it."

"I... They gave me some spare paper when I got the rod. I wrote the address on it."

"You wrote... Where is it?"

"You... You do know it's raining out there, right? Like really coming down. It was paper. It got wet. I lost it a good four blocks away."

"Damn it, you... Without that paper, this rod is worthless."

"What? The mages can't just tell that the rod is the prototype?"

"Well... I guess so... It's just... It's not as valuable without the certificate of authenticity."

"Well, seeing as how you said it was priceless, wouldn't that even it out a little?"

"Are you kidding me?" The Contact asked. He pulled the case out of Eric's grip, sliding it back under the table. "Do you have any idea what... that thing is worth?" He eyed the area, as if he expected someone to be listening in on the deal. "To have one of them still working with the world the way it is now? No, without the certificate, I'd say this rod is worth about... I guess a working iPhone 30. I could get you one of those, if you'd like."

"The deal was the briefcase for the rod," Eric insisted. "No one said anything about-"

"Help," the girl screamed. She was still on the stage, still in the ice tower. The next act was standing at the base of the stairs behind The Contact, staring up at the girl with an annoyed expression on his face. The girl was standing on the other side of the ice from him, banging into the wall with her fists. "I can't get out." The next act just rolled his eyes at the girl.

"A likely story," he said. "Just get out of the way. Some of us actually want to sing without all... that." He waved his hand at the ice tower, a sneer on his face like the performance had somehow offended him. "Some of us don't need to throw around our power to attract attention."

"Help," the girl yelled again.

"Maybe we want to move out of the way," Eric said. "We really don't want that kind of attention right now."

"No, I think this is exactly the kind of attention I want right now," The Contact said. "You're trying to cheat me. That's not the real rod, is it? That's why you don't have the certificate. Forget the iPhone. I'll give you twenty bucks for it. It's barely worth ten these days."

"What?" Eric asked. "No way. I'm not leaving here without that case."

"Well, you're not leaving here with the case. So, I guess you're not leaving here."

"Don't worry, lassie," someone called out from the crowd. "I'll set you free." The tall man was wearing a dark, blood red coat that skimmed across the floor of the bar as he made his way through the throng towards the stage. His beard, kept short and trim, was a much brighter shade of red, though his head was shaved clean. Beneath his coat was a red tartan, which matched his accent. "Just need to light a fire to melt your fine work."

"Let's get out of here," Eric said, eying the oncoming Scotsman. "We can discuss this somewhere away from... them."

"No, we'll discuss it here," The Contact said.

Eric got up from his chair, sliding it backwards in the process. He was already up against the far wall, leaving him nowhere to escape to. The back of The Contact's chair was right up against the corner, and he had pulled the table closer to him to block any approach. This, of course, also blocked his escape. Eric tried not to look at the case as he eased his hand towards it.

"Don't," The Contact said.

The Scotsman pressed his hands against the ice tower, right on the other side of the wall from the girl. The hands started to glow, first a light red but quickly turning to a bright blue. The tower hissed its outrage at the fire as it lanced its way through. Two holes, the size of the mage's hands, were suddenly in the wall, allowing the Scotsman to reach through to the girl. However, the rest of the wall was slow to follow.

"Strong stuff, ain't it," he said. Eric didn't notice that the man's accent had changed.

A loud cracking sound rent the air, silencing the conversations of the bar. Everyone, Eric and his contact included, stared up at the ice tower. Small fissures started to flow out from those two holes in large spider webs as they expanded outward. The girl trapped inside still battered her fists against the wall, causing those cracks to hasten and expand as they spread over the entire surface of the tower. When the cracks had almost reached the ceiling of the bar, a large chunk of the wall slid forward, leaning out dangerously over the crowd.

Everyone scrambled to get away from the wall. The Contact stood up, pushing the table away from him as he desperately tried to flee from the tower as it started to come apart. As the first section started to topple forward, another one came out in one large slab from the side of the tower, heading for their table. Eric rushed forward, grabbing the rain rod from the table right before the slab took it out. He just managed to get out of there before the table broke into splinters, showering him with them.

The Contact was standing against the wall, staring at the large block of ice that had only just missed him. The front of his pants took on a darker tone from the rest of them as the smell of urine permeated the air. He took one look towards the tower next to him, one look towards Eric, before running for the door behind everyone else. The crowd had already hit the hallway, blocking the entrance as they all desperately tried to get through first. Popping sounds came from out of the cacophonous collapse of the tower as some of the mages tried to teleport away. The safeguards that were in place over the building, over most buildings, had them immediately bouncing back into view, right where they had just been standing. This didn't stop them from trying over and over again as the hallway continued to provide no escape from the destruction.

The tower crumbled inward as the whole structure buckled. Several pieces of ice hung onto the ceiling, large icicles that quickly took on the shape of deadly spears as the rest of it fell away. The wooden support beams whined in protest, as they were not designed to handle the water soaking them through. As the ice toppled inward, the girl in the tower, the mage that had constructed it to begin with, was crushed under its weight. The Scotsman used his hands to ward off the falling ice, melting it as quickly as he could with the heat. As a large piece fell from the ceiling, he got hit in the head, knocking him out and sliding him across the floor and free from the destruction.

Eric stayed where he was, pinned against the wall. Several times, the smaller pieces of ice got hurled away from the structure and made for him. He held up the rain rod, his one and only defense against the onslaught. The smallest of pieces, barely larger than normal sized hail, bounced off of the shield that the rain rod projected. The larger pieces skimmed the edge, heading just enough away from him as to not do any damage. He closed his eyes as the last of the structure came down, squeezing them tightly as his only safeguard against it.

Eventually, the screams of the people drowned out the sounds of ice crashing down. Eric opened his eyes, looking around at the destruction that the two mages had caused. The pile of ice that had once been the stage had a noticeable blood red tint to it. There was no sign of the next act, though the debris around the stairs could just as easily have claimed two lives rather than just the one. The Scotsman was standing to the side, his hand to his forehead. He reached out, touching one of the blood stains where it had escaped the girl's tomb. His hand came back bloody, but before it moved far from the ice, the blood seemed to disappear, soaking into his hand. Once the blood was gone, the gash on his forehead healed on its own. He looked over at Eric, giving him a single wink, before teleporting away. Whoever, whatever, the Scotsman was, the safeguards against teleporting were no match for him.

The crowd was still clustered around the hallway, though it slowly grew smaller as people made it through. Two of the teleporting mages had managed to hit each other when they bounced back, causing them to merge in a disgusting mess near the center of the bar. The mess moved every once in a while, but it wasn't clear if either of the mages had survived the encounter or if they had somehow spawned some new creature out of their gruesome death. The bartender was still working behind the bar, having shown little interest in the destruction that the rest of the room had seen. A few blocks of ice had found their way to the bar, taking out some of the bar stools. But the bar itself had gone completely unscathed.

Once Eric managed to get control of himself again, he looked around for the briefcase. It had been under the table when the ice crashed into it, but he hoped that it had somehow managed to get out of there in one piece. He doubted that he'd be able to find a replacement for it anytime soon, though his mission would need to go on without it if that were the case. The scene of the bar made it quite clear to Eric that the world couldn't continue the way it had been. There was no sign of the case around where the table was, but a glint of silver flashed out of the corner of his eye, drawing his attention to a table three over from the corner. There, under the table, was the metal case.

Eric ran over to the case, not bothering to look at the crowd near the door. His contact was long gone, consumed by the frantic people over there. He picked up the case, brushing off the ice and wood that had coated the outside. With the rest of the area mostly destroyed by the ice, he headed towards the far end of the bar, the furthest from the stage he could get while staying in the room. It would have been where he would have chosen to have the exchange, where he felt most comfortable around those mages.

"What'll it be?" the bartender asked him as he sat down on one of the only barstools that had survived.

"Just a water," Eric said. "A regular water. A normal water. None of that magic created crap."

"Tap water it is." He could hear the tap turn on as one of the floating glasses sailed over to it. The pipes groaned as they spit out the water, the science struggling against the magical forces conspiring against it. Eric knew that, in a few years, maybe sooner, the pipes would go too, leaving the world at the whim of magic and those that wield it. "If you're worried about a magic allergy, though, we filter all the magic water we get before serving them. We kind of have to, after that one fire mage started to choke. Well... I guess the filters are magic, too, but that's light magic. You don't look like a darkness mage." The bartender eyed Eric's poorly bleached coat, giving him a curious look as the now full glass floated over to him.

"No mage," Eric said. "Is that a problem?"

"Not here. You might get some problems uptown, but we don't judge here. I guess you'd probably know that by now, huh? You look like you've gotten chased out of a few places over the years."

"This kind of thing happen often?" Eric asked. He pointed behind him towards the scrambling people as the last group made it through the hallway.

"More often than some would think, though not many deaths. That blood mage kind of made things interesting. Actually, now that you mention it, you might want to get out while the getting's good. Once that hallway is clear, The Authority is going to be sending someone. The water guild is going to want their pound of flesh, and it's not likely the blood guild is going to give up one of their own. They might just decide a pure blood is as good of a suspect as any."

"Thanks for the tip," Eric said.

He slipped a silver coin onto the bar and stood back up from the stool. Once he was certain his legs were steady, he started to make his way back down the hall. Already, he could make out the last remnants of the fleeing crowd at the far end of the hall, lit up by the ambient glow of the fire mage at the door. The entire group disappeared as one, immediately replaced by a group of four mages. These new mages, each wearing one of the four major colors, also wore long, pointed hats that matched their coats. At the center of the brim on these hats were sigils, symbols of the four elements, the four major affinities. They also wore matching scowls as they glared over at the fire mage before making their way towards Eric.

Eric hugged the wall as they passed, trying to give them as wide of a birth as he could in the narrow hallway. The one in blue managed to step on his foot, but the snicker that came off of the man suggested that it wasn't an accident. As soon as he was clear of them, he ran the rest of the way down the hall. He barely paused at the desk to give the fire mage hostess a wave goodbye before heading out into the night. When the door closed behind him, it slammed home with a sense of finality.

While he was inside, the night had fallen in earnest and the storm had left the area. The roads still ran deep, the water flowing past him quickly and loudly. Apophis could be seen in the distance, glowing its usual eerie orange light and drowning out Luna as the good old moon trailed behind it. Despite seeming bigger than Luna, Apophis was one ten thousandth of the size, and the difference in mass was even larger. The new moon was so small and light compared to the old one that it had little impact on the world, other than bathing it in mana and destroying any technology that had ever existed on it. Eric stood there, looking up at his nemesis, cursing its very existence.

With a deep sigh of frustration, Eric made sure that he still had the metal case in his hand and the prototype rain rod in his pocket. Again, he lamented that he couldn't verify the case's contents. But when you're trying to change the world, there were things that you had to get used to.

Chapter Two
First on the scene

Bethany

Bethany was home alone, trying to catch up on her reading. Every year they came out with new spells, new ways to do the same old things. She had been twelve when Apophis fell into orbit, old enough to have some understanding on how the world worked. Or, more accurately, how it didn't. Since then, she had spent her entire life working to understand her magic. When the Mage Authority had been put into place, she had been one of the first to join up. She knew what worked, how best to use her skill, and didn't need any of the new generation, the one that didn't even remember the old world, to tell her differently. However, she still read the new books, making sure that her way was better.

The low fading light of the day still came in the window, giving her enough light to read by. As a fire mage, she could glow in the dark when necessary, so she had no intention of lighting the ever-burning candles that were strategically placed around the room when the sun went down. They were set to light when her husband came home, but as the quorum was in session, that was unlikely to happen for hours. Maybe days. She should have known that she would have married a politician like her father.

The instant the incident happened in the bar, as soon as a life was taken by magical hands, the signal went out to one of the teams on call. It just so happened that Bethany's group was next in line. Her badge started to glow, radiating heat from its usual spot on the other side of the room by her landing pad. She just saw it out of the corner of her eye, flickering there in the corner. If she hadn't noticed it, the glow would have gotten brighter, the spell emitting a more tangible signal to her, before turning audible.

Bethany sighed, shaking her head as she put down the book. "What now?" she asked the dead air, as she got up from the couch. The Authority didn't have a uniform beyond her guild coat and The Authority hat and badge, so she didn't need to change from her t-shirt and jeans that she usually wore. In seconds, she was decked out and ready to go. But, when she triggered the teleport on the badge, it didn't work. Something was blocking the teleport on the receiving end, undoubtedly a group of bystanders just trying to get out of the way of the danger behind them.

Every few seconds, Bethany triggered the badge, waiting for it to go through. The teleport network, centered around the landing pads, was put in place for everyone's safety. No one wanted to teleport into a wall or another person. If she needed to be on the scene immediately, she could have forced the badge to send her through, or to the nearest unoccupied pad. But the badge had already started to abate its heat, telling her that the incident was probably already contained.

When the badge finally let her through, bringing her to the entrance to the bar, she barely batted an eye when Greg, Dan, and Igloo landed right next to her. As long as they all had been holding their badges, similarly trying to get through, hers would have triggered theirs so that the entire team would arrive together. As Bethany pulled her magic into her, she could feel her team doing the same around her. Instantly, mere seconds after they arrived, they were ready for anything short of a high mage.

The four of them walked cautiously down the hall. Before they got far, a man came out of the darkness, rushing towards the exit. From the scared expression on his face, it was clear that the man was little more than another of the bystanders, just trying to flee before they were next. Bethany knew that she would be able to track him through the teleport network if needed. However, as the group made their way to the main room, the front door to the building slammed closed behind them.

Bethany turned around, shocked that the man had left through more conventional means. No one bothered to go outside anymore, not in the city. There were parks for that. And beaches. Places specifically set aside for people to use, even deserted islands that could be rented for privacy. There was no need to go outside anymore.

"Hey, boss," Dan called to her, pulling her back to the matter at hand. She shrugged it off, figuring that the man must have just been too panicked to teleport himself away.

The room was a mess, with ice and blood everywhere. However, there were no active mages, so she relaxed her stance, letting her mana stores deplete back into the air. She pointed towards the one witness, signaling for Dan and Greg to interview him. Igloo would stick close to her as she examined the scene, though it didn't take her long to ascertain what happened. Magic gone awry, which pretty much described her entire job. It was only one in ten calls that had intent behind it, but she needed to follow through with each anyway.

After interviewing the bartender, Dan went over to the ice and started to interview the water as it dripped down. It always made Bethany queasy whenever he did this, but his water affinity was specifically adapted for that sort of thing. She had never learned how to listen to fire. Even if she was interested in learning, she didn't have the years it took. Besides, she had heard that fire wasn't overly helpful, as it was a rather vein element to work with.

It didn't take Dan long to hear the whole story, straight from the horse's mouth as it were. The water knew everything that had happened, and was eager to talk about the whole thing. It kept denying fault in the death, blaming it on the blood mage that drew strength from it. Hearing that part of the story didn't make her happy. The last thing she wanted to do was deal with the blood guild, though it was the lesser of the three high guilds.

When Dan got to the part of the two pure bloods sitting in the corner, Bethany pulled him up short. "Is it sure they were pure bloods?" she asked.

"No, Bethany. It's not sure of it. It's water. All it knows is that they weren't water mages. From how it described them, though, I'm thinking that guy that went out the door earlier was one of them."

"I knew we should have gone after him," Igloo said.

"Well, then why didn't you say something?" Bethany asked.

"You didn't ask. I've learned a long time ago not to offer my opinions if I don't want my head bitten off."

"Relax, he's a pure blood on foot," Greg said. "How far can he get? Igloo, think you can track him?"

"Track him? How? I never learned how to do that."

"It probably works the same way Dan talks to water," Bethany said. "Not exactly standard training in The Academy."

"Oh, please," Dan huffed. "There is no standard training in The Academy. All the professors were just making it up as they went. But, that's kind of how magic is, isn't it? At least on the cause side of things. You have to feel your way to the desired effect."

"That's very zen of you," Bethany said. "I would have expected it from Greg, but you?"

"Yea, I know. I think I pulled something with that."

"It ain't easy being green," Greg said, as he adjusted his green hat.

"Look, I can try tracking the guy, if you want," Igloo said. "I just don't think I'd have much luck."

"Don't sweat it," Greg said. "I can get a feel for the earth along his route. If we're going to catch up with him, though, we should leave now."

"We can't leave until we've sealed the scene," Bethany said. She pulled her badge off of her hat, tapping it several times in a specific pattern. This would send out a signal for a crime scene team to come in and handle the site, freeing them to follow the suspect. Her group was a first response and investigation team, first to come in for those rare instances when the mage responsible wasn't done by the time they arrived. With the all clear signal sent out through the badge network, they had to sit and wait for the next CSI team that was available.

"Think they left behind fingerprints?" Greg asked. Greg was the oldest of the team, almost fifty-five, and had been a cop before everything happened. It had been thirty years since then, but old habits die hard. He often brought up the thought when an identity was unknown.

"Fingerprints do still exist," Bethany said. "But, how would they be lifted? Compared to the database? Without computers, that would take years, wouldn't it? It's going to be faster to just hunt the guy down."

"And even if there was a system in place, what are the chances he'd be in it?" Dan asked. Dan had no idea what they were talking about, he was barely thirty, but the subject had been brought up so often that he knew the arguments by heart. Greg always seemed like a fish out of water, one of the old guard, stalwart and steady in his methods. It was that mindset that lent well to his earth affinity.

"Where are these guys?" Igloo asked. Impatiently, she looked towards the entrance to the bar. "If we want to chase after this guy, we should leave now. There's no one heading for the entrance to block their arrival. They should be here."

"I just put out the call like a minute ago," Bethany said. "The CSI teams don't need to have the same response time as we do. It could be--" Bethany was interrupted by a signal coming through her badge. She held up a silencing finger, though she was the one that had been talking, as she tried to catch the signal pattern. After the first few beats, she realized that it was a longer communication, coming in through Morse code. "They're going to be a while," she said, putting her badge back onto her hat.

"How long?" Igloo asked. She sat down heavily onto one of the few chairs that hadn't been overturned or destroyed in the destruction or mass exodus. There was a half empty drink in front of her and she moved to drink it. When she saw the lipstick marks, she put it back down on the table.

Bethany pulled her blood book out of her pocket. As usual, it reminded her of the fact that so many of the tools that have come out since Apophis's arrival, replacing the technology of the past, had come from fantasy, and named more for those predecessors than their actual use. For instance, the blood books had nothing to do with blood, or the blood guild or blood mages. Rather, it was named after a similar set of books that, up until about two years after The Arrival, didn't actually exist.

She paused to feel the thick leather cover of the book for a moment before flipping it open to the latest page. The older pages all showed communications that had come through the badge network, some short and some much longer. When she got to the end of the writing, to where the call was transcribed, she paused. As part of the call, the more drawn out communication had the actual coordinates to the landing plate, in both latitude and longitude and GPS coordinates, despite no one being able to actually use GPS anymore. On the next page, below her own drawn out signal of all clear, the full communication was still coming in. The writing was spreading across the page as if it were being written by an invisible pen. The pen, of course, was in the dispatch headquarters, down in DC, and really was being used as she watched, writing out the long handed message.

CSI team 9343428 will be inbound to your location in three hours. They are still finishing up their old scene and will need to close that out first. No other team is available to satisfy your request. Please maintain the scene until their team arrives.

"You gotta be kidding me," Greg said, looking over her shoulder. "Three hours? There's no chance we'd be able to catch up with the pure blood then."

"Hold on, hold on," Bethany said. She pulled a pen out of the binding of the book, the only pen that was specifically designed to work with the book. Designed as a safety measure, the pen wasn't supposed to be attached to the book, in case the book was ever stolen. However, no one ever actually followed that rule. Too many pens were lost, too many books needing to be replaced in full, and the natural hole in the binding was a perfect place to stow it.

Let it be known that a suspect has fled the scene on foot. Requesting permission to split the team to chase after him. Suspect is believed to be pure blood.

The response was quick, and unsurprising. Bethany had suggested chasing after a lone suspect before, splitting the team to watch the scene. Even the words were no different from the last time she had suggested it, barely two pages earlier.

Negative. Remain on scene.

"Forget it, I'm going," Igloo said, after reading the orders over Bethany's shoulder. "You can write me up if you want. There's no point in all four of us sitting on an empty room. Get the bartender to do it. He's not doing anything else."

"I am actually very busy," the bartender said from the other side of the room. Despite his words, he was still cleaning the same glass as he was when they came in.

"There's a reason why they pair us up in groups of the four elements," Bethany said. "If you get attacked by an earth mage out there, you'd be completely vulnerable."

"I'm not going to be attacked. No one is going to attack me. I'm a member of the Mage Authority. It would be stupid, foolish, suicide. This sigil is the only shield I need."

"Except maybe the suspect," Greg said. "We only think he's a pure blood. He could be a void mage; they present like pure bloods if you don't know what to look for."

"Void mages are the highest of the high mages," Bethany said. "The rarest, too. I know all the void mages on sight. It's easy enough, seeing as how there's only ten in the whole world. Why don't you?"

"I do," Greg said. "At least, I know the registered ones. There might be a few out there that just didn't bother to register. If he had resources outside of The Authority, gold or silver coins perhaps, he might have been off the grid this whole time. That means he might never have been tested for an affinity. Which means he could be anything."

"Hey, bartender," Bethany called over to him. "Did that guy who left last pay with coins?"

"Coins?" the bartender asked. "No. Of course not. We're supposed to report that sort of thing, aren't we?"

Something about the way he said that didn't sit well with Bethany. She glared over at the man, but he never looked up from the glass, shining it to perfection and beyond. It seemed almost meditative to him, a way to alleviate whatever stress he was feeling about a woman dying right in front of him. Or, maybe, it was some nervous tick that he had. Either way, his denial wasn't reassuring to her.

"No one is going anywhere," Bethany said.

"But, Ma'am," Igloo whined.

"I said stand down. There's something about him that we just don't know yet. I'm not letting any of us go up against him alone."

"If he was a void mage, the four of us together wouldn't stand a chance against him anyway," Dan said. "Just saying, it's not any more dangerous to send her off alone. Plus, if she gets herself killed, we'd finally be rid of her."

"Yea," Igloo said. "You'd finally be rid of me."

"Except then they'd send an even greener recruit to replace you. The answer is no. That's my final answer."

Greg snickered when she said that. "Are you sure you don't want to phone a friend first?"

"What's a phone?" Igloo asked.

Chapter Three
The Rent is Due

Ardith

Ardith stared down at the earring she had on her workbench. The mounted magnifying glass gave her a close up look at it, as she tried to see the minor imperfections that were causing her the problems. She had put a lot of money into buying the small thing, the small sapphire stud that was the base of her enchantment. It was so simple of an object, but the perfection that needed to be in place was no small thing. Perfection costs money. Once again, she promised herself that it would all be worth it once she cashed in on the patent.

After making sure, once again, that there were no minor gashes or misaligned grips in the stud, she leaned away from the earring. She moved the magnifying glass out of the way and stood up, facing the desk. With a deep breath, she steadied herself as she started to pull more mana out of the air around her. At school, her teachers had always discouraged her from holding her breath as she held in the mana, but it was a habit that she never managed to break, no matter how old she got.

Once she had centered herself and drew in as much mana as she could, she opened her eyes again. She focused on the earring, small as it was, almost too small for her to see properly. The magnifying glass would have helped, but it blocked the flow of her spell, wasting both the spell and the magnifying glass. Her hands twiddled and waved through the air as she started her incantation. Neither had any real impact on the spell itself, though they helped her concentrate on the effect that she wanted, on the dweomer that she was trying to form. She had used the spell by itself often enough to know that it worked. And to know that she was casting it properly. The issue was tying it to the earring in such a way that it would last.

She could feel the spell forming in the air over the earring, could sense it as a tangible, almost visible thing hovering there. Once it was almost completely solid, with just a few lasting tendrils to weave together, she started to push those tendrils around the earring, trying to find places to attach them to the gem and rod. If she did it right, the earring would take the spell, holding it in place for the rest of time.

If she did it right.

The earring sent off a spark as soon as it came in contact with the spell, this time melting into a small gold puddle beneath the mount. The sapphire tumbled forward, spilling onto the desk, then the floor. Ardith cursed loudly, slamming the desk in front of her. As she did so, her elbow bumped into the wall behind her, draining what was left of her focus.

"Are you sure you're a water mage?" came a voice from the other side of the room. It reminded her that she wasn't alone in the small office. Ardith's officemate, Carissa, snickered at her from across the distance. She was sitting against the far wall at her own desk, though hers was full of papers, documentation for her spells, invoices for her clients. She even had a few design documents for her own enchantments, though they didn't seem as ambitious as Ardith's was. The office just had the two desks, smushed together in the back, with the rest of the space set aside for more elaborate spellwork.

Carissa, such a common name, Ardith had always thought. Her parents, neither of which were mages, hadn't bothered to give her a proper name, one worthy of a mage of their caliber. Carissa was a fellow member of the water guild, though two years Ardith's junior. The blonde bitch was always showing her up, always doing everything in her power to make Ardith look bad in the eyes of the guild. Both of Ardith's parents were mages, her dad the head of the earth guild. Although, a person's lineage had no impact on their power. It just came down to the gene that decided if you belonged or didn't.

"The thing was defective," Ardith swore defensively. "Something must have been wrong with it. Maybe it was made by a fire mage, though I had insisted on an earth mage's work at the jeweler. Stupid pure blood doesn't even know the difference. I'll be demanding my money back."

"Oh, yes, you definitely should," Carissa said. "After all, your half of the rent is still outstanding for the past... three months is it now? If you can't pay up, I'll just have to evict you and find a decent mage to share the space with. You know, one that can actually cast an enchantment. Maybe you'd be more at home in the factories. You're certainly not skilled enough to get that position in management that I know you've applied for."

"What? How did you... Did you--"

"Oh, don't be silly, little one," she sniffled. "I saw the application. It was on your desk for weeks before you sent it in. What would dear old dad think of his precious little girl if she can't even get a simple spell to work? Does he know that you applied? Is he pulling every string he has, every favor, just to get your application to the top of the pile? I'm sure it's not nearly impressive enough to do that on its own. Certainly not as impressive as mine."

"You..."

"Watch yourself, little one," Carissa laughed. "This time next month I might be your regional head. I might just make my first act casting you out of the guild entirely."

"What? You wouldn't. You can't."

"Of course, I can. I've seen your work. You're no water mage. Everyone will know, everyone will see. You'll be set out to live with the rare talents."

"Ha, like your parents?" she scoffed.

"Exactly," Carissa said, without missing a beat. "That's why I know how miserable it is over there, how you'd be ostracized from the entire guild. You'll be a laughing stock. You'd never dare show your face in civilized society again. Enjoy it here while you can."

"Bitch," Ardith hissed.

"Anyway, I'm off. I have some work to do for actual clients. You know what those are, right? People who actually pay you to do enchantments and spells for them. I have so many clients these days I don't even have the time for them all. Maybe I won't bother getting another officemate. I could just expand my own space. All the more reason to kick you out."

"You can't," Ardith said. "We have an agreement."

"One you're already in breach of. Get me the money by the end of the week or you're out on your ass."

Carissa snapped her fingers twice, once to dispel the safeguards in place over the space that would block outgoing teleportations and once the teleport away. Ardith felt when the safeguards slammed back into place just a few seconds later. Carissa had been the one to do the enchantment over the entire building, so of course she was able to disable it whenever it suited her. Heaven forbid she walk the five steps to the landing pad by the door.

Ardith cursed the empty air that Carissa had just vacated. She grabbed up the now cooled puddle of melted gold, meaning to throw it across at Carissa's space. The small pebble that it had become didn't want to let go of the desk.

Ardith scraped her well-manicured fingernails along the edge of the metal, trying to pry it loose of the wood. When her fingernail just managed to cut between, pulling loose a sliver of metal, she ended up only slicing her finger open for all the effort she had put in. She cursed again, punching the desk, the newest of several gold inlays spread across its surface, and her chair for good measure. Only the chair showed any sign of acknowledgement to the effort.

The bottom drawer of the desk slid open a crack under her fury. It had always been defective, ever since she moved into the space. The landlord had said it was a holdover from the old days, back when the place was an ad agency. Ardith wasn't quite sure what an ad agency was, or even what an ad was, but she imagined it had something to do with sending out information in a persuasive format. These days, there was no point to advertising. The marketplaces were all still too young for competition to blossom. If you wanted a rain rod, you'd end up paying the same thirty credits whether it was from the corner store or the home delivery services, though it cost an extra five to get it delivered instantly.

She righted her chair and sat down heavily in it, staring down at the floor. That was when she noticed the drawer, cursing it along with everything else broken in her life. She kicked the drawer closed, but put too much force behind the motion and the drawer just ended up opening further. In the drawer was her three remaining earrings, part of the same package as the last seven, and an old bottle of whiskey. She scooped up the packet first, then the bottle, staring at the packet as she slammed the bottle down onto the desk. The earrings were such small items to have given her so much trouble over the past week and a half. She took a closer look at the package, scanning the small words closely, looking for some admission of fault, of guilt, on the part of the goldsmith or jeweler. All that the words said, though, was "Enchantment Blanks, Earrings, Sapphire and Gold".

"Stupid pure bloods," she cursed, tossing the packet back into the drawer. She stared at the bottle, another holdover from a previous tenant, though obviously not as old as the desk. On the label was a tornado logo, showing that the whiskey was made by the air guild. There were still some of the old distilleries out there, still run by the same pure bloods that had run them for generations, but their booze always paled in comparison to what the mages could brew up in a fraction of the time.

Ardith pulled open the top drawer of the desk, taking out the glass she hid in there. The glass was dirty, having been put back in the drawer the previous night when she was too drunk and too tired to bother to clean it. She rolled it around between her hands, blowing into the top and putting just enough magic into the effort to summon enough water to fill the glass for just a split second. The water splashed out of the top, disappearing instantly, and taking all the dried booze, dust, and other substances with it. She slid the glass onto the desk, letting it bump into the magnifying glass mount before coming to a stop. Her hand was on the much-abused cork, ready to pull it free, when she was interrupted.

The front door to the office slammed open, hitting the wall behind it. Ardith stared daggers over at the door, and the person standing outside. She was shocked, not that someone would come to see her there, but that the door actually worked. Neither mage had ever thought to bother checking to see if it was locked. The thing had never been open the entire time she had been working out of that office. Granted, she had only been there since she became a full member of the guild, three months earlier, but that was a long time for her. She slipped the bottle back into the bottom drawer, hitting it closed as she stood up.

The man rushed into the office, pulling the door closed behind him. He wore an old, beat up coat of seemingly random shades of gray, marking that he didn't belong to any of the mage guilds. Immediately, she assumed he was a pure blood, but he could just as easily be a rare talent. It was still rude to dismiss the rares outright, or she would have just kicked him out just on her mood alone. However, the man also stunk, even from across the space. That might have been enough of an excuse.

Once the door was closed solidly, the man turned around, giving his back to it. He even leaned against it for support, getting his pure blood filth, sweat, and stink all over the old wood. Ardith figured it would take a thorough cleansing before she ever went near it again. His eyes darted all around the room, barely pausing on Ardith in his search for whatever he had come there for.

"Is... Are you Carissa?" he asked.

His voice was old, raspy, and more worn than his appearance would have suggested. The man was barely older than her father, maybe mid to late fifties, with hair grayer than his coat. The old suit that he wore was out of style by about five decades and was frayed and torn in several places. She knew then, without a doubt, that the man was a pure blood. Or maybe worse, maybe a demon or Hulandan, though neither group have shown their faces out in public for years.

"Maybe," Ardith said, wanting to be as unhelpful as she could. "Who wants to know?"

"Someone who will pay," he said. He pulled out a coin purse, shaking it and its contents, though he never left the door. It no longer looked like he was using the door to support him, so much as holding the door closed. Though why he expected someone else to use the old thing was beyond her.

"Pay for what, exactly?" she asked. She looked towards the pile of mail in the corner, just as another letter, another bill, popped out of thin air and fell onto the top. It wasn't just the rent for her workspace that she was behind on, and the bills always knew where to find her.

"Nuh uh. Not until you agree to help me."

The door bumped into him, jostling him away from it for a moment, but he pushed back against it right away. This surprised Ardith to no end. Not only did this one pure blood come in through it, but there was someone after him, someone coming through the door as well. Or trying to, anyway. It was clear, from the fear in his eyes and the weight of his purse, that he was in a lot of trouble, and quite desperate for help to get out of it.

"Fine, I'll help you," Ardith said. A wide smile spread across her face as she started to think of how easy it would be to take advantage of this one pure blood. "Now hand over the purse."

"Not so fast," the man said. He pulled the purse away from her, even hiding it behind his back, as if he expected her to pull it out of his hands even across the distance of the office. Had she been better at air magic, she might have been able to, though she had enough trouble with her own element at times. "You know the drill."

"The what?"

"The oath. I'm not giving you this purse until we have a magic bound oath." Someone slammed into the door behind him again, but he managed to hold his spot.

"Fine," Ardith said, rolling her eyes. She raised her hand, sending just enough magic through it to make it glow. That was enough for any oath to be locked onto her magic. She wouldn't be able to break it without risking her magic. "I, Carissa Von Strucker," she tried not to smile as she said the name of her officemate, rather than her own. After all, Carissa was who this man had come to find. "Promise to help you for that purse." She really did smile as the second loophole went in.

"Help me do what?" he asked, not fooled the least bit by her choice of words.

"Help you... what?" What exactly was she helping him with? "You wouldn't tell me what we're doing until I gave the oath, but I can't give a more specific oath without more information."

"Help me complete my quest."

"Quest?" she laughed. Her hand went down and the spell was broken, the oath as it was originally worded locked in. She felt a brief flutter around her heart as the first oath solidified there. "Seriously?"

"Yes, quest. It's a quest. An important one."

"Sure, sure. Okay. I'll help you on your quest."

"Help me complete my quest. Swear it, on your magic."

"Fine." She raised her hand again, letting it light up. "I promise to help you complete your quest."

"Good," he said. He pulled his hand out from behind his back, but the purse was no longer in it. When he moved forward, his empty hand extended, the door got bashed into again, sending him flying. "Now let's get out of here."

"Nuh uh. Purse first."

"You'll get the purse when the quest is done," the man insisted. "Not a minute before it. Besides, we'll be far too busy escaping here to do much shopping. The first step on this quest is to escape here."

The door got bashed into again, this time the hinges groaned under the abuse. Without the man standing behind the door, the frame took the entire brunt of the assault. The old, heavy door was meant to keep people at bay, to keep animals and weather and burglars out. But it had also been there a long time, and not maintained at all for decades. Ardith wasn't sure how long it would last against the barrage from outside, but she knew it wouldn't be long. He was right; they needed to get out of there, and quickly.

"Fine. Fine," she said. "Where's your linking book?"

"My what?" he asked.

His ignorance stunned her for a moment. He knew about the mage's oath, but not what a linking book was? How exactly did he get around without a linking book? How did he even get to her office? It wasn't like the stairs still worked.

Was he really a pure blood or was there something more about the man, something that went beyond what she could readily see? All that she could readily see suggested that the guy was a moron, way over his head in the world.

"Your linking book," she said. "The book you use to teleport around?"

"I don't..."

"God, seriously? I mean, you obviously don't have the power to teleport yourself, so how do you get around without a linking book?"

"I walk."

"Everywhere? Like around the world?" The door splintered under another hit from outside. The upper corner stretched inward, showing the hallway outside.

"I don't get that far. What can I say? I don't get out much."

"Fine, fine," she said. "Well, that's too bad. I don't have a linking book. I haven't needed one since I was eight."

"Can't you teleport us out of here?" He turned around staring wide eyed at the door as it got hit again. The crack spread further as the top hinges gave way. One more slam and it would break free, slamming right into them.

Ardith made her way quickly across the room. She pulled as much magic into her as she could, not trusting her ability to do a ride along. Teleportation is air magic and she had never managed to do a ride along in all her years trying. "Hold your breath," she said, as she wrapped her arms around him, pulling him tightly against her chest. "This could hurt... a lot."

She took a deep breath, holding it for a few seconds, as she centered herself, focusing on her apartment as their destination. It would help to land somewhere familiar, somewhere that she knew well enough not to bump into anything. However, it would only help with the landing. It was still quite possible for her to leave half of the man in the office while taking the other half with her.

Right before she teleported away, the door broke open, revealing who it was that was after the man. Four mages stood outside the door, the earth mage standing in front. His hands were extended towards the door that was no longer there, the follow-through for the spell that he had been hammering into it. She just made out the badges on their hats before they got away.

They were high ranking officers in the Mage Authority.

Chapter Four
The Scene of the Crime

Bethany

It took a lot longer than three hours for the CSI team to show up the previous night. By the time they did, it was closer to morning than evening. Igloo and Greg had snuck off together, perhaps to catch some sleep. Bethany wasn't sure, and didn't much care. Dan spent the time communing with his water, which just weirded Bethany out like usual.

As soon as the team arrived, Bethany jumped up from her chair. She tapped on Dan's shoulder, though he didn't need the prompting. Apparently, the water told him they had arrived, as he was already starting to stand when she went to him.

"The others?" he asked, motioning towards the back room.

Bethany pulled her badge off of her hat again, tapping in the command to regroup the team. Igloo appeared before her, practically standing at attention, though Greg was on the floor at her feet, sleeping. Bethany kicked him but didn't bother to wait for a response.

"Let's go," she said.

"Team 843452?" one of the CSI guys asked as the group approached him. "I'm here to--"

"Yea, yea, yea," Bethany said, annoyed. "It's about time you guys showed up. If our suspect got away because you people were dilly dallying, don't be surprised if you get written up in our report."

"Dilly dallying?" the CSI guy asked.

"Come on," Bethany said, ignoring the rest of the CSI team as they came into the bar. "We have a lot of ground to cover."

"Perhaps not as much as you might think," Greg said. He yawned audibly through much of that, though he seemed to have some plan as to how to address the large lead the suspect had over them. "He probably would have had to sleep at some point as well. Plus, with magic on our side, we can move much faster than him."

"Except we have to waste time tracking him," Bethany said.

The group was just making it to the end of the hall. She paused there, staring at the landing platform. The flat, brown stone had intricate carvings in it. The carvings might have seemed beautiful at some point, but they were the same as on every landing platform that had ever come off of the assembly line. Considering all of the enchanted objects that had been manufactured in those thirty years, of course they all had to look exactly the same. Without them, most people in the world would have long since starved to death. The world wasn't ready for all of its technology to be destroyed in one fell swoop.

There was no one at the desk that was positioned right next to the landing platform, though she remembered seeing someone the night before. A book, probably forgotten in the panic, rested in a little nook hidden behind the desk. The book heralded at her, an echo of her own power, telling her that it belonged to a fellow fire mage. It distracted her just long enough for the others to get impatient.

"Huh?" Bethany asked, when she noticed the expressions of the others.

"I said, we don't really need to slow down much to track him. We just need to pop between blocks to make sure he's still on the same path. There's no teleportation blocks outside."

"Right," Bethany said.

Still, she dawdled at the door, staring at it. It took her a moment to realize why. Most of their suspects, the ones actually responsible for the injuries and deaths that they respond to, were still on the scene when they arrived. Fewer run from the scene, though it was quite easy to track people through the landing platform network. It was part of the spellwork that ran through them. Fewer still ran outside. So few of the buildings those days even had front doors; there was no need for them. She couldn't remember the last time she went outside through a door, let alone chased someone through one. Certainly not through the streets that waited for her outside.

"You alright, boss?" Greg asked.

"Yea," Bethany said. She shook herself before stepping over the landing platform. It wasn't necessary, the platform wasn't going to go off without her using it. But it still felt wrong, that tangible connection to one of the symbols of the era before heading out into something from the past.

The sun, shining down the street, greeted the group as she pushed open the door. Bethany looked at her wrist, more out of habit than anything else. No one had quite managed to figure out how to make a watch with magic just yet. Still, the old scar on her wrist, where her old watch had blown up on the day of The Arrival, reminded her of the old simplicity of marking time. The suspect would have almost ten hours lead over them and they needed to make up the time as quickly as possible.

"Alright, Greg, you're up," Bethany said. She stood just off to the side of the doorway, looking out at the city around her. Bethany grew up in the suburbs, back when the suburbs were a thing, so she didn't remember actually seeing a city all lit up, like they described in books. The tall buildings loomed over her, making her almost feel like she was inside. It was nothing like the parks that were set aside for the much more sensible uses of the outside world.

"He went that way," Greg said, pointing off to the south from the door. "The trail is faint, perhaps ten hours old or more. It should get stronger as we go along."

"Fine," Bethany said. "Igloo, think you can land reasonably close to the next block over?"

"Of course," Igloo said. Teleportation was an air spell, after all, her specialty. As if to demonstrate her aptitude, she teleported down the road to the next intersection, waving over at them from the distance. Immediately, she teleported back, though the distance was far enough away that, for a split second, she seemed to be in both places. The speed of light was one of the few things that hadn't changed upon the arrival of Apophis, though humans were no longer subject to that limit. "See?" she said.

"No showing off," Bethany said. "Teleport back there and pull us along with you. Greg won't be able to teleport without a linking book, and these individual intersections won't be in it anyway. I wouldn't want to test my own skills, for that matter. I'd be likely to land in a wall or something."

"I could just pull you guys along. I've done ride along teleports before."

"Igloo, use your badge. That's what it's there for. You just teleport over there and trigger the regroup command."

"I... I've never done that before. I don't even think I know how."

"Nothing to it, kid," Greg said. "You just hold the badge, give it a little of your juice, and think 'regroup'. It always kind of reminds me of this old show I used to watch when I was a kid, much younger than you. I don't think it was 'regroup', though."

"I miss TV," Bethany moaned, nostalgically. "Now, let's get to it." She shooed Igloo along.

"Oh... kay..." Igloo said, hesitantly.

She teleported down the block once more, to the same spot she had been earlier, only she didn't wave this time and stayed longer. The three of them were stuck in place, watching impatiently, as Igloo reached up to her hat, pulling her badge free. The instant her hand touched the badge, though, Bethany felt the familiar pull of someone else's teleportation spell hitting her. The three of them were instantly pulled across the distance, landing right next to Igloo. Bethany landed with her heels just inches away from the wall and she had a strange feeling that her butt wasn't as large as it used to be.

"Right," Bethany said. "That easy. Just be careful with your spacing, alright? Not too close to the buildings." She tapped the wall behind her to emphasize her point.

"Right, sorry," Igloo said.

"Yup, still south of here," Greg said. "We lost a little time on that one, but that's alright. We'll get a pattern going soon enough."

"Igloo?" Bethany said, signaling her to continue.

They continued like that for an hour, though the suspect had changed directions soon after leaving the bar. He started heading west, towards the older sections of the city, and the group was quick to follow. Each block took less than a minute, though it would have taken the suspect three to walk them. It was slow, but steady, arduous work making their way across the city.

"It helps that there's only the one guy out here," Greg said, as they came into another block. "Ooh, and it's here."

"What's here?" Bethany asked. She always hated when Greg played the pronoun game.

"His tracks here are a lot fresher than the last block, which means he camped down somewhere along here."

"Are you sure it's the same guy? It is possible for more than one person to be out here."

"Possible, but unlikely," Dan said. "I mean, two people, out on the street, on the same day? What are the chances of that happening? I never go outside in the city besides for work. It's disgusting out here."

"It's the same signature," Greg said. "I'm sure of it. And, now, it's less than an hour old. We're close."

"Good," Igloo said. She was doubled over, leaning on her knees, and panting heavily like she had just run a marathon. In a way, that was exactly what she was doing. "I don't know how much longer I can keep this up."

"We could take a break," Greg suggested. "Five minutes would only cost us two, in the long run. We'll catch up to him in the next half hour or so, anyway."

"Why aren't you tired?" Igloo asked. "You've been using your magic as much as I have."

"Tracking is a much simpler spell than teleportation. Plus, I've had more experience using my powers for long periods of time and have built up my muscles."

"And, he's just generally a more powerful mage," Bethany said.

"Yea, says you," Igloo said.

"No, says the tests. Remember, I know all of your scores. He tested better than you in all elements except air."

"Think we should look for his camp site?" Dan asked. He looked all over the block, but he didn't seem to find anything worth noting.

"Greg could find it if we need to," Bethany said. "But later. Let's catch up with the guy, then see where he camped out. There might not be a point to it anyway. Igloo, you good for a few more?"

"How much better?" Igloo asked.

"She's ready," Dan said. "Hop to it."

Igloo rolled her eyes before checking with Greg on the direction for the next jump. It was starting to seem too easy to Bethany, like the suspect was somehow drawing them towards where he wanted them. She knew that he was a pure blood, incapable of using any magic. But that didn't bar him from knowing their tracking abilities, or using some type of enchanted object to mask his path suddenly. Or worse, perhaps he was leading them on a wild goose chase, only to teleport away with a linking book at the last minute. Out there in the old city, so far away from the usual landing pads, they would be hard pressed to track any teleport. A few of the old buildings were still being used, but mostly for magic labs. It was safer to try untested magic in areas where casualties would be limited.

"Uh, I lost him," Greg said, just a few minutes after their brief break.

When he said this, Bethany was barely surprised. This was it, she thought. This was where they lose him. He must have teleported away.

"Maybe he teleported away," Dan said. "We can't track a teleport out here. Unless Igloo can."

"Oh, no. That's... I'm way too tired to even try right now."

"You guys, relax," Greg said. "It probably just means--" He broke off in mid-sentence, pointing off into the distance.

Bethany looked off in the direction he was pointing, instantly spotting the pure blood. He was standing there, just outside the door to one of the buildings, looking at a sheet of paper that he was holding in his hands. The man looked between the paper and the buildings around him, probably looking for the numbers on them. The buildings were all so old, so worn away by the weather and the more wild magics of the area, that even those that had numbers in the past no longer did. He started to count the doors on the block, pointing at each one as he went, until he came to the door that the group was standing next to.

The man froze there, his finger still pointing towards the group. His lips were parted awkwardly, like he was trying to say something, perhaps a number, but had forgotten what. He was like that for a few seconds before he clutched the paper to his chest and started to run.

"Did no one think to go after him?" Greg asked, as they all just stood there, watching the man flee.

"Don't look at me," Igloo said, though no one was looking her way. "I'm exhausted."

"On foot it is, then," Bethany said, the comment an order as she led the way after the suspect.

The man had a decent lead over them and, unlike the group, he was well rested. Without Igloo teleporting them forward, they weren't likely to catch up with him, though he wasn't about to lose them either. The streets were too open, too deserted for him to disappear on them again. The simple fact that he was running from them, that he fled without them having to say anything, told Bethany all she needed to know. The man was up to no good and should be stopped before someone got hurt.

Two blocks over from where they spotted him, the man seemed to swerve in mid step as he made a quick dash to his left, heading for the door to the building. Bethany figured he must have seen the number he was looking for. Unfortunately, when the group got to the spot where he disappeared, they saw that the building had three doors, each with different numbers on them. The suspect wasn't visible through any of the doors, but Greg quickly tracked him again, sensing that he went through the middle one.

No words passed between the members of the well-oiled team as they jumped into action. Greg pulled open the door to the building, letting Bethany lead the way. Igloo knew well enough to stay out of the way of the other three as they went in. She instantly fell in behind Greg to take up the tail of their group. Had they been expecting more trouble, she would have let Greg take the end, as his affinity went well with defense.

In the front room, there was a set of old elevator doors. The doors showed signs of rust, with a gaping hole in one of them. Through the hole, the elevator car could be seen, though not much else. It was dark inside, both the building and the elevator. Bethany didn't stay long enough as they passed to light the interior of the elevator, though she knew nothing could open those doors shy of brute force.

When they got to the stairwell, around the corner from the front room, they heard a slamming door ahead of them. Bethany raced up the stairs, following the echo of the slam. She pulled out her own tracking capabilities, specifically tracking the body heat of the suspect. It was easier to do when closer to the target, and with only two other people in the building there was no doubt which was the one they were after.

Bethany pulled up short in front of the door that the suspect had just gone through. She could see his form through the heavy wooden door, as well as another one further into the room. There was an old nameplate on the door, but the name had been scratched out ages ago and was no longer legible. There was no telling what they would find through that door, but she could feel the teleportation blocks in place over the building. The only way in was through that door, unless they went back out of the building and teleported onto the landing pad. However, she couldn't tell if the room had a landing pad in it, and it would take far too long to try.

The others were next to her in seconds, falling into their normal formation. Greg took the front, placing his steady form between them and the potential danger. Dan was to her left, far enough away that his affinity wouldn't block hers should the fighting get confusing. Igloo was on her right, standing there with a stupid, gleeful smile on her face, bouncing up and down on her heels.

Bethany tapped Greg on his shoulder, a silent signal for him to break down the door. She could feel him pulling mana from the air, forming it into a battering ram spell. The spell slammed home into the center of the door, which didn't show any sign that it noticed. She wondered, worried, that he was too drained from the tracking outside, but he quickly started to spin up another spell. The second one was bigger, harder, stronger, faster, longer, hitting the door solidly in its center. Other than a few flecks of paint falling free, the door just stood there smiling at them. It took several spells, hitting the door in a decent rhythm, for it to start showing that it would come down, and several more before the hinges started to whine.

When the door broke free, Bethany was about to move forward, into the room. But something caught her eye, claiming her attention fully. She stood there, stunned, as she watched the suspect and the other occupant of the room disappear before her eyes.

"Igloo, track them," Greg called out when Bethany didn't move. She was too stunned to do anything.

Igloo stepped into the room, bumping into Bethany as she did. She pulled her badge off of her hat again, using the tactile connection to it to aid her in her efforts, though just having it on her should be enough to do it. Bethany took a few steps away from the door, leaning heavily on the wall across from it.

"I... I can't," Igloo said. "There's... It's weird. I'm accessing the landing pad network just fine. I can even read a clear teleport a few minutes before we got here. But the one that just happened? It's all jumbled up, like they weren't going anywhere. Worse, like they were going everywhere, all at once. If they survived that... I don't know. It seems that, whoever the suspect was here to see, whoever that young woman was, she's probably one of the best air mages the world has ever seen."

Bethany let out a single bark of a laugh before retracing their steps back out into the day.

The entrance to the bar was packed with reporters when Bethany and her team came back. She was already annoyed by having just missed the suspect when he teleported away. When the reporters came at her, asking her questions faster than she could answer, in a collection of voices she couldn't begin to decipher, her fiery rage sprang forth, as did her fire magic. Twin flames formed in her hands, soaring to the ceiling overhead. When it became clear to the reporters that she wasn't in the mood, they backed down.

"No need for that," Greg said. "A simple 'no comment' would do."

"Oh, like that would have stopped them," Bethany said. As the group started to head down the dark hallway, she glared at the reporters, causing them to scurry further from her wrath. Most of them were pure bloods, with the news being one of the few high end careers they had left to them. There were even a few air mages in the mix as well. It was clear that the press was taking this incident very seriously. Perhaps too seriously, given what they knew of what happened.

The CSI team had done their work while they were away. The entrance to the crime scene was blocked off by a sealing spell, keeping most of the onlookers at bay. An earth mage was standing guard, his well-muscled heavy form designed to stop those few that were powerful enough to pass through the barrier. As Bethany passed through, her sigil glowed above her head, sending a warm feeling through her entire body. The badge was designed to let the Mage Authority representatives go in and out of such spells without trouble.

The scene inside had changed since she had last seen it. The ice tower had since melted, destroying much of the evidence of the original incident. The crushed remains of the water mage had been removed by the coroner. Even the splinched mages were sent to The Authority's failed spells ward, in the hopes of restoring them. It wasn't looking favorable, though.

The bartender, still behind his own protective barrier, continued to tend the bar, though the place wasn't open to patrons. He was cleaning a mug, as usual. When he saw the group come in, he started mixing them some drinks. The enchanted glasses flitted about in the air back there, playing tag or fighting each other, it was too difficult to tell. The enchantment on them was one of those weird, advanced spells that worked, though no one actually understood how. The inventor was something of a madman, and killed himself soon after having succeeded. The glasses had been manufactured long before anyone figured out that they were the cause of his suicide.

Bethany sat heavily down on the one good stool, with a loud, equally heavy sigh. Greg, Dan, and Igloo took up positions around her, with Igloo leaning against the bar right next to her. Igloo was one of those people who just didn't get the idea of personal space, tending to sit way too close to the other members of the team. Bethany knew it would get her killed one day, but she was tired of trying to discourage the girl.

"Don't worry," Igloo said. "We'll find him."

"That's not what I'm worried about," Bethany said.

"Well, you don't really think he was involved in all of this, do you?" Dan asked. "That water mage obviously got herself killed, trying to pull off magic she wasn't ready for. From what the bartender said--"

"I know what the bartender said," Bethany said. "I know what happened here. And, no, I don't think the pure blood had a hand in any of this. That wasn't why we were chasing him down."

"Well, hey, you're the senior Authority here. It's your ballgame. I'm just here for the hotdogs."

"What's a hotdog?" Igloo asked.

"I don't know," Dan said. "It was just something my dad used to say."

"Ugh, don't remind me," Greg said. "I miss hotdogs."

"No, seriously, what's a hotdog?"

"It's a glorious tub of unidentified meat that tasted glorious," Greg said, fantasizing about the meat byproduct.

"It was a kind of sausage-like product, a casualty of culinary science not working like it should," Bethany explained.

"Oh. So, not related to canines? Or was it canine meat?"

"No one really knows," Greg said.

"Usually pork or beef," Bethany said. "Can we stop talking about food? I have more important issues on my mind."

"What? Like our escaped... witness?" Dan asked. "I keep telling you, he had no hand in this. The water told me as much."

"Yes, but what did the water tell you?" Bethany asked. "Not just that he was innocent."

"Oh, wait, this isn't about the deaths here, then?" Dan asked. "I thought... I mean, yea, of course it's not about them, right? It's about the black market deal."

"What was he buying? Who was he buying it from? What is so important, so valuable, for it to be worth an original prototype?" And why, she wondered more than anything else, did he have to get her daughter mixed up in all of that?

Chapter Five
Accomplice

Ardith

It was probably the worst landing Ardith ever had when teleporting, even compared to those that she had when she was only just learning the spell. The first time she managed to disappear, her landing placed her in the janitor's closet of her school, three rooms over from where she was supposed to land, with her foot in a bucket. When she landed in her apartment, she landed on her head, hitting hard enough to give her a concussion. She slid across the hardwood floors, coming to rest at the base of her bed.

"Ow," she grunted, when she hit.

Ardith lay there for a few moments, coming to grips with what it was that she had seen before disappearing. There was no doubt who they were, or what it meant that she got him out of there when she did. The Mage Authority was the only source of law and order in the world, after all the old governments fell when Apophis dropped into orbit. She had just helped a known fugitive from the law escape from the group that had been duly appointed to arrest him.

"Or did I?" she asked.

She realized that she hadn't heard anything from the man, hadn't seen him since they left the office. She figured that he might not have come along with her at all. Fighting against her pain and dizziness, she managed to sit up, using her bed for support and stability. She looked around her apartment, over towards her landing pad. The apartment was new, made only three years earlier, so the apartment didn't have a door. There was no hallway either, just a landing area near the center of the building that could be expanded for deliveries.

The landing area was empty for a split second, before her pile of bills from the office appeared in the small mail box on the floor. The letters piled up neatly, one on top of the other, before spilling over again. They spread out across the floor in a mess. The idea was that she would never lose her bills, but it didn't help if she couldn't pay them. Fortunately, they wouldn't follow her if she went out, just to locations that she could claim ownership to.

More importantly, though, was that there was no sign of the old man. He must not have made the ride along like he was supposed to, not leaving the office when she did. Ardith would have cursed herself for her inability to pull him along, for her lack of ability in air magic, but that worked out better for her. For once, her incompetence saved her from a much worse infraction.

However, that relief, that joy, was short lived. Before the smile could spread across her face, the man suddenly appeared from thin air. He landed perfectly in place on the landing platform, head up and solidly on his feet. His eyes were closed and his arms were stretched outward, as if he were still holding onto Ardith. It took him a few moments to realize that she wasn't there, for him to pull his arms towards his chest. Only then did he open his eyes.

"That didn't--" he started, but he couldn't get out more than that before he was doubled over. Vomit spilled out of him onto the floor. Her bills, too close to the man to avoid being hit by the vomit, cried out in disgust. They tried to skirt away from him and the sick that was coming out of him. Most of the bills managed to escape the onslaught, but a few were hit full on. Those few that were properly soiled hung in the air for a moment, still struggling to escape. But between the vomit and the fact that they were the oldest bills in the pile, the enchantment on them quickly dissipated. Ardith couldn't help but wonder if her creditors would know of the destruction.

"You asshole," Ardith said. She managed to get to her feet, but not much further. As soon as she stood up, she started to feel lightheaded. She took a few steps forward, toward the man, before tipping over and falling onto the bed.

"Sorry," the man said, once he was done vomiting. "I hope those letters weren't important."

"Not the bills, you moron," Ardith said. She was much more stable just lying there on the bed. "You... You made me an accessory after the fact."

"A what now?"

"You were escaping the Mage Authority, and you made me help you. Why didn't you tell me you were a fugitive?"

"I'm... I'm not... not really."

"Uh huh."

"No, seriously. I... I was just at a bar that got hit by a mage attack. They only want me for questioning. The problem was that would involve them asking questions that I couldn't answer, not without putting my quest in jeopardy."

"Oh, not your stupid quest again." She managed to sit up on her bed, though she kept her feet up on it. Stars started to dance in front of her eyes for a moment, but then they faded. "I really couldn't care less about your quest."

"It's more important than you know. The fate of the world is at stake."

"God, melodramatic much? Maybe if you actually told me what this quest of yours was, I'd understand how important it is."

"I just told you," the man said. "My quest is to save the world."

"Save the world? Seriously? That's your quest? Save it from what?"

"Um... how do we get out of here?" he asked. He was looking at the wall behind him, back where the door would have been on an older building. The wall had a picture hanging on it instead, some old thing that her mother had given her for a housewarming gift when she moved in. It depicted a nymph dancing in a forest glen and used to belong to her grandmother before she died. Her grandmother was a light mage and it was meant to remind Ardith that she would always be looking over her.

At that moment, it just reminded her of how disappointed her mother would be in her.

"I don't have a door. Seriously? How could you never have been in a new building before? How can you survive in this world without a linking book? How... How are you even possible?"

"Like I said, I don't get out much. Some friends of mine and I sort of... bunkered down when everything happened."

"You mean... You mean to tell me you haven't been outside, like really out in the world, since Apophis arrived?"

"That about sums it up. My life has been a bit sheltered as of late." He laughed at his comment for some reason, though Ardith had no idea why.

"That was like thirty years ago. Most prison sentences are shorter than that. Wait... were you in prison? Are you an escaped felon? That would explain the law being after you. Did I help an escaped felon escape the law?"

"No, seriously. I didn't do anything wrong. Did... There was an accident at a bar downtown. You must have heard about that? Three dead, that I know of, all by magic. How would I have had any part in that? I'm a pure blood. They still call us that, right? Pure bloods? Or is there some other word for it now, seeing as how it's not just demons and Hulandans anymore."

"Yes, you're still called pure bloods. We're just mages... well, mages and rares, for rare talents, though we both might as well be the same group. It's all in how the gene manifests."

"How do they even know it's a gene, though? Wouldn't anything that could have determined that be adversely affected by Apophis?"

"Huh?" Ardith asked, trying to unpack the question.

"The equipment used to extract... to pull DNA out of a cell, that's all based on science. Science doesn't work with Apophis overhead."

"It doesn't work when it's set, either. No, I don't know how they know it's a gene. That's just what they taught us in school."

"Well, however they know, I don't have it. I am quite useless in this world."

"And, yet, you think you're going to save it? How? You never did tell me what your plan is."

"Let's just say there's a package that I need to get somewhere and leave it at that... for now."

"And where is this package?" Ardith asked. She looked him over, trying to see if he was hiding something somewhere. Even with his coin purse tucked into his belt behind his back, she could still see it, bulging out through the coat. Unless the package was small enough to fit in a pocket, it didn't seem like he had it.

"I stowed it somewhere. It's too valuable to risk losing it while I put the rest of my plans in motion. Once we have everything set up to get it where it's going, I can retrieve it."

"Assuming it's still there. You're not the only one worried about their place in the world. There are scavengers everywhere, looking for anything valuable. I hope you hid the thing where no one will look for it."

"Oh, don't worry," he said. "I'm pretty sure no one will ever think to look for it there."

"Oh... kay... Anyway, I don't think I caught your name. If we're going to be working together, and that's a big if, what am I going to call you?"

"Call me... The Scientist," he said. He laughed again for some reason that was a complete mystery to Ardith.

"The Scientist, huh? That's a bit of a mouthful. How about TS? That good?"

"Umm... sure, I guess," TS said.

"Good, 'cause you do know that the whole myth about given names is just that, right? A myth?"

"What?"

"There's no more power in a person's given name than their use name. A name is a name. If it's yours, it has power over you."

"Huh? Wait, what do you mean if we're going to be working together? You gave me your oath. I thought you couldn't break that without risking your magic or something."

"Well, my magic isn't that great to begin with. Besides, I'd rather have my life, my freedom. With the Mage Authority after you, I might be better off without my magic than with helping you." Not to mention the fact that she was pretty sure the loopholes she put in place would keep her from the brunt of the impact of breaking the oath.

"I don't think it will come to that. Once the whole thing blows over, they won't see a reason to keep chasing after me. What exactly are they going to charge me with? Fleeing the scene of a crime? Of an accident? There were tons of people there. They all fled. It's not like anyone would ever think I had something to do with it."

"How do you know I don't think you had something to do with it?" Ardith asked. She eyed him warily. After all, he already admitted to having been at the scene, claimed to know nothing about the world, and was fleeing from The Authority. There were plenty of enchanted devices that can kill and make it look like a mage did it.

"What?" TS asked. "Are... Are you serious? I didn't even know those people."

"Then why were you there?"

"I was there to talk to a contact, to get the package. He chose the place, not me. He would have been more likely to have had a hand in it all, though he's as much of a pure blood as I am. Please, you... You gotta believe that I had nothing to do with it. Nothing at all. I swear." He almost seemed close to tears. His eyes still wandered around the room, perhaps looking for a way out of the enclosed space. The only way out through conventional means, though, was through the window, and it was a ten story drop down to the ground below.

"Alright, alright, just calm down," Ardith said. "Look, if you want my help, we need to set a few ground rules. First, if we see a way for you to reach out to The Authority without you ending up arrested, we do it, alright?"

"Sure, I can agree to that. It would help to get them off my back, if we can. I don't think we can really pull this off with them chasing after us."

"After you," Ardith corrected. "They're chasing after you." She moved towards the edge of the bed, dropping her feet down onto the ground. She was already feeling stronger from the botched teleport spell and wanted to get going. The sooner she could get rid of the guy, the better for all involved. "Second, you're going to tell me everything about this whole mission, quest, whatever, of yours, or I walk."

"Well... I don't think that will work," TS said. "If I do tell you, you might just walk anyway, and I need your help to get this whole thing working. Once everything is in place, once you see the whys and the hows of it all, it won't... Well, it won't seem as dangerous, as hopeless, as life threatening as you'd think it is now. Just... trust me."

"How?"

"What?"

"How exactly am I supposed to trust you? I don't know you. I don't know anything about you. You haven't said anything that even remotely suggests that you're on the level, even on the little that you've told me so far. How exactly do you expect me to trust anything you've said? How do you expect me to follow you into the unknown, without even knowing your end game? I might as well just turn you into

The Authority myself, save us both a huge headache. They'll probably know of a way to get the oath removed without it being triggered. I'm sure there are lots of people that made oaths without knowing the full story beforehand."

"You know what? You're right," TS said.

"I'm what now?"

"You're right. You have no reason to believe anything I said, though I'm sure there's some kind of... lie detector spell or whatever that you could use."

"Sure, but... well, it's an air spell, and I'm not all that good at air spells. Why do you think I had so much trouble getting us here?"

"I don't know; it seemed like a perfectly fine teleport to me."

"Trust me, it wasn't."

"Anyway, there is one thing that could prove that I'm on the level, something far better than my word."

TS reached into the inside pocket of his coat. Ardith jumped to her feet, expecting him to pull out the weapon that he claimed that he didn't use on the victims at the bar. She hadn't heard anything about an attack, but she wasn't about to let a pure blood get the better of her. While most defensive spells were earth magic, there were a few that she could work with water. She pulled mana into her from the air around her and started spinning up the spell.

When TS pulled his hand back out of his coat, he was holding a long rod in his hand. He looked over at Ardith, seeming oblivious of her defensive posture, of the spell she was starting to form between them. It was only when TS extended the rod to Ardith that she recognized what it was. She had seen far too many rain rods over the years to think it was anything but. In curiosity and shock, she dropped the spell before it was fully formed, letting her mana reserves escape back into the air around her.

"Here," TS said, handing her the rod.

"What? It's just a rain rod. What's so important about that?"

"It's not just any rain rod. It's the prototype."

"What? No, it isn't. That should be in a museum somewhere. There's no way you have the prototype to the rain rod."

She rotated it in her hands, feeling the weight of it, probing it with her magic. It felt just like any other rain rod, no different from her own that she barely used. But, then again, that was the whole point of the prototype. It was meant to be the first of its kind, duplicated exactly down to the smallest detail. The more perfect the baseline components were, the easier the original enchantments could be melded with it. But it also helped in manufacturing, as making copies of the copies of the copies meant more of them could be duplicated per hour. If the original was imperfect, the duplicates would be more so.

Ardith walked across her loft apartment, heading into her kitchen area. She had one drawer that was dedicated to all the odds and ends that she barely used. Pulling that drawer open, it took her barely a minute to find her own rain rod. With the two of them in her hands, she could do a more detailed examination of them, comparing the feel of each of them side by side. Still, there was no difference, no sign that the one TS had given her was any different. She was about to turn back to him, to tell him as much, but then she saw it.

Along the base of her rain rod was a line of numbers, engraved in the handle. They were barely noticeable, taking a play of the light for them to show up against the stainless steel surface. It was the serial number of her rain rod, showing that it was the five millionth one to come out of the factory, give or take. She held the two rods up to the light, side by side, gradually rotating the one that TS had given her. Only after spinning the prototype several times did she realize that it didn't have a serial number on it. Beyond that, there were further imperfections around the edges of hers, which she only saw after she started to believe the man's claims.

"Okay," she said. "Okay, I'm willing to admit that this might be the prototype. I'm no expert on this stuff, though, so I'd need to see proof on that. But, so what? So what if you have the prototype?"

"That thing is worth quite a lot of money, isn't it?" TS asked.

"Enough money to kill for, sure. Was this what you went to that bar for? Is this the package you got there?"

"No, that was supposed to be the payment. I'm just saying, that's how important my quest is. That's how expensive the package is."

"Then someone really is sure to find it, wherever you stashed it, and make serious bank off of it. Either you're that stupid, or..."

"Or that desperate." He nodded his head before reaching out his hand for the prototype. Ardith didn't give it back easily. She was starting to think she should have held out for a bigger payout than that small purse he had shown her. "Now do you believe me?"

"No, not entirely. I'm willing to admit that you might be telling the truth, though. What now?"

"What do you mean?"

"I mean, what's the next step to the quest? Where do we go from here? If not straight to jail."

"Well, I have the package," he said. After putting the rain rod back into his pocket, he pulled out a pile of papers. The pile was messy, folded and refolded so many times that they looked like so much trash. He stood there, flipping through them for a moment, before continuing. "I have the water mage, now, namely you. Next, we need an air mage. I'm guessing you're not going to be able to help me with some of the spell work we'll need to get the package... where it's going."

"So, wait a minute here. This quest is a delivery mission?"

"Sure, I guess you can think of it that way. I have to get the package to somewhere, while it's in one piece. To do that, I'll need you, an air mage, and a couple of other things. Once we get the package to where it's going, you'll get the pouch."

"Now we're talking. Why didn't you just tell me that to begin with?" She spun back around to the still open drawer of miscellaneous things. When she was looking for the rain rod, she had seen her old linking book. Figuring it would be easier to get around with that instead of relying on ride alongs, she pulled it out of the drawer and tossed it over to TS. He caught it, but ended up dropping half his notes to do so. "Let's get started."

Chapter Six
Getting Blood from Stone

Bethany

Bethany wasn't sure how Ardith managed to block their attempts to track her. She had never been all that strong of an air mage, like Igloo had suggested. The way that she had described the teleport that had happened in that room wasn't sounding all that promising. However, with no reports of dismembered bodies popping up on the network, and she did check, she had to hope that her daughter managed to land somewhere safely. Ardith was an adult, and she kept reminding herself that she had to trust her to do the right thing, once she figured out what that was.

The blood mage that had left the scene at the bar, however, was much easier to track. He hadn't done anything to block his signature, which came up as the two hundred eighty-fifth entry on the landing platform. Even though he hadn't actually used the platform, forcing his way through the barrier that was put up over the building, his teleportation still registered on the nearest platform. There were no other platforms in the building, or even the neighboring buildings, as the old city was almost abandoned. It was easy enough to find him in the registry, as he was the only blood mage to teleport in or out of the building in the twenty-four hours prior to the incident. There was one up side to so few blood mages being out there.

One of the downsides, though, was that they quickly closed ranks when one of them was in trouble.

"What exactly are we hoping to get here?" Greg asked.

The four of them were staring up at the blood logo over the door. They were at Guild Row in DC, the former site of congress. The old building was destroyed soon after The Arrival, when the then president of the United States had his awakening. He was there to discuss how the government was to address the sudden loss of technology and the "plague of mages", as he put it, that was starting to spread across the globe. The entire building, including all of its occupants, disappeared instantly, leaving only the president behind. A lot of people at the time found it a bit ironic that the leader of the free world was the most powerful void mage to ever be identified. He went from being the leader of the free world to being the leader of the magical world in a single afternoon.

In place of the old building, nine towers were erected, and held in place, through magic. In the center of where the old building stood were the guild halls for the four main elements, earth, air, fire, and water. The water hall was a large ice tower, not too different from the one that the water mage had tried to make in the middle of the bar. Earth was solid rock, reaching up into the sky. Air was crystal, reflecting and refracting the light from the sun and bathing the area. Fire was constantly flowing magma, pulled up through the earth around it.

On either side of the square were light and dark, with light being in the south and dark to the north. The two towers were echoes of each other, light being solid white and dark being solid black. Both were carved of solid marble, though neither showed a single speck of the opposite's color.

These six made up the main part of guild row, the symbol of the Mage Authority. However, the guild hall they stood before wasn't one of them. Most people ignore the three much smaller towers that stood to the east of the main six. This was where the high mages had their guilds, one for each of blood, death, and void. The void guild stood empty and dark in the middle, appropriately so. Their numbers were so few that none of them had stepped forward to be their guild master. While each of their members were known to The Authority, only the president had ever revealed himself to the world at large. He had his own office at the quorum hall, which had replaced the White House, though the original building had survived The Arrival and that first year. Few liked to look upon the death guildhall, as it was made from bones piled high in a disgusting display. It, too, stood empty, as most of its members were in hiding or on the run from the law.

However, the one they had come to see was the blood guild, the blood red tower that stood three floors tall. Rumor had it that the building was made from solidified blood, hardened into a stone that was harder and stronger than steel. Members of the guild often bragged that, had they the resources to do so, they could have built their tower into space, pushing beyond the limits that Apophis would have allowed. No one knew just how far that was, though, as space travel was a casualty of the loss of science.

"Hoping?" Bethany asked, once Greg's words registered to her. "Not much. What we'd want is for them to surrender the mage that destroyed the tower at the bar. He's the true culprit, the one responsible for the mage's death."

"Glinda," Dan said. "Her name was Glinda."

"God, these Magic-Touched names. Stupid condemned."

"Aren't you a condemned?" Greg asked. "I mean, I'm a Centennial. Pretty sure that makes you a condemned."

"Yea, yea, yea. But, when it came to naming my daughter, I went with a real name. Ardith may be rare, and old, but a real name."

"Glinda is a real name," Igloo said.

"No, it's the name of a faery."

"A witch," Greg corrected.

"There's no such thing as witches," Igloo said. "Faeries, though..."

"Back to the matter at hand," Greg said. "What are we expecting to get out of this?"

"Our asses handed to us," Dan said. "Do you really expect them to just hand over their guildmate?"

"No," Bethany said. "But we have to at least try. He's a suspect in an ongoing investigation. The treaty says they're supposed to hand him over to The Authority. Whether or not they do, that's another story."

"What did the boss say when you told him about this plan?" Greg asked.

"I haven't yet. It's still within my purview on how I want to handle this investigation."

"Yea, but only until we report in to The Authority," Greg said. "We should have done that already."

"We're still in pursuit of the suspects. Once they stonewall us, I have one more card to play. You know me, I hate to just leave things out there like this."

"I don't get it," Igloo said. "If we know that they're just going to stonewall us, why do we try?"

"Oh, Igloo, honey," Dan said. "You do know we're cops, right? It's a dirty job, and no one likes us for doing it, but it's gotta be done."

"And if we don't do it, who's going to?" Greg said.

"Besides, there's still a slim chance that they might just hand the guy over," Bethany said. "Just... remember, if they turn on us, our magic is going to be blocked. Don't try to be a hero. If you sense your affinity going down, run."

"Well, wait for the others," Greg said. "But, yea, run."

Bethany smiled and nodded at Greg before leading the way into the guild hall. The main entrance was for members only, blocking anyone that didn't have the affinity in question. It was this entrance that had the blood logo over it. Just next to it, with a logo of the Mage Authority, was a visitors' entrance. The guildhalls were supposed to let anyone in as a visitor, to request an audience with the guild, but the high mage guilds didn't follow that rule. As the group headed through the visitor's entrance, they felt the barrier over it move across their skin, letting them enter the building. Pure bloods would be hard pressed to make their way through it, but any mage worth their affinity would be able to come in.

The entry chamber for the visitors' entrance was small, just barely allowing the four of them to be in there together. Across from the entrance was another door, one leading into the guild hall proper. To their left was a desk, blocked off by magic proof glass. The blood mages didn't need that kind of protection, but the receptionist might not have been a member. She was sitting there doing a crossword puzzle, seeming oblivious to their arrival. It was hard to tell anything through the glass, though her red framed glasses suggested that she was a lesser mage. No self-respecting blood mage would leave their eyesight as anything less than perfect. Their egos were too big for that.

"Hello," Bethany said, trying to get the attention of the receptionist.

"We're not accepting petitioners today," the receptionist said, without looking up from her crossword. The paper looked old, fragile, perhaps even from before The Arrival. But as she wrote in pen down the middle of it, Bethany wondered how even someone working for the blood guild would be that wasteful.

"When do you accept petitioners?" Igloo asked.

"We don't accept petitioners any day."

"We're not petitioners," Bethany said. She pulled her badge off of her hat, slamming it against the glass. "We're Mage Authority." The receptionist barely showed the slightest reaction to the act.

The glass hissed defiantly as the enchantments of the badge battled with the protections interlaced through every molecule of the glass. Rumor had it, magic proof glass had been around longer than Apophis had been, though no one really knew why that would be. The enchantments on it were so strong that even the president himself couldn't break through it.

"We're not accepting Mage Authority today, either," the receptionist said.

"Come on, Bethany," Greg said. "Let's just go. We don't need this kind of trouble."

"We have reason to believe that your guild is harboring a fugitive from the law at this moment," Bethany said, through gritted teeth. "I demand to see your guild master."

"The guild master isn't in, but if you'd like to file a request for an appointment, the forms are on your right."

Bethany looked to her right, but there wasn't anything there. The glass ran the entire length of the wall, with barely a ledge along its length that made up the desk. Beyond that was the door itself, which took up the entire far wall. Behind her, though, was another table, holding several boxes along the near side. Each box was labeled with the forms that would go in them, including a request to see the guild master. However, each box was completely empty, even of dust.

"You're out of forms," Bethany said.

"Oh, well, then you'll just have to wait until we get more printed off. That should be sometime next year. If you'd like to come back at that point, I'll be happy to accommodate you."

"You are aware that you're required to grant the Mage Authority access to your guild when on official business, are you not?"

"We have given you access," the receptionist said. "You're inside the building, are you not?"

"Who is the ranking member on site?" Bethany asked.

The receptionist slammed her pen down onto the desk and finally looked up at her. She seemed to glare with a fiery passion at Bethany through the glass. Suddenly, the fire mage was thankful that the protection of the glass went both ways. "Look, I don't know how your guild handles things, but we don't track the comings and goings of our members. Even if the person you are looking for was here at some point, it is unlikely that they are still here. We don't house our members here. Unlike the more pretentious footprint of the other towers, we don't have the room to even house the guild master. Which, of course, is why he's not here. Now, if you will excuse me, I have some very important matters to handle here."

"What about access to your landing pad?" Bethany asked. "Certainly that wouldn't be too much to ask."

"We don't have landing pads in the guild. Thank you. Have a nice day."

"Let's just go, boss," Greg said again. This time, he placed a restraining hand on her, turning her towards the door.

Bethany glared behind her, first to the receptionist, then to Greg, and finally to the door barring their way further into the guild hall. No matter what the receptionist said, she knew he was in there. She knew that the man responsible for the deaths at that bar was through that door. If only she could get through it.

And why not?

Bethany turned around, pushing her way out of Greg's grip. She squared off against the door, her enemy, the one thing standing in her way, blocking her from getting to the man they should have been after all along. Her magic flared up without her needing to pull it into herself, soaring as her rage was given its head like a wild stallion. The glass between them and the receptionist might have been protected from magic, but what were the chances that the door was, too. She saw red as she let her flames flare forward, forcing their way through the air and to the wooden door. They licked at the wood, salivating at the feel of it in their mouths, their tongues licking every inch of it. The wood caught on fire quickly, the flames turning blue with heat. The door was quickly consumed in the conflagration, and the fires edged forward, searching for new things to burn, more things to consume in their fiery hunger.

Instantly, the flames died, disappearing and dropping the small room into darkness. Bethany could no longer feel her magic. The loss of it felt like a bucket of cold, icy water to her face. At the same time, it felt like the blood in her very veins was on fire, burning her up from the inside as it boiled within her. She had never felt that kind of heat, not since The Arrival. Even when her flames were at their hottest, it was little more than a warm day on the beach. Yet, she could feel her skin start to pinken, start to burn under the barrage of magic coming at her from the guild. The door, which had been her enemy, her nemesis, suddenly seemed like her only protection from the haunting visage before her. The gaping maw waiting to draw her in. To consume her. To cook and eat her alive.

And, just as suddenly, it was over. The fire left her, making her feel more drained than before. Her magic was still blocked, still lost to her, but her blood started to calm down once more. She shivered in the cold as it surrounded her, a steady breeze playing out across her skin giving her goosebumps. The lights slowly returned to the front room, as the ever burning torches flared back to life. The steady form of the receptionist claimed her attention, still sitting in the same chair, still working on the crossword as if nothing had happened.

With a loud boom, a door popped back up in the doorway, once again blocking the way further into the guild hall. With its return, Bethany's magic was released from the block that had been on it. She pulled it close to herself like a warm blanket, using its heat to guard against the cold that still surrounded her. It was only then that she realized that she was alone in the entry area. Her team had left her, had fled before the magical might of the guild members on the other side of the door.

"Th-th-thank you," Bethany said. She hated that her voice was no longer steady. Hated that she couldn't get it out in a single try. Hated that she thanked the woman at all, as she was very much not helpful. Still, it was the only thing that came to mind before she turned tail and ran for the front door.

Greg, Dan, and Igloo were all standing at the foot of the stairs that led up to the front door. When she exited, they all turned towards her, in various forms of defensive stances. It took them a moment to realize that it was only her, that she wasn't running from a troupe of blood mages at her back. Then, they suddenly seemed very relieved to see her coming out of the building under her own power.

"Thank god," Greg said. "We were worried that we needed to come rescue you."

"What happened to you guys in there?" Bethany asked. "I thought you had my back."

"We were following orders," Dan said. "You told us, in no uncertain terms, that we were supposed to run when we felt our magic go away. My magic went away, so I ran."

"I remember some part about not leaving your team behind, too."

"Boss, I hate to say it, but that was you," Greg said. "What the hell was that in there? Why did you go off at them? I've never seen you this... angry before."

"I have," Dan said. "That's not it. That, in there, that wasn't anger. That was something more. There's something you're not telling us. What's going on? Why is this case so important to you?"

"Just what were you expecting to accomplish by barging your way in there?" Greg asked. "They're high mages. The lowest of the highs, sure, but still high. Just one of them can block every one of us. Just one of them can take out the entire Mage Authority."

"Well, not technically," Dan said. "I mean, we'd need help from a light and dark mage--"

"Shut it, Dan. Boss, you could have gotten us all killed in there. Dan's right. This case... I'm heading back to The Authority to check in. You should, too."

"No," Bethany said. She shook her head, not out of defiance but resignation. "You guys go on ahead. There's one more thing I need to try before... You guys go on. I'll be fine."

"No more stupid stunts that are going to get you killed?" Greg asked.

"No more stunts. Just... Just a lunch date with my husband."

Chapter Seven
The Air Bar

Eric

Eric thought that the linking book was weird. Each page was set aside for a different location. The pages themselves had some writing along the top, followed by a picture that took up almost the entire page. When the book was moved, the picture shifted, the point of view rotating in place. When Eric moved back and forth while holding the book, though, the picture didn't move, as if the camera that took it was mounted in place but could swivel around.

"Cool," Eric said, as he played with the book a little.

"Can you focus?" Carissa, the mage, said. She seemed exactly like he had expected most mages to be, selfish and entitled. She had been born with her power, grew up probably knowing that she would become what she was. There was no point in her trying to be anything else. It reminded him of the rich families that ruled the world from the boardroom back before Apophis had supposedly changed all of that.

Carissa pulled the book back from him and started to flip through the pages haphazardly. Eric managed to catch glimpses of the first few pages, which showed a forest glen, a torch lit room filled with a lot of kids, and a dark room that was lit only by the light from the windows. It seemed like those were probably important locations for Carissa, from when she was growing up. That was probably her park, her preschool, her childhood home, yet she flipped past those pages like the locations meant nothing to her. There seemed to be a couple hundred pages in the book, and from what he could see they all seemed to be full of one of those pictures.

When she got to the middle of the book, she found an empty page, the first that Eric had seen. On the other side of the book from it was another scene with kids in it, though these were older, perhaps ten or so, and were running through the picture down a long hallway that extended into the distance. The view looked weird without the sounds to go with it, but the book was silent. Carissa moved the book over to the table, blocking his view of it, and started to write along the top. Her quick scribbles were completely illegible to Eric, but the book seemed to understand what she wrote. He watched from over her shoulder as the picture started to form in the empty space below her scribbles. It was foggy at first, but a crowded room slowly formed into the view.

"There," she said, nodding in approval. She held the book out to him, the new page open and pointed at him. "It's my book, so I'll have to hold it for you to be able to use it. Don't worry that the book won't come with you; that's part of the safeguards on it."

"Um... okay," Eric said. He hadn't known what to expect, but the book coming with him was pretty far down on the list. "What... What do I do?"

"You've really never used a linking book, have you. Just put your hand on the picture."

"Then what?" Eric asked. He reached out his hand towards the page, sensing the magic as it poured off of the book. "Should I click my heels together, or--" His words were interrupted the instant his flesh touched the paper.

Eric was still nauseous from the first teleport. The second did not help things. The room started to spin around him before he landed at his destination. When he did land, the ground fell out from under him and he went down hard onto the landing pad. Hands grabbed his coat, pulling him up from the ground, though he couldn't focus on the room enough to understand why or who it was. All he knew was that the hands were stronger than he expected from the girl.

A pair of stylish black boots appeared on the platform next to him. The toes curled up onto themselves, looking like they belonged to one of Santa's elves. Moments later, they were obscured from view as a long blue coat flitted down around them, grazing the floor. That was when he noticed that the floor wasn't all there. At first, he thought he was losing it, more so than he already had. But then he noticed that his own arm extended down past the landing platform that he was lying on.

"Oh, god," he shouted, staring down at the empty space below him. The restraining hands were actually saving him from plummeting through the air to his death. Below him, any possible sight of the ground was obscured by clouds floating past. He wasn't sure if he really was at a high altitude, if the ground was just beneath the cloud cover, or if it was some kind of illusion and the floor was actually just a few feet down.

"Watch that first step," someone said in a bad impression of Daffy Duck. "It's a long one."

"Can we rent some clouds?" a more familiar voice said. "He's a pure blood and I've never been that great at air magic."

"Sure, sure. Five credits. I'd better get them back in one piece."

"You'll get them back in more or less the same state as we get them. They're clouds. Can it really be considered to be a distinct piece?"

"Touché. The cover is twenty credits, each. Comes with a drink."

"I don't plan on staying that long."

"Hey, the cover is the cover. Don't use the drink voucher, no sweat off my nose."

"Ugh, you'd better be worth this," Carissa said. She gave Eric a sideways kick for good measure.

Eric was starting to get his senses around him. The view of the long fall helped with that, setting adrenaline coursing through his veins. However, as the nausea faded, fear took its place. Whenever he tried to pull his arm back up, he would overbalance, tipping precariously towards the ledge to his side. The landing pad seemed highly inadequate to hold his hulking form.

"Oh, get up," Carissa said. She pushed him over, flipping him off of the landing platform to fall through the air. He let out a loud scream as he fell onto his back, staring up at the sky above him. The sun was similarly blocked above as the ground was below, but he could see the bright ball blazing through the clouds. He flailed around, reaching for some handhold, something to hold onto. It took him several moments of screaming to realize that Carissa's smiling face above him wasn't moving, wasn't fading, wasn't disappearing above him. "You done?" she asked, once Eric's breath ran out.

"Noobs," the bouncer muttered. He was huge, a lumbering fat man sitting on a stool next to the landing pad. The stool itself, though, wasn't on anything. No cloud, no floor, just open sky. It was as solid hanging there in midair as it would have been on a hard floor.

Once he was certain he wasn't about to fall to his death, Eric rolled over onto his stomach. Beneath him was a cloud, but it held him up. He reached his hand down, pressing against the white fluffiness of the cloud. His hand went through it, but not all the way. Instead, he found enough resistance to push himself up onto his feet. The cloud felt more like an oversized pillow, hugging his hand in fluffy, wet comfort.

As Eric stood up, the cloud seemed to adjust to him, shrinking to a much smaller size beneath him. He spread his feet wide as he tried to balance himself on the cloud. The cloud was small, but there was plenty of space on it for himself. It reminded him of the old skateboards he used to use as a child, though it was as wide as it was long. Once he was certain of his balance, he looked around for some way to control the thing.

Around him, several faces were staring his way. Most of them showed humor, making it clear that they thought the pure blood the funniest thing to come in that place in a while. A couple just rolled their eyes before returning to the conversations he must have disturbed by his less than graceful entrance. While some of the people there were riding clouds like Eric, most were hovering there without the need. Yellow coats were everywhere, shining brightly in the sunlight.

"Where are we?" Eric asked. He looked back over to Carissa, who was just getting on her own cloud. Hers was on the opposite side of the landing platform from his, so he didn't see much of the cloud itself. But as she stepped down from the platform, she didn't go tumbling through the sky, so he figured it was a cloud holding her up.

"It's the Air Bar," she said.

"Should I know what that is?"

"I guess not. It's the big hang out for most of the young air mages, fresh out of The Academy. If you want to find someone to do your air magic for you, this would be the place." Once Carissa was solidly on her cloud, she folded her arms, looking very much like a genie. Or, at least, very much like how genies used to be depicted. The cloud seemed to move forward under its own power, moving around the platform and coming in front of Eric. It turned her around so she could face him square on. "Are you coming?"

"How do you move this thing?" Eric asked. He folded his arms like she had, thinking forward, but it didn't move. After that, he tried pushing against the air with his foot, like he would on a skateboard. That didn't help either, though it drew a few more laughs, including from Carissa.

"Will you stop that," Carissa said. She flapped her hands at him dismissively. "You have to lean forward, but subtly. If you lean too much, the cloud will shoot off too fast for you to stay on it. People actually race these things, but I don't recommend someone like you to try it."

"What do you mean someone like me? You mean a pure blood?"

"No, I mean an old person. I've seen pure bloods run circles around air mages on one of these, though that's largely because the air mages aren't too familiar with them. It just takes more practice than anything else. If you spent, oh, about three years running around on one of those, maybe even you could do a decent job in one of the races. One of the starter races. Against children. You'd still come in last, though."

"Oh, ha ha. Just lean forward? That's all? What about the arms?"

"What about the arms?" she asked, confused.

"Nothing," he said, smiling. "Never mind."

Eric relaxed his arms, letting them fall back to his sides. He leaned the slightest bit forward, barely digging his toe into the cloud beneath him. The cloud moved forward quickly, drawing him closer to Carissa. His eyes went wide, fearing that he would collide with the girl. Instinctively, he leaned backwards even more and the cloud started racing in the other direction. His arms went wide, desperately trying to find some new balance as the cloud seemed to take on a life of its own. Behind him was a wall of clouds, and he was heading towards it too quickly for him to stop.

The bouncer grabbed him up by the front of his coat, right before he slammed into the wall, or passed through it to the open sky beyond, he wasn't quite sure which. The cloud kept on going, punching through the wall and heading out. The wall parted under the impact, showing a bluer bit of sky before reforming into clouds. Barely five seconds after the cloud disappeared, it came soaring right back in, sliding over to a stack of the things that stood next to the bouncer.

"Careful, noob," the bouncer said. "You go out there, you ain't never coming back."

"Yea, they don't have the races at this altitude," Carissa said. "If you go out there, you'd pass out and fall to your death. Maybe we should get you a different cloud. Got any ones meant for babies?"

"Babies?" the bouncer asked. "In a bar? Not in this or any world, girl."

"What about a rope? Maybe I'll just pull him along behind me."

"Oh, yea, 'cause that won't be humiliating at all," Eric said.

"Would you rather be humiliated or dead? 'Cause it's looking like those are your choices."

"Just... Give me a second, alright. I'm new at... all of this. Mind setting me down?"

"Are you going to fall again?" the bouncer asked.

"I'm not planning on it."

The bouncer grunted his amusement before setting Eric back down onto his feet on the landing platform. He reached over to scoop up the returned cloud, sliding it out over in front of the platform. Eric walked forward, stepping down onto the cloud one foot at a time, making sure the first one was settled properly before easing the second one down. Once settled onto the cloud, he didn't so much as move a muscle, letting his natural balance keep him in place. Instead, he simply thought about leaning forward, without actually doing it. The cloud seemed to notice something, as it started to ease forward slowly.

"See? I can learn," Eric said. He moved over in front of Carissa, coming to a stop right next to her. "Now, did you have someone in mind or should we just ask around?"

"Well, if you're done embarrassing me, I can start showing you around. I'm sure there will be someone here I'll recognize. I may not have ever been good at air magic, but I knew some people at The Academy. One of them is bound to show up around here at some point."

Eric looked around at the bar, getting a decent look for the first time. The inside of the bar was huge, stretching further than he could see. Even so, the place was packed by the patrons, literally dancing on air. The entire area was enclosed within the clouds. Everything in it was either made of wood or clouds. The cloud bar had wooden accents and a wooden top. The wooden bar stools had clouds for seats. The melding of the two seemed odd to Eric.

"Isn't wood supposed to be part of earth?" Eric asked. "Earth and air are opposing elements, right?"

"Wood is part of light," came a voice from behind Carissa. They both turned around to look at the newcomer, who was wearing white instead of yellow. Still, she floated on air just as easily as the air mages. "It's a gift of the goddess, a part of life itself. Trees are so much higher than the earth that birthed them."

"Ignore her," Carissa said. She came over next to Eric, pulling him, and his cloud, away from the light mage. "She's just another self-righteous light mage, thinking her power is some divine gift to the world. As if someone like her would be given by god."

"I don't know," Eric said. "If God were to grant us a gift in the form of a woman--"

"Ugh, men," Carissa said. She let go of his arm and pushed him away from her. Eric had expected the move, though, so he managed to keep his balance and his place on the cloud. He laughed as he slowly turned circles around Carissa.

"I was just kidding," he said. "You're pretty, too."

"As if I care what you think of me. I just want to get you your air mage, get the delivery done, and get on with my life." She started drifting away from him, heading through the crowd.

"Oh, don't be like that," Eric said, as he slowly followed her. He still wasn't overly comfortable with the cloud, though he had to admit he liked using it. It was much easier to use than a skateboard, except he could never forget the fact that falling off of it would be so much worse.

They made their way to the bar, the crowd reluctantly parting for them. The clouds were actually lower than the level that the air mages were floating on, with Eric's knees on the same level as the mages' feet. Everyone was just looking down at them as they passed, sneering as if they were afraid to step on them. Eric appreciated the fact that none of them did.

As the crowd lost interest in the newcomers, they went back to what Eric assumed had been their activities prior to their arrival. Most of the mages there were dancing in place, bumping into the people around them, both intentionally and unintentionally. Eric didn't hear any music playing, but it seemed that the mages did. Every once in a while, as they made their way through the crowd, he peeked back at Carissa, wondering if she heard what the others did. If this was just a mage thing, an air mage thing, or some additional magical device that they didn't have.

When they got to the bar, the clouds stayed low. Eric could rest his arms on the bar without needing to duck down or sit, and Carissa had to jump up onto one of the stools to be seen. There was only one stool free, so Eric ended up hovering next to her. There was no bartender behind the bar, with the animated glasses doing the work themselves. Eric wasn't sure how to get their attention, or even if they had attention to get. He decided against ordering anything anyway, what with his stomach still rolling around on itself.

They stayed there for a while as Carissa scanned the crowd. A couple of times, she jumped back off of the stool, taking the cloud out into the crowd. Each time, she called back to him to stay there and hold her stool for her. With the crowd circling around the bar, eying the stool like vultures, he wasn't about to let it go unattended. He trusted that she could handle herself in that crowd, certainly better than he could.

After about an hour there, Eric was starting to worry that they wouldn't be able to find anyone that she knew. Eric didn't like the idea of approaching someone at random, it was bad enough that he had to rely on Carissa and she had come highly recommended to him. However, he knew that his plan would require a full powered air mage. Even if Carissa was capable enough at it, he still would have wanted another one. He was only going to get one shot at the delivery, and nothing could compromise it. Still, as the hour aged, he was about to suggest that they try figuring out which stranger seemed the most trustworthy.

"Ardi," someone shouted over the general din of the room. Carissa's eyes went wide when she spotted the person that called out. An air mage, wearing her yellow coat flapping open in the wind, flew her way through the crowd. Under the coat, the girl was wearing a white, billowy dress that kept threatening to fly over her head. As she approached Carissa, she threw her arms around her, pulling her into a huge hug. "Why didn't you tell me you were coming?"

"Um... hey, Dorth," Carissa said. After a few seconds, she hugged her back. "I... I didn't know you were going to be here today."

"Yea, I got off work early," she said. "Big scoop, so I got my story in for tomorrow already. I'd tell you about it, but you're just going to have to buy the paper tomorrow like everyone else. No special treatments, not after you--"

"Dorth, please," Carissa said. She glanced over at Eric pointedly. "Not in front of the pure blood."

"Oh," she said. She glared down at Eric like he was something that she had accidentally stepped in. "You two are together? Or, I mean... Are you guys like... together?"

"What? Ew, no. He's like... fifty or something. No offense."

"None taken," Eric said. "I am fifty or something. Did you call her Ardi?"

"Yea," Dorth said.

"No, she called me RD. Arr Dee. It's short for... Radiant Diva. It... was a nickname I picked up at The Academy from a bad round in a party game. You had to be there."

"No, wait, what?" Dorth asked.

"Shh," Carissa hissed. "I'll explain later." She said it low enough that it was hard to hear over the crowd, but Eric had excellent hearing, especially for someone his age.

"Whatever," Eric said, letting the matter drop. "What about her?"

"What about her?" Carissa said.

"What about me?" Dorth said.

"Well, she's obviously an air mage, right? Yellow is air?"

"Yea, she's a... Oh, no," Carissa said. "No. We're not... No."

"What am I missing here?" Dorth asked.

"You said we were here to find an air mage that you knew. Did you have another one in mind? Is there a reason why we can't use..."

"Dorth," she said, reminding him of her name.

"Dorth? Really? Is that short for Dorothy?" While Dorth's skin suggested a middle eastern or Indian lineage, he had heard all sorts of weird names since leaving the bunker.

"No. It's not short for anything. It's fine just the way it is. As am I. I'm in."

"Dorth, no," Carissa said.

"You're not keeping me out of this. If you're in, I'm in. Whatever it is, whatever comes our way. I want to be a part of it."

"You don't... I don't... I don't want you to come. It... It may be... risky."

"All the better for me to come with you. The two of us, working together again. We'd be unstoppable. Whatever you got yourself into, I'm coming with you. There's no talking me out of it. If you leave me behind, I'll just follow you."

"What about your job?" Carissa asked. "I'm not even sure how long this whole thing is going to take, but something tells me we're not going to be done tomorrow."

"I'll just tell my boss I'm working on a huge scoop. I'm guessing that, whatever this is, there will be a point that I can go public about it, right?"

"Um... sure, I guess," Eric said. "I mean, once it's done, it's not like it can be undone. Sure, why not? I'm sure everyone will want to know all about it. But no publishing anything until it's all done, okay?"

"You got it, boss man. I'm sorry, what's your name again?"

"Just call him TS," Carissa said. "He's being all mysterious about his real name."

"TS, RD, I feel a bit stupid using my real name."

"Have a code name in mind?" Eric asked. "I can call you Ishmael, if that would make you feel better."

"Ishmael? I don't get it."

"Dorth, you don't need a code name," Carissa said. "Your real name is awesome enough as it is."

"Good," Eric said. "Now that we have our air mage, do you think we can blow this popsicle stand? I'm either getting motion sickness or vertigo. It's too close to call."

"Don't you have someone to tell you're leaving?" Carissa asked Dorth.

"No," Dorth said, shaking her head emphatically. "As always, I'm all yours."

Carissa blushed at that remark, which spurred Eric's interest a little. However, he figured it wasn't his business, so he slowly led the way back over to the landing platform. Even as packed as the place was, there were still people steadily coming into the place, practically streaming off of the platform. The bouncer, ever vigilant at the entrance, didn't seem concerned in the least with the numbers coming in.

"Isn't there like a fire code?" Eric asked while they waited for the platform to clear off so they could use it.

"Why would there be?" the bouncer asked. "We have a fire mage on duty, somewhere in that mess, so any fire that starts up in here would be easily contained. Besides, nothing in here is flammable."

"Don't you ever run out of room in here, though?"

"Dude, we're in the sky. There's always more room." As if to demonstrate, he leaned against the wall behind him. It stretched out against his pressing and started to actually move away from him under its own power. The little indent in the wall caused a wave to flow out across the entire expanse, creating a bigger space. The patrons of the bar quickly moved to occupy the new space, continuing to dance to the music that only they could hear. "That's the problem with you pure bloods. You can't grasp the concept of the infinite possibilities that magic gives us."

"I can grasp the concepts just fine," Eric said. "Doesn't mean I gotta like it. Doesn't make it any less dangerous."

"No one has ever fallen out of this place... Well, at least not without wanting to. It's never hit anything; the whole place can move around anything that comes its way. It even floats around the world so it's always light in here. This place is safe as houses, dude."

Suddenly screaming filled the space enclosed by the clouds. Fire flared up behind them, making Eric flinch away from the heat and sudden brightness. The cloud under his feet started to shake and Eric had a strange feeling that the thing was scared. Worried that it would run off into the sky beyond the wall, taking him with it, Eric jumped off of the cloud and onto the recently cleared landing platform. This gave him an excellent view of the mayhem that was happening in the middle of the room.

And, also, of its cause. He had to smile with nostalgia at the large, fire breathing dragon in the middle of the room as it flapped its heavy wings against the clouds. There was a large gaping hole in the floor of the room, showing where the dragon had come in. The hole only got wider as it continued to throw fire all around, batting its wings feverishly to stay aloft. The mages that were in the middle of the room pushed against those further away, trying desperately to get away from the fierce creature. This only clustered the already congested people further, making progress across the room impossible.

"See?" Eric asked. "Fire code."

Chapter Eight
Politics as Usual

Bethany

There was a large storm cloud over DC. From the shape of it, almost cubic, Bethany was certain that the cloud wasn't naturally occurring. She reached for her badge, wondering why she hadn't been flagged for the investigation before she remembered that she was still technically on a case. There were plenty of members in The Authority, but it sometimes felt like she was the only competent one in the bunch.

"If they need me, they know how to contact me," she said to herself.

Bethany was just leaving the Earth guild. The rest of her team had headed back to the office. She had stopped by the guild not long after leaving the blood guild, making sure that John hadn't gone back after the quorum session. The sessions were known to run for days sometimes, and rarely for shorter than twenty-four hours. The fact that he hadn't reached out to her and hadn't gone back to the guild to check in suggested that he was still there, that the session was still running. However, even in the longest stretches, they always stopped for lunch.

She looked back up into the sky to check the time again. The sun was almost overhead, though blocked by the storm cloud. If she was going to catch him, she'd need to put things in motion quickly. She pulled out her linking book, as it was always more reliable than her memory and it had one great advantage over teleporting herself all over town. One by one, she flipped through the book, running through the list of John's favorite restaurants among those that actually did take out. The picture in the first few showed a long line, so she kept flipping. The third showed one that might take twenty minutes, but the sixth only had two, so she jumped at it. Minutes later, she was in front of the quorum hall, two steak sandwiches in hand.

The quorum hall was an interesting meld of science and magic. The original building, the White House, was still there in part. Crystal and stone were grown up strategically around the building, fortifying it and supporting it and generally making the old house look more like a castle. The hybrid building captured the light of the sun shining down on it, spreading it out across the grounds even in the middle of a storm. Bethany waited patiently, sitting on a bench across from the main entrance. Several other people were waiting around, sitting on other benches or just standing there staring at the doors. She felt like a parent waiting for her child to be released from school, reminding her of her daughter's more innocent days. They all waited there, some more patiently than others, for about twenty minutes before the large clock that was suspended over the building tolled the hour.

Minutes after the clock went off, a stream of people headed out of the building, most of them disappearing the instant they made the base of the stairs. With the leadership of the world in that building, there were no landing platforms inside and the teleportation blockers ran the entire perimeter of the place. There were also other safeguards in place, including lockdown capabilities where the building actually folded in on itself to protect against attacking mages. The place was ten times more fortified than the original White House had been in its heyday, without needing hundreds of guards to protect it.

The people coming out were an interesting mix. While several of them were wearing guild colors, not all of them did. Each of the old countries, at least those that still stood, had their own representatives on the quorum. While most of them were pure bloods, other factions had representation as well. There were representatives from the Hulandans and demons, though neither faction had much of a presence. Even so, the mages made up the bulk of the people coming out of the doors. There were a lot more yellows than blues, greens, oranges, blacks, whites, and reds, as the press corps came out with the rest of them. It was difficult to tell the difference between the guild representatives and the press, but one yellow garbed individual stood out among the rest. The guild master, the center of one of the congested yellow areas, wore a yellow baseball cap with the guild sigil in the middle, much like the hats of The Authority. Plus, instead of a yellow coat, he wore actual robes much more similar to the mages from works of fiction. Several of the other guild masters were coming out, but the splattering of green drew Bethany's eyes away from all of them.

When Bethany spotted John, she waved at him feverishly. He was standing at the top of the stairs, pulling his own green ball cap off and using it to wipe at his brow. At first, he was too far away and too preoccupied to notice her. The other people waiting for their own lunch dates were waving similarly, so she was briefly afraid that he wouldn't see her there. She needn't have worried though, as his eyes found hers the instant that he left the protection of the building. He smiled, running towards her while laughing loudly enough for her to hear across the open field.

As soon as John got to Bethany, he scooped her up off of the bench, twirling her around and laughing loudly. Her lips found his willingly, desperately, hungrily. Despite the fact that the two of them had been married for decades, had a child together even, they were still desperately, madly in love with each other. He was her whole world, the only man she ever truly loved. While she had a dalliance or two over the years, they were nothing compared to what she had with John.

"Hi," he said, simply, when he pulled away from her for a breath of air.

"Hi," she said, back, smiling and laughing right along with him. "I've missed you."

"It's been twenty-seven hours," he said. "Yet, it still feels like a hundred. Well, with how things are going in there, it might be hundreds before we're out." He let her slip out of his hands and back onto the ground in front of him. The height difference wasn't much between them, so it wasn't a long fall. "So, to what do I owe the pleasure of your company this fine afternoon?"

"Do I need a reason to come visit my husband for lunch?"

"No, but I know you have one anyway. Otherwise, you would have brought a picnic basket. Two sandwiches from that place in Philly says 'spur of the moment' to me."

Bethany handed him one of the sandwiches and the two of them went back to sit on the bench. The crowd around them slowly dispersed, most of the people heading off into DC or teleporting away to other locations. With no limits on teleportation range, other than staying on the planet, nobody ever worried about needing to get back in time. Their lives were their own, their off times their own. The world was their oyster, and they fed deeply.

"So, shoot," John said, before taking a bite of his sandwich.

"I need access to the guild master of the blood guild."

John choked on his bite of sandwich, coughing up the bit of steak and bread. It fell down to the ground several feet away from them, where a braver than usual pigeon started pecking at it. The pigeon only managed to get two pecks in before it had to fly away to avoid being hit by a fireball from a fire mage that was sitting next to the stairs. The remnants of food took the full force of the blast, leaving nothing but a charred remnant behind.

"You want to talk to who now?" John asked, once he was done choking. "Are you insane? You actually want to talk to the blood guild master? Why?"

"Because I have reason to believe they're hiding a suspect in the guild. They teleported into the guild last night and the guild receptionist refused to grant us access."

"Beth, that's not going to happen. I can't even get access to him sometimes, and I'm the earth guild master. He's supposed to be in on the quorum, but he never attends. We're just lucky he sent a representative this time. I might, emphasis on might, be able to get you a minute with that guy. But, the guild master? No. Just... no."

"John, this guy killed, or at least caused the death of a girl, not even as old as our daughter. She was nineteen, way over her head on her magic, and he just..." She snapped her finger, indicating just how quickly the blood mage had killed the girl. "From what the witnesses were saying, he actually enjoyed it, soaked up the power from it. That was how it was with the death mages before they started taking them to task."

"And you want to start rounding up the blood mages, too?" Jack asked. "Do you remember that war? How things played out? How many people died? Blood mages might not be as strong as the death mages were, but there's a lot more of them. Not to mention that they're a lot more powerful than we are. They're high mages. Who do you think is going to take them on? You? The president?" He shook his head before taking another bite of his sandwich.

"I don't know," Bethany said. "I just... Sometimes, I feel so helpless in this job. If I was a stronger mage, if I had a stronger affinity--"

"Then you'd be as spoiled and self-righteous as the rest of the high mages," John said. "I like you the way you are. Power corrupts, and all that. Besides, not all of the blood mages are like that. If they hadn't helped us out, we never would have taken down the death guild. We owe them a lot."

"Not that much. Not a life. Never a life. This guy, he needs to answer for this. If the guild protects him..."

"That's what the guilds are there for, to help us. Maybe not this far, but... Anyway, can you close the case any other way? Do you know his name? How to find him outside of the guild? Can't you just track him to his place?"

"No," she said, shaking her head. "We got his signature off of the landing platform, but not his name. You know how it works; we can only track him to the next point that he went to. We need access to the guild's landing platform to get his next destination, assuming he didn't just leave through the front door."

"Well, what about his previous destination? Certainly he had to come from somewhere when landing at the scene."

"I thought of that. It was a dead end. He teleported in from an open location. No source point to track."

"You seem more dogged about this than usual," John said. "Is there something you're not telling me? Is this just how young the girl is?"

"Not exactly." Bethany sighed heavily, staring at her barely touched sandwich as she decided how much she was going to tell him. She looked over at the other people in the area, though they all seemed well preoccupied with their own conversations and taking no interest in theirs. "There was another suspect, a pure blood, who fled the scene on foot. He was involved in an unrelated issue."

"Well, that simplifies things, doesn't it?" John asked. "Couldn't he have had something to do with the death as well? Not that I think you'd ever give up so easily, but I think this blood mage is a non-starter. If this guy is guilty of something else, maybe whatever he was doing had an adverse reaction to the victim's continued existence."

"If only it were that simple. No, I wasn't even tempted to pin it on him. Not after..."

"Not after what?"

"We chased him halfway through the city. He left on foot, if you can believe that. But... When we found him..." She looked around them again, making sure that no one was listening in on their conversation. Even then, she leaned in close to her husband, whispering the words that had been torturing her the entire day. "Ardith is with him."

"What?" John asked. He bolted to his feet, his half-eaten sandwich tumbling to the ground, forgotten. "Why are we worrying about some blood mage?" he yelled. "Why aren't we chasing after this guy? I'll kill him. I'll kill him with my own hands."

"She went with him willingly," Bethany said. She placed a staying hand on his arm, pulling him back down to the bench. "He didn't kidnap her. He hired her, I think. She teleported him away before we got in the door."

"But... Wait, why are you still on the case, then? Why weren't you pulled off the moment that your team found out about Ardith?"

"Because they didn't find out. Something went wrong with the spell; you know her and air magic. But it went wrong in the right way. We couldn't track them. Her name isn't on the lease of the space, as she has a separate agreement with her officemate, and the officemate had a rock-solid alibi. I let Greg take the lead on all of that, so it couldn't be called into question later. Besides, I was just so stunned by the fact that it was her. That it was her office that he went to. That she actually helped him. I just..."

"Hey, hey, hey," John said. He pulled her into a much needed hug, holding her tightly to his side. "It's alright. Have you heard from her today? I've been in the quorum all day, so..."

"No, nothing. No reports of unidentified splinching victims, though, so she had to have made it out of the teleport alright. I just... Why hasn't she reached out to me yet? If she's in trouble, she should have contacted me. A fire letter at the least."

"Maybe she was out of the paper for it. She's a water mage, so she can't use fire magic without an enchantment. She was never all that good with keeping her supplies filled up. Last I heard she was working on a big project, so she's probably strapped for credits right now. I'm sure fire paper is pretty low on her list of priorities, somewhere below toilet paper."

"Yea, you're right. And I guess a lot depends on how closely this guy is watching her. I just... I mean, I don't trust him, obviously."

"Well, no, of course not. But, she's our daughter. I don't think we would trust him even if we knew who he was. Who is he, though? You said he was a pure blood?"

"Yea. I have no idea. All I know is that he was involved in a black market deal. And I only know that because the water told us."

"Well, it's a good thing water can't be called to testify, then. Just try to put it out of your mind. Let Ardith reach out to you when she's ready. She's an adult, as hard as it is for us to remember. We taught her the best we could. We need to trust that she knows what she's doing. In the meantime, what are you going to do about this blood mage?"

"I guess I'll have to take you up on that offer to meet with the quorum rep, when he gets back from lunch," she said.

"Yea, lunch," John said.

He looked down at his lost sandwich, which had already attracted more pigeons. The sandwich was too close to the two of them, so the fire mage by the stairs hadn't attacked the new flock. Even if he had dared to cast a fireball so close to other people, their respective hats of authority would have dissuaded him of the idea. Still, the man glared annoyed at the birds that had become more and more of a pestilence lately.

Something about magic was making them breed out of control.

"Here," Bethany said, handing him the rest of her sandwich. "I have to be getting going anyway. I've been in the field too long for today, and with the rest of my team back at the office, the lieutenant will be chomping at the bit to start yelling at me. I'll be back in..." She looked up at the clock overhead, trying to figure how long the blood mage in question would be gone for. "Fifteen minutes? Think you can get him to give me a few minutes of his oh so precious time?"

"I'll try," John said, taking a bite out of the rest of her sandwich. "I'll try."

Chapter Nine
Fire in the Clouds

Ardith

"Dragon," someone yelled in Ardith's ear.

"Yes, thank you. That's quite helpful," she said. Reflexively, she pushed the yeller. The girl hadn't been expecting the reaction and she started to topple off of her cloud. Her hands flailed out, trying desperately to grab onto something. She grabbed onto Ardith's hand and pulled her with her, the two of them tumbling towards the floor together.

The air bar floor wasn't designed to hold people. The idea was that the smaller clouds would hold those people incapable of their own levitation or flying spells. However, the floor was solid enough to stop their fall, if only for a moment. The floor had the same flexibility as the walls did, so it bowed beneath them, stretching out and trying to make room. This only made their clouds to be even further above their heads. They were designed to hold their altitude when not controlled. Quickly, the two girls were too far away from the rest of the room to get themselves out of there. It was only a matter of time before the floor stretched beyond what it was capable of and let them fall to their deaths on the ground below.

"Help," Ardith called out, looking up at the people above her. She couldn't tell one pair of shoes from the other, besides the heeled boots from the flats. One or two had a red sole, but they all seemed the same as the floor beneath her suddenly jerked down another story. "Please," she begged the crowd above. However, they all seemed preoccupied with the dragon in their midst.

"Ardi," came a call from above. Ardith looked around for the source, quickly spotting Dorth. The girl was hovering over by the landing platform, TS standing next to her. The pure blood was just staring down at her, at a loss for what to do. Dorth, though, was already deep within the throws of spellcasting. Ardith just had to hope that her spell would save her from the certain death that awaited her.

When the spell hit Ardith, her first instinct was to block it, to throw the dweomer away. It was weak, and came at her slowly, so she could have done it. She could have thrown what little mana she already had at her disposal to turn it away from her and send it through the cloud floor. However, it was Dorth that was casting it, and she knew that the girl would never do anything to hurt her. Not after that last semester at The Academy.

As the spell made its way through her, Ardith started to feel lighter. The levitation spell took some time to build up in her system, took time to lift her up off of the floor. When she started to drift away, the screamer grabbed onto her leg. At first, her weight kept Ardith down on the cloud floor, but the levitation spell continued to build until the two of them were starting to make their way up together.

By the time they left the cloud floor, they were about ten stories down from the rest of the action. It was impossible to see what was happening, besides the rapidly moving feet of the bar patrons as they scrambled to get away from the dragon. People were already making their way out through the landing platform, but with the limited space, made even smaller by TS and Dorth standing there, it was slow going. The gap around the platform was quickly filling with scrambling people, blocking Ardith's view of her friends.

Several more people were dropping down from their clouds, landing heavily on the cloud floor which was already lower than it should have been. Ardith noticed the girl in the white coat from earlier as she screamed her way all the way down to the floor. A few of them bounced back up off of the floor as if it were a trampoline. The rest were hitting other people, eliciting screams of pain and outrage. Distracted as they were, by the dragon above their heads and the impacts with other people, none of them noticed when the girl in the white coat suddenly disappeared through the clouds. There was no sound of her screams, drowned out by the louder ones above or simply blocked out by the cloud floor that swallowed her whole.

Still five stories down from the landing platform, Ardith started flapping her arms like wings, desperate to get back up to the landing platform and out of there. Tears of fear and frustration were already flowing down her face as she tried desperately to shake off the girl that still clung to her leg. This only made the girl hold on harder, grabbing her other leg in the process and holding the two of them together with all her might. Ardith's blue coat barely kept the girl's fingernails at bay. She could feel them clawing at her legs, trying to find a purchase that wasn't there. The coat was enchanted for added protection against the elements and some minor spells, but only the original cotton kept the nails from her skin.

When she was three floors away from her friends, she heard her name called out above. Looking up, she saw TS and Dorth again, far away from the landing platform and over by where the cloud wall had moved. TS was holding his head, which had started bleeding, but the two of them were floating freely in the air. Ardith had no power over the levitation spell that was gradually drawing her towards them, so she didn't have to shift it. She didn't have to do anything. Yet Dorth continued to wave her forward, one hand flapping at her emphatically like she was reeling her in while the other was extended over to TS, keeping him afloat.

"What are we doing over here?" Ardith asked, when she was only a story away. The four of them were sweeping out through the empty space that stood on the other side of the landing platform from the dragon. No one was bothering to go much further than the platform, as intent as they were to get out of there before they were fried.

"It's ridiculous over there," TS said. He pulled his hand away from his head, revealing the large gash that he had down his face. It was bleeding profusely, as most head wounds did. Ardith certainly had her fair share of them at The Academy while trying to learn how to properly utilize her affinity. "We couldn't stay on the platform a moment longer. They were pushing me off just to get more room for themselves. It's nuts. Can you really believe all this? I mean, seriously, what ever happened to manners?"

"I think they went out the door the moment the dragon swooped in," Ardith said. She was just coming up next to Dorth and TS, with the other girls still grappling with her legs.

"First off, I think that went out the door a long time ago," TS said. "Second, that's no dragon."

"What are you talking about?" Ardith asked. "It's big, red, has wings and scales, and breathes fire. What do you call that?"

"A charizard. I'm surprised they actually exist. But I guess I should stop being so surprised with all the things this world has managed to come up with in these past thirty years. I mean, seriously, it's like a bunch of children playing with fire and wondering why people keep getting burned alive."

"What the hell is a charizard and how is that in any way different from a dragon?"

"Well, it's... I mean, um... Wow, I guess it's not that different from a dragon. Anyway, it's hard to explain what a charizard is without explaining a lot of the culture from my generation. Actually, I think it was more of a Millennial thing, really, so my parent's generation. Anyway, there were these thousand or so monsters that people spent their lives collecting and training and battling against each other."

"And you call us children playing with fire," Ardith said. "You actually did that sort of thing before magic? How? And what happened to all these monsters that they're not still around today? I would have thought magic would have helped out monsters."

"Well, they weren't real," TS said. "I mean, they were fiction, from video games and TV shows."

"Can we discuss the finer points of monster rearing when we're out of here?" Dorth asked. "How are we going to get back in there?"

"Let's not," Ardith suggested. "Let's just stay over here until everything calms down. The fire mage can handle the dragon."

"Ardi, the fire mage is already dead," Dorth said. "I saw it before things started turning to shit. He went up to the thing like it was a lost puppy and it just barbequed the guy."

"What about you?" TS asked Ardith. "You're a water mage. Just hit it with a hydro pump or a surf or something. Fire pokemon are weak to water."

"Oh, no, I'm not a battle mage. I barely passed my battle magic classes. I do enchantments, transformations, things like that. Battle? No. I'm not going in there. I'm just not. You can't make me. I'm not--"

"Ardi, it's okay," Dorth said. "We're not sending you in there. We're staying right here like you said, right? The crowd will clear out eventually, or the dragon will get bored and head off on its own. It probably doesn't even know how it got in here or how to get out."

"Oh, god," TS said. "No, we can't stay here. I can't stay here."

"Oh, what are you on about now?" Ardith said.

"The Mage Authority. Wouldn't they be coming to respond to this?"

"Uh, do I get a vote?" said the girl that was still hanging down from Ardith's legs.

"No," Ardith and Dorth said together.

"Why do you care that the Mage Authority would be coming?" Dorth said.

"Yea, TS. Why would you care?" Ardith said. She wasn't quite sure how much she believed his earlier story of being at the wrong place at the wrong time.

"Hey, I don't wanna be here when they come either," said the girl.

"Shut up," Ardith and Dorth yelled.

"The platform is blocked right now," Dorth said. "No one is coming in until that crowd clears out."

"Why an air bar would have just as much protection against teleportation as the rest of the world, I'll never understand," Ardith said. "Isn't air supposed to be all about freedom?"

"Freedom, yes, but we also like to stay in one piece, and not be splinched by any idiot teleporting in here," Dorth said. "The platforms are a channel for our safety, not just to keep people from stealing anything."

"They could have built in a buffer for incoming traffic," TS said. "That would allow the outbound traffic to head out and keep the platform clear for the inbound to hit safely."

"Magic doesn't work like that," Ardith said. "What you just described... That sounds more like science."

"Yea," Dorth said. "Now science was a dangerous thing, damn near destroyed the world. Who is this guy again?"

"Uh, guys, I don't think we can wait around here anymore," the girl said.

"Oh, shut up," Ardith yelled down at her. "Who asked you?"

"No, really, um, I think we need to get out of here. Like now."

She lifted one of her arms, risking falling off of Ardith's legs to point out at the crowd. None of the group had been paying much attention to the rest of the bar, and the ongoing conflict with the dragon. The crowd had thinned out near the center of the room, giving the dragon as much space as possible. While most of the people were running for the platform, only so many of them were on that side of the dragon. Those that couldn't make their escape were all clustered against the far wall, constantly pushing that wall further away from the dragon and stretching out the already stretched space. The clouds that made up the walls, ceiling, and floor were starting to thin out, to become more transparent than opaque. It made the room brighter, but it also suggested that the walls had a limit to how far they would go. As more people fell down from the dancing layer, they all passed through the floor and into the open air below.

"This bubble is about to pop," the girl said.

"Didn't you say something about this place being at a high altitude?" TS said. "If the place goes, we go with it."

"Yea, okay, I can see that being a problem," Dorth said.

"What are we going to do?" Ardith asked. Her mind was reeling as she tried to come up with some solution to the problem. It didn't help that her training was in water, and they were as far away from water as possible. "Maybe I can strengthen the clouds? I mean, they're just water vapor, right?"

"Even if you knew the enchantment they used, that would just be a stop gap measure," Dorth said. "Maybe we could pull some around us, saving us over the rest of them. I think it's a little too late to save anyone but ourselves at this point."

"There's also the angry dragon that's getting low on toys to chew up," the girl said.

Her words drew their attention back to the crowd. Several of the people that were stuck between the platform and the dragon were letting their spells lapse, dropping through the air and through the cloud floor, opting for the uncertain death of the fall over the more certain death at the hands of the dragon. Several dead bodies were floating there around the creature. They were all burnt to a crisp, but their spells still held them in place. At some point, those would fail too and they would fall to the earth below. In the meantime, they did little to draw the dragon's attention away from the victims that were still alive. Still kicking. Still trying to get away from the dragon. A few of the mages were actually trying to fight it, throwing lightning bolts and tornados at the thing. But it mostly dodged those efforts, sending back long bouts of flames at the much less protected mages. Even though the dragon was still preoccupied with plenty of tasty mages, its play toys were dwindling quickly enough that Ardith was no longer sure which death would come sooner. Or which she would prefer.

"I'm open to ideas," Ardith said.

"I got nothing," Dorth said. "If we stay here, we die. If we try for the platform, we'll just be bogged down there until we die. If we go outside, we die. If we try to go after the dragon, we die. I have no idea what to do."

"We need some kind of protection against the dragon," Ardith said. "It'll come for us before the place goes to hell."

"If only we could get away from the teleportation block so we could teleport away," the girl said.

"Well, why can't we?" TS asked.

"Altitude," Ardith said. "Like you said. Magic hasn't changed that."

"No, but it could save us from it, couldn't it?"

"Wait, he's right," Dorth said. "We don't need to do the whole cloud layer. We just need to keep from not dying until we get far enough away to teleport. Guys, all of you just hold onto me."

"Can I just stay here?" the girl asked. "I don't think I can move."

"Sure, we can leave you behind," Ardith said. "Just let go."

"That's not..."

"Ardi," Dorth scolded her. "Let's just get out of here, all four of us. Then we'll argue about who should be left behind."

"I vote her," Ardith said.

"Just hold on tight."

"I feel like I'm missing something here," TS said. "What are we doing?"

"This was your idea, doofus," Dorth said.

After that, Dorth ignored them as she focused on her spell. Ardith had to smile at the face that she usually made when she did this. She was sort of scrunching up her nose like she was warding off a sneeze. The screams of the dying and dead around them, and the roars of the dragon and its fire, was a constant reminder of the very real, very serious danger they were in. Still, all Ardith could think about was that last day they had together. Dorth had saved up for that private beach all semester, even though they only had it for the one day. She wished that they were still there. Still on that beach. Still together, their whole lives in front of them.

Ardith felt it when the air solidified around them. She could no longer move her arms, could no longer feel the girl squirming on her legs. The position that the girl had ended up in wasn't the most comfortable. But as long as she wasn't moving, Ardith no longer feared that her struggles would pull them both out of the sky. Ardith was stuck facing right between Dorth and TS, getting a halfway decent view of both of them. TS looked like he was struggling against the spell, his neck muscles taught and pulling at the collar of his shirt. His face looked like he was trying to take the biggest dump on record. And, yet, Ardith couldn't even smile, let alone laugh at the sight.

The four of them started to drift through the air, making their way towards the nearest cloud wall. Ardith tried to breathe normally, but her lungs wouldn't cooperate. They tried to pull as much oxygen from the air as they could and her breathing started to get fast. No matter what, she couldn't forget the fact that outside that wall the air was going to be too thin to breathe at all. Consciously, she trusted in Dorth, knew that she wouldn't put them wrong. Unconsciously, she was a ball of nerves and doubt and fear.

Before they made it to the wall, the entire structure snapped back together, contracting back to its original form. They were already outside of the boundaries of the original bar, so the wall came at them like a charging horse. Ardith felt the wall pulling at her as it passed, trying to dislodge her from Dorth's spell. But the spell held. The four of them stayed together as they were suddenly dropped out into literal thin air. The screams were instantly cut off. Not because people were no longer dying. It was because the dying could no longer draw breath. The air could no longer carry the sound of those that already had breath to scream with.

Ardith could no longer blink. She wasn't sure if that was the spell or the horror of the sights around her. People were raining out of the clouds, falling to their deaths on the ground below. She knew they had been for a while, but it was suddenly all she could see. There were no longer any clouds keeping the sight from her, no longer anything blocking out that scene of men and women falling out of the sky. She wondered where they would fall. How badly their bodies would break against the rocks below. How many people would be hit by the falling bodies. How many would die before they even hit the ground. How many would die at all that day. It was certain that many more than just those in the bar were dead already.

And, then, suddenly, it was all gone. Blackness engulfed her for a moment before blinding light replaced it. Ardith could suddenly breathe normally again, and the air that held her in place slackened before she knew where she was. She fell down to the ground, but not hard enough to break anything. Something softened the blow, forcing her forward onto her hands and knees. An audible grunt came to her ears, but she was certain she hadn't made it.

Spots replaced the brightness and her vision slowly came back to her. She was lying down in the middle of a field, a familiar field, yet she couldn't place it. Beneath her was the girl, no longer attached to her legs. Instead, her arms were wrapped around Ardith's torso, holding her in a huge bear hug that she seemed as unwilling to break as she had before. Above her, or more accurately next to her head, she could see Dorth sitting up in the grass, smiling around at the area they had fallen in.

"See?" she said. "I knew it would work." The sounds of TS retching in the bushes accented her words nicely.

"Where are we?" Ardith asked.

"Don't you recognize the place? It's the old teleportation practice field at The Academy."

She pointed off into the distance behind Ardith. Ardith tried to roll over, but the girl wrapped around her chest made the motion impossible. Instead, she just looked back over her shoulder at the group of gawking teenagers behind them. Mrs. Duckworth, the teleportation instructor, had her usual stern look about her as she impatiently waited for the four of them to clear the field.

"Oh," Ardith said. "Home sweet home."

Chapter Ten
A Stern Yelling At

Bethany

"DeSalvo," the captain yelled into the bullpen the moment that Bethany teleported in. She wasn't sure how he knew it was her, or even how he knew that anyone had come in. The captain's office was around the corner from the landing platform, out of eyesight of any new arrival.

The landing platform in the Mage Authority building was different from those used around the world. The logo of The Authority was ingrained in the center, instead of the normal pattern that was on all the others. This added engraving housed the added layer of protection on the platform, making it so that no one could enter or leave the building without a badge or being accompanied by someone with a badge. There were no doors and windows to the place, so there was no way out without destroying a wall. This did keep breakouts to a minimum. Plus, the platform was in the center of the bullpen, so everyone coming into the office would instantly be surrounded by the Authority mages.

"You'd better get in there," Igloo whispered to her. Igloo's desk was right next to the platform, giving her the best view of the new arrivals. It also meant that everyone entering or exiting the station would walk right past her desk, often bumping it in the process. All of the junior members of The Authority were stuck with the worst desk placements. "The captain has been on the warpath since Greg reported in. It's not pretty."

Bethany nodded to Igloo before making her way through the bullpen. The space was kept just bright enough to read by with ever-burning torches strategically placed around the room, on the walls and the support beams, plus some suspended in air. The ceilings were high, disappearing into the darkness above. No one really knew where the place was, other than the higher up in the organization and those earth mages responsible for carving it out. There were hundreds of thousands of officers stationed in that one location, with a couple hundred in her bullpen alone. Thousands of other similar areas were spread throughout the large place. Each bullpen was connected to the others through long, winding tunnels, where they housed the offices of the captains and chiefs.

The officers were separated by global regions, each group taking a large swath of the countries of old. Bethany and her team belonged to the North East United States division, or NEUS for short. Some of the older officers joked about them being Newsies, though Bethany didn't get the reference. They covered from Maine to Illinois, and as far south as Virginia. While there were still local police departments, and even lesser tiers to the Mage Authority, that handled the lesser crimes and magical incidents, the majority of the legwork fell to Bethany's team, and the other teams in her division.

As Bethany walked through the bullpen, her fellow officers diverted their eyes from her, focusing on the paperwork in front of them. Paperwork was one of those things that didn't go away because technology did, though it made it harder to fill out. Ballpoint pens no longer worked, blowing up after they were used for more than five minutes and spilling ink everywhere. Pencils still worked, but anything but the most basic of sharpeners didn't, and their supplies of them were limited. No one had quite come up with a magical alternative, so most officers were stuck using quills to fill out their forms. Protecting their hands from the ink became an excellent use for the old evidence gloves they could no longer use for collecting evidence.

Before Bethany made it to the edge of the cavernous room, the captain poked his head out into the hall to stare down it. He pointed his finger emphatically at her and she could feel the first few wisps of a spell coming off of it. She picked up her pace, practically running over to him so he wouldn't need to finish the spell. It wasn't exactly encouraged for Authority officers to use magic on each other, but that had never stopped the captain from picking up an officer and pulling them towards him when they had properly outraged him. It was looking like that was the case here, yet Bethany wasn't sure why.

"Yes, captain?" she asked, when she made it to the edge of the room. She was still several desks over from the hall, but the cubicles were aligned so that her voice would be channeled towards him. Besides, it made it easier for the officers around her to eavesdrop. They were obviously only feigning their focus on their work.

"My office," the captain said. "Now."

He turned around, heading back into the office that he was still hanging out of. The door swung back to the doorframe like he had slammed it as he passed, but the door quickly opened back up again of its own accord. The remnant of the spell that opened the door was still in the air as Bethany passed it. Once she was inside, the spell disappeared and the door slammed home once more. Bethany jumped at the sudden noise right behind her. She stood in place while the ringing in her ear subsided before slipping into one of the two plush chairs in front of the captain's desk.

Unlike the other officers in the division, Captain Bennett didn't have any clutter on his desk. No pictures of children or loved ones. Not even a divider to keep private memos private. There was just a pad to keep his quill from damaging the desk. The mountain of paperwork that he was expected to read and sign were held in two perfect piles off to the side of his desk. They didn't so much as flutter from the brief gust of wind that came from the door's closing. The captain didn't seem the least bit concerned about the pile, so whatever dweomer had kept them in place must have been cast long ago. On the many instances that Bethany had been in his office, she had often wondered about those piles. She had even tried reaching out with her magical senses to see the origin of the spell. But that was in those few instances when she wasn't about to be yelled at.

The captain was staring daggers at her, loudly drumming his fingers on the hard wood of the desk. This wasn't a good sign. It was never a good sign when the captain didn't speak first. Unlike Bethany, his anger was low, seething just under the surface, building to a crescendo before exploding. It was clear that an eruption was imminent. Bethany ran the events of the past day through her head, trying to figure out just which of her choices was likely to get her in the biggest trouble. There was nothing that came to mind that she would want to undo, given the chance. Bethany sat there for a while, smiling over at the captain. It was clear that he expected her to say something, to be the first to blink. To defend herself and her actions against his rising ire.

"So," she said, once the unsettling silence got the best of her. The single word wasn't phrased as a question, more as a prompting for more conversation to come. When the captain didn't respond, when the unsettling silence returned to the office, interrupted only by his continued drumming, Bethany moved to stand up from the chair. "It was nice talking with you, captain."

"Sit your ass back down in that chair," he yelled. His yell was emphasized by a blast of magical wind, knocking her off of her feet, which weren't quite under her just yet, and back onto the chair. It was just the prompting he needed to start his diatribe about whatever it was that had gotten him so riled up. "How dare you?"

"How dare I...? What? You'll need to be a little more specific, captain."

"Oh, you know exactly what you did, what I've had to fix over the past hour. The barrage of fire letters that have come through over the course of a single minute was staggering. They almost filled up my office." He flapped his arms around wildly, almost as if to demonstrate his office, though it was clear what he was talking about. Yet, for all his concern, the office didn't seem the least bit marred by the fire letters, if any had actually come in. If they came in at the rate that he had suggested, the damage to the office would have been noticeable.

Bethany was about to point out that fact, to openly declare that she didn't think the letters were that plentiful, when a fire letter popped into the room. It came in like normal, starting out as a tiny spark that came out of nowhere, popping into midair. Instead of fizzling out like a normal spark, it got bigger, forming into a proper flame as it spun around. After about three seconds, the ball of fire was the size of a fist. That's when it suddenly bursts out into a larger configuration before the fire disappeared entirely. Once the fire faded, the single sheet of paper gradually glided down onto his desk, riding the hot air that was caused by its arrival. When a single sheet of fire paper is sent, it's never a problem, with the flames staying in the air and away from anything flammable. However, the enchantment wasn't designed to stay out of the way of other fire papers when they came to the same address. If more than one arrived at the same time, they would end up fighting each other over the space. One paper, usually the first one sent, would flare out first and be knocked down to the floor, singed by the remaining paper. The more that arrived, though, the larger the conflagration became, until the entire area was alight. Bethany had been to the scenes of three deaths caused by fire paper so far that year.

"See?" the captain said. He pointed at that single sheet of paper, as if it were indicative of the claimed rain of fire that he had been subjected to earlier. "They keep coming." He scooped up the single sheet, glancing at it for the briefest moments, before slamming it on top of one of the piles of documents. It was then that Bethany noticed the singe marks on the edges of half the pages of the larger pile. It wasn't clear if all of those pages were the fire papers in question, or if they were simply attacked by them.

When the captain removed his hand from the pile, Bethany caught a view of the blood guild logo placed strategically at the top of the page. That logo on the paper was tantamount to an official letterhead from the guild, perhaps even from the guild master's office itself. Bethany doubted that. If the guild master didn't have the time to be bothered to show up for the quorum, she very much doubted that he would be troubled by her going to their guild. In the grand scheme of things, especially in the eyes of the blood guild, she was little more than a gnat buzzing in their ear.

"That... is odd," she said.

"That's it?" he asked. "That's all you have to say for yourself? That's odd?"

"Um... yes?" she asked.

"Do you have any idea what I've been doing this past hour? How many letters I've had to write back to? How many times I've had to pop over to personally apologize for your actions? Oh, how I miss the days when I would just be getting a messload of phone calls instead of having to deal with all this... stuff. You know, there were plenty of people you shouldn't have pissed off back then, too. But the worst they could do was get you fired. These people? They can have you killed. And probably will."

"No," Bethany said. She shook her head a little, denying his words. "They wouldn't have you killed. They'd probably do it themselves, and get a buzz off of it while they're at it.

Why do you think I went to the guild to begin with? They're hiding my suspect."

"I don't care," he shouted. His voice resonated off of the walls and door, vibrating her chest while it did. She suspected that it was magically charged, but it was hard to separate the two sensations. "I don't care if they killed the president himself, though, honestly, I'd like to see someone try. They're the blood guild. You don't go breaking down their doors, no matter what they do. If you wanted to talk with someone in there, you should have come to me. I would have sent in a request--"

"And the perp would have been long gone before they so much as considered the request," Bethany said.

"And where do you think he is now?" he yelled. "He's already long gone, probably before you even got there."

"Because I was stuck at that crime scene--"

"No, because he's a blood mage. He went to the guild because he knew they would hide his trail. He may not have even landed at the guild before teleporting away again."

"It still would have registered in the network. If I could just get access--"

"Not if he teleported outside of the network. Come on, DeSalvo. You should know this. You're not some noob like Igloo in there. Think, DeSalvo, think. He's gone."

"What about matching his signature to their roster? It might take a while, they have a few thousand members, but not all of them were in the states when this happened."

"And if he was a lower mage, I might actually let you," the captain said. His ire had started to play itself out and his voice had returned to a more normal level. However, it was clear that he wasn't about to allow his resources to be spent on such a fool's errand. "He's a bloody blood mage and his guild is backing him one hundred percent. You've got no eye witnesses, outside of a bartender that was on the other side of the room. You've got no evidence, outside of the water that disappeared in transit. And, don't go spouting any conspiracy theories about that. It was magically created, and the mage is dead. What didn't evaporate dissipated. You've got more evidence to convict that pure blood that you went running after for this murder than you do the actual killer. What about him, by the way? Dead end? Dead?"

"Dead end, for sure," Bethany said. She liked the fact that he wasn't shouting anymore, that he seemed to think this other line of investigation more fruitful. But, with Ardith mixed up in that, she had to be careful as she danced around the information that he wouldn't have access to just yet. She had to hope that she could contact Ardith before she ended up being booked as an accomplice. "I've never seen a teleportation register on the platform like that before. No destination, sure, but all possible destinations? Not even the high mages can do that. Do you think this is some kind of new form of teleportation?"

"No such thing," he said. "Teleportation is simply moving from one location to the other, instantaneously, without passing through the space between. There's only one way to do it, the normal way, the way the landing platforms are designed to track, to allow through the barriers that keep it from happening otherwise. A new way of teleporting would be a lot more scary of a thought that a murderous blood mage on the loose. Think you can deal with the air guild without stepping on everyone's toes?"

"The air guild?" she asked, confused.

"If anyone knows about the signature you're looking for, they would. The air mage's signature, not the blood mage. Don't go looking for the stupid blood mage, okay?"

"The air mage? Oh, the mage that helped the pure blood escape?"

"Isn't that what we've been talking about this whole time? If there is some teleportation cloaking spell, which is the only explanation for this jumbled up entry..."

He pulled a sheet, seemingly at random, off of the stack of fire papers. The papers didn't move at all, despite the extracted sheet being near the bottom. As he lifted the page, two more fire letters came in in rapid succession. The two papers started fighting each other, bucking and tossing, trying to get priority over opening in front of the desired target. When the fires flared up, they threatened to take the paper that the captain was holding with them. He just managed to get the report out of the literal line of fire by tossing it over at Bethany. With the report out of the way, he reached out to the two balls of fire that seemed hell bent in igniting his entire desk. He reached out with his magic, forming two protective barriers around the balls of flame, separating them and stopping their fight as quickly as it had started. With the two of them away from each other, they flared out, popping their respective pages into existence in front of him.

"Why don't people just mail these notes?" he asked, as he placed the new sheets on top of the pile. "Envelopes are so much more civilized than fire paper. They just pop around, following the recipient like a lost puppy."

"Well, in a way, fire paper is like a puppy," Bethany said. "Biting anyone that touches them when they don't want to be touched and destroying the furniture."

"Plus, I guess the envelopes require proper addressing," the captain said, answering his own question. "It's a lot easier to send fire paper when you don't know the name of the person that you're sending it to. But, seriously. You think you can talk to your guild and get them to tone down the fire on the next batch?"

"I'll see what I can do."

"Now, where were we? Oh, yes, the report. The only way that could have come out of the landing platform, without the mage really splicing themselves like that, is some form of cloaking spell. That's the only explanation. It's not some new way of teleportation. Not a thing. Not going to happen."

"I don't know. This new generation that's just coming up is pretty creative. The offspring of the Magic-Touched. They're going to be the most creative with their magic."

"That's what they say about every generation," he said. "And I do mean every generation. We Millennials were supposed to be the future. Then the Centennials. How'd that turn out? No, there are things that just can't happen, no matter how creative you get. Even magic has its limits."

"I have yet to find any," Bethany said. "When my back is to the wall and it's me or them, I've always found a way to use magic to save my ass."

"And you will, every time, until the last. Now get out of here. Go talk to the air nerds at the guild. Figure out just how this happened, how to track the mage that did it, and get your pure blood. Let's close at least part of this case, shall we? And, it's not too late to pin the whole mess on the pure blood. I know the blood guild would just love that."

He pulled the three letters he had gotten since Bethany had been there in front of him, studying each one in turn and completely ignoring her. It was the only signal she was going to get that the meeting was over. Slowly, silently, Bethany got up from the chair, trying not to disturb him any more than she already had. The door creaked as she opened it but, when she looked back at him, the captain showed no sign of noticing. When she pulled it closed behind her, the door refused to latch properly. She pulled it closed as tightly as she could. But when she let go of the doorknob, it just swung open once more, swinging freely on its hinges, creaking back and forth. This pulled a single sigh of annoyance from the captain before he sent another wave of magic at the door, slamming it shut in her face.

"How'd it go?" came a voice from behind her. Bethany jumped, her hand automatically going to her heart to stay its wild rhythm. There was no one there, the area as empty as it was when she went in the door, but the voice seemed to have come from right next to her. When her startled expression didn't go away, the voice continued talking. "Oh, sorry. Right. Forgot."

Igloo, Dan, and Greg appeared out of nowhere, the invisibility spell fading from them as Igloo twirled her arm in front of her. Dan was ducked down low to the ground, his ear right next to the door, still trying to hear what the captain was saying. Greg, on the other hand, was leaning against the wall, his arms crossed over his chest and his eyes closed in feigned sleep. Bethany knew that the elder member of her team was just as interested in the scolding she had to endure as the rest of them were.

"Well, you heard enough of what went on in there already," she said, figuring they heard everything. "How do you think it went?"

"We didn't hear a thing," Dan said. He pressed his ear against the door as much as he could, but still showed no sign of having heard anything. "I think he spelled the door since the last time you were yelled at."

"So, since yesterday?" Greg said.

"It wasn't yesterday," Dan said. "It was last week."

"It was three weeks ago," Igloo said.

She was flipping through a tiny notebook that she had pulled out of her hat, which was tucked under her arm. Her raven black hair had fallen down around her shoulders, though she usually kept it up and tucked under the hat. Bethany thought she looked better with it down, but she wasn't one to judge. Her own curls were usually cut short to keep them out of the way.

"Last time it was because we left the crime scene before the CSI team showed up," Igloo read, "to chase after that one pure blood with the ripped up linking book that he stole off of that nun. Damn near got into the Vatican with that one."

"Oh, like anyone cares about the Vatican anymore," Dan said. "Organized religions should have gone away when the demons showed up. Just an old relic of a time that no longer exists."

"There are plenty of people who still go to church, Dan," Bethany said. "Most of us think the arrival of magic is proof that God exists, and loves us, rather than that he doesn't."

"Anyway, how did it go in there?" Igloo asked again. She pulled out an old pencil, priming it over her notebook, ready to take extensive notes. The old pencil was worn down almost to the nub, looking like one of the old pencils they used to give out at the bowling alleys that were used for scoring, in the older alleys that had never gone to the electronic scoreboards. Bowling had gotten a lot more interesting since magic came onto the scene, but the scoring was all manual.

"Well, I'm not fired," Bethany said. "That's a plus."

"Ah, man," Greg said. He snapped his finger in annoyance before passing a silver down to Dan, who accepted it without looking in his direction.

"Bad bet," Igloo said. "The last time he fired her was three months ago."

"It was due," Greg said. "And, I mean, she really pissed the blood mages off."

"He didn't take me off the case," Bethany said. She waited for a moment, but no one seemed to have taken that bet. "And, he expects us to go to the air guild to see about the possibility of the teleportation spell being cloaked. Not exactly glamourous work, but I'll take it."

"Ah, man," Igloo said. Bethany smiled over at her, at her echo of Greg's words, but she wasn't paying out a bet. "I don't wanna go to the guild."

"Hey, it's your guild," Greg said.

"Yea, but that doesn't make it any more fun. It's like going to church, only worse."

"We're not going to be hanging around for a meeting," Greg said. "We're just going there for research."

"Yea, but our meetings are on Tuesdays, which means I'm going to be pulled into it anyway."

"Do you have any contacts with the research team, at least?" Bethany asked. "Maybe you can just hide out in there. That's where we're going."

"Pfft, the nerds? Hells no, I don't know any of them. I was a jock in The Academy. They're probably all afraid of me. Maybe you should just go without me."

"You're going," Bethany said. "That's final. Come on. Get your stuff. We're out of here in ten."

Chapter Eleven
The Demolition

Ardith

TS was kneeling down on the hard cement sidewalk, his head in his hands. Ardith and Dorth were giving him his space, keeping to the other side of the street from him. The place seemed weird to the two of them, like it was out of some old story of the world that was. The sidewalks were all broken, falling apart with the passing of time. The plants that once owned the land were reclaiming it from the people that had conquered the area. While the street was currently dry, Ardith could tell that water had often passed through there, her affinity giving her the sense of a recurring river.

As far away as Ardith was, she wasn't sure if TS was crying. It seemed like he was crying, though the old man didn't look like one to cry. His usually stoic features had cracked the moment that they had arrived there, teleporting straight over from the practice field at The Academy. While TS had provided the coordinates, largely in relation to Ardith's office, it was clear that the rubble wasn't what he had been expecting to find there.

"What do you think used to be here?" Dorth whispered. She gestured towards the rubble pile, as if Ardith needed the clarification.

The entire block had been leveled. The buildings that once stood there, an echo of a time long forgot, were little more than a pile of stone, steel, and glass. Hanging over the pile was a large banner, suspended by air magic, declaring that the block was the future home of a new apartment tower. The earth mages had done their work, dismantling the old buildings that had been there, before they managed to fall down themselves. The steel that the builders of old had used to support the structures frequently gave way under the continued exposure to mana. Those old buildings were no longer safe, and there was no longer an interest in keeping them around for nostalgia.

Soon, perhaps in the next day or so, the fire and light mages would come by, melting the old materials, and the ground around it, and shaping them into the new tower. The entire process would take a few hours, much faster and more efficient than the old way of building things. The new tower would last for centuries, millennia, before ever showing the smallest amount of age or decay.

"Buildings," Ardith said, shrugging. "Whatever was here, it must have been important to him. Maybe his old house?"

"No," TS said, his voice traveling across the road. "Not my old house. That's a few miles south of here. No, this is where I stashed it."

"Stashed what?" Ardith asked.

"The... item I need delivered. It should have been so simple. Get the case, get a couple mages, get it all squared away. But, no. Instead, people just keep dying around me and I stash the case in the one place that I thought was safe. It's where they always stick stuff in the old movies."

"Movies?" Ardith asked.

TS stood up, shaking off the melancholy that had claimed him before turning around to the two of them. "It was an old bus station. There were lockers inside. I thought it would be safe there. Maybe it still is. I mean, the lockers were solid metal, right? They couldn't have destroyed that, too. Maybe they survived intact."

"Survived a whole building falling on them?" Dorth muttered.

"Can you guys, I don't know, lift the rubble?"

"Oh, sure, no problem," Ardith said, nodding. "Do we look like two large strapping pure bloods?"

"No, you look like mages. I just thought you could use your magic to do it."

"That's earth magic," Dorth said.

"So?" TS asked. "Magic is magic, isn't it?"

"God, what rock have you been living under?" Dorth asked. "No, not all magic is the same. I'm an air mage. That means I'm best at air and lousy at earth. And don't even get me started on this one."

"I... I don't get it. I know that there are different types of mages, but... I just thought that was like preference or something."

"It is and it isn't," Ardith said. "Think of it this way... Are you left handed or right?"

"I'm a southpaw," TS said.

"You're a what now?"

"I'm left handed."

"Well, can you throw a ball with your right hand?"

"Sure, can't you?"

"Alright, think of it like this," Ardith said. "My affinity, water magic, is like writing with my right hand. I can do it the easiest, without even thinking. Air and Earth are more like writing with my left hand, sloppy and weird and awkward. Fire magic, though, is more like... like writing with my feet. I could probably do it if I really really tried, but no one is going to be able to read it."

"And, with magic, the mana needs to be able to read it," Dorth said. "Sort of."

"Well, yea. It reads our intent, helping us shape it the way we want. Mana wants to be used like that."

"So, it's like midichlorians?"

"Ooh, I know that one," Dorth said, getting all excited. "May the force be with you and all that. Luke, I am your brother. Live long and--"

"No, stop," TS said. "Just stop."

"Most of us are elemental mages," Ardith said. "Fire, earth, air, water. We're born with a certain affinity for one of those elements and develop as a mage as that type. Our weakest element is always the opposite, fire and water, earth and air, while our strongest is the one we have the affinity in. Some of us can use the side elements easily enough."

"Like me," Dorth said.

"While others are shit in everything but their own," Ardith said.

"Like her," Dorth said.

"You said most of you, though? What about light and dark and all them?" TS asked.

"Light and dark mages are one step above elemental. They're more rare, like one in one hundred for light mages and one in a thousand for dark. They can do all elemental magic equally, but there is light magic and dark magic that only they can do. Healing spells are all light magic, so most of the medical professionals are light mages."

"While some of them slum it in construction," Dorth said. "Making buildings that look pretty, instead of the crap that's around here."

"Hey," TS said. "The crap that's around here is designed to actually stand the test of time. I'd like to see how your buildings would work without mana constantly being pumped through them."

"That's not how it works," Ardith said. "They're made of crystals, grown through magic, or something. They'd stand just fine if Apophis just suddenly stopped giving us mana."

"Yea, that wouldn't really be a problem," Dorth said. "Though everyone inside would be trapped."

"What?" TS said. He seemed surprised by this revelation, and even looked a little sick. "What do you mean?"

"Doors aren't just outdated," Ardith said. "I mean, they are, but that's not the only reason why we stopped using them. The buildings... well, they won't be... Crap, I remember this. Dorth?"

"Hey, don't look at me," Dorth said. "I slept through that class."

"Anyway, something about the buildings not being able to stay up on their own with doors in them."

"You mean the structural integrity of the buildings?" TS asked.

"Yea, that," Ardith said. "Anyway, no doors means that, with no magic, everyone would be trapped inside. They talked about it in school when I was young, back when they thought it might actually end. But, I mean, it's been decades, hasn't it? Magic isn't going anywhere."

"Right," TS said. There was a weight behind that one word, something that he wasn't telling her, something off about him. At the time, she mostly wrote it off as being because he was a pure blood, one of the many people locked off from the magic world. Worse, he was old, a member of a generation before hers, someone that didn't grow up in that world, or a world that at least knew of it. He would have been set in his ways, averse to change, especially when that change dropped him in status so deeply.

"Right," Ardith said.

"What about... Wasn't there a blood affinity or something like that?" TS asked.

"Ah, yes, the high mages," Ardith said. "Blood, death, and void. The rarest of the rare. Like light and dark, they have their own magic, mostly surrounding life, death, undeath, life draining, and other less appetizing magic. We don't talk about them much."

"Mostly because they're assholes," Dorth said. "They're more powerful than all the other guilds put together, even with our larger numbers. We should thank our lucky stars that they didn't gang up together and take over the world."

"Well, the void mages do rule the world," Ardith said. "But, yes, it could have been much worse. Instead, the bloods and the voids joined the rest of them when they went against the death guild a couple of decades ago. We don't really remember it much, as most of it happened before we were born."

"Ah, the benefit of the young," TS said. "And those of us that lived under a rock. So, you can't help me move the stone, then?"

"Nope," Dorth said. "You'll need to get an earth mage for that."

"Great. How exactly am I going to get the funds to pay for one? I don't really have anything to pay you. I already promised all the money I had for Carissa to help me."

"Why do you keep--" Dorth started to say. Ardith, knowing she was about to blow her cover, grabbed her arm, trying to be as subtle about it as she could as she gradually squeezed it. "Ow," Dorth said.

"I don't suppose you'd take an 'I owe you', would you?" TS asked, seeming oblivious to the exchange.

"Oh, don't worry about me," Dorth said. She waved her offended arm at the man, trying to smile it off. "I'm just here to keep this one out of trouble. Something about you says you draw it in, and I know she is one to as well. Let's just say the two of us can make our own arrangements." Dorth smiled over at Ardith, waggling her eyebrows suggestively. Ardith's eyes went wide as she hastily shook her head. "Anyway, if you already knew you needed an air mage, why did you already promise all your money on the water mage?"

"There was the matter of an Authority team on his tail," Ardith said. "There wasn't time to count silver."

"Wait, he's paying you in silver? That's big. Is it a lot?"

"Yes, it was a rather large bag of it," Ardith said, shaking her head. "Don't get any ideas, though. I have bills to pay."

"We'll probably need some supplies, too," TS said. "After we get the case that is. I still can't believe... I mean, why today? Why not put a notice up or something? What if someone was living in there?"

"Living in there?" Dorth asked. "Why would anyone want to live in one of those old buildings? Were there apartments above the station or something? You said it was a bus station, right? What exactly is a bus?"

"It was one of those long metal things, right?" Ardith asked.

"Pulled my horses?" Dorth asked.

"No, dogs. Greyhounds, or something, right?"

"God, I miss home right now," TS said.

"Can't you just get another one?" Dorth asked.

"What?"

TS seemed stunned by this suggestion, despite the fact that it was the most obvious. There was nothing that was a one of a kind anymore, not with the magical replicators found in every factory. Anything that was inserted into it would be replicated down to the very last detail. Even money could be duplicated, which was why the economy was moved off of solid currency and replaced by the credit system. It still took resources to make items, though, so silver coins had managed to keep their value, despite them being illegal.

"Yea," Ardith said. "You can probably just go back to the guy that sold you the first one and just buy another one. Whatever it is, if he told you it's rare, he was probably lying."

"Nothing is rare these days," Dorth agreed. "Except for people like her." She nodded towards Ardith, smiling over at her. Ardith blushed deeply at the compliment.

"I'm not even sure how to get in touch with the guy. After what happened at the club, he ran for it. It wasn't like I set up the meeting to begin with, and it took weeks the first time around. I don't have weeks."

"What is this thing that's so important?" Dorth asked. "What's worth all this effort? A case, you said? What's in the case?"

"I... I can't tell you," he said. "I'm sorry, but you can't know what's in the case. If that's a deal breaker for you, I'll understand."

"Yea, I don't really have much of a choice in the matter, though," Ardith said. "A promise is a promise, especially when it's made on your magic. Anyway, maybe we'd be able to track the guy down if we had at least some idea on what you're looking for. I have a few connections of my own."

"I'll say," Dorth said. "You think you'll call--"

"No," Ardith said. "I can't bring her into all of this. Not with him on the run from the law."

"Oh, right. That complicates things. Who are you thinking of, though?"

"Jack, of course. His dad..."

"Jack? Really? Are you sure?"

"Don't worry. He's over all that mess... I think."

"I wasn't talking about him. I was talking about you. I mean, you two were pretty tight before..."

"Care to fill me in on this little inside story of yours?" TS asked.

"No," they both said, shaking their heads emphatically.

"But we will need to know what kind of thing you're looking for," Ardith said. "We'll need to make sure the right connections are used."

"Well, it's old," TS said, hesitantly. "The case... Well, the case was designed to block out mana. The item inside... I need it to still work."

"Seriously?" Ardith asked. "You're trading in iPhone 30's? Why didn't you say so? I know a guy. I don't even have to reach out to Jack."

"Yay," Dorth cheered. She wrapped her arm around Ardith's neck, pulling her close to her in a hug. "No Jack."

Chapter Twelve
The Limits of Teleportation

Bethany

Bethany didn't think the field trip to the air guild was worth the time. But she couldn't explain that to her group or to her boss without telling them that it was Ardith that helped the pure blood suspect escape. So, the group ended up right back on Guild Row, just a couple of hours after they had left it. This time, however, they approached the tower of air. The elemental guilds were a much more friendly bunch. Plus, they had an active member in good standing in tow. It was one of the many benefits to their team orientation.

The soaring crystal spire of the air tower pierced the sky in front of them. The sun, now past its zenith, shone brightly overhead, reflected and refracted through the crystal. It was both beautiful and blinding, the colors spreading out around them perfectly to fall on the fire, water, and earth towers. Each of those guilds' colors lined up with their towers, emphasizing those colors that were already there. Not many noticed that the reds refracted off of the spire also fell on the blood tower behind it, though Bethany couldn't help but look towards that direction as they approached the tower. The blood red stone looked twice as bloody with the added red light.

Unlike with the blood guild, there were plenty of people coming and going from the tower, even on foot. There was only one entrance at the base of the tower. The air guild was too popular and too friendly to require a separate entrance for guests. Also, instead of going up a set of stairs to the doors, like with the blood guild, the group had to go down a flight, heading down under the tower before coming inside. The crystal was grown much like the apartment buildings that were starting to fill the world, replacing the old ones of cement and metal. They wouldn't allow for doors to be carved in the walls.

Under the tower, the light from above was as bright as if they were still outside. Right after they came down the stairs, there were two tunnels leading off to either side of them. At the entrance to each was a carving in the walls, one showing the symbol for water and the other for fire. Those tunnels led back over to the other guilds, with similar branches on the other side of the main pathway. The tunnels were meant to show that, deep down, the elemental guilds were united as one. Although, they were mostly used to sneak around without the upper guilds noticing. They became quite invaluable during the war with the death guild.

At the center of the basement area was a reception desk, long and large, running around in a circle. Behind the desk was the main entrance to the guild, a small controlled tornado that pulled people up to and down from the levels above, depending on where one entered it. Behind the desk were several people, all air mages. All wearing the customary yellow coats. All smiling broadly as the group approached them.

"Um, hey," Igloo said. She waved apprehensively to the mage closest to the main path. He was standing in the dead center of his section of desk, staring down the hall at the large number of people heading his way. The smile on his face looked as authentic as the others, but the slack expression on his face suggested that his brain had gone on a long vacation. As the group approached him, he waved them forward, towards the gap in the desk to his left.

"Hello, Igloo," the man said, in a tone that reminded Bethany of a scary movie she once saw when she was a kid. She was pretty sure it was the last movie she ever saw, though she couldn't remember the name of it. "Welcome home."

"Yea, thanks."

"The meeting will begin in twenty minutes. Please proceed to the main meeting room."

"I was afraid you were going to say that."

"Unfortunately, your guests are not allowed in the meeting, as this is a closed-door meeting," he droned on.

"Lucky," Igloo said. Still, she made her way around to the gap in the desk. "Don't worry, the rest of you will be able to get in just fine. Just don't try to get into the meeting room is all."

"God, this place always gives me the creeps," Greg said.

"Really? I like it," Dan said. "Maybe it's because it's the guild for your elemental opposite? I never liked it over at the fire guild."

"What's wrong with the fire guild?" Bethany asked. "And, no, I think it's creepy too. I have a feeling they found some way to remove their brains while standing watch or something."

"Wait, seriously?" Igloo said. "I'm the only one that knows about this? Wow, this is a rare treat. Can I just enjoy this moment for a bit?"

"Enjoy it while moving," Bethany said. She pushed Igloo into the tornado in front of her and she instantly disappeared. After a few seconds, she followed after her, jumping in herself.

Bethany hated the feeling of the tornado, often avoiding interactions with the air guild just to escape it. Unfortunately, there was no way to do so that day. The instant that she stepped inside the tornado, the world started to spin around her. There was no sense of movement, no inertia or pressure against her skin. The world spinning around her was the only indication that she was moving as she quickly ascended up through the cathedral ceilings of the chasm below the tower. And, then, she was inside.

In the moment before her lunch tried to escape her, she took in the usual sights and sounds of the entry hall of the air guild. Framing the giant hole in the center of the room were several troughs, specifically set aside for exactly the purpose she started using it for. All of the recent arrivals to the tower were stooped over the trough, voiding their stomachs the hard way. All mages were highly susceptible to motion sickness, a fact that made the air guild's choice in stairs that much more illogical, bordering on unethical, and should very much be illegal.

Once she got past the nausea, she was able to take in the rest of the room. The place was huge, much larger on the inside than the outside. Still, the entire ground floor of the tower was one room, stretching out to the outer walls of the tower itself. While on the outside, the light shining off of the tower was too bright to attempt to look through, on the inside the brightness was muted. The walls were perfect windows, showing the comings and goings of the tower's many visitors. However, due to the extradimensional properties of the room, the images were distorted, stretched around, making the windows look more like funhouse mirrors.

Inside the room itself, there were several sitting areas, situated around the room like numbers on a clock. These were set aside for meetings with visitors that weren't allowed in the more inner areas of the guild house. Most of these were filled with people wearing yellow coats, eating a late lunch or an early dinner. Bethany also figured it was possible they had forgone eating until after coming in for the meeting, so they wouldn't have anything in their stomach for their entrance. The floor of the room, other than around the hole, was mostly carpeted, blocking the view from the tunnels below. Not many people wore skirts or dresses anymore, but a transparent floor was never a good idea.

Bethany took a step away from the hole, jumping over the long trough, right before Dan and Greg joined them. Dan instantly lost some vomit, despite the fact that his hand was solidly across his mouth. The red tinged liquid hit the floor just shy of the trough, but disappeared quickly after from the same enchantment that kept the troughs empty. He spent a good two minutes doubled over the trough. However, when Greg arrived, he was glowing green. The glow quickly dissipated once his feet touched the ground, but with it went his own nausea. It was the only spell Bethany had ever been envious of, the one spell she was never able to get to work, despite the fact that she wasn't too shabby in earth magic.

"Which way is the research library again?" Bethany asked Igloo, while Dan was still voiding his stomach.

"You'll need to use the eighth crystal on the right over there," she said.

She pointed to a row of crystals that were lined up in a circle in the space that the northern sitting area would have taken. Each crystal, the same shape as the tower itself, was the size of a fist. They floated in midair, perfectly spaced between each other and at shoulder height for Bethany. Travel within the tower was much more sophisticated than getting in and out of it, which seemed appropriate to Bethany considering that most teleportation and travel spells belonged to the realm of air. Bethany always figured the more extravagant entrance was due to the pride of the founding members of the air guide and their attempts to keep any interlopers off kilter.

"Alright, let's meet back up here after the meeting," Bethany said. "I doubt we'll be much longer in the research library. This whole trip is a rather moot point, I think."

"I don't know," Greg said. "There's always room in life to learn new things. Most of it is stupid crap that doesn't help any, but it's still nice."

"I'll just stay here," Dan said. His head was still dangling over the trough, but he had stopped vomiting. "If I move, I'm just going to throw up again."

"Yes, let's not do that," Greg said. "Think you'll be alright going to the meeting alone?"

"I won't be alone," Igloo said. "That's kind of the problem. But, no, it'll be fine. I'm sure I'll know someone there that I can sit with. You guys have fun learning that there's no way for us to track whoever the air mage was."

Instead of heading for the crystals, Igloo walked around the perimeter of the room until she found an open seat near the wall. She sat down, pulled her magic towards her, and disappeared with the wave of her hand. The seat vanished with her, so that no one would think to sit down in what would have appeared to be an empty seat. Bethany doubted it would work for long, as the guild workers were certain to notice a missing chair. Plus, seeing as how invisibility was an air spell, she had no doubt that many had attempted to use it to get out of meetings over the past thirty or so years.

Bethany and Greg headed over to the teleportation crystals. A low hum seemed to come off of them, radiating out and vibrating the very air around them. Bethany could feel the power emanating off of the crystals, a charge that would allow for anyone, even a pure blood, to teleport throughout the tower, even with the safeguards in place. They were some of the more dangerous enchanted objects known to man, displayed so haphazardly out in the open. However, she also knew that no one would ever be able to steal them, to reconfigure them to teleport a person to a different location, like say the quorum room. No one could even touch them, with their hands or their magic, without triggering them. It took an entire greater coven of mages, a gross of mages, to create, set, and configure each of the crystals, working simultaneously to keep them attuned to each other. Of course, being an elemental guild, the air guild had them to spare.

She pointed at each of the crystals as she counted out loud. Before she got to the second one, though, Greg reached out and grabbed the eighth one, instantly teleporting away.

Still, she counted the rest of them off before touching the same one Greg did, making sure that he hadn't made a huge mistake and gotten himself teleported into an abyss. She wouldn't have put it past the air guild, or any guild, even her own, to do just that. Hidden deep within each of the towers were secret, hidden rooms where the most valuable and powerful magics were stored. Only the highest members of the guilds knew about them, and, from how her own husband reacted when she questioned him about them, were so secret they couldn't even tell their spouses.

Or, you know, they were just urban legends.

The instant her flesh touched the crystal, she felt the familiar pull around her stomach as the teleportation spell took effect. She felt a brief moment of vertigo before her eyes settled on the room that she arrived in. Despite knowing that she was still within the tower, still within the limited space that the crystal provided, the room that she was in seemed to go on for eternity. She appeared in the middle of a row, tall shelves to either side of her extending up to the ceiling that was a good four stories above her head. The shelves were full of books, each written by a member of the air guild on a certain subject. Despite how brief the magic world had existed, there were hundreds of millions of mages, almost a quarter of which would have been air mages. There was no doubt that the library held at least as many books within its seemingly infinite space.

"Greg?" she called out, hoping her voice would carry to her teammate. The problem with teleporting into an extradimensional space was that there was no way to be precise. Even as safe as the crystals were, there was still a splinching victim coming out of the guild once every month or so. Bethany shuddered at the thought when she realized just how narrow the row that she was in was. Had she been facing the other direction, her shoulders would have brushed against them on both sides.

"Over here, Beth," Greg called out. His voice echoed around her, making it impossible for her to track the source. "Head towards the end of the row."

"Which end," she asked, but she ended up just heading in the direction she was facing. It was as good as anything to go on.

The row ran the length of ten shelves before breaking off into a wide corridor. The open space had several tables, each running the length of three rows. Some of the tables, far down the corridor, were occupied, though it was mostly by younger mages, all of whom looked about school age. For a moment, Bethany thought she saw her daughter in the distance. When she noticed that the girl was wearing yellow, instead of blue, she knew she must have been mistaken. Still, she kept her distance from the look alike, not wanting to draw Greg's attention towards her.

"Greg?" she called out again. This time, she was answered by several shushing hisses from all around her. Bethany just glared down at the students until they all returned to their work.

The table next to her was leaden down with several stacks of books, though no one was sitting there. Two of them were sitting open in front of two of the chairs, suggesting that someone had just left the area, or was still there and sitting invisible in the chairs. She waited, watching the open books, half expecting one of the pages to be flipped by an invisible hand. When the pages on the one on the left started to move, she wasn't entirely sure if that was the cause, or if the crisp binding of the book refused to keep the pages flat. Or, even, if she had accidently done it herself, willing the pages to move without noticing it.

"Beth?" Greg said. His voice came from right behind her, making her jump and let out a very high pitched, very girly squeak. When she turned around to look at him, his expression was very wisely schooled. "You okay?" he asked, his voice taking on the humor that his face refused to show. Sometimes, it paid to be a stone.

"I'm fine," Bethany said. "Any idea where the researchers are?"

"I imagine most of them should be on their way to the meeting. That's not really why we're here, though, is it?"

"What do you mean? That was the assignment. Talk to the researchers to find out how that air mage--"

"We both know it wasn't an air mage. Ardith somehow messed up the ride along teleport in just the right way that we weren't able to track them."

"What?" Bethany asked. Her stomach plummeted when he mentioned her daughter. "What are you talking about?"

"I recognized her the moment the door opened. I was there, in front, with the best view of the group. It was kind of hard to miss her. Don't worry, I don't think the others know it was her."

"But... Why? Why didn't you say something?"

"Because I don't think she knew what she was getting herself into. Have you heard from her? Have you tried to reach out to her? She's probably worried about what you think of her."

"I doubt very much that she cares at all. She was out of that room the instant after we got in. She might not have even known it was my team looking for the pure blood. I should have recused myself from the start. Let's go back to The Authority and tell the captain--"

"We're not telling anyone anything. If you recuse yourself now, it'll only get us both in trouble. I've already had to hide the sublease agreement with her name on it."

"What?" her outburst elicited another bout of hisses from the few people hiding out in the library. "That was... I stayed out of that whole part to keep from doing just that. Why would you risk that?"

"You know why. We've worked together for how many years now? Since soon after you left The Academy? I saw that girl grow up. My own daughter babysat for her. I wasn't about to let her go down for… what is it we're chasing after these people for again?"

"Black market sales," Bethany said. "Probably dealing in illegal goods. We won't know until we talk with him. Either way, the captain is probably going to want to pin the murder on him as well, to get the blood guild off his back. Why we're capitulating to them is beyond my understanding though. We took down the death guild. We can take them down too, if it comes to it."

"You're forgetting that a lot of people died that year to take down the death guild. Do you really think we can handle going through that again? There's a lot more blood mages than death mages, and we won't have the help of any high mages to do it. The war would be bloody, they'll see to that more than anything else. Plus, we'll lose. No, we don't want that war. Trust me."

"You forget, I was in that last war. It wasn't that long ago. In fact, if it wasn't for that war, I wouldn't have Ardith. As for our chances against the bloods, I don't think it would be that bad. Besides, unlike with the death mages, where they gained power by killing people, the blood guild just has a few bad apples, ones that are spilling blood. If they would just stop defending those…"

"What about the fire guild? Would you want them to stop defending you because they were told that you were harboring a fugitive?"

"I'm not harboring anyone. Ardith is just on the run. But, no, I wouldn't want them defending a guilty person, even if it was me."

"That's easy to say now, but just wait till it comes to it. You'll go hiding out in the fire guildhall, hoping they won't just turn you in to The Authority."

Bethany shook her head, refusing to admit what she knew was true. The guilds were established for just that reason, to help protect the wrongly accused. When magic first came, when people first realized what it meant and how the individual affinities played out against each other, most were afraid of a much larger war, one spanning across all affinities. Air against earth, water against fire, light against dark, blood and death against life itself. The guilds were put in place to keep the peace, where no peace seemed possible. It was only after the demise of the death guild that anyone realized there was no need, no desire, for a larger war to be had. And, if they went up against the blood guild, that larger war was exactly what they could expect.

"Let's hope it doesn't come to that," Bethany said. "What are we going to tell the others?"

"Nothing," Greg said. "They don't need to know that Ardith is involved."

"No, what are we going to tell them about the investigation? If we don't have any researchers to ask about the missing teleportation tracking?"

"Oh, that. That's simple. We tell them what we already know."

"What we already know about teleportation? You're an earth mage. What could you possibly know about teleportation?"

"The same thing everyone knows. The same thing everyone needs to believe to sleep at night. There's no new way of teleportation. The safeguards are still in place, blocking all but the high mages from teleporting through the protections. We'll probably just throw them a bone, say that the researchers said the garbled entry was just a rare artifact, a mistake made on the mage's part, rather than something intentionally done to hide their destination. That's true, right? Ardith didn't suddenly become an expert in teleportation, did she?"

"Not that I know of. But, then again, that's not exactly something she'd tell her mother. I'm beginning to think there's not much she would tell me about her life. Oh, my God. I don't even know my own daughter, do I?"

"You know her about as well as anyone can know anyone. When this is all over, how about you, John, Martha, the kids, and I all get together for a picnic or something, eh?"

"Yea, that would be nice," Bethany said.

Chapter Thirteen
A Little Time Alone

Ardith

With a plan in place, and a little extra time on their hands before they could implement it, Ardith and Dorth left TS to his own devices for a bit as the two of them headed off to grab some dinner. They hadn't seen each other since graduation, and they had loads to catch up on. So, they ended up in the back corner of an old diner a few blocks over from the teleportation training field. It used to be their place, the place the two of them would always go to in order to be alone. As usual, the place was practically empty when they got in.

The old lady that ran the place nodded to them with a knowing smile as they came off the landing platform. She gestured towards their usual table without a word and the two of them simply nodded to her as they passed. The woman was a pure blood, having owned the diner since before The Academy was The Academy. Back before The Arrival, the area was some old college town known as Prince Town, or some sort. It was one of several such schools that were reappropriated for the teaching of magic. With teleportation being so common, the fact that the schools were all spread throughout the country had no real bearing on their unity. There were far too many newly discovered mages to house them anywhere else during their training, and it wasn't like the schools were going to be used for anything else.

Contemporary education, centered around sciences and maths, had to revamp itself completely. With science gone, for the most part, no one needed to learn it anymore. Math was still math, but it was no longer relevant in any real way. Beyond simple arithmetic, which was still taught, no one really needed to know it. Magic was an artform, learned through practice and interpretation and not through direct study. While some of the technical schools survived the transition, it was mostly education in the humanities that had taken over the training for the pure bloods, the Hulandans, the cambions, and the rare talents. Even business schools fell out of use, with everything about business needing to change around under the new practices and resources.

From what the old lady had told them about the place, the diner hadn't changed much over the years. The old lamps that once hung overhead were replaced by ever-burning torches set in the same brackets that had once held the lamps. The menu had changed only as much as it needed to, with sausages and hot dogs no longer available and chicken becoming harder to come by. The decorations were mild, mostly pictures of old celebrities that no one recognized anymore, decorative windows with missing glass panels, and plastic plants that were half melted by the residual magic from The Academy.

The back corner of the diner was around a large partition, which blocked the view from the door. No one would see them back there if anyone walked by, or even bothered to come to the diner. The food wasn't great and the ambiance had much to be desired, which was a death sentence for most businesses those days. But the place had somehow managed to survive over the decades. Of course, the lack of traffic made the place perfect for Ardith and Dorth. They got privacy in a public place without needing to pay for it.

Ardith giggled stupidly as she slipped into her usual spot, the side of the booth that faced the door. Her mother had taught her to never give her back to the door, though Dorth didn't seem to mind. Dorth had a similarly dopey grin on her face as she slid into the other side. Before they had settled into the booth, the old lady was there, sliding their usual drinks onto the table and placing the menus in front of them. Without a word, she retraced her steps, leaving the two to their peace and privacy.

"So," they both said at the same time, eliciting more giggles from both of them.

"So," Ardith said again. "What have you been up to? You're a writer now, right? The AP?"

"Yea, it's great. Real job security, too. Everyone always wants to know the news. As long as I get a story or two in each week, something unique that's not been reported by anyone else, I'm golden. Tomorrow, I'll write something about an inside view of the dragon attack. No one else was there... Well, no one that survived. Can you believe that? What was up with that?"

"Can we not talk about it?" Ardith asked. "I swear I'm going to have nightmares for weeks on that one. So many people died."

"Meh," Dorth said, shrugging. "Honestly, I don't even think that ranks the top one hundred magical massacres of the past decade. Maybe top twenty for the year, though. Not that we keep track of it. It's just that I see it all the time. Hell, I write about it all the time. You kind of develop a thick skin about it all. Or, well, or you go insane. Three reporters last year were committed when they just snapped. But, well, they were all pure bloods, so good riddance, eh?"

"Can we not bash the pure bloods today? We could have just as easily been one of them if we had been born without the gene."

"Yea, but we weren't. We're mages. Maybe just elemental mages, but mages nonetheless. In a few more decades, the pure bloods will start dying out, and we'll out number them. We practically already do, at least in the job market these days. I mean, come on, who wants to hire a pure blood when they can have one of us?"

"Yea, we'll out number them, if we don't die out first. What would happen if these deaths take all of us out? Then the pure bloods would be stuck, with no science and no magic. That's the end of the human race right there."

"Oh, nonsense. Sure, we've had a lot of deaths, especially with Africa."

"Yea, Africa," Ardith said. The two of them dropped into an unprompted moment of silence for the millions that died when the continent all but blew up. Too many of the inhabitants of Africa became mages upon the Arrival, all having their awakenings at the same time. The overload of power decimated the continent, killing all on it.

"But the world was already overpopulated. By a lot. As long as we don't go below a couple of billion, there's no danger of us dying out. And isn't the Mage Authority supposed to be making sure the mages don't die out first?"

"No, they're just trying to keep the peace between the guilds and punish the most dangerous of the out of control mages. Mage or pure blood, everyone is protected equally."

"See? I've missed this. We need to get together more often, like old times. Discussing the pros and cons of killing all the pure bloods."

"You know, you have graduated," the old woman said, drawing attention to the fact that she had come back to take their orders. "I remember when the two of you came in with your cap and gowns. No need for further debate over academic issues as such. Not all of us pure bloods are as useless as some of you seem to think."

"Sorry, Mary," Ardith said.

"Yea," Dorth said. "We totally don't include you on the list. Your apple pie is magic all its own."

"Speaking of which, we'll have two slices."

"And a plate of fries."

"I don't know where the two of you skinny girls put it all, but alright. Three plates of empty calories it is." She scooped up the two menus, still unopened, and left them to their discussion.

"See?" Ardith said. "Not all pure bloods are useless."

"I never said they were all useless, just that we should let them die out, if they're going to. Have you seen the new employment stats?"

"Ugh, stats? Seriously? You're going to quote math at me?"

"Pure bloods have a twelve percent employment right now. Twelve. Versus eighty-seven for mages."

"I wonder what side of that I'm on," Ardith said. "You do know this is my first assignment all year, right? And I'm still not having any luck with my enchantments. If pure bloods can't afford the services of mages, those of us that don't have paying jobs will be out of luck. The whole economy can collapse in on itself. Too much is already covered by the enchantments we already have in place. Something has got to give."

"Oh, god, can we just... I didn't bring you here to discuss politics," Dorth said.

"I know, I'm sorry."

"So, things aren't working out like you hoped?"

"Things are pretty horrible," Ardith said. She stopped talking when she noticed the old lady coming back their way, carrying all three plates on one arm. It was times like that that made her wonder if the lady was a rare talent after all, whose talent was simply being able to balance plates. But, if that were the case, Ardith figured she would advertise it, perhaps even put on a show, if for no other reason than to draw in traffic.

"Here you go, dearies," Mary said. She let the plates slide down her arm one at a time, placing them strategically around the table. "Bon appetit."

The two women waited for the old lady to turn back around the corner before digging into the pie. "This pie makes up for some of it, at least," Ardith said, around a large bite.

"Hey, it was your idea to go off on your own like that. We could have moved in together, found a nice home, settled down."

"Dorth, I wasn't going to be a kept woman," Ardith said. "I wanted to see if I could make it on my own. Besides, it was your decision, not mine, to just... break up like that."

"Hey, it's not that simple and you know it. I wanted more of you, not less. It wasn't enough for me, Ardi. Not anymore. It still isn't."

"And how did that work out for you? Did you... Did you meet someone else? Are you happy?"

"There's no one like you, Ardi, and you know that. No one in the world. No one in the universe that can captivate me, aggravate me, annoy the hell out of me like you can."

"Yea, well, I've missed you, too. But, even if I decide to give up on being a professional mage, I just... I can't. Not now. Maybe not ever."

"And, that's fine," Dorth said. "I never asked you to give up your career. I just wanted us to do it together, to be together. Though, I know, my dad would not be happy about it. Or your dad, for that matter."

"Yea," Ardith said. "Sometimes, I want to just tell my mom. I know she'd be cool with it. Maybe she'll have some idea on how to handle my dad. I just... Sometimes, I feel like a middle child, not an only child. He just doesn't get me, when he even bothers to try. Or, maybe we just don't tell them, any of our parents. Just leave them behind and out of our lives." She grabbed a fry off the plate, dipping the overcooked stick into her pie and then waving it around as a scepter in her proclamations. "They don't matter, not when true love is at stake."

"True love?" Dorth smiled at the thought, but it was clear that she was trying not to laugh. "Who would have thought it, eh? The daughter of the earth guild master in love with the daughter of the president of the world. I mean, not exactly Romeo and Juliet... or, would it be Juliet and Juliet? I don't know. Anyway, in any case, the political ramifications alone would be a nightmare. Besides, you know how gung ho my dad is about spreading the mage line. If I don't marry a guy and start popping out some kids soon..."

"You know, back in the day, there was this thing, something akin to a turkey baster. I'll bet it still works."

"Ah, biology. The only ology that still ologies." They both laughed at the old joke, though it was no longer funny. It was more out of habit and the reminder of the simpler times of their youth. "But, no, seriously. Not going to happen. I actually told Dad that... well, that I like girls."

"What?" Ardith said. All mirth instantly disappeared. "W-What did he say?"

"He damn near had another awakening. I swear, I could feel the power emanating off of him. He was quite literally about to blow. I just got out of there, haven't been back since. That was... Three? No, four months ago. I've heard from Mom, so I know the house didn't explode. She sent me a fire letter to tell me she was starting to look into arranged marriages. I mean, seriously? Our family gave that up like three generations ago. Or... At least I think so. Both my parents are Indian, but I just figured that was like a coincidence or something. They can't really expect me to..."

"So, your life is about as bad as mine, then?" Ardith said. She tried not to laugh at the fact that Dorth, despite seeming as put together as always, was just as miserable without her as she was without Dorth. "Granted, I imagine if I told my dad that I was in love with you, mine would still end up being worse than yours. Procreation may not be that high on his list of priorities for me, but he is still super religious. This is despite the fact that the demons had pretty much confirmed that God was gone, like decades ago. Half a century ago. I mean, he still thinks the gays chased him off. Then to find out his daughter was one of them? He wouldn't just chase me off. He'd straight up kill me."

"You're his daughter," Dorth said. "Maybe he'd surprise you. Maybe it'll get him to change his mind."

"Nope. He'd kill me. Even if those torture camps were still a thing, he'd still just kill me. And, with Mom investigating the crime, he'd get away with it."

"Oh, come on. Your mom is awesome. She'd never take his side over yours. But you've never--"

"No, she tells him everything. If I even came close to telling her, he'd know. Then--" She rubbed her finger across her throat while clicking her tongue. "I mean, yea, she'd probably feel bad about it afterwards, but she'd still clean up the mess."

"Ah, if only we could have the excuse of living on the other side of the world to hide behind," Dorth said. "Sometimes, I really hate how small the world has gotten since this whole thing started."

"Yea, the world would be a better place if teleportation wasn't as big of a thing. Or, no, if we had managed to get that Mars colony up and running before this whole thing started. Then we could just run away to Mars."

"Except Apophis wouldn't reach there," Dorth pointed out. "Plus, we'd have to get there without science, which would mean we'd need to be able to teleport there, which would totally be possible if Apophis reached there. But, then, that would just defeat the whole purpose of moving to Mars. I mean, it's Mars."

"Exactly. It's Mars," Ardith said. However, where Dorth sounded disgusted by the prospect, Ardith always loved the idea of living on another world, one beyond the limitations of the one she was born on. If only there was a way to get there, she would have left everything behind to go. "But, yea, our chances of getting away from our parents are about as good as our chances of getting to Mars. No sense in teasing ourselves that it would work. Even if we tried, they'd just track us down and punish us for the attempt."

"So, we're in the same place as we were nine months ago," Dorth said. "Stuck between a rock and a hard place, with nary an earth mage in sight."

"Well, there's one chance, one possibility that had come to mind. If we do this, if we help TS make the delivery, we'll be coming into a lot of money. I mean, yes, it's in silver, so we'll need to convert it to credits, and launder it in the process. But, once we do, we'll be able to..."

"To what? To escape? If it was just a matter of money, Ardi, I have enough to make both of us disappear. All the money in the world isn't going to hide us from my dad if he decides to hunt me down. He's only the most powerful mage in the world, in all of known existence. There's no power in the 'verse that can hide us from that. I want to, really I do, but ... I just think... The best we can hope for is, well, roommates."

"No, there has to be a way. Light magic or, no, blood magic. What if we somehow tie ourselves together? Like a magical marriage or something. Something that not even the most powerful void mage in the world can break without killing us both."

"He'd still try," Dorth said. She shook her head. "Don't you think I've been trying to figure this out this whole time? If we even go to a blood mage, they'll tell Dad. Everyone knows I'm the first daughter. Well, for some reason TS didn't seem to know, but he's apparently been living under a rock all this time."

"Seriously, that dude is clueless. I sometimes think I got the better end of the deal with all of this. I mean, a delivery? That's child's play, if he ever actually finds the thing he needs delivered. Granted, if it was a simple delivery, he would only have needed an air mage, not a water mage. He seemed convinced he needed both." She shrugged, unsure of herself as always. In the silence that followed, she finished her pie, staring at Dorth's half of the fries as her friend slowly ate.

Dorth gave her half a smile before spinning the fries around. "Don't say I never gave you anything."

"You've given me everything," Ardith said. "I just wish it was enough."

Chapter Fourteen
Missed Opportunity

Bethany

Igloo hadn't managed to stay hidden the entire time that
Bethany and Greg had been in the library. Dan had watched
from the sidelines as air guild orderlies swept into the entry
room, swallowing up all the people lagging behind there. They
had sent out a pulse, something akin to the radar of old, that
displayed all the mages that were hiding out in there. Some
were invisible, some not. Once spotted, the orderlies literally
pulled them by their ears over to the meeting room crystal. By
the time they had managed to extricate Igloo from the
meeting, it was past time to clock out for the day. With no
new leads on the quickly cooling case, Bethany dismissed the
others and decided to head home.

Bethany had expected the place to be dark when she
teleported into her apartment. She shielded her eyes against
the light from the ever-burning torches, though they adjusted
quickly enough. The smell of dinner permeated the air,
reminding her of her half-eaten lunch. When she looked over
to the little nook that was their kitchen, she was pleasantly
surprised to see John there, wearing an apron and little else.
He was standing in front of the stove, a wooden spoon in his
hand as he stirred his famous sauce.

"Perfect timing, as always," John said, without having to
turn around to see her. He would have noticed the displaced

air, known what it would mean. Bethany could feel the wards in place, blocking anyone from arriving besides John and herself. Even Ardith, no longer an occupant of the apartment, would need to send a letter to be allowed in. The two of them were as alone as alone can be, with no one and nothing to interrupt them.

"Had I known I had you to come home to, I might have left early."

"But then you'd be early, and the sauce wouldn't be almost ready. What would we possibly have done with all that extra time?"

"Oh, I can think of a few things," Bethany teased. She came up next to her husband, leaning against the counter next to the stove. Standing next to his nakedness, she felt remarkably overdressed in her usual attire. "I'm just glad you're home. I had a rather shitty day."

"I figured," John said.

He stirred the pot a little before taking out a large scoop of the sauce, offering it for her testing. She leaned forward, sticking the entirety of the spoon in her mouth so she could take every last drop of the sauce. An explosion of flavor hit her tongue, washing away all the ills of the world. Her eyes closed of their own accord and she hummed her enjoyment, her encouragement. She let the sauce linger in her mouth, trying desperately to hold onto that flavor for as long as she could.

"When you hadn't come back to meet with the blood guild rep, I figured something had come up," John said. He retrieved the spoon, now empty, from his wife's mouth before sticking it back into the sauce as is.

"What?" Her eyes bolted open again and the sauce flitted down her throat before she was ready to let it go. She coughed a few times as the liquid threatened to go down the wrong pipe. "What?" she asked, again. "Crap, I totally forgot. Sorry. I think getting yelled at by the captain totally wiped it from my mind. Can we set something up later?"

"Don't worry about it," he said. "When you didn't make it back before the guy did, I figured something had waylaid you, so I approached him myself. I'm not as useless as you sometimes think. Besides, with Ardith mixed up in all of this, I figured it was as much my duty as yours. Anyway, I knew enough of your case to ask what you would, or most of it anyway. While he won't be able to get you into the guild as a visitor, he assured me that there was no fugitive hiding out in there."

"That's it? Wait, how would he know? The quorum was in full swing when I got the notification of the incident. The perp could have popped in without this rep knowing."

"Like I said, I'm not completely useless, Bethy. I said something along those lines myself. There's no place in their guild to straight out hide. They have some rooms set aside for visitors, but they were all in use with the quorum in session. It's easier to just crash at the guild than risk teleporting home when too tired to walk straight."

"Isn't that what linking books are for?" Bethany asked. "Some people are just so lazy, even in a world where everything is at everyone's fingertips."

"Well, not everyone," John said. "But, yea, laziness abounds. Anyway, I got him to make a copy of the logs for the twenty-four hour period around last night. That's what you needed, right?"

"Yes, thanks," Bethany said. She pulled on his apron strings, pulling him closer to her so she could give him a nice, long kiss full on the mouth. "You are truly perfect," she said, after a few moments of their lips locked together.

"Just as God made me," John said. "It should be on your desk first thing tomorrow, if it's not there already."

"Wait, it might--"

"You're not going back to work right now," John ordered. He moved over to stand in front of her, extending his arms around her torso as he leaned forward against the counter. "You're all mine for the night. No work, no talk of work, no talk at all if I have anything to say about it. It has been a very long thirty hours and I intend to bed my wife before I sink into a coma."

"What about dinner?" Bethany said. The comment was more a tease than anything else. Her thoughts were nowhere near her stomach.

"We can do both. It'll be messy, but oh so worth it."

"Oh, there's nothing I want more. It's just... Ardith."

"She's not invited," John said. "I want you all to myself. Besides, she wouldn't want to see what I have planned for you."

"I'm not talking... No, she's still out there, still in trouble. Doesn't that bother you?"

"She's an adult, barely but still. She can take care of herself. And, if she's in over her head, she knows how to reach out to us. The fact that we haven't heard anything at this point, one way or the other, is starting to seem like a good thing."

"Ugh," Bethany said. "I'm sorry. I just can't turn off my brain right now. Maybe I should try to send her a fire letter. I should have sent one when I first saw her at her workshop."

Bethany broke out of the loosely restraining arms, heading over to her supply of paper. As she passed, John gave her a teasing pat on her rear. She let out a sharp cry of surprise, eyeing him seductively over her shoulder before continuing across the room. He smiled after her briefly before going back to his sauce. The sauce was starting to bubble over, as it wasn't getting the attention it required, so he turned off the heat and started to decant it.

By the mail slot, there were three boxes of paper, one for mail, one for fire paper, and one that was just regular paper. Bethany pulled from the third box, scooping up a quill from a fourth. Using the wall as a writing surface, Bethany scratched into the blank paper "Are you OK? --Mom." with the dry quill. Nothing showed up on the page, but as she tilted it back and forth in the light from overhead, the scratches showed up in the paper. She pulled mana from the air, shaping it into a spell as she thought of her daughter, wherever she was. The paper quickly lit on fire, going up in smoke as it disappeared in her hand.

"There," John said, happily. He had already pulled the pasta out of the other pot, placing a huge pile of it on each of two plates. John held the plates aloft over the kitchen table, seeming unsure if they were eating there. "Now, table or bed?" he asked.

"Tempting," Bethany said. She feigned thinking about it for a moment, but then she shook her head. "Better to eat at the table." She walked the three steps back over to the table, pulling her usual chair out before falling heavily into it. "I don't want to have to clean the sheets before actually sleeping tonight." At the mention of sleep, she yawned broadly. As she stifled the yawn, she remembered that she hadn't gotten any sleep the night before, standing watch over the crime scene. Despite the fact that John had a similarly long night, he seemed properly rested. "Wait, when did the quorum session break?" she asked, accusatorially.

"Um... Soon after lunch," John said. He placed the plates down on the table before taking his own seat. He quickly took Bethany's hands, both of them bowing their heads as they said grace. "I'll admit I got a nice long nap in. It was nice. I did, however..." He trailed off, raising his finger in the air when he remembered something. The chair scraped as he jumped back up to his feet, swiveling around the chair to head over to the counter. A familiar scent reached Bethany's nose as he returned to the table, carrying two mugs and one of the few modern marvels of the last couple of centuries that survived The Arrival.

"Coffee," Bethany said, with a level of ecstasy that went beyond anything that John had ever given to her. She gazed into the French press longingly as John pushed down on the plunger. Her usual mug found its way into her hands before she could think to move. John poured the cold coffee into her cup, instantly becoming warm by her magic. The smell only intensified as her magic did its work. "They really need to come up with a way to make coffee through magic," she said to her mug before taking a long, deep draught. The caffeine did its work quickly, perking her up once more.

"Coffee is magic," John said, as he poured himself a cup. His remained cold, but he often said he preferred it that way. "I think making it with magic would just spoil the whole thing. Besides, the beans are starting to become hard to come by. The pure blood farmers are getting lazy again."

"Yea, either that or the remnants of global warming is impacting the growing seasons," Bethany said. "We may have stopped pumping carbon into the atmosphere, but there's only so much of it that can be pulled back out by the air council. The world is a big place, after all."

"I would have thought, what with science not working and all," John said.

"Oh, come off it. You know as well as I do that science never stopped working. We stopped being able to control electricity and most machinery gets jammed up. But science is science, no matter what magic is doing. The carbon is still up there, still heating the world up. It's just not as bad as it would have been had Apophis never come."

"One of the many ways that the world is a better place because of magic," John said. He raised his coffee mug in a toast, one that Bethany failed to notice with her attention on her plate. "So, after dinner, will we be adjourning to the bedroom?"

"This sauce really is amazing," Bethany said, letting the question die in the air. She smiled over at him, knowing he wouldn't take that for an answer, but not wanting to supply one just yet. Even with the letter away, her mind was still on her daughter and her potential problems with the law. She feared that, once the case was all over, she would end up forced to arrest her own daughter, sending her away to the mage prison for years.

When their plates were almost clean, and the coffee was fading from Bethany's system, a fire letter arrived in the middle of the table. It flared out, filling the space between them, before falling down, just barely missing both of their plates. The page was smaller than the standard size, suggesting that the sender had cut it in half before sending it. On it were just three words.

"I'm fine. --Ardith"

"There," John said, pointing to the paper. Despite his earlier bravado, he did let out his own sigh of relief at seeing those words on the paper. "She's fine. No need to ruin our evening with unnecessary worry, eh? Now, then. Shall we adjourn to the bedroom?"

"Sure," Bethany said, with half a smile. "I could really use a nap. I hear they're all the rage."

"Aw," John said, sounding thoroughly disappointed.

"After the nap... Well, we'll see."

Chapter Fifteen
Black Market Dealings

Eric

Eric was convinced that the world was working against him. He had never been that religious of a person, it was hard to be when growing up around scientists. But, with everything that had been happening since he left the bunker, a unified force hell bent to stop him seemed the most likely source. It stood to reason, at least to him at the time, that the arrival of magic to the world may have heralded something else, something more powerful. Or, perhaps, there was something that came with it. Perhaps Apophis itself was alive and he knew exactly what Eric was trying to do.

While the girls went off to get reacquainted, Eric mostly spent the time moping around the city. He still had Carissa's old linking book, she had even done something to it so that he could use it without her. However, he didn't particularly like that method of travel. It was nothing compared to riding his old motorcycle down the open road, even though it was faster. It baffled him how such a thing, such a simple thing that fit in the palm of his hand, could break the very laws of physics like it did. Everything about magic just rubbed him the wrong way. Being out in the world had done nothing to sway him from his mission.

Soon before sunset, he found his way back to New Chicago, just a few blocks over from the old bar. He didn't dare go much closer, knowing that the place was probably being watched. The Mage Authority was no doubt still hunting him, and the last thing he wanted to do was help them with that hunt. Still, some part of him longed to go back. That bar had been the last place he went before the ground started to fall out from under him. The most illogical parts of him was thinking that, if he could only go back to the bar, he could go back to his old life. Before the mission. Before the quest. Before things started going south.

"What are you doing here?" The voice was whispering harshly at him from the shadows of the alley next to him. Eric hadn't noticed the alley, his eyes just glossing over the small gap between the building he had been standing near and the one next to it. The darkness of the alley itself seemed to take on a form, but it swiveled and swerved in his vision, never quite taking shape. "They can track you."

"I know," Eric told the shadows. "I wasn't going to get closer."

"You're already too close," came the voice. It was feminine, despite the anger in its tone, and somewhat familiar, but he couldn't quite place it. "You were supposed to be here already."

"Where?" he asked. "Who are you?"

"What? Oh, god, you really are a stupid pure blood aren't you. It's Dorth, you dork. You were supposed to meet up with us twenty minutes ago."

"Oh, god, sorry," he said. He looked to his wrist, forgetting that he had left his watch back at home, so as to save it from the effects of the mana filling the air. "I'll..." Eric trailed off as he looked down at the linking book in his hand with disgust. He was pretty sure that there was a page in there that would lead him to the meeting place, but the book had a couple hundred pages to it, most of them full. Without having seen the place already, he had no way of knowing which was the right page.

"Oh, forget it," Dorth said.

The form spiraled away from the street in a whoosh, disappearing as it merged with the shadows native to the alley. Eric let out a sigh of relief, once the strange form was gone. Its presence unsettled him deep down. However, his relief was short lived as the feeling of unsettlement was replaced with something else, something worse. The now familiar feeling of a hook in his guts, trying to pull his stomach out through his belly button, signaled that he was about to be teleported away. He looked all around the street, trying to see the source of the spell, but the street quickly disappeared around him. He was surrounded by darkness for a split second as he lost all sense of gravity, of up and down, of outside of his body and inside. When he landed on his feet again, he didn't stay there long. He doubled over at the waist, leaning heavily on his knees as his still empty stomach tried to vacate itself onto the ground at his feet. The group was supposed to have split up to get dinner, but Eric already knew that he wouldn't be eating much until his quest was done.

"There you are," Carissa said. She was standing right next to him, or at least he was pretty sure she was. All he could see was her blue coat, blocking his peripheral vision on his left.

"The idiot was back near the crime scene," Dorth said. She took up a position to his right, but all he could see was yellow, reflecting the lights from the area harshly into his eyes. "I swear, if it wasn't for his binding over you, I'd've let him be caught. As it was, I had to bounce him through three guilds and a museum just to drop any chance of being tracked."

"No wonder why I'm about to be sick," Eric said.

"That and someone else teleported you," Carissa said. "You seem remarkably susceptible to that for a pure blood. Most pure bloods I've heard of love the feeling of disorientation. Do you usually get motion sickness?"

"Only when I'm not driving."

"Driving?" both the girls asked, obviously unsure of the meaning of the word.

"Oh, right, like in those old books," Carissa said. "You actually got to drive? Just how old are you?"

"Old enough. I was in my early twenties when that thing arrived."

"That thing, as you call it, is the best thing to ever come to Earth," Dorth said. "Have some respect."

"Where are we anyway?" Eric asked. He tried to look up but his stomach didn't like his view changing suddenly and he had to look back at his feet.

"At the meeting place," Carissa said. "Where you should have been half an hour ago."

Eric looked up again, this time taking his time and doing it in fits and starts. The cobblestones beneath his feet reminded him of the street he had just left, though that one had originally been paved in asphalt. It had only looked like cobblestones because the street had been broken up so completely by the rising waters of the lake during the heavy rains. The sky was much lighter than it was in New Chicago, and the old street lamps had been replaced by ever-burning torches. The area was as bright as day, though it was clearly mid evening. Despite them being quite obviously outside, there were actual people everywhere. It reminded Eric of the bustling city streets of his youth, from back before the world had gone crazy around him.

The buildings on either side of the road seemed as new as the ones in New Chicago, though these had been kept in repair by expert hands. The familiar glass, cement, and steel of the buildings were clean, with none of the panes broken, none of the cement chipped. Eric could even make out a group of people milling around inside one of the buildings, sitting at tables together and eating what looked like normal food. Everything was bright and clean, not run down like most of the old neighborhoods.

More than that, everything there looked normal. No one was throwing magic around. No one was trying to show off to their friends. No one was dying from completely preventable accidents. Everything seemed like a normal day in the city, with everyone just going about their business, ignoring everyone else. He loved every minute of it. The only signs that magic had claimed their world were the torches and the fact that the only car within sight had long since been stripped for parts. Even that seemed normal to Eric. He felt like he had finally come home.

"What a dump," Dorth said. She sneered at the scene around them, like she was above it all. "Why does anyone even go outside anymore?"

"Maybe because not all of us want to rely on magic," Eric said. "Where is this place, anyway? I know this was the rendezvous, but where is it?"

"Panama City," Dorth said. "I don't think Panama got much in the way of mages after The Arrival, so they mostly went with these pure blood cities. They're kind of a refuge for your kind. RD and I aren't all that welcome, thus the odd looks from the people."

"What looks?" Eric asked. He looked around at the people that were walking by, but none of them seemed to take much notice of the three of them. Dorth and Carissa did stand out, in their color coded coats, but they didn't seem to be attracting any more attention than Eric was. What attention they were getting seemed more due to the fact that they were new there, after having just teleported into the middle of a city with minimal magic.

"Let's just get out of here," Carissa said. "My contact is just up the road."

The three of them walked along the street, melding into the crowd that was passing through, heading in the same direction. Eric was elated with the familiarity of it all, a reminder of his college years in the city, before the world had gone to hell. He hadn't seen so many people, normal, non-magical people, in one place in so long he could barely remember it. Remember the feeling of not being surrounded by people that could kill him with just a snap of their finger.

Even his time in the bunker, with his people, was not nearly as satisfying as that one short walk.

Two blocks down, on the left side of the street, was an old subway station. The stairs leading down looked familiar, the black metal running down at an angle before merging with the cement of the sidewalk. The lettering over the entrance, white on black, was in Spanish, but just as satisfying as if it had said Sixth Street. It probably did say Sixth Street, or something along those lines, but Eric wasn't enough of a linguist to know. People were actually going up and down the stairs, though he knew that there was no chance for any form of train running along the tracks. With the station open to the air above, the subway system would have been permeated by the mana just as much as the rest of the world. The not so subtle reminder of his mission made Eric focus on the road ahead, on getting to Carissa's contact, hopefully getting what he needed, and moving on with his next task.

"How does someone like you even know someone like this?" Eric asked Carissa.

"What do you mean someone like me?"

"Her old boyfriend was into all this stuff," Dorth said. "He used to collect these old sort of pamphlet thingies with pictures in them. Grown men wearing tights and beating up bad guys, or whatever. Now that people can do that for real, I guess the draw of the old things was lost. Anyway, it's just the old collectors that have them anymore, and they're all in places like this."

"I think there was a motion to make them illegal at one point," Carissa said. "My dad was annoyed by that when I was growing up. As bad as my dad is sometimes, he's a big proponent of free speech."

"I bet he loved Jack," Dorth said. "Wondering why you're not still with him."

"Actually, no, he didn't like that he would take me to places like... Well, like this place."

"Really? I figured my dad would be like that, wanting to burn the whole place down. Probably could, too."

"Can we focus?" Eric asked. "Who is this guy? How are we going to know which is him? Is there some kind of signal?"

"No," Carissa said. She seemed the think the idea rather stupid, even laughing at him a little to her friend. "We're just going to this club up the street and asking for Paul at the bar. The guy at the bar is supposed to point us in the right direction."

"So... Like a signal?" Eric asked.

"Oh, I guess so. Whatever. Anyway, I think it's..."

She pulled over to the side, getting out of the flow of the foot traffic. The narrow sidewalk made this a bit difficult, so the girls actually walked out into the street. Eric stared at them, surprised that they would just walk out into the street like nothing was about to hit them. Then again, as he looked up and down the road, he realized that it was actually the case. None of the locals seemed to key off of the fact that there were no cars coming up and down the road, no threat to anyone that they were about to be hit by anything. Everyone just stuck to the sidewalk anyway, perhaps more out of habit than anything else. It was ingrained, built into them, like birds instantly flying away from a cat.

"Nope, it's over there," Carissa said, pointing further down the road. Rather than coming back into the safety of the pack walking down the sidewalk, the two girls walked brazenly down the middle of the road, taking the easier and less crowded path. It was that, more than anything else, that suddenly drew the attention of the crowd around Eric. They all started to gape openly at the two mages, thumbing their noses at the norms of yesteryear.

"Hey, TS, you coming?" Dorth asked, before walking straight at the flow of the foot traffic, disappearing in the masses.

Eric continued to walk with everyone else, opting not to push past anyone and attract more attention than he already had. As he walked beside these people, his people, he started to wonder where they were going, where they were coming from. It was about the right time for this to be the rush hour traffic of people heading home from work, but he had never heard of an overabundance of work to be done. Not in the cities, and certainly not by pure bloods. Most of the mindless tasks of the past, those that hadn't relied on technology, had quickly been automated, not by machines but by magic. If they were coming from work, the jobs probably didn't pay that well, which might be the better explanation for why they were all walking the blocks, perhaps even miles, between work and home. If none of them could afford a linking book, walking was their only option.

As Eric passed another of the seemingly endless doorways, four arms reached out, pulling him out of the throng. He let out a short grunt of surprise, but when he noticed the two girls there, he quickly stifled it. Carissa led the way into the building that they must have been pointing out from the street. Just inside the door was a small bar, barely big enough to sit three people, though no one sat there. The man behind the bar barely glanced over at them as Carissa passed through the door on the far side of the room, heading deeper into the building. The hallway beyond stretched far into the distance. The light from outside barely went past the entrance, and with no torches, no light sources of any kind, he was quickly plunged into darkness.

"Are you sure this is the right way?" he asked. Dorth's hand on his arm was a steady presence as the three of them continued onward into the dark.

"Yes," Carissa said, simply, from the front of the group.

"I don't like this," he said. Eric had an unsettling feeling as they continued into the dark. The hallways seemed to go on for forever, with no end in sight, literally or figuratively. Then, suddenly, he was being pulled to his right, coming around a corner that could easily be at the back of the building. As they continued down this other path, the darkness that had surrounded him started to get lighter.

Another turn to the right dropped the group into a large room. A single ever-burning torch was hanging down from above, giving the room just enough light that no one was bumping into anyone, but little more than that. And there were people there, loads of people. The room, which seemed as large as the building outside, was jam packed with tables, displaying a large assortment of wares of all manners. People were bustling around everywhere, all of them calling out and talking over each other. Eric wasn't sure if he was at a bazaar or some kind of stock exchange.

Carissa and Dorth continued further into the room, pushing their way through the throng as they made their way to the far wall. The further they went into the room, the more the general din faded around them. The wares that were being sold further into the room were apparently much less in demand, resulting in the sales being more muted, more in tune with what Eric would have expected from an underground marketplace. It seemed strange that such a place would be so close to the main thoroughfare. Then again, a lot of things about this world seemed strange to Eric.

"How do these people get away with selling things so close to the people outside?" Eric asked. "Don't the local authorities care?"

"Not particularly," someone said. It was one of the merchants to his left, currently devoid of customers. On his table was a spread of several comic books, all laid out in their original protective sleeves. The sleeves showed wear, the plastic worn away by the mana that filled the air, and the books themselves were starting to show a similar reaction. He couldn't help but notice Sue Storm on the cover of one of them seemed to bear a striking resemblance to Dorth. "The locals don't care much about anything but the booze that keeps coming their way. The Authority might care, except we pure bloods don't rate much on their priorities list. Anything I can help you folks find?"

"We're looking for an iPhone 30," Carissa said.

"I never said I needed an iPhone," Eric said. "I said it was like an iPhone."

"Shh," Carissa hissed, but the merchant had already heard him.

"Well, now, that's a rather fancy item," the merchant said. He started to lick his lips as he eyed Eric up and down. "I'm assuming you have the... coin to pay for such a rare item?"

"He does," Carissa said. "Not that you'll be getting any of it." She lifted her fist threateningly, pulling power from the air and surrounding the fist with a thick layer of ice. It was enough to show the man her power, to show that she wasn't a pure blood like him, though the coat should have already done that. The merchant didn't seem to back down in the least, though, barely showing any reaction at all.

"I'm just making sure he's not wasting our time," the merchant said. "There is usually a finder's fee for an item like that, but I see you're in a bit of a hurry. The iPhones, and similar electronics, hadn't been holding up as well as some other items, so I'm guessing you'd want the ones in cases. Those are exceptionally valuable--"

"Do you know where to find them or not?" Carissa said. Her patience was obviously wearing thin, and her fist was only getting thicker as the ice continued to swell.

The merchant just smiled broader, his fingers rubbing together in front of him. Eric rolled his eyes before reaching into the pouch he had strategically placed in a hidden pocket of his coat. He pulled out two silver coins, making sure not to rattle the rest of them too much. With a flip of his thumb, he sent them towards the merchant, who quickly caught them out of the air with a single hand.

"Back corner on the right," the merchant said, finally. He pointed furiously towards the corner, though his eyes had become locked on the fist that was threatening to freeze his face off. "Don't tell them I sent you."

"Thank you," Carissa said. As her ire faded, so, too, did her ice. With its departure, Eric actually shuddered, like the room was colder without the ice than with it. She offered him a small wave as the two women left to follow his pointing.

As they left the merchant, Eric distinctly heard the man muttering "Damn mages think they own the whole planet." He didn't disagree with the sentiment.

They passed by several other merchants, with varying goods for sale. All of the items there were from the old world, from his world, from before The Arrival. Everything was showing its age, the plastics eaten away, the paper worn by the normal passing of time. Anything metal had tarnished. One merchant was only selling one piece of metal, a long rod that shined in the light from above. This merchant was old, with wrinkled skin and heavy bags under his eyes. He smiled as they passed, pointing to his prized possession, that one metal rod gleaming there. No one bothered to look at it, no one bothered to even check it out, knowing that the metal rod was enchanted. That was the only way for iron to stay that pristine. Only the more precious metals, the golds and silvers, managed to survive the effects of mana. In fact, even without needing to look at it, Eric was relatively certain that the rod was a rain rod, much like the one he still had hidden away in a deep pocket of his coat.

Once they managed to get past most of the merchants in the room, heading for the more expensive and, therefore, less desired items, the back corner fell into view. And, more importantly, the merchant they had come to see. Once Eric saw him, he lost a step. He recognized the man instantly, the very sight of him filling him with a mix of emotions. It was the man from the other night, the one that had originally sold him the briefcase. When the shock wore off, Eric figured that this would only play out in his favor. That, for once, the universe was playing for him, not against him.

"Oh, it's you," The Contact said. "Come to stiff me again?"

"You know each other?" Carissa asked.

"I never stiffed you in the first place," Eric said. "You ran out without the rod."

"Yes, well, you still owe me. I'll add it to the bill. What do you want now?"

"The same thing I wanted last time. It... I lost the case."

"Oh, well, well, well now. What's this? You actually lost that precious thing that you went through all that trouble to procure?" The Contact smiled broadly, a cat with his catch. "That item was quite hard to come by the first time. A second one, well, that's going to be three times as much. Plus the cost of the first one. That is quite a steep price."

"Oh, screw you," Dorth said. "He doesn't owe you shit. It's not like he ran off with the thing, did he?"

"He left with it. I didn't leave with my pay. I'd say that counts as running off with it."

"So, call the cops," Carissa said. "Oh, that's right. You can't. This stuff is illegal. Well, maybe I'll just call them for you. I'm sure they'll be happy to take all of your items off your hands, for free."

"Yea, and her mom--" Dorth started to say.

"Dorth," Carissa said. "Not a good idea."

"Right, sorry."

"As I was saying, I think you'll just have to give up on the first price. As for whatever new price, for the second one, I'd say it's better to keep it more reasonable."

"As I was saying, little lady," The Contact said, "these items are not easy to come by. Why, it just so happens that I was able to procure one since our last meeting, but that was mostly through blind luck. I'd say the cost of my hardship should be included in the price, otherwise it wasn't worth my time. It'll have to be, oh, I'd say, about, three million."

"What?" Carissa spat.

"Outrageous," Dorth shouted.

"Oh, it's not that much more than the last one, is it?"

"What kind of iPhone is this?" Carissa asked.

"iPhone?"

"I said it was like an iPhone," Eric said. "I never said it was an iPhone."

"But three million? That's ridiculous."

"The last one was two and a half," The Contact said. This seemed to quiet the two women.

"Yes, and last time you said this was priceless," Eric said. He pulled the rod back out of the inside pocket of his coat, placing it down on the table. Its shine echoed the one from the other table.

"Last time I told you it was worthless without the certificate of authenticity," The Contact said. "It still is."

"Oh, come now," Carissa said. "A man like you? There's no way you don't know someone who couldn't fake that certificate. It's not even like it would be lying."

"What... What is that?" Dorth asked. "That's not..."

"Yea, it is," Carissa said. "Stay with us here, honey."

"But..."

"Just come off it," Eric said. "It's the original deal. It's still good."

"It would be, if I didn't have to go find a new one, now would it? No, I think you'll have to sweeten the deal a little."

"How? It's not like these things are easy to come by."

"No, but that's not my problem."

"Oh, forget it," Carissa said. "The asshole probably doesn't even have another one anyway. Let's just go. I'm sure there's someone else we can go to."

"For this item? Not a chance," The Contact said. "And, of course I have it. In fact, it's right here. Something told me you'd come looking for another one, what with The Authority on your tail. And, yes, I know all about your problem with The Authority. No point trying to threaten me with it. You'd want to stay out of their way just as much as I would."

The Contact reached below his table, pulling out a familiar looking case. It looked just like the first one. He moved several other, similar looking cases out of the way, pulling them off of his table to make space. The Contact held a staying hand on the case as he spun it around to face Eric. His other hand was at the latch as if he were about to open it, though both of them knew he wouldn't. The contents would be quite worthless if he had.

"It's pretty much the same model as the first one," The Contact said.

Eric looked over the case for a moment, not sure what he was supposed to be looking for. He wasn't even sure how The Contact could tell this case apart from all the other cases that he was moving around on the table. Was there a mark on it somewhere? Something that he didn't see before? "Pretty much?" he asked. "I'd say it's exactly like it." He pointed towards the only familiar, yet out of place, marking on the case, a single notch that marred the otherwise pristine handle. "I'm pretty sure that nick right there came from when the case got shoved under the table. At the bar. This is the first one, the same one you sold me yesterday."

"I don't know what you're talking about. That nick could have been from anything."

"No, I know it's the same one. That nick was digging into my hand the entire time I was carrying it. That's kind of hard to forget. How did you find it? How did you get it out from the rubble?"

"What rubble? What are you talking about? Don't try to cheat me on this deal... again."

"Dorth?" Carissa said. "How about a truth spell? You always liked those in The Academy."

"Ooh, sounds like fun. I wonder what kind of secrets we can get him to spill." Dorth smiled broadly, evilly, rubbing her hands together as a slight, lilty giggle slipped out of her.

"Oh, alright," The Contact said. "No spells. Yes, it's the same case, but I didn't take it out of any rubble. After I managed to escape that death trap--"

"You mean after you ran out of there like your hair was on fire?" Eric said.

"Yes, after that. I just tracked the case." He pulled what looked like a rubber ball out of his pocket. The ball lit up in a slow pattern, getting faster the closer he brought it to the case. "It's an insurance policy for my larger items, for those times when people try to cheat me, like you did last night. It's paid off more than just the once."

"I didn't try to cheat you," Eric said. "This was the agreed upon price. I'll overlook your... underhandedness if we can stick with it."

"And give us the tracker while you're at it," Carissa added. "We don't need you tracking us or stealing the case back again once we're out of here."

"Fine, but payment first. And that rod isn't enough. Not anymore. You'll need to add..." He paused, thinking for a moment. As he did so, he ran the tracking ball across his chin, back and forth, until it seemed to shock him. "Add the cost of the counterfeit certification. That seems valid and appropriate. After all, if you hadn't lost the certificate in the first place, the deal would have finished and we would have been out of that bar before anything happened."

"And, then, you would have stolen the case back anyway," Carissa said. "No deal."

"No," Eric said. He reached back under his coat, heading for the coin purse again. "What's the cost of the counterfeit?"

"That's not credits, mind you," The Contact said. "I only take silver."

"Wait, that's my silver," Carissa said. "You said--"

"I said the silver in the pouch, not any specific amount. There will be plenty left over for what you were expecting. Now, how much?"

"A thousand. That would get me a decent enough certificate to get my money back for the rod. I am a merchant, after all. It's what I do."

"He'll probably make twice as much off that rod as the case is worth," Carissa said.

"Yea, probably," Eric agreed. Still, he reached into the pouch, feeling around for a few moments until he found what he was looking for. With a tug, that he had practiced often enough, he pulled out one of the smaller pouches that he kept inside, all without moving the main pouch from the hidden pocket of his coat. He tossed the bag onto the table next to the rod, causing Carissa's eyes to bug out of their sockets.

"But..." Carissa said.

"It's not the same pouch," he assured her. "I figured a mage of your reputation would have recognized that pouch for what it was the moment you laid eyes on it. Maybe I'm paying too much for your services."

"But..." she said, again.

"Don't worry. Once my mission is over, I won't have a need for that coin purse anyway."

"Fine," The Contact said. "The rod and this purse for the case. I'm assuming I don't have to count them."

"Pfft, can you count that high?" Dorth asked. "Without taking off your shoes?"

"That would only get him up to twenty," Carissa said. "At best, a hundred, but I doubt he'd figure that out on his own."

"Actually, if he used binary, he could get to a thousand just on his fingers," Eric said.

"What's binary?" Dorth and Carissa asked together.

"Ah, mages," The Contact huffed. "They think they know everything, when they really know nothing. No one actually counts coins that high, anyway. They weigh them. It's just a figure of speech to say count them."

"Now, then," Eric said. "The case? The tracker?"

"Yes, yes, yes. All set," The Contact said. He slapped the ball down on the table next to the case. When he let it go, the ball bounced a few times before settling right on the center of the case, staying there perfectly still as if it were glued to the surface.

"Pleasure doing business with you," Eric said. "Again."

"Maybe this time you can leave without trying to steal from me," The Contact said. "Now would be good."

Eric grabbed the ball with one hand as he scooped up the case with the other. Despite its appearance, the ball came away from the case easily, readily, resisting for only a moment as if it were magnetically attached. The case seemed somehow lighter to Eric, causing him to worry that, once again, he had been cheated. He glared over at The Contact, who only glared back at him, until he turned and left the table, reluctantly giving The Contact his back. Once he managed to get back to the main crowd of the room, the two women fell into lock step behind him, flanking him and protecting his back from any knives that were aimed his way.

"Think we can actually get out of here before any more bad things happen?" Eric asked.

"Oh, sure," Dorth said. "Once we make the hallway, we can teleport away. This place doesn't even have the usual teleportation shield. I would have expected a place like this to have prison level anti-magic safeguards, but I guess they rely on secrecy."

"Those safeguards are too easy to track," Carissa said. "The Authority really locks down the unauthorized use of them. It would have only drawn their attention."

"Wait, anti-magic safeguards?" Eric asked, his mind lighting up at the possibility. "What exactly do those do?"

"Everyone stay where you are," someone called out. Their voice was obviously magically amplified, coming in over the noise of the front of the room. Eric turned back towards the direction of the voice, back towards the entrance to the room, to see the familiar forms of a team from the Mage Authority.

Eric didn't have time to swear his annoyance before Dorth grabbed his arm and the three of them teleported away.

Chapter Sixteen
Back for More

Bethany

In an odd stroke of fate, the team arrived back at headquarters the next morning within a few seconds of each other. They had agreed to get an early jump on the investigation that morning, which usually meant that Greg and Bethany would get there around seven and Dan and Igloo would stumble in closer to eight. However, soon after seven thirty in the morning, all four of them arrived, ready to get back at it, though none knew what approach to take.

Igloo yawned broadly as she stepped off of the landing platform, the last to arrive of the group. Ever the best teleporter in the group, she sometimes seemed like she could teleport in her sleep. The other three had barely gotten past her desk when she came over. She seemed to fall into her chair rather than actually sitting in it. It took her a moment to even notice they were there, notice that they were staring at her.

"What?" she asked around another yawn.

"I don't think I've ever seen you in the office before eight," Bethany said. "Did you even go to bed last night?"

"Of course, I did. Then again, I had a nice long nap during the meeting yesterday. I don't know why they insist on everyone being there when all they're going to talk about is the usual crap. Dues, research, upkeep of the tower, totally boring. I don't think there was an open eye in the place. Even old man Drummond was asleep on stage."

"Well, I hope everyone got some good sleep last night," Bethany said. "Hopefully we'll have some good ideas on how to track someone who has proven to be untrackable."

"Are we still on this pure blood?" Greg asked. "I would have thought we would go back to the blood mage. That side of the investigation is much more interesting."

"I'm expecting some new information on that part of it this morning," Bethany said. "Let's head over to my desk to see if it's here yet. However, I know that we are quite capable of dealing with two ends of a case at the same time."

"Wouldn't it technically be two cases?" Igloo asked. She reluctantly got up from her chair as the other three started to head down the aisle towards Bethany's desk near the back. "I hate having to do double the work."

"I think that's why we're not separating it," Greg said. "Two cases means double the paperwork."

"That and I was afraid if I suggested it to the captain yesterday, he'd bite my head off," Bethany said. "Maybe he'll be in a better mood today." A part of her was hoping that he wouldn't be, that she could keep using that as an excuse to stay on both cases. If she gave up on tracking the pure blood, she wouldn't be able to help Ardith once they find them. On the other hand, if she dropped the wrongful death, whoever picked it up would surely try to pin it on the pure blood, taking both cases for themselves.

"I was thinking about tracking," Dan said. "If we could get something of the pure bloods, or of the mage that helped him escape, couldn't we do some kind of locator spell? That's more your realm, Bethany, isn't it?"

"We'd need to know a general vicinity," Bethany said.

They had gotten to her desk, so she swiveled around into her cubicle, leaning against the old filing cabinet in the corner. The thing was so old, and unprotected from the magic, that it was starting to rust around the edges. The paint had fallen off ages ago, leaving the metal bare and exposed to the elements and mana. She glanced over at her desk, expecting to see some kind of envelope, maybe a fire letter. But the surface was bare of all but her current case folder, the pile of paperwork that she hadn't started yet.

"And... And they'd need to stay still for about five minutes. Not exactly something we can rely on," she said, haltingly, as she tried to regain her thoughts. "It was a good thought, though, just tough to manage. Earth or air tracking spells are more reliable, you just need a start to find the finish."

"But neither work through a teleport," Greg said.

In the silence that followed his comment, Bethany started to hear a rumbling coming from behind her. At first, she thought her filing cabinet was about to surrender to its age and collapse underneath her. So, she stepped away from it, turning around to stare at it. However, when it didn't move, when it didn't show any sign of warping under her weight, she relaxed. And, yet, the rumbling continued, only piquing her interest more.

"What do you have over there?" Bethany asked.

She peaked over the partition at the back of her cubicle to the one next door. Her neighbor was an earth mage, the leader of the team one junior from her own. The man was older than Greg, and quite close to retirement, yet he still enjoyed the chase of a good case. He smiled up at her, motioning his head over to a small ball that was on his own filing cabinet, an echo of hers. As she looked at the ball, it settled down in place, only to start shaking again all on its own. No stranger to enchanted items, she just figured that the red and white ball just did that. However, she couldn't figure out the purpose of a ball that would shake intermittently. It must have been made by the light mages, she figured. They were known for creating annoying things like that, claiming they were meant to help enlighten the masses.

"It's a pokeball," the earth mage said, smiling broadly.

"Wait, seriously?" Greg asked. He turned around to look over at the ball, his eyes all aglow. "Does it have something in it?"

"Don't you know it. Did you hear about that dragon attack yesterday?"

"We were a bit busy with our own case yesterday," Bethany said.

"Well, I would have thought you would have heard about it. A couple thousand dead at its hand. But, when we went over there to handle it, it wasn't a dragon. Not really, anyway."

"Dragonite?" Greg asked.

"Charizard," the mage said.

"Awesome."

"What are you guys even talking about?" Bethany asked.

"Must have been before your time," the mage said. "Certainly before these two."

"Huh?" Igloo asked, obviously not paying attention.

"Anyway, we tracked it to this underground market last night. Some guy in South America has been breeding these things. They almost had the full first one hundred and fifty of them. Marge is down with the others, checking them into evidence. We're going to be tracking the guy down today, if you guys are interested in tagging along."

"Tempting," Greg said. "Very tempting. You'll have to show me them this weekend, if they let us take them out of evidence."

"Speaking of which," Bethany said. "Why isn't that in evidence now?"

"Because it keeps shaking," the mage said, as if that were obvious. "If it breaks out while it's in evidence, it'll just destroy the whole place before anyone gets to it to stop it. I figure, let it stay here, surrounded by some of the best mages in the world, ready to step in before it does any damage."

"Wait, it can do that? Break out like that?"

"Sure," Greg and the mage both said together.

"DeSalvo," came a call over the general din of the room. The tone was familiar, though the voice wasn't. "My office. Now."

"Who's that?" Bethany asked, looking over in the direction of the voice.

"New boss," the mage said, uninterested. "Same as the old boss, only meaner."

"They replaced the captain?" she asked. "I just saw him yesterday."

"I wouldn't keep the new boss waiting," Greg said. "First impressions and everything. Don't worry, we'll keep brainstorming. Think we could ride the charizard?"

Just like the day before, when Bethany got to the side of the room, no one was waiting for her in the doorway to the captain's office. Without knowing for certain that the new boss had taken the old office, she continued along the wall, peeking into each office as she passed. Each of the officers within were familiar to her, their heads bowed over their mounting paperwork, just trying to be as invisible as possible without actually disappearing. One of the officers, Sergeant Jeffers, actually was invisible, his pen scribbling on the paper with no visible hand holding it.

Right before getting to the captain's office, she steeled herself, drawing her magic into herself just enough to gain strength from it, but not enough for it to be noticeable. The door was open, giving her the perfect view of the office as she came around it. Not much had changed in the hours since she had last seen the place. The desk was as sparse as the day before, with just the two neat piles of paper off to the side. The captain's old hat was even still on the coat rack in the corner, suggesting that he would be back for it at some point. The only difference that she could see was the person sitting in the chair. He was smaller than the old captain, though the fury on his face suggested that he wasn't one to be trifled with. However, the biggest difference between this captain and the last one was the coat. Bethany had expected another white coat, signaling the captain was another light mage. Most of the officers were light or dark mages, their more powerful affinities placing them on the fast track to a more senior position. As Bethany came into the room, she lost a step when she noticed that the coat of the new captain was red.

Blood red.

"Sit," he barked. His voice filled the room and then some, though she didn't detect any magical amplification to it.

Bethany focused on putting one foot in front of the other and not running from the room in terror. What was this about? Why would they put a blood mage in charge of a group that was in the process of investigating the guild? Was it intentional? Had the higher ups wanted her to drop the case so much that they decided to put the blood mage in place to order just that? She hadn't even thought that there were any blood mages in The Authority to put in charge anywhere. Yet, the man's hat, a red matching his coat, was hanging from the same coat rack as the old captain's white one. He was in The Authority, though the appointment could still be new as of that morning.

She fell backwards into the chair, her legs giving out when she tried to sit. The new captain continued to glare at her, though he didn't show any indication that he noticed the fumble. His hand was placed firmly on the desk, as if he were holding it down where gravity failed to do so. Beneath his hand, she could make out some kind of form. The words were in the familiar scrawl of the autowriters that produced them. The captain's hand was blocking much of it, though. She couldn't make out what type of form it was or what it would mean to her and her team. Was she being demoted? Reassigned? Whatever it was, she knew she would have no say in it. She just had to hope that, if someone else was taking over the group, it would be Greg. The last thing she would tolerate was Dan being in charge of the group. Or worse, Igloo.

"Well?" the new captain asked. "What do you have to say for yourself?"

"I'm sorry?" she asked.

"Sorry isn't going to cut it this time. You really screwed the pooch. Do you have any idea how much trouble you are in?"

Enough trouble for her to have gotten her last boss fired? Probably. Enough trouble for her to get fired? Likely.

"Um..." she said.

"Let me be perfectly clear. Your investigation into this... unknown blood mage?"

He glanced over to the top page of one of the piles, drawing Bethany's own eyes to it. That was when she first noticed her old captain's signature, at the bottom of his resignation. It was true. She had somehow managed to mess up so badly that her old boss had to quit in shame. Why hadn't she had to? Or was that what this was?

"Your investigation is over," he said. "Whatever interviews or investigations you had scheduled on this line of inquiry, cancel them. You are now fully on this pure blood. He is the one you are to look into. To find. Immediately. All efforts are to be turned to him and his accomplice. They're both to be arrested for this wrongful death. Am I being perfectly clear?"

"But, sir, I... I mean, he was fleeing from a related, but completely different, charge. He had nothing to do with--"

"Am I making myself completely clear, detective?" he yelled. His voice, still unamplified by magic, resonated in her chest, causing her heart to skip several beats.

"Yes, sir," she said in a low voice.

The captain gave a little smile, showing that he thought her properly mollified. "Now that that has been settled, we move onto another matter. From my review of your case file, it would appear that you have come to a roadblock in tracking this pure blood. And, so, I've decided to reassign someone to your team. Don't worry, I won't be taking away any of your current members. I know the dynamic of these teams is fragile enough at the best of times without me making unnecessary changes. However, as part of my restructuring process, I will be assigning high mages to each team going forward. All four member teams will now be five member teams, with the new roles to be filled on an as needed basis. Your team needs a tracker, someone actually capable of tracking people without needing proximity or... whatever it is that you need. Make no mistake, DeSalvo. Despite you still being the team leader, for now, this new member of your team answers to one person and one person only. Me."

He pointedly slid the sheet of paper under his hand across the desk towards Bethany, releasing it from his firm grip only when it was on the edge of the desk. Once his hand was free of it, he reached over to the top pile of documents to his left, suddenly ignoring Bethany. It was clear that that was how the new captain ended his meetings. Slowly, Bethany reached out to pick up the form, standing up from the chair at the same time. She tiptoed her way out of the office, trying not to draw the captain's attention, or his ire, as she fled from him.

When Bethany left the office, she spotted her team right where she had left them, over by her desk. She had expected to find them outside of the office again, trying to eavesdrop on her conversation with the new captain. However, looking over at the group that was starting to gather at her desk, it was clear why her conversation hadn't been the most interesting thing happening. Two blood red hats were sticking up into the air right next to them, one on a man aggressively talking to Greg while the owner of the second hat was too short to see over the cubicle walls. The one man's voice carried over the distance, making it clear that her and her group was the matter being discussed.

"I don't care what you think," the man said. "I'm on your team now. There will be a new pecking order. I follow no one's orders but my captain's." He had a very thick French accent, which was odd considering most of the division was from America. In a way, it made him sound more stuck up and overbearing than he might have sounded otherwise.

"And I'm telling you, you're not taking over the team. Bethany is our team leader. No... vampire is going to take over it."

"Vampire? How dare you. I am a blood mage, not a vampire. I should pull your affinity out of your dead, lifeless corpse for that."

"Woah," Dan said, stepping between the two men. "No need for threats. Let's all just calm down and wait for the boss lady to tell us all that there was some huge mistake. Right, Bethany?"

"I'm afraid not," she said, when she came up next to the group.

As she came around the corner to the cubicle row, the shorter of the two blood mages came into view. The woman was old, older than Bethany's mom when she passed, and probably only kept alive by her affinity. Her blood red lipstick was haphazardly applied, making it look very much like she had blood for breakfast. The two of them stood taller, standing in defiance against the looks of denial from the rest of the group.

"We're getting a blood mage added to our group. A..." She looked down at the sheet of paper, trying to find the name in the jumble of words. As powerful as the new captain was supposed to be, his handwriting was much worse than the last one. "Renard Cauliflower."

"Renard Chalifour," the man corrected. "That would be me."

"But he's going to be leading the group?" Greg asked, despair plain in his voice.

"As I should," Renard said.

"No," Bethany said. "I'm still leading this team. However, apparently Renard doesn't report to me, but to the captain directly."

"Pah, a technicality with no difference. I don't report to this woman. She reports to me."

"No, I also report to the captain. Neither of us report to the other, and there's nothing in here," she quickly skimmed what she could make out of the rest of the form to be sure, "that says the rest of the group reports to anyone new. That means I'm still team leader. They report to me. You're just..."

"A tick," Greg said.

"An attaché," Bethany said, figuring the French word would go far with the man.

"What about... her?" Bethany's earth mage neighbor asked. "She's claiming a similar set up for my team."

"That may be the case. The new captain was saying he was going to start assigning blood mages to the teams. Well, I think he said high mages, but I doubt we'll be seeing any void mages added to teams. And, last I checked, death mages were still arrest on sight. So, that just leaves the bloods."

"Leeching off our good names," Greg said.

"Greg, that's enough of that. Like it or not--"

"Not," he said.

"We're going to be working with these people now. You'll need to get used to it eventually. Who knows, maybe us working together will build more good will towards each other's communities."

"Pah," Renard said.

"I'd check with the captain on the assignments before bringing anyone into the field, though," Bethany said, looking down at the old woman. She seemed well beyond the age that they usually forced the Authority mages into retirement. Would the woman even be able to keep up in a foot chase? Would she try and get herself hurt?

"Why the hell is this new captain assigning us blood mages?" the earth mage asked.

"Because he is one," Bethany said. She looked pointedly at Greg. "So, it would be best if we all avoid using certain slurs going forward."

"Oh, like vampire, tick, leech, blood bag, bleeder," Greg listed off.

"Tampon, maxipad, flow," Igloo added.

"Sunlight averse, garlic allergy, pile of dust waiting to happen," Dan said.

"I actually do know a few blood mages with a garlic allergy," Igloo said. "We went to The Academy together. It was hilarious."

"Pah," Renard said, again.

"In any case," Greg said, "on the team or not, no matter what the chain of command is, or becomes, it's not nice to open other people's mail." He held up a long manila envelope, motioning it towards Bethany.

"Not nice?" Igloo said. "Hell, isn't it illegal? You do know we're the cops, right?"

"Some enchanted mail even self-destructs if someone other than the addressed opens it," Dan said.

"I have a feeling that this particular item was too important for that type of enchantment," Greg said. "It's probably related to that matter we were discussing earlier, so..."

"Right," Bethany said. She scooped up the manila envelope, the enchantment within it resonating out when her skin made contact. It was clear that there were some protections in place, but thankfully Greg's quick work made that unnecessary. "I'll be back. You four... get acquainted, I guess. You'll be spending a lot of time together."

"Maybe," Greg said.

"For now," Dan said.

"Welcome to the team?" Igloo said.

"Yea," Renard scoffed.

Bethany swung around the corner, ducking back into her little cubicle. As she passed the entrance, she tapped the crystal on the wall by it. Instantly, the low buzz of the office disappeared. The crystal had a low-grade sound dampening spell, making it so that all but the loudest shouts in the office were completely blocked. It also meant that she could talk to herself, or someone else in the cube, without anyone hearing it outside. She wasn't sure if her now four team members were still talking out there, but she'd hear it if any of them started trying to kill another.

She practically jumped into her chair, spinning it around so that her back was to the door. An old mirror was mounted on that wall, letting her see if anyone was snooping around near the entrance. The mirror was silver, and often polished when she had the time, so it still shined under the light from above as if it were new rather than the one remnant she had from before The Arrival. It had once belonged to her own mother, and she had on occasion planned to give it to Ardith one day. However, if her daughter continued to be as reckless as she had been lately, that was growing less and less likely.

Bethany flipped the heavy envelope in her hand a few times, trying to figure out just what was in it. She had some idea, but with the new arrivals that seemed less likely. If the blood guild was making a concerted effort to pull her off the trail of the blood mage from the bar, what was the likelihood that they would be sending her exactly the information she would need to track them down? On the other hand, letter bombs, and similar attack methods, had become much more dangerous with magic, as well as making them harder to detect.

She pulled open the bottom drawer to her filing cabinet, which she kept empty for just such questionable letters. She stuck the letter inside the metal drawer before opening it. When nothing went off and her hands didn't disappear, she pulled the letter back out and pulled out the papers from within. It took her a moment, staring down at the jumble of numbers and symbols, to realize that the letter was exactly what she was looking for. There were no timestamps or notes of any kind to mark off the time period, and there were several sheets of paper in the bunch. She started to skim the first few pages, looking for the signature of the unknown blood mage. She knew that the signature would have to show up at least twice over the stretch of the documents, and she had no way of knowing just what that would give her. The information was already stale, already two days old. The blood mage could have circled the globe several times since that night. Hopefully, though, it would get her closer to him.

There was a knock at the entrance to her cubicle, the reverberations on the partition passing through the dampening spell. Bethany dropped the pile of papers back into the still open drawer, slamming it shut before her visitor noticed them. Standing at the entrance were Greg and Renard. Renard's lips were moving, but she couldn't hear anything that he was saying. She liked him a lot better that way, present yet silent. It broke her heart a little to reach over and tap the crystal again, dropping the dampening field.

"--etant tracking?" Renard finished.

"I'm sorry, what?" Bethany asked.

A snicker slipped past Greg's otherwise stoic appearance. "Renard wants access to the evidence we collected from the office of the air mage so he can start tracking her. Apparently, since he's so new to The Authority, he doesn't have access to the evidence room yet. I told him he'd need your permission for it."

"Oh," Bethany said.

Her face fell and her stomach plummeted, as she realized just what that meant. If the blood mage had a better way of tracking her daughter than her team did, that meant he might actually be able to find her. And that was the last thing she would ever want to happen, at least before she had come up with some way to get her out of her pending accomplice charges. Yet, she knew there wasn't an explanation that would keep him away from the evidence. Not with another blood mage as her boss, looking over her shoulder. Then again, if Ardith kept on the move, no one would be able to track her quickly enough to catch her.

She hoped.

"Um... Sure, why don't you walk him down there, Greg? I have to... finish up some stuff here."

"You sure?" Greg asked. He looked pointedly at her, trying to mentally signal that he didn't think it was a good idea. They both knew why it wasn't.

"If he's going to be on our team from now on, he'll have to know where the evidence room is eventually," she said. "I don't think our new boss would appreciate us trying to bench the new teammates."

"Right," Greg said. He sounded as frustrated about the whole thing as she felt.

Renard sneered right back at Greg. "I can find my own way down there," he said. "I don't need this one babysitting me."

"Fine, why don't we all go down there?" Bethany said. She glanced back at the drawer, at the papers within that she desperately wanted to get back to. But with her daughter's freedom, perhaps even her life, she wasn't about to let the blood mage have open access to the very evidence he would need to get everything pinned on Ardith and the pure blood.

Chapter Seventeen
Anti-Magic Safeguards

Ardith

As usual, the Great Wall of China was crowded. But, for all Ardith cared, she and Dorth could have been alone, sitting on the ledge of the wall and watching the sunset in the distance. It had become the oldest structure on Earth after The Arrival, with the rest of the wonders of the world being destroyed by the awakenings and rampant mages. As such, it had become the biggest tourist trap in the world, with landing platforms and souvenir stands at every few feet along the entire top of the structure, and half as many along the bottom. Here, the pure bloods lucky enough to have jobs at all hocked their wares. Recently, it had become the murder capital of the world, though only the pure bloods were dying off. Still, this fact never entered her mind as Ardith sat there, watching the sun drift down over the horizon.

TS was vomiting in the distance, his occasional grunt the only indication that he had survived the trip. Dorth had been a little overzealous as they left the black market. Despite the fact that the Mage Authority officers that arrived on the scene never called them out specifically, she was convinced that they were there for them. Dorth pulled the other two along for several teleports in a row, taking breaks at a few parks along the way. The confusing pattern, stretching over three hours of the night, was so erratic that no one would ever be able to follow them through it. Just for good measure, she had laid out several false trails that just led back to their old positions, leaving anyone that tried to follow them running around in circles. It was enough to make anyone nauseous, but TS seemed to be taking it a lot worse than Ardith was.

"All our nights should be this beautiful," Dorth said. She pushed a stray lock of hair out of Ardith's eyes, making the movement feel so natural, so subtle, that Ardith barely noticed it.

"Yea, the sunset is nice," Ardith said.

"I was talking about you, but, yea, that's nice, too." Ardith blushed, despite the fact that the cheesy comment was typical of Dorth.

"We should probably find a place to lay low for a while, let the heat around TS die down a little. If they were after us, they found us way too easily."

"I was thinking the exact opposite. They did find us too easily, and that's the problem. If we lay low, they're going to find us again. We need to keep on the move, make about twenty jumps a day. More, if TS can handle them. The sooner we rid ourselves of him the better."

"Except they're probably onto me, too," Ardith said. "In fact, I'm probably easier to track than he is. That's probably the one good thing he has going for him, with being a pure blood luddite. No one knows who he really is, not even me, and he doesn't have a signature that's easily spotted or tracked. Even tracking our teleports, they're tracking you not him. Heck, I'm surprised they didn't just track me from the office home. We should have never been able to meet up with you at the air bar."

"So, I've been thinking," TS said.

Ardith jumped at his sudden arrival, falling off the edge of the wall. Before she could get far, before her mind could even think to start screaming, let alone for that command to get to her mouth, her fall slowed greatly. She came to a stop halfway between the top of the wall and the ground beneath her. As she hung there in midair, she slowly spun around and around, flipping head over heels in place. When she was upside down, she tried looking back up towards Dorth, who was standing on the ledge looking down at her. After hanging there for a few moments, Ardith started to float back up to the two of them. When she got closer, she saw that Dorth had her arm stretched out over the ledge. She could feel the magic flowing off of her. Ardith levitated up, over the heads of Dorth and TS and the other onlookers, before flipping over one last time and coming down onto her feet on top of the wall.

"Oops, sorry," TS said. "I thought you saw me come over. I think that's why you're not supposed to sit on the ledge." He pointed to an old sign that was posted a few feet away from where the two women were sitting. The old sign was rusted through in several points, but the English section was still legible.

"That sign is older than me," Ardith said. "No one pays attention to that anymore." She pointed up and down the wall, where half the people were sitting on the edge like she had been. Only a couple of the closer tourists came down from the ledge after seeing her fall off. One couple actually jumped off the ledge together, tumbling around in open air like Ardith had. After seeing this, several more joined in.

TS rolled his eyes at the spectacle. "Anyway, as I was saying, I was thinking. You--" He paused, placing his hand over his mouth for a moment, as if expecting another round of vomit to come forth. Ardith took a pointed step further away from him, but after a moment he resumed talking. "You mentioned yesterday about anti-magic shields or whatever."

"Yea, for prisons and stuff," Dorth said. "Sure. What about them?"

"How exactly do those work?"

Ardith and Dorth looked at each other for a moment. Neither of them had been expecting the question. The anti-magic shields that they had placed around prisons, and certain other places like The Academy's detention rooms, were just a normal part of their lives, their world. No one ever thought to ask how anymore. All such questions usually just came down to the fact that it was magic. But it was clear that TS was expecting more of an answer than that.

"It's magic," Dorth said, shrugging.

"No, I mean, yes, obviously. What I mean is, inside of the shield, is there like no magic? At all?"

"That... wouldn't really work, would it?" Ardith asked. "I mean, if one side of the shield had no magic in it, wouldn't the whole thing just collapse?" She laughed it off a little, the idea seeming quite funny to her. How could anywhere in the world not have magic?

"Is there no way to test that?" TS asked.

"Ooh, I got this one," Dorth said. "No."

"Like we said yesterday, there's no way of getting one. Even if there was, The Authority would track it in an instant, the moment it went up. The idea is to stay off their radar, not wave a red flag and shout hello. Even if we could get one, and somehow keep it off their radar--"

"Or suddenly not care if we did," TS said.

This comment confused Ardith to no end. Ever since she had first met the guy, he had been on the run from the Mage Authority. Was he just going to surrender to them? Take whatever punishment they were going to dish out, for whatever crime they're actually going to arrest him for? What about his mission? What about her oath?

"Or... that," Ardith said. "In order to test that it would hold the magic outside of the shield, you would have to be able to find somewhere to deploy it that didn't already have magic. And, since the shield works on magic, it wouldn't deploy."

"Except... Okay, so what I was thinking was, placing the anti-magic safeguards around a place that is shielded from magic and then... well, drop the shield. Would it keep the magic out? Or, well, enough of it? I know there would be some between the shield and the safeguards, but that would dissipate without direct contact with Apophis, right?"

"Oh," Ardith said, thinking she got what he was asking. "So, hypothetically speaking, you have some place, like a hole in the ground, that you want to keep safe from magic. You want to put the safeguards around it to keep the magic out, thinking that it would keep magic from flowing in and let the hole in the ground stay safe from magic?"

"Well... yea," TS said.

"Dorth?"

"No," Dorth supplied.

"It wouldn't work."

"Not at all."

"Not in the least," Ardith said.

"How do you know?" TS asked.

"For starters, no such place exists. Even if this proverbial hole in the ground weren't exposed to the air outside, mana is everywhere, and flows through everything." TS glanced rather pointedly down at the briefcase that was leaning against the wall. The hard metal shell glistened in the lights from the ever-burning torches as they flickered overhead. The sun had set in the distance, though the women had missed the best parts of it. "Okay, but that's small. You're talking about something big enough to actually house a person. Even if you knew of such a place, and where to find it, the protections would only last so long. Nothing can stand against the overwhelming power of mana for long."

"I know," TS said. "I know."

"Look, sorry to break it to you, but what you're thinking... It just isn't possible. Even if such a place actually existed, the safeguards don't work that way. They absorb the mana flowing through them, or something, greatly reducing the amount inside. There's still magic, but not enough to do anything serious with it."

"Remember about that one kid in detention that managed to unlock the door with magic?" Dorth asked. "That was badass."

"Okay, well, it was just a thought," TS said. "A hope that... Well, let's just forget it, shall we?"

"Great," Ardith said. "Now, what are we doing next?"

"Pardon?"

"Well, we have the case." She pointed at the metal case next to her. "We have the water and air mages."

"That's us," Dorth said. Dorth smiled broadly, crossing her arms over her chest as she hopped right back up onto the wall. She seemed to wobble a little on landing, but a rather pointed breeze came up, seemingly out of nowhere, to hold her in place. Ardith just laughed at her unintentional representation of her air magic awesomeness.

"What's the next item on your list of things you need for this little quest of yours?"

"Oh, that," TS said. He seemed to perk up a bit at her mention of their progress. "Right, well..." He trailed off, his sudden perkiness fading as quickly as it came up. "We... I guess we'd need some raw resources."

"Perfect," Ardith said. She smiled, thinking that they were close to completion if they were working on something so remedial as raw resources. "What kind are we talking about? Silver? Gold?"

"Gems?" Dorth asked.

"Iron, I guess," TS said. "Or, well, I think titanium would be best. Something solid and lightweight."

"Oh," Ardith said. That wasn't good. Of course he would think of the one thing that they couldn't use anymore. "Does it have to be metal?"

"Well... I... I don't know," TS said.

He took a few steps away from them, heading over to a clear stretch of the wall. The ever-burning torches were specifically designed to not drown out the stars. This gave the three of them an amazing view of the brightest stars in the sky as the sun's last rays fled. TS stared off into the sky, his eyes searching in the distance as if he were looking for something specific.

"I don't know," he said again. "It's always been metal. Isn't there something? Like the case?"

"I'm honestly surprised the case lasted as long as it did," Ardith said. She picked up the case by the handle, her hands searching the surface for some sign of the normal decay that all metal went through. Though she didn't find any on the case itself, there was some rust forming around the nick in the handle. She brought the case over to TS, twisting and turning it in the light so that the rust would be more noticeable. "Even the case will someday rot away. Anything that... Well, whatever this was made of, even the raw material for that would have been exposed. In a few decades, all of this will be gone too. Only magic lasts forever."

TS laughed at the comment, though he didn't explain what he thought was funny about it. "I'd hate to ask, but what about crystal?"

"What about crystal?"

"Well, can we shape it into something for our use?"

"Sure," Ardith said. "If we had a light mage."

"Great," TS said, sarcastically. "I don't know any light mages."

"I do," Ardith said with a shrug. Her mind instantly went to her ex-boyfriend.

"No," Dorth said, automatically. Her stern look told Ardith that she knew exactly who she was thinking of.

"Any other ideas, then?" TS asked. "This is the next item on my list, something that I can make airtight that's large enough for me to sit or stand up in and actually move around a little. Thoughts?"

"Hmm," Dorth hummed.

"It has to be airtight?" Ardith asked. She was wracking her brain, trying to come up with something that would work. There were several obvious answers, but she quickly crossed them off. Stone was too porous and hard to move. Crystal they would need a light mage for. Wood had both issues. Without adding anyone else into the mix, there was only one thing left that came to her mind. "I could make an ice box."

"An ice box?" TS asked. "Wouldn't that be made of metal? That's the whole problem, isn't it? Besides, would it really be an ice box without all the electronics added onto it?"

"What?" Ardith asked. She shook her head in confusion, figuring whatever he was talking about was a remnant of the old age, something that no longer existed and, therefore, no longer mattered. "No, an ice box. A box made of ice."

"Oh. You mean... like the tower that... Like a structure thingy that is made out of ice?"

"Yea," Ardith said. "It's simple enough, and if I make it tight enough it should hold out the air."

"But... well..."

"I mean, there was something you needed a water mage for, wasn't there? Why not this?"

"Because, well... It just won't work, not with what I need you to actually do as part of this. No, I... I mean it would just melt. Or worse, I'd freeze to death."

"What? Why? How? You... You still haven't actually told me what you need me to do. Maybe if you did, I'd be able to figure out what it is you need for this."

"Oh, well," TS said, hesitantly. He dithered in place there, staring out over the wall as he thought about her request. There was obviously something heavy on his mind, something he didn't want to discuss. Not yet, anyway. It made Ardith a little sad, seeing him like that. She wondered if he ever had anyone to talk to, to confide in.

"You're going to have to tell me eventually," Ardith said. She slipped up next to him, taking the stretch of the wall between where Dorth and he were standing. Facing out from the wall, the night seemed darker, more eternal than it did looking inward. The light from the ever-burning torches stretched out only so far, and the night claimed the rest of the area.

"I'll... I'll need you to fill it," he said.

"Fill what? With what?"

"Whatever container we settle on. I'll need you to fill it with water. Hold it in place, completely filling every square inch of the container. While I'm inside."

"What? Why? Won't you drown?"

"Just... It'll just be for a little while, shorter than I can hold my breath for anyway. Then, once I signal you... There would need to be some way for me to signal you. Then, you'll have to be able to take all the water out of the container, not leaving even a drop of it behind, without opening the container. You... you can do that, right?"

"Well... Sure," Ardith said. "It's pretty advanced stuff, of course. Not all mages could. It's all water, though, so I'll be able to handle it no problem."

"But, see, with an ice box, as you called it, the water would freeze to the sides. Some of the ice will melt into the water and some of the water will freeze into the ice. No matter what, the ice box will be contaminated by the water. It just... Well, it won't work."

"Oh, okay," Ardith said. "So, no ice box. Got it."

"Sounds like the only thing that would work would be metal," Dorth said. "Or glass."

"Glass?" Ardith asked. "Wait, that would work, right? We can get glass to melt together along the seams and form an airtight seal. It might take some doing, but we can manage it, right?"

"I guess," TS said, shrugging. "Where are we going to get that much glass, though? Some kind of junkyard or something? It's not like we can call Safelite."

"Who?" Ardith asked. She had stopped caring about these references from his youth, but the question came automatically anyway. "Well, you're right. Not many people are working in glass anymore. It's all crystal. No doors, no windows. But we don't need new glass, exactly. We just need a lot of it. If we get enough glass, we can make a house out of it."

"Well, not exactly," TS said. "Plus, well, it would need to be really thick. As much as we can find of it, I think a smaller box would be better than a bigger one. Besides, you'll still need to lift it."

"Lift it? Me?" Ardith asked.

"No," TS said. "Your girlfriend over there." He nodded over to Dorth, who seemed to perk up at the mention of her, then smile broadly when the title registered to her.

"What?" Ardith asked, her face going cold. "Girlfriend? What are..."

"Don't you kids still use that term? Girlfriend? Friend who's a girl and all that?"

"Oh," Ardith said. She smiled in relief, though she couldn't quite figure out why she cared whether or not the man knew of her feelings for Dorth.

"Whatever," Dorth scoffed. She seemed almost insulted about something or another. "I have an idea on where we can get some glass. Besides, we've stayed here long enough. Much longer than I would have liked to have. Let's go."

Not bothering to jump down from the wall, Dorth grabbed hold of both of their hands, reaching around Ardith to grab onto TS. Without any other warnings, she teleported them away, leaving the wall to the rest of the tourists.

Chapter Eighteen
All Evidence to the Contrary

Bethany

The evidence room was down three flights from the bullpens. Unlike with the guild hall towers, where the guilds were showing off more than anything else, the Mage Authority complex didn't have anything magical to get people up and down between floors. Instead, the group was left with walking down the three flights of steps. This gave Bethany some time to think, some time to come up with a way to keep this blood mage away from her daughter. When the team had been tearing up Ardith's workshop, she had been too stunned with her even being there to pay attention to what, if anything, of hers they had grabbed into evidence. There was no way for her to redirect Renard away from the items that would be best to track Ardith with.

When they got to the floor that the evidence room was on, Bethany was surprised to find a line running the entire length of the hall, all the way over to the base of the stairs. It was mostly quiet, with people waiting patiently in line to turn in their evidence. For the most part, only one or two people of a team would need to bring the evidence down, depending on how heavy or awkward it was. Conversations between teams were rare, with the exceptions usually centered around cubicle neighbors and the like. Sticking a bunch of random officers into a line with no real order, conversation wasn't likely to happen. However, it also didn't take long to check in evidence. She didn't remember hearing about an overabundance of cases coming in. No more than usual anyway. When the line hadn't moved between when she spotted it and when they got to the base of the stairs, she knew something out of the ordinary was happening.

"What is this?" Renard said when he noticed the group getting into the line. "I thought... Why is there a line for the evidence room? I'm not going to be waiting in line."

"Oh, shut up, leech," said the person at the back of the line. He turned around, sneering at Renard, openly snubbing the blood mage. "I was here first. You can wait like everyone else."

"I won't stand--"

"Stow it, Renard," Bethany snapped. "The lot of you wait here. I'll go see what the holdup is. Maybe I can help move things along."

"No cutting," said the person at the back of the line.

"Oh, I wouldn't dream of it."

Bethany gave a slight nod to Greg, trying to signal that, if she was able to, she would do whatever it took to keep the evidence out of Renard's hands. Unfortunately, she knew there wasn't going to be much she could do, whether or not she risked her job or her freedom in doing it. She slipped out of line, moving along the space that was kept free for the people coming back from the evidence room. This was a narrow space, as much of the hallway was allotted to account for the bulkier evidence that often came through. As she passed by some of these bulkier items, a wrecking ball that fought against the officer's grip on it, a reindeer that kept growling like a lion, even a stand up piano, several people would grunt at her that she was cutting.

"Not cutting," she said. "Not cutting. Just trying to see what the holdup is."

As she neared the end of the hall, she noticed that the usual order of the line got lost near the front. Instead of a single file against the wall, there was a large clump near the front. Several people were crowded around the desk. Those near the back of the crowd were stretching taller, trying to look over the shoulders of those in front of them to get a better look at whatever it was that was happening up there. When Bethany came up to the last person in line that stayed along the wall, the earth mage just rolled her eyes at her, silently signaling her annoyance and incredulity.

"What's going on here?" she called out over the heads of the crowd.

The back of the crowd turned around to look at her. Those that recognized her as a team leader started to peel away from the crowd, heading back to their place in line along the wall. This had little impact on the mass itself, though, and she was forced to push and prod her way through the clump to the front. The crowd didn't back down readily, annoyed at someone trying to take their place, and their view, in the crowd.

"What's going on here?" she asked again, once she made it closer to the front. She could make out the entrance to the room, but the desk that separated it from the hall was still blocked from her view. A few more members dropped away from the crowd, giving her a little more breathing room. This also removed the last obstacle between her and the desk.

"Oh, hey, Bethany," Marge said. She was standing at the desk, looking rather sheepishly as she glanced back at her. "Sorry for the delay. There's a lot of these." She pointed back to the desk, at the large pile of balls rolling around on it. They all had the same red and white pattern as the one in her neighbor's cubicle, each rocking back and forth in place. A few were even rolling away, as if trying to escape. Only Sergeant Howard's fast reflexes kept them all on the desk.

"They're a bit much to handle," Howard said. "It would have been easier if she had labeled them all before coming down here."

"I'm telling you, that one is the magikarp and that one is the snorlax. Neither of them are moving much, though, so maybe they're both asleep."

"One can only hope," Howard said.

"Who cares?" Bethany asked. "Label them all poke-whatever and let's get on with it. I thought you guys were keeping them out of the evidence lockup. What happens if they escape?"

"No, only Mick thought that would happen. Or, at least, that's what he said. I think he just wanted to keep the charmander upstairs."

"No, this is the charmander," Howard said. He held up one of the balls, which had already been labeled "Charmander" in thick black ink on the white portion of the ball. "Now stop confusing me."

"God, no one cares," Bethany said. "Just label them whatever. It's the same case. Why does it matter? Can't you see this long line of people waiting to check in evidence? The whole world doesn't stop so you guys can geek out over there."

"I care," someone said in a low voice behind her. When she turned around to see the source, everyone was making a point to not be looking in her direction.

"Just get this cleared up and do your job... please, Sergeant."

"Oh, alright," the sergeant said. "We'll get to these later." He reached back to grab a large cardboard box that was on the shelf behind him. With a quick sweep of the table, he slid the entire lot of the balls, some labeled some not, into the box. Once they were all in there, the box started to rattle, making it difficult for him to hold with one hand. He dropped the box to the floor and kicked it under the table. "Next?" he called out.

Marge just stood there for a moment, at a loss for words about what had just happened, before turning around and heading back down the hall. The crowd willingly parted to let her through, forming back up into the line that they had abandoned before. Unfortunately, the line didn't wait around for them, so there still wasn't much room at the front of the hall. This kept Bethany pinned against the desk, with her unwilling to push her way back down the hall.

"No cutting," the fire mage that was next in line said.

"I wouldn't dream of it," Bethany said. "However, while you're helping these fine people out, Sergeant, I was hoping that you could help me out."

"No--" the fire mage began to say again.

"He can multitask, can't he? I mean, I know he's a man, but... Anyway, it's more of a request for when my group, which is all the way at the end of this line, comes up here."

"And, why is it, pray tell, that you can't ask for it then? If this is something I can do while I check this... What is this?"

"A self-swinging golf club," the fire mage said. "It wasn't content to only swing at balls. Well... Golf balls that is. Apparently the original enchantment didn't specify."

"A self-swinging golf club? Geesh, how lazy can you get. I mean, it's golf."

"We have a newcomer to the group," Bethany said. "I don't want him to have access to the old evidence, if we can avoid it."

"A new team member? So, Igloo finally failed out?"

"Worse," she said, surprised that the news hadn't already traveled that far. Even with no phones, the rumor mill was working as quickly as ever. "The new captain is putting blood mages on teams."

Several whispers stemmed up behind her, ranging from "We have a new captain?" to "Filthy leeches." It was clear that this news was as unpopular there as it was with her and her group. Several people looked down the long line, trying to spot the red coat in the distance. A few of them even stepped out of line, though it wasn't clear to Bethany what their intention was as they strolled back down the hall towards the stairs, surrendering their spots.

"Anyway, I was hoping that, whatever was taken from the workshop yesterday, could somehow be... misplaced momentarily?"

"No can do," Sergeant said. "As much as I hate the blood mages--"

"No more than me," said someone from the line. "Damn vampires killed half my family."

"I just can't go against the captain. If this guy is on your team, he's on your team. You wouldn't want me to hide things from you if the roles were reversed, would you?"

"Well, no, but--"

"What would he even want with the evidence anyway? You missed question five. Fill it out properly. No, no, not here. Back of the line. Next."

"He wants to track someone so they can frame him for a wrongful death, though I know he had nothing to do with it."

"I hope you're not thinking they're going to be planting evidence in here that would lead people to that assumption. I run a tight ship. Speaking of a tight ship, are there people in this?" He raised the ship in the bottle up to his nose, gazing through the thick glass at the long line of people waving up at him from the deck of the ship. "Ever think of trying to get them out before bringing them down here? Try bringing it to the light guild. I'm sure they'd love a challenge. Next."

"I wouldn't dream of insinuating that you would do anything wrong, Sergeant. He's already been placed at the scene, by me. They wouldn't need more evidence to convict him. He just wants to find him. And, I... well, I can't let him do that."

"I'm sorry, you're just going to have to figure out another way to stop him, then. I can't help you. I can't risk my job, with a new captain in place, on a whim like that. Just imagine what they could do if they get a blood mage in charge of the evidence room. Instead of one framed man, you'll have them all framed, with the bloods free to do whatever they want. The streets would be running with... well, blood. Seriously, Neddly? Another one?"

"I don't think it's another one," Neddly said. "I think it's the same one. It keeps coming back to my desk. I think it likes me or something."

"Alright, I'll put it in the vault. Maybe that will help things. But, seriously, if it comes back to you again there's not much I can do about it. No one even think of trying to jump the desk. The safeguards are in place."

The sergeant turned away from the desk, taking the strange object with him. Bethany hadn't gotten a decent look at what it was. Her curiosity piqued, she didn't even notice that the sergeant had suddenly considered their conversation over. She was stuck standing there for a few moments, half expecting the sergeant to come back quickly to continue talking with her. However, the silence that surrounded her was rather deafening. She was left standing there wondering just what she could do, how she could help her daughter. She even considered hopping the desk, like he had said, but she could feel the magic buzzing through the air. The safeguards really were in place, like he had said. If she tried to hop the desk, she might be electrocuted or randomly teleported away. The effects of the safeguards largely depended on the sergeant's mood on any given day. In any case, she wouldn't be able to help her daughter if she wasn't there to do it.

Bethany waited for about a minute before turning around and making her way back down the hall towards the others. While the silence didn't change much as she went, the weight of it somehow lessened as she passed those that would have heard her conversation. She didn't worry about any of them blabbing to the new captain about her attempts to thwart the investigation. None was likely to volunteer that information, though it was bound to make the rounds of the rumor mill. There was no love lost among the Mage Authority when it came to the blood mages. In fact, she often thought that the only people that actually liked the blood mages were the blood mages.

There wasn't much information on how a person's affinity was determined. However, the one tendency that people had noted was when it came to the blood mages. When The Arrival happened, the blood mages numbered in the tens of thousands, somewhere around forty or fifty thousand, though no one knew the exact number. Since then, their numbers had only grown. At the time of the last census, they were closer to a hundred thousand, almost doubling in the time that other affinities had barely increased by ten percent. Most of these new blood mages were the offspring of two blood mage parents. Meanwhile, mages of other affinities, even same affinity pairings, had offspring whose affinities varied greatly. There were even two light mages whose oldest son was a rare talent. With the blood mages keeping to themselves, this disparity of their numbers was only going to grow.

And, now, they were starting to take over the Mage Authority. That hadn't been what they said, not exactly, but Bethany had this unsettling feeling that that was exactly what they were intending. Why else would they suddenly be there, in The Authority, taking over a captaincy, forcing themselves onto the teams. If it was just to shut down her one investigation, there were easier ways to do that. It had been all but done already before the new captain arrived. Now, as she came into view of Renard once more, she had a renewed interest in the case, a new push to make sure that it is the blood mage, and not her daughter, that ended up in prison.

Renard was standing apart from the others, on the other side of the stairwell door. His sneer fell on Bethany the moment he spotted her, making it clear that he felt insulted by the others of the group for some reason, and that it was very much her fault. There was a large, broad smile on Igloo's face, while Dan and Greg's expressions were both well steeled.

"What now?" she asked, as she slid in the large gap between them.

"My honor has been insulted and I demand retribution," Renard said.

"Do you even have honor?" Dan asked. Igloo snickered at the comment but was able to stave off any further laughter.

"See? That is exactly my point. I didn't come here to be insulted."

"Where do you usually go to be insulted?" Greg asked. Bethany knew him well enough to know that the comment was automatic for him, a conditioned response to the phrase, more than anything else.

"Why exactly did you come here for, then?" Dan asked. "It obviously wasn't a desire for spreading justice, like the rest of us."

"Speak for yourself, I'm here for the steady paycheck," Igloo said. "It's getting harder out there for new graduates. It was either this or politics, and I can't lie with a straight face."

"Yes, we all remember that from poker night," Bethany said. "But, seriously, what is this about? I asked you all to behave, to help Renard get acquainted with the group, not ostracize him more."

"This is us getting him acquainted with the group," Dan said. "If he can't take a joke, he'll be at our throats in a week."

"He's at your throats now," Bethany said. "What did you say?"

"I... Well, I just suggested that he was in league with the blood mage that fled the bar the other day. If I were that guy, I think I'd try to get on the team investigating them, too."

"Except you're not investigating him," Renard said. "You're looking for the real culprit, this pure blood fellow and the air mage that is helping him, no?"

"I really can't tell if you're being serious right now," Dan said.

"I really can't tell what he's saying at all half the time," Igloo said. "Do you think you can speak American?"

"I'm French, you--"

"Enough, all of you," Bethany said. "Obviously there is some bad blood between us--"

"Yea, him," Dan said.

"But, like it or not--"

"Not," Igloo said.

"We're expected to work together. And, in the spirit of working together, no, we're not only looking for the pure blood. He came on our radar as part of the investigation, but not in the wrongful death charge. The new captain--"

"Captain Blood," Dan said.

"The new captain is insisting on placing both charges on the pure blood. The trail on the blood mage has gone cold, so we are focusing on the pure blood, temporarily. Once that part of the investigation is completed, make no mistake I intend to follow up on tracking the blood mage as well."

"The captain isn't going to like that," Renard said.

"Well, too bad. We don't investigate crimes according to one captain's likes or dislikes. We don't even investigate them to our own likes or dislikes. We investigate them where the clues lead us, where the trail leads us, no matter what. If you can't do that, then you have no business being in the Mage Authority. Understood?"

"He has no business--" Dan started.

"Dan, stop," Bethany said, putting a staying hand on his arm. "That's enough. You're not helping."

"I'm not trying to help."

"Well, then go home."

"What?" Dan asked, stunned.

"Go home. That goes for you two as well. I don't like it any more than you do. I don't trust this blood as far as I can throw him."

"Hey," Renard said.

"But we're stuck with him, for now. So, either put on your big boy, and big girl, pants and put up with it or go home. That's your choice. Just don't be surprised if your spot gets filled while you're away."

"But, I," Dan said.

"No buts. Those are your choices. Decide. And, in the meantime, shut up."

In the silence that filled the hallway after her speech, the line started to move forward again. Bethany looked towards the front of the line, just barely making out the sergeant in the distance. He didn't show any sign of noticing her, of even looking in her direction, focusing on his work in front of him. Renard hung back on the far side of the stairwell door for a bit, wisely giving the rest of them their space as they dealt with adjusting to the new team member. Once they were far enough away from him that whispers wouldn't carry, Greg pulled Bethany off to the side.

"You know, I almost believed you meant all that stuff you said," Greg said.

"I did mean it," Bethany said.

"Really? Even the part about investigating things against our own feelings? You know that would mean letting the leech track Ardith and arrest her, right? Are you really ready to do that to your own kid?"

"What? I just... That's not what I meant."

"Exactly," he said, pointedly winking at her.

He was right of course, though she didn't like it. Her trying to get Ardith out of trouble was exactly like the captain forcing her to arrest the pure blood for a crime he didn't commit. It was trying to bend justice to her will, trying to circumvent it. In a world of evidence that didn't melt, of rules that couldn't bend, of people that didn't automatically mistrust the pure bloods and those working with them, she could trust for the system to see that her daughter would go free. Whatever the pure blood has her wrapped up in, Bethany couldn't believe that she had gone along with it willingly. There had to be something to it, something that forced her hand. She just had to hope that she could find out what it was before it was too late for Ardith.

She stewed internally a while as the line got steadily shorter. It was easy to fall into her internal argument with herself once peace had been restored to the group. Renard tagged along with the rest of them, keeping a healthy distance, though as the line grew shorter, so too did that distance. By the time their turn had come up, Renard had not only joined them again, he led the charge towards the desk.

"How may I... Oh, uh, how may I help you?" Sergeant said. His words stumbled when he noticed Renard's red coat. Even with a healthy warning from Bethany earlier, he obviously hadn't been expecting the blood mage's arrival at his desk.

"I need all evidence gathered from the second scene on case 564-3568, specifically any evidence that has DNA on it."

"Uh, sure, it's just, well, I don't... We can't really determine if anything has DNA on it anymore. You know--"

"I know, I know. Obviously, we can't test for that anymore. I meant... Oh, just give me the entire box."

"It's twelve boxes, actually. The CSI team catalogued the entire site and carted everything up. Did you have something specific that you were looking for?"

Bethany smiled at that, at him. Fortunately, Renard wasn't looking at her, focused as he was on the sergeant. A hint of a smile fell on Sergeant's face as well, though he quickly steeled himself under Renard's vengeful gaze. Bethany wasn't sure if he was being intentionally unhelpful in order to help her or if that really had been the case. She just hoped that, if he really did hand over twelve boxes, a few boxes from other cases might "accidentally" get mixed in.

"Fine, just... Just have all twelve be sent up to my desk. I'll go through them and see if I can get a trace on the owner."

"Which desk is that?" Sergeant asked.

"Oh, um," Renard said, seeming at a loss.

"Don't look at me, I have no idea which desk is his," Bethany said. "We came right down here. Normally, new Authority members get desks close to the entrance."

"Wait, am I going to have to move?" Igloo asked.

"I'm not going to be getting a desk near the front," Renard said. "Everyone is going to target all their abuse at me as they come in."

"Oh, trust me, it's much worse than that," Igloo said. "It's not even all intentional. Though, with you, I imagine it will be around fifty-fifty."

"Just... send the boxes to her desk for now," Renard said, pointing at Bethany. "I'm sure I'll be having her desk soon enough."

"Yea, not if I have any say in it," Bethany said, knowing full well that she didn't. "Sure, fine, send them to me. We'll deal with it there. We'll also make sure you get an actual desk, somewhere in a dark, dank, enclosed space will be nice. You know, out of sight of most of the decent, hardworking agents of the Mage Authority. For their own gratification, more so than yours."

"You really want all twelve of them in your cube?" Sergeant asked. "Some of them might be a little... dirty."

"Sure, why not. If we had a better place to put everything, we'd do it there. But I'm sure this place is going to get a bit crowded with all the new... personnel coming in."

"Alright, you got it," Sergeant said.

The sergeant turned around, pointing a long, thin stick in the direction of the door behind him. The stick very much conjured the word wand for Bethany. She had plenty of experience in bringing evidence into the room, but it had been a good three years or so since she had to personally request it to be sent up to her. So, she was a bit surprised by the wand, especially when the sergeant just pointed it towards the ceiling before turning back to the team.

"New gadget," Sergeant said. "Love this thing. The boxes should be in your cube... Or, well, reasonably close to it. My aim isn't great."

"Are you sure you gave us the right boxes?" Renard asked.

"Reasonably sure," Sergeant said, but his growing smile seemed to say otherwise.

Chapter Nineteen
The Grand Junkyard

Eric

By the eighth teleport after the Great Wall of China, Eric was wishing he had never left the bunker. Dorth the dork seemed insistent that the Mage Authority was about to track them down at any moment, though he found it hard to believe that he ranked that high on their list of priorities. After all, it wasn't like they actually knew what his plans were. If they had, he never would have made it out of that bar.

He counted each teleport as they went along, using that brief moment in time where his stomach stopped trying to claw its way out of his gut as the cue. Nine teleports, ten teleports, each one worse than the last, seeming to last ten times longer, though the teleports themselves were supposedly instantaneous. He was starting to believe that the trick to instantaneous travel wasn't just that it was magic, rather that the spell bent time around the traveler, taking more time the farther they teleported. If they kept jumping around like that, he feared he would age prematurely. Not that he had many more years to play with. Then again, any delay of his own death would have been greatly appreciated, if it weren't spent in such nauseous agony as with teleporting.

On the twelfth arrival, he suddenly had an unsettling feeling that something was wrong. His senses were still all messed up from the teleports themselves, but when his feet didn't feel like they had ever hit solid ground, he knew something was wrong. Of course, Dorth saying "oops" solidified the thought in his mind. Suddenly, he was being pulled again, just like with teleporting, only without the clawing of his stomach. There was no nausea beyond the remnants of the last spell. Air was rushing past his ears, leaving him with a whistling sound. When he realized they weren't teleporting again, he braved opening his eyes, regretting it instantly.

They were plummeting towards the ground below, several hundred feet up. A large spire could be seen below them, pointy, deadly, calling out for them to land on it. Eric had no control over his fall, had no way of stopping it, of slowing it. As always, he was a hostage, a slave, a victim of gravity, with no magic and no technology to save him. He wondered in those brief moments as they headed down to their certain death, if parachutes even still worked in the reduced scientific state that the world existed in.

Well before they hit the spire, their fall started to slow. Eric could sense the feeling of magic filling the air, a feeling he had slowly become accustomed to since leaving the bunker. Spending the past couple of days almost entirely with those two mages did much to speed that acclimation. As Dorth worked her magic, literally, Eric tried to take in the views of the world beneath him. He tried to relax as he put his very life in the hands of the air mage, who seemed a world more competent than his choice in water mages.

As he got closer to the spire, he realized that it was actually a pile, loaded high with garbage and other refuse. It looked a lot more pointy from above than it actually was because there was a steady pouring of trash on top of the pile, coming out of what looked like a distortion in the sky. From above, it looked like barely more than a glimmer, shining in the light from the sun. But, as they passed it, the other side just looked like a large, black hole in the world. The trash came out of it in a steady, continuous flow, as if it were water coming out of a faucet. Some of the trash was easily identifiable, left-over food, old clothes, a dresser, the rusted remains of a car in its entirety. Some of it was less identifiable, until Eric realized that it was because it was multiple items merged together to form some large clump of trash. A hairbrush merged with a rusty beer can looked more like a stuffed animal than what it actually was until he got closer. A pillow was struggling against itself, the raccoon that had been searching for a meal having fallen in at the same time that the pillow was added to the source. He had remembered hearing something about splinching when it came to teleportation and he started to wonder if it applied to portals as well.

The pile seemed to go on for forever, though it was hard to judge. They started to flow away from the pile and it soon became difficult to make out the individual items. Without being able to tell how quickly they were falling, the pile could have been ten stories as easily as a hundred. When they left the shadow of the pile they were falling near, he could make out three others that were similarly forming behind it, and another two on the other side, behind him. It was clear that this place was the global dumping ground of all discarded items, though it could just as easily be one of many.

It took them a while, flowing outward from the large pile, to find a stretch of land beneath them that was free of the trash and debris. When they got to a few feet above the ground, their fall stopped but they continued to fly out across the area. Carissa was quiet as Dorth focused on moving them around in the sky. Eric figured it would be safest to follow her example and kept quiet himself. Most of the questions that were flowing through his head at that point fell into the category of "you don't want to know" anyway.

The base of the mountain of garbage merged with those around it, so they had to fly out and around another two piles before they found empty ground. Even that was a small island in the sea of junk around them, slowly sinking beneath the waves. The sounds of trash falling on trash was everywhere, loud but not deafening. When they finally settled down on the solid ground again, Eric was not greeted with a desire to embrace it in any way. He almost wished they could just fly away and keep going.

"What now?" Eric asked. At some point in their flight, his stomach had settled, despite, or perhaps even because of, the very disgusting smell that surrounded them. He looked all around at the four piles that bordered the island, but the trash was churning too quickly for them to find anything useful.

"That is the question," Carissa said. "This was your idea."

Eric looked between Carissa and Dorth, slow to realize she had been talking to him. "Was it?" he asked. "This wasn't exactly what I was expecting when I said a junk yard. I was thinking something a little more... or a little less... Something that people could actually get raw material from. This is just... disturbing."

"Why?" Carissa asked. "It's gotta go somewhere, doesn't it? Better one, out of the way place than several. No one has to cart the stuff around, send it out to sea only to pollute the ecosystem. The base of this place was coated with crystal, blocking the pollution from seeping into the ground. But, yea, I guess it's not very useful for raw materials. It just sort of all goes here."

"And what happens when the piles get too big? Or when the... Those are portals, right? What happens when the piles reach the portals?"

"That's like asking what happens when today reaches tomorrow. The portals just go higher, obviously. They were careful to choose a place that no one would miss, that goes on for miles in every direction. Why else would they call it Nevada?"

"Wait, we're in Nevada? Well, okay, yea, I guess it makes sense. This was where they tested the nukes and stuff." Eric instinctively glanced down at the briefcase, which Carissa was holding. He wasn't sure when that happened. But given that he probably would have forgotten it on the wall, with how little warning Dorth had given them, he was glad they still had it. "I'm sure someone will miss Vegas, though. Or was that saved?"

Carissa and Dorth shrugged. "They didn't say anything about Vega in school," Dorth said.

"Yea, it's not like we actually know everything about everything," Carissa said. "We just know what they taught us at school."

"And some stuff we figured out along the way," Dorth said. She eyed Carissa seductively, causing her to blush under her scrutiny.

"Well, if we're going to try to find glass here, I imagine we're going to want to find an older pile. Do they retire piles?"

"No idea," Dorth said. "Why would we want an older pile?"

"Besides the fact that these piles are too--"

"Watch out," Carissa called out. She leapt forward, pushing Eric out of the way. Dorth had jumped back, lifting off of the ground and out of her reach, at her call. Seconds later, the remnants of a large, old truck bounced down the mountain of trash behind Eric, plowing right through where he had been standing, before slamming right into the next mountain over. In an instant, the truck was buried by the trash as it flowed down the mountain, no sign of it remaining behind.

"Dangerous," Eric finished, once he could catch his breath.

With the immediate danger gone, Carissa got off of Eric, helping him up once she did. Once he was off the ground, he noticed a splattering of coins spread across the space he had fallen into. Carissa's eyes went wide when she saw this and she quickly scooped them up, even using her power to pull them out of the way of the rising tide of garbage around them. As she did, Eric checked the bag in its pocket, making sure that the spillage was minor and that the bag itself was still intact. There were a few loose coins in the bottom of the pocket, but the bag seemed fine. It did feel a tad lighter, though.

"These piles are too dangerous," Eric said. "Plus, like you said, they're not using glass much anymore. Everything is crystal. The glass would be in the older stuff, or the newly discarded old stuff. I couldn't tell if that truck still had its windows in place. Did either of you?"

"It did," Dorth said, still hovering off to the side. "You're welcome to go digging for it."

"Nope, I'm good," Eric said. He looked towards the mountain that had swallowed the truck, unable to even see where it had gone in. "Think we can find an inactive trash mountain? Or at least one considerably less active?"

"We can try," Dorth said. "This place goes on forever, though. Not sure if that's a good thing or a bad thing for our search."

"What we need is some way to track the glass. I'm not even sure how much of the stuff we're going to need."

"Well, you're The Scientist. Shouldn't you know?"

"Says the mage that just said she only knows what she learned in school. Science doesn't work that way. I don't just suddenly know everything. Besides, even if I knew the appropriate thickness of one kind of glass, I'd need to know what kind of glass we're working with. That's kind of hard to do without knowing the source and without a mass spectrometer."

"There are different kinds of glass?" Carissa asked. "Why?"

"For different uses. Windshields, like the one that's buried over there, are different from the windows they used on the space shuttle or in submarines. If I knew it was strengthened against atmospheric differentials, we could use it at two inches thick. Whereas, if it's for visibility and safety, like windshields, we might need as much as five or six. I think a sixty-four cubic foot interior box would be the smallest I could put up with for... for what I'm using it for."

"I don't quite understand what this box has to do with delivering something," Carissa said. "That is the whole point of this mission, right?"

"Right," Eric said. "You'll understand how this all fits together in the end, I promise."

"When is that going to be, exactly?" Dorth asked. "Is that going to be today? Soon?"

"It'll be a lot sooner if we can find the resources and get out of here," Eric said. "Why don't you fly around a little, see if you can find someplace that will work? You'd probably go faster without the two of us weighing you down."

"Well, yea, you are rather heavy. RD, though..." She hung there for a moment, looking down at her girlfriend with longing.

"Go on," Carissa said. "I'll be fine here with The Scientist."

Dorth looked around at the mountains that bordered the island, then down at Carissa once more, before heading off. She flew out and around the mountains and disappeared in the distance. She really did fly much faster, much smoother, without the two of them hobbling her. Carissa watched her as she left, longing obvious on her face. It was clear to Eric, even from the beginning that they were in love with each other, that they belonged with each other. He wasn't sure why they weren't though, and it wasn't his place to ask.

"Don't worry," he said. "She'll be back soon enough. Think we can find anything around here that can help us in the meantime?"

"What?" Carissa said, obviously not paying attention. "I doubt it. You saw what happened to the truck. Most of this crap is just that, crap. I don't even know what you expect to find here that would be worth the effort. But, well, you're the boss, right?"

"If that truck had landed in the clearing here, we could have removed the windshields, and that would have been a start at least. Maybe we should try to find some abandoned neighborhoods instead, somewhere where the vehicles are still parked on the streets, left where they had broken down when Apophis arrived. From what I remember of back then, I think it happened rather suddenly. Besides, that truck had to have come from somewhere. Maybe there are others there. Think you could track where it came from?"

"Not without having access to it. Even then, it would be iffy at best. If it was passing through water, sure, no problem. Tracking its progress through air would be more Dorth's strength."

"Well, maybe a piece of it had fallen off at some point. How much of it would she need?"

"More than paint chips but less than the whole thing, I'd guess. I didn't see anything fall off of it."

"Neither of us were paying much attention at the time," Eric reminded her. "You did kind of tackle me to the ground. Thank you for saving my life, by the way. I don't think I properly said that."

"It was nothing," Carissa said. "Seriously, nothing. If you die, the oath gets broken. So, you know, don't die."

"Well, it came through over here," Eric said.

Eric motioned with his hands, mapping out the space that the truck had plowed through earlier as if he could hold the space itself. It was a habit he had picked up from some of his former bunkermates. With that space mapped out, he followed what he remembered of the truck's trajectory. It wasn't easy, given the fact that both neighboring mountains were constantly resettling, changing in size and shape from moment to moment. From what he remembered about where he was standing, though, he was relatively certain of the path of the truck's passing.

He called out in victory when he saw a single, large scuff mark on the ground. While it had been a good long time since he had seen a tire mark in person, its shape was unmistakable. With the path marked out, not just by his own memory, but that very real mark, he started to look around the area for any small piece of metal that he might have missed. There were three small pieces that he had spotted almost immediately, shining in the light from above, but they were all glinting pieces of something much bigger that was buried in the ground beneath his feet. None seemed likely to be connected to the truck or anything with glass in or on it. He was pretty sure that one of the pieces of metal was part of a crowbar, but the other two escaped identification.

After a few more minutes of searching, he had managed to find three bolts, of varying age, a thick pipe, that looked vaguely like it might have fallen off the truck's exhaust system, and a harmonica. The harmonica looked like it might still work, but it was way too dirty for him to try. Eric pocketed the harmonica, figuring he might get the chance to clean it properly before his quest was over.

"What do you think?" Eric asked, showing her the pipe. "I'm pretty sure this came off of a vehicle of some kind, maybe not that truck but another one."

Carissa shrugged. "What do I know about cars? I'm a mage."

"You're also a girl, but that doesn't necessarily mean anything," Eric said, smiling broadly at his lame joke. "I mean, would this be enough for Dorth to track?"

"It should be, unless it was here for the past several months, like most of the crap around here. Tracks fade, even those tracked through magical means."

"Well, it doesn't need to be precise. Just, well, the general vicinity of the neighborhood that it came from. I'd settle for the city."

"Look, magic isn't that exact of a tool. It's an artform, not a science."

"Well, obviously," Eric said, snickering. "It's the exact opposite of science, so much so that it killed science completely."

"Yea, well, maybe science had it coming," Carissa said.

"What's gotten into you?" Eric asked. "I know Dorth left, but she'll be back soon enough. If she found something we can use, great. If not, maybe she can track the pipe back to the point that the truck came from. We're getting closer."

"No, we're not," Carissa said. "Because you keep moving the goalpost."

"What? What are you talking about? The goalpost has always been the same. Deliver that to where it needs to go."

"And where is that? Huh? Why do you need to go with it? Why do you need an airtight box? Why do I need to flood it with water? What exactly is that going to do? Are you ever going to tell me any of this?"

"Carissa, calm down. Of course, you'll know everything. Soon. Once everything is in place. I'll explain everything once we're almost finished."

"Why?" Carissa asked. "Why not now? We have the time. But, no. You're not going to tell me anything. Why?"

"Well, because you might not help me if you knew what I was planning on doing," Eric said. "Even with the oath, I'm not going to force you to help me. And I really do need your help. This whole plan... It's nothing without you. You and Dorth and whoever we can get to forge the glass box. Seriously, Carissa. I'd be lost without you."

"God, my name's not Carissa," Carissa shouted. "How can you be so smart yet so thick? Dorth has been calling me RD this entire time and you don't get it. My name is Ardith. Ardith DeSalvo. And, you know what? If you're basing all of this, all of your plan, your whole entire quest, on my oath, well, I've got some news for you. That oath is crap. You have no power over me."

Chapter Twenty
Ninety-Nine Boxes of Evidence in the Cube

Bethany

Renard led the charge back to Bethany's cubical. He was so eager to get back, to start going through the boxes, that the rest of the team had trouble keeping up with him. Bethany wanted to get ahead of him, to lock him out of her cube for a few precious minutes before letting him have access to the boxes, but the man was just too fast for her to get ahead of him. The stairs were barely wide enough for two to walk side by side, and those few opportunities she had to pass him were blocked by people coming the other way.

When they got back to the bullpen, there was blood red everywhere. The new captain was wasting no time fulfilling his promise to expand the teams. No one seemed the least bit happy about the new arrangements. Most of the team leaders that Bethany knew were in the process of screaming their heads off at the blood mages that were insisting they now belonged on their teams. From the few passing words that she heard, it even sounded like many of the blood mages were insisting they were the new team leaders, much like Renard had tried to do earlier. That was not going over well. The one thing that a lack of TV had given them was a lot of spare time to come up with new curse words. Many of them were being used openly that day.

The noise of the bullpen had gotten so loud, Bethany would have liked nothing more than to slip into her cube and shut it all out. However, when they got to the cube, getting into it was the last thing she would be capable of doing. Renard had come up short at the entrance to the cube, too focused on the mountain of boxes within to notice the other four slam into him from behind. Bethany had been expecting only twelve boxes, like the sergeant had said, but from the look of them it looked more like a hundred.

"What the hell?" Renard said. It was hard to make out over the noise of the room, but the sentiment was echoed among the group.

"Think he accidentally pulled in boxes from other cases?" Bethany asked.

"Just how much did those CSI guys take from that workshop?" Dan asked.

"Looks like all of it," Greg said. He smiled broadly over at Bethany, silently reminding her that this was a good thing. If Renard couldn't find something to use to track Ardith, he couldn't find her.

"Never mind," Renard said. "I don't need to find anything specific, just something to use to track the air mage."

"What about the water mage?" Greg asked. Bethany's cheeks flushed at the correction, her eyes going wide as she stared daggers at Greg.

"The who?" Renard asked.

"Carissa Von Strucker, the water mage that owns the workshop. The actual leaseholder. At least some of the stuff in there belongs to her. If you just pull something out and track it, won't you just find her more often than not?"

"She could just as easily be an accomplice to all of this. If she was there--"

"She wasn't," Igloo said. "We checked her alibi that first day. She's clean. She left before the pure blood entered the building. There's nothing there. She's as angry at her workshopmate as we are."

"Yet, she didn't tell you the identity of this workshopmate? Didn't you find that a little convenient? What if this Carissa was the one helping the pure blood and the workshopmate was the one with the alibi?"

"She was of the opinion that it wasn't her workshopmate at all," Dan said. "We were, are, looking for an air mage, right? The workshopmate is a water mage, too. Besides, Carissa Von Strucker is an up and comer. The captain... the old captain didn't want to push her. People are saying she's on the short list for the new water guild master when the current one retires next year."

"What people? I haven't heard anything like that."

"Uh, water people, obviously," Dan said, pointing at his blue coat.

"Right," Bethany said. "So, if you're looking for something from this air mage, you might just be looking for a needle in a haystack here. Most of this will fall into belonging to either of the... tenant water mages. If you want to find something from the air mage..."

"It's not as hopeless as you four seem to think," Renard said. "I don't know how you usually handle things like this, but I can make short work of all of this. That is, of course, if you don't get in my way. Now, I'll need a space to work with. Who do I go to for cube assignments?"

"All the cubes are full," said someone from around the corner. The woman peeked over to him, her red coat coming into full view. "I stole someone else's. They're working on getting them for us. Hey, Renard. I thought that was your voice I heard."

"Petunia," Renard said, nodding to the woman. "Glad you decided to join us."

"Working in the Mage Authority? How could I miss this? You guys have ruined some of my best schemes. It's about time I can return the favor."

"This place really is going to hell in a handbasket," Dan said in a low voice so he couldn't be heard over the noise of the room. Bethany, standing right next to him, barely managed to hear him. "That's Petunia Flowers, one of Western Europe division's frequent fliers. They could never quite pin anything on her, though, no matter how hard they tried."

"I wonder if they're doing it intentionally," Igloo said. "Putting these Europeans in the American divisions so there's no conflict."

"No conflict?" Bethany asked. "They're blood mages."

"No, I mean, well Petunia and Renard are from France, so much more likely to... bend the rules there than here. So, we wouldn't have run into them, tried to arrest them, or have an open grudge against them."

"But, they're blood mages," Greg said. "There's a grudge anyway."

"No, I see what she's saying," Bethany said. "No more of a grudge than any other group."

"Wanna help us find a needle in a haystack?" Renard asked Petunia. Apparently, they had been talking while the group whispered behind their back, though none of them heard a word of it.

"Sounds like fun," Petunia said. "What's the separating factor?"

"The owner of the object. Or maybe the last person to touch it?"

"Last person is easier. Stronger imprint. I think one of the conference rooms is open. I'll get my team to help lug the boxes over. I needed to test their willingness to have me as their leader anyway. How broken in is your team?"

"I'm getting there," Renard said. He eyed the rest of them over his shoulder, daring them to correct him, to counter his authority, even though he had none. "Let's hold off on slave labor for now."

"Oh, you're no fun. My team folded like a house of cards. But, what do you expect from an air mage team leader?"

"Hey," Igloo said.

Petunia blew strongly at her, laughing at her own joke before heading off to find her team. Renard followed her, laughing his full head off. They quickly disappeared around the corner, their voices drowned out by the arguments of the room.

"Let's just get out of here," Igloo suggested. "We're not going to get any work done here anyway."

"Yea, not with these... people here," Dan said.

"I keep offering to teach you to center yourself," Greg said. "I could work in the middle of a hurricane."

"And you would, too," Igloo said. "We're all very impressed by your work ethic."

"What work are we going to do?" Bethany asked. "As long as we're stuck on this case, we're at a standstill. Nothing to do until Renard gets us this new lead."

"What about the, uh, envelope?" Greg said. "Can't we follow up on that a little?"

"Not with him looking over our shoulders. It's looking like I might need to outsource that, if we're going to be saddled with the nanny cam."

"What's a nanny cam?" Igloo asked.

"It's a small camera they used to use to record people having affairs on," Dan said.

"What's a camera?" Igloo asked.

"Don't they teach kids about electronics at The Academy?" Bethany asked.

"No. Why would they? It's not like they work anymore. There might have been an elective at some point, but no one took it."

"Now, that's something they should re-invent," Greg said. "Cameras. I miss TV."

"What's--"

"That's enough of that," Bethany said. "Can we focus?"

"Where are the boxes?" someone asked.

Bethany turned towards the voice. A full team was standing at the corner, looking over at them with questioning faces. Bethany recognized the air mage, though she couldn't remember her name. She was one of the older members of The Authority, older than Greg even, with just a few months before retirement. It was no wonder why she hadn't fought Petunia too much for leadership of the group. That close to retirement, no one wants to rock the boat.

"Right in here," Dan said, pointing towards the cube. "Better you guys than us."

"Oh, you're helping," Renard said. His head popped out from behind the far partition wall. "Or, do I have to go to the captain?"

"He's right, I'm afraid," Bethany said. "Did you find a conference room that will work? Most of them are used for actual meetings, you know."

"Not today," Petunia said. "They're mostly used for people without cubes. We had to kick three lesser mages out of this one, but they were used to it and didn't put up much of a fight. Only one bloody nose." She sounded actually disappointed about that, like she would have loved to have bloodied all three of their noses, and maybe even killed one of them. Knowing how blood mages tended to work, that probably wasn't far from the truth.

"Everyone, grab a box," Bethany said. "Greg, other earth mage, take the bigger ones. It shouldn't take too long. Besides, I'd like my cube back at some point today."

"Sounds fine to me," the former team leader said, shrugging. She came over to the front of the cubicle, grabbing the large box that had been blocking the entrance herself. Although she seemed small, light, a little on the frail side even for her age, she managed to lift the box easily enough. Bethany could feel the magic flowing off of her. It was clear that a mage's power is one thing that doesn't fade with age.

Once the first box was cleared out, the rest were easy enough to manage. Only two of them were on the large side, though it wasn't clear from Greg or the other earth mage if they were heavy at all. Between the ten of them, they managed to get most of the boxes over to the conference room in one trip. The room that the blood mages had managed to co-opt for the efforts was the nicer one that was three doors over from Bethany's cubicle, making the trip easy enough. Once the first set of boxes were in, the two earth mages ran off to grab the last ones, looking like little more than two kids racing for the fun of it.

As soon as the boxes were inside the room, Renard and Petunia went to work. Instead of taking each piece out one by one, like Bethany had expected them to do, they both sat cross legged on top of the table, their eyes closed and their hands in their lap. They sent out their magic, wrapping the closest of the boxes in it. Bethany could almost see the dweomer as it went to work, the air thick with the spell. One by one, the objects were pulled out of the box by their power, held aloft in the air momentarily before being placed back down on the table. After the first five or so, the objects started coming out faster, two at a time, one for each of the mages. In no time at all, they made short work of the first box, quickly moving on to the next.

Bethany started to worry as she saw them tear through the evidence. Soon enough, she knew they would find out the truth. That there was nothing to find. That there were only ever two mages in that workshop. It quickly became clear that where they were placing the object corresponded to one of the two mages, Carissa and Ardith. While Carissa's pile was the larger of the two, it was her workshop after all, Ardith's pile had more than enough to track her with. If the blood mages were able to do that without her general vicinity, as they had claimed. Once it became clear to the two of them that there was no air mage, they would just grab the first item off of Ardith's pile and that would be it.

Greg nodded to her, trying to get her attention. He slipped out through the door, leaving the blood mages to their work. Bethany followed, hoping that he had a plan, some idea that would help save Ardith from the justice heading her way. She hated the fact that she had to save Ardith from anything, that she was even in the danger she was already in. But there was only so much she could do without getting herself in trouble. Greg didn't go far, just the next door over, in front of the office next to the conference room. He eyed the area around them, looking for eavesdroppers or the like.

"What are we going to do about this?" he asked. "Are we really going to leave Ardith's fate in the hands of... of them?"

"Oh, hell no," Bethany said. "I was hoping you had some plan. As soon as they figure out the truth, they'll be off after her and the pure blood. I just hope she had the good sense to leave him behind. Far, far behind. They're still looking for an air mage, so, as long as she's not actually with the pure blood when they find her, she might be able to get away with it. Neither of us are going to identify her as the mage in question. I'm not sure about Igloo or Dan, though."

"I can try to slip them notes. Air messages maybe? But, well, you know me and air magic. You'd have better luck with that."

"God, air messages," Bethany said. "I feel like I'm back in high school. Let's just see what these blood mages come up with before tipping our hands too much. Maybe, just maybe, it won't come to it. Maybe they'll find something that we're not expecting and take it the wrong way. Maybe this will all just come out to nothing. There's an awful lot of junk in those boxes back there."

"Yea, maybe our luck with change," Greg said.

"Found it," came a victorious cry from the room behind them. Renard popped his head out from around the doorway, something small and gold in his open hand. "I found the needle."

"You, wait, what?" Bethany asked. Stunned, she tried to see what it was that Renard was holding. It was small, barely visible just a door away. She came closer, holding her hand out to ask for the object. Renard held it from her, though, protectively.

"No, no touching," he said. "It's mine. I found it. You can see it when we've tracked it to the source."

"It's mine, my own, my precious," Greg mumbled. When he noticed the curious looks from the group around him, he just shrugged.

"It's rather small," Igloo said. "Can you actually get a read off of that?"

"Yea, enough of one to track the air mage down without knowing anything about her location?" Bethany asked. "What is it, anyway?"

"I think it's an earring," Renard said. "Or, at least, it was at one point. It's a bit melted. Not going to fit in anyone's ear now. And, yes, there's enough of a residue on it that I can track the person who last touched it anywhere in the world. Well, in this case, the owner. It's the stronger signature. Anyway, that's the beauty of blood magic. It's just so much more powerful than you... lesser mages. God, I hate even calling you idiots mages at all. You're as beneath us as the pure bloods are beneath you."

"You sure this belongs to an air mage?" Dan asked. "How can you even tell?"

"The signature is completely different from the two water mages that work in the workshop. I can't know for certain that it's the air mage, but it's different. And, it's also the only different signature in the entire collection of items."

"How can you know?" Dan asked. "There are still three boxes left in there."

"Only three?" Bethany asked, surprised they had managed to go through the objects so quickly. It had only been a couple of minutes since the two of them had left the blood mages alone.

"And they're the smaller ones."

"What are the chances that two random mages entered the workshop, while the original tenants were gone, with a pure blood in there as well, over the span of a few minutes to an hour after the water mages left? If this isn't the air mage, they'll at least be in league with her. This is it. It's been days since this case opened and I solved it in, what, an hour? Come, let's find this girl before they kill someone else."

"He says that like he actually thinks the pure blood was responsible for the wrongful death," Greg muttered. "He does know there was a blood mage involved in all of this, right?"

"I don't think he cares," Bethany said. "If he really thinks we're so below him, he must look at the pure bloods like little more than flies. No wonder why their egos are so big."

"The tracking spell is easy enough," Renard said. "We can track her from the road, once we've narrowed down the area a little."

"Great," Bethany said, all feeling vacant from her voice. "Let's see what we can see from this tracking."

Chapter Twenty-One
You have no power over me

Eric

"What?" Eric asked. He was stunned, completely confused. He had gone to that workshop looking for Carissa, but that wasn't who he found? Carissa... Ardith... She had said she was Carissa, didn't she? It was Carissa he had meant to find, Carissa he had meant to bind into the oath to help his cause. If this wasn't Carissa, what had he done? Was she even a water mage? Could she even do what he needed from her? "But... Why?" was all he managed to get out.

"You promised me silver. I needed money. I'm low on credits right now, in debt up to my eyeballs. It's not like Carissa would need it." It was clear from the way she said her name that she not only knew who Carissa was, but that she hated her guts. Was that a good thing or a bad thing?

"But... The address..."

"We work in the same space. You had actually just missed her, by the way. She left like minutes before you barged into my life. Oh, and if you had actually met her, promised her money to help your lost cause, she probably would have just laughed in your face. Maybe even turned you into The Authority just to see you squirm. She definitely wouldn't have made that stupid oath without knowing what you needed. God, I was so stupid to do that. No, not stupid. Desperate. I was desperate, and you took advantage of that.

But, what can I say? You are a stupid pure blood. Ha. Pure blood. What's so pure about you? Dorth is right. You almost destroyed the planet, almost destroyed the human race before Apophis came along and changed everything. For the better, I might add. Fortunately, your little quest, I don't have to bother with it any longer. It or you."

"But... What? What about your oath? You made an oath to help me, on your magic. Breaking that..."

"I made no oath. I used Carissa's name, because you thought I was her. There's no oath to break. Had I made the oath under my actual name, then, yes, you would have gotten me over a barrel. But, there's a reason why the name needs to be in the oath for it to be official. Without it, well, it has no power over me. It or you. I'm as free as a bird. Anyway, now that I'm no longer even pretending to be shackled here, I'm off."

"What?" Eric said. He looked around himself, at the constantly flowing trash. The little island they had landed in was quickly shrinking around them. Instead of several hundred feet across, it was so narrow that the two of them were standing right next to each other. "You can't just leave me here." He motioned around at the trash, though he needn't have bothered.

"You have my linking book and your stupid case." She pushed the metal case solidly into his chest, forcing him away from her and dangerously close to the trash. "Just don't try using any of the pages in the linking book with the lock symbol on it. Those locks are tuned to my signature and anyone trying to use them will end up in a deep, dark, and scary place. Other than that, you'll be fine. Plenty of pure bloods make it out in the world these days. You'll be no different, once you give up your hopeless quest. God, seriously, who does quests anymore? This is 2066, not 1566."

"But..." Eric's words fell on deaf ears. He had no idea how to follow that single word up, how to convince her to stay on, to help him with his cause. The only way she would even think of considering helping him would be if he told her what the quest was, and that was one sure fire way to get her to leave. He had been relying on the oath, counting on it. Without it, he had nothing. No amount of silver in the world would push someone into doing something they didn't want to do, to change their entire world around in a way that went against their own wellbeing.

"Good luck, Scientist. You're going to need it." With those words left in the air, she turned away from Eric, lifting her hands over her head, stretching towards the sky. She flickered a few times before disappearing. And, with that, she was gone, and he was alone in the middle of the largest trash heap that had ever existed.

Eric waited there for a moment, half expecting her to come back. To say that it was all just some stupid, twisted joke. That she really was Carissa and he hadn't made a huge mistake choosing her. Not that he ever actually had a choice. All he had coming out of the bunker was the rain rod, the silver, and the name. And, now, all he had was the silver.

His hand unconsciously reached for the linking book in his pocket. It was his only escape from the trash that threatened to bury him at any moment, yet he no longer cared about it. He was on the run from the law, or whatever this world had in place of it. He had no one to turn to for help. All of his contacts had been transactional, and those transactions were completed. Without being able to track down a new water mage, and a new air mage for that matter, he was stuck. And, with him being on the run, none would help him without putting their own lives in jeopardy.

He had nowhere to go besides back to the bunker, returning home empty handed, his quest a failure. Sure, he had the briefcase. But, without a way to deliver it safely, there wasn't much he could do with it. It was dangerous carrying it around like that in any case. He should return home, if for no other reason than to stow it properly, in a place that wouldn't be destroyed as soon as he left it. Then again, he had no way of knowing just how well the bunker had held up in his absence.

Eric pulled the linking book out of his pocket. He looked between the book in one hand and the case in the other, struggling to think of a way to flip through the linking book without putting the case down. The way the trash was coming on, if he put the case down, it might just get buried before he could pull it back up again. Already, the trash was starting to hit his feet. Desperately, he started trying to use his chin to open the cover of the book, but he couldn't position his hand properly so that it wasn't in the way.

A high-pitched laugh coming from behind Eric clued him in that he wasn't alone anymore. He spun around, his eyes searching the sky for the source. Dorth was just hovering there, looking down at him in complete glee. She seemed extremely happy about his predicament.

"You must think I'm so stupid," Eric shouted up at her.

"Well, yea, a little. You know you could put the case down, or like tuck it under an arm or something."

"No, about your girlfriend. About... Ardith. This whole time, you knew. You knew I thought she was someone else. The both of you must have had a great laugh about it behind my back."

"No, not really," she said, shrugging. "I mean, yea, a little, at first, but once I realized how desperate you were about all of this, it quickly lost its humor."

"Well, of course I'm desperate. I don't know anything about this world. I'm like an alien. An alien on my own planet."

"I didn't just mean you. She was desperate enough herself. She really needed that money. You must have annoyed her something fierce to have told you the truth. Where did she go?"

"Oh, I don't know," he said. He waved his hand, the one still holding the linking book, off into the distance, in the direction Ardith had been when she teleported off. "She teleported off a couple of minutes ago. Speaking of which, a little help?"

Dorth looked off in the direction he had pointed for a moment, like she should be able to see Ardith off in the distance or something. Then, she looked back down at him, the trash starting to pile up at his feet. When she didn't immediately react to help him, he had a sinking feeling in his stomach. Something told him that she wasn't going to help him either.

"You know, I grew up thinking all pure bloods were worthless, useless, a holdover from an age long dead. You and your people practically destroyed this world, damn near killed all of us off. I mostly figured the whole lot of you could just go to hell."

"Well, there's plenty of room in hell these days," Eric said, only half joking. "I've heard it's almost nice now that the demons aren't there."

"But spending time with you these last few days? My opinion hasn't really changed that much. If you want my help, you're just going to have to help yourself first."

"What? How does that even make sense? How can I just help myself out of this? I'm going to die."

"Well, then, maybe you should," Dorth said. "You're a scientist, right? What do your people say about natural selection? Survival of the fittest and all of that? I'm thinking that magic just put that sort of thing on fast forward. It's just nature running its course. If you can't get yourself out of the mess you put yourself in, then you don't deserve to live. Oh, by the way, that little mission you sent me off on? There are no dead mountains. They're all like this. Have fun looking for those raw materials you wanted."

Without moving from her spot in the air, Dorth just disappeared, teleporting away like Ardith had. Eric thought he had heard a witch's cackling as she left, though it might have just been his imagination. Half expecting, half hoping, that Dorth would come to her senses and come rescue him, he watched the space of thin air that she had just left for a while, until his feet started getting buried by the trash tumbling down around him.

"Alright, Eric, think. You're The Scientist. Work your brain already."

He stepped up, pulling his feet out of the growing pile of trash around him and stepping on top of it. That only helped so much, as the trash was unstable, moving around under him as he settled his weight onto it. Still, the trash continued to come down, sliding around him and continuing to grab at his feet. His mind racing, he stuck the case under his arm like Dorth had suggested. It didn't free up his hand completely, but it was enough for him to open the linking book.

Not even looking at the first page, he slapped the book down onto his thigh, holding it in place with two fingers as he inched the other onto the picture in the middle. Once his flesh touched, he felt it, that familiar feeling of a hook pulling his guts out through his belly button. Worse, though, was that his feet were being pulled at the same time. This was new, something he hadn't been expecting, something that was obviously not supposed to happen. Even as a magical luddite, he knew that couldn't be good. But it was already too late to stop it.

The world around him started to blur away, something that also hadn't happened the last time he had used the linking book. It seemed that, whatever power the book had, whatever spell it performed, it was somehow being slowed down. He was teleporting away, but slowly, agonizingly slowly. He wondered if he would be able to teleport away before the trash buried him completely.

Eric tried to move his fingers, tried to take them off of the picture or push them further on. He wasn't sure if it was something with the trash clawing at his feet or the weak connection with the book. In either case, he couldn't move, his fingers stuck just barely touching the picture. As the world slowly disappeared around him, he noticed that the hook at his gut was turning into more of a knife, pulling at him and digging into him deeper. He started to have an unsettling feeling that only part of him was teleporting away, while the rest of him was stuck in the trash. The image of a black hole popped into his head, the idea of only part of him being sucked into the spell at a time. Could a teleportation spell spaghettify a person like a black hole could? Did that mean that only part of him was stuck? Was frozen by the spell?

He tried to move his feet, but those were still pinned beneath the ever-increasing level of trash. Failing that, he tried to wiggle his toes, any sign that his lower half wasn't as paralyzed as the rest of him. At first, he thought that was just as much of a failure, but then he started to feel his toes hitting the insides of his shoes. With that as a clue, as one last glimmer of hope, he put as much force, as much strength, as much will into lifting his right foot as he could manage.

The world was almost gone around him and his stomach was on fire. The burning was starting to spread, starting to consume every inch of his torso. Something told him, if the sensation got to his heart, he would die. However, he had no way of knowing for sure, no way of knowing if the rules of science would govern something so ingratiated in the world of magic. He tugged, pulled, yanked his foot up as much as he could, as hard as he could, as fast as he could. Yet, still, it wasn't enough.

Then, suddenly, finally, his foot started to slip free of the trash. He wasn't sure if the stream slowed or if the teleportation spell was starting to affect it or if it was just blind luck, but his right foot finally slipped free of its entombment. As soon as it did, as soon as his shoe entered the open air, all feeling left him, all sight and sound left him, and he was hurled face first into the darkness.

As slowly as the teleportation had been, his reentry into the world was that fast. He hit the ground hard, crumpling into a ball in the grass. His eyes were closed, prolonging the darkness, but he feared to open them. Feared to see what had happened to his body. The pain was gone, but no sensation had replaced it, no sense of self, no sense of body left behind. He wasn't sure if all of him had made it there, wherever he was. He wasn't sure where he was at all. More than anything else, he was too scared to find out the answer.

The first sensation he did feel, other than the ground beneath him, was a hard stick poking at his stomach. He let out a reflexive squeal, which turned into a complete belly laugh. Eric wasn't even sure why he was laughing, if it was the fact that he was alive, that he must have arrived intact, or the reminder of the old commercials from his youth. Either way, he quickly sat up, opening his eyes and looking on at the glorious day that greeted him.

Eric was lying in a field, surrounded by a bunch of teenagers. One of the younger ones was holding a stick pointed in his direction, the person that had poked him before. What surprised him the most, though, was how familiar the place was. He had been there, barely a day earlier, when they had fled the air bar. Carissa... Ardith, had named it the teleportation training field of The Academy. That made sense, both the teenagers, the students, that surrounded him and that it would be one of the first pages in the linking book.

"Hello, kids," Eric said. He waved stupidly at the students around him. "Nice to see people taking an interest in education. Stay in school, and all that."

"What kind of idiot are you?" the boy with the stick asked. "Of course we're going to stay in school. We need to learn how to use our magic before it kills us. We're not suicidal."

"Right," Eric said, nodding. "Right. Anyway, I should be off."

"Yes, you really should," said one of the older girls. "Now would be nice."

"Yes, I know," Eric said. "I just... I don't think I can move right now."

"That's stupid," the boy said. "Why not?"

"I... I think I just tried to teleport a mountain." This caused a lot of laughter from the students, and a little from Eric.

"That's stupid," the girl said. "Why would you go and try to do a thing like that? You could have gotten yourself killed. What kind of stupid pure blood are you? You're lucky you didn't end up in three pieces."

"Oh, only three?" Eric asked. "Wait, my case. Where's my case?"

"It's right next to you," the girl said. "My god, you're stupid. I guess my daddy is right. All pure bloods are stupid."

"Not all of us," Eric said, though his voice was barely loud enough to get to his own ears. "Not all of us."

"What's all this," came another voice.

Eric tried to look in the direction it was coming from, but the students were blocking his view. In any case, he had a feeling that it would be best not to be there when the owner arrived. Staying where he was, lying there on the ground, he flipped the linking book back open. He quickly leafed through the pages, trying to find something familiar, something closer to the bunker. The first one he noticed was to Ardith's workshop, but it was locked. He was halfway through the book before he recognized his alma mater, U of C.

With a smile, Eric grabbed the case tight with one hand and hit the page with the other. This time, the teleportation was much quicker, though just as unsettling as always.

Chapter Twenty-Two
Finding the Trail

Bethany

Bethany was nervous as the six of them stood out in the middle of a field a few blocks over from Ardith's workshop. She had no idea what to expect, from the two blood mages that were casting the tracking spell. From the results of that spell. From wherever that spell was going to take them. The fact that Renard and Petunia had found a different signature at all was surprising enough. Could that signature actually belong to someone else? To an air mage, perhaps? What would happen if, when, they found the owner of the melted earring?

Petunia had insisted on helping out with the tracking spell, though she said she wasn't going to follow the group to where it led. Apparently, the more blood mages working a spell, the easier and quicker it was accomplished. This was something specific to the blood mages and their strange affinity, though. No other mages Bethany had ever heard of were able to cast a cooperative spell like that. The magic would have to be attuned just so in order for their powers to work with each other rather than against each other. That alone was worth the trip.

"It's like two people trying to send out the same message on the same frequency without creating noise," Greg said. As always, Greg had a way to explain things that only confused people more. "It would be hard enough doing it as a source and repeater, without having chips for brains, but two sources? Impossible."

Bethany's team was standing off to the side, keeping far away from the two blood mages that were sitting cross legged on the ground. They had found a flat, heavy stone to use as a table, something solid that had never felt the effects of a spell directed at it. The earring had been placed dead center on the stone for their spell. Two other, similar looking stones were in the grass behind the mages, thrown away when Renard had declared them both contaminated by someone's magic. Bethany couldn't tell the difference, they all looked like stones to her. What shook her more was that Greg had echoed her assessment. Yet, somehow, these blood mages had been able to detect it.

Then again, they could have just been full of shit.

"Maybe if the rest of us could work together like that, our affinities wouldn't be looked down on by the higher mages," Igloo said. "Did you ever think of that?"

"No," Dan said. "No one ever does. Because it's stupid."

"Hey."

"No, not your idea. The fact that we're looked down on. That we're somehow lesser. Even in our own affinities, there are ranges. Some are stronger than others, weaker."

"Yea, except our strongest is half the mage of their weakest," Greg said. "And if we ever try to go up against them in combat, we might as well be throwing stones at a tank."

"What's a tank?" Igloo asked. "Like a fish tank?"

"An old armored vehicle with a huge honkin' cannon on top," Dan explained. "Think air battle mage with an earth mage's shield around it."

"Against someone throwing a rock? Geesh, even we think we're as beneath the blood mages as the pure bloods are beneath us."

"No, that's just how their affinity works," Bethany said. "Don't they teach that sort of thing at The Academy anymore? Blood, death, and void affinities block all, and only a combination of the others together would ever block them. The four of us against just one of those two wouldn't stand a chance. But bring in a light and dark mage and both sides will be throwing rocks."

"Yea, so don't piss them off," Greg said. "Too much."

"Too late," Dan said, smiling cockily.

"Fact of the matter is, with the death mages out of play, it's just ten people stopping the blood mages from taking over the world," Bethany said.

"Yea, and those ten people are practically hermits," Greg said. "Did you hear about Herman?"

"Herman the hermit?" Igloo asked.

"No, Herman Rockefeller," Bethany said. "That's four of them, right? Four void mages to go missing. That can't be a coincidence."

"Sure, it can," Greg said. "It's not like they show up much anyway. Heck, I don't even know the last time I saw President Geller. For all we know they could be at some retreat somewhere, trying this very spell, and they just never told anyone."

"Speaking of the spell, when are they going to start already?" Igloo asked.

"As soon as you four shut the hell up," Petunia said. "Like Groot over there said, this isn't easy."

"Groot?" Greg asked. "I am not Groot."

"Whatever. Your name isn't important enough for me to remember. Now shut it the lot of you."

Silence filled the area at her shout. Even nature seemed to be afraid of her, as the sounds of bugs and birds dropped off as well. Bethany held her breath, crossing her fingers behind her back as she hoped that their spell went awry, fizzled, or simply tracked someone else. Perhaps the owner of the earring was just some pure blood, not the one they were supposed to be tracking but a random homeless one that lived under a bridge and ate rats. She even willed that description at the earring, trying to send signals at it. But she never once considered actually using her magic to make it so. There was no telling what would happen if she tried. If her spell would properly interact with theirs or if theirs would simply block the effort. She couldn't even hope that the attempt would go unnoticed.

Like in the conference room, the dweomer of their spell was almost tangible. It was just barely visible as it spread out from the two mages and towards the center, towards the earring placed carefully on the stone. Even as far away as she was, even though the spell was directed inward instead of outward, Bethany could feel the raw power of it, could sense the disturbance in the air, in the flow of mana that always surrounded them. The hairs on the backs of her arms stood up on end, screaming at her to flee. To run away from these powerful mages like she was a deer and they were monsters.

And they were monsters to her, their clawing hands coming for her little girl. Whether the tracking spell worked or not, they would come for her. Whoever got pulled into this mess next, they would come for her. As long as she was with him, they would come for her. Even if she left him, they would have no way of knowing that, and they would come for her. She was a mama bear trying to protect her cub, but the forces aligned against her were too great for her to do anything to stop it.

The tracking spell didn't take long. The dweomer extended inward from the two mages, crossing the distance between them in a few seconds, hitting the earring dead on. Just a few seconds after impact, the spell ended, the dweomer dispelled into the air. Bethany held her breath, hoping that something went wrong. Hoping that nothing came of the spell and they would give up the hunt.

"She's close," Renard said. His words were a bullet to her heart. "She's over in the merchant district a few blocks that way." He pointed towards the south, though none of them really knew where the merchant district was in comparison to them. It wasn't like they were going to walk there anyway. "She's been there for a couple of hours now, so maybe she's given up running."

"If she was smart, she would have surrendered by now," Petunia said. "It's what I would have done, you know, if I was a lowly, pitiful air mage." She shuddered at the thought of it.

Dan grabbed hold of Igloo's arm as she jumped forward, pushing against his restraint to get at the woman. Her hands were waving wildly in the air, trying to form a spell, probably an attack spell, to hurl at the blood mages. There was no way to know if it would have worked, if it would have helped anything, as her spell, her magic, her very affinity itself was blocked by the blood mages. They didn't even seem to notice Igloo's attempts against them as they continued discussing the hunt for Bethany's daughter.

"Thanks for your help, Petunia," Renard said. "I could have done it myself, but it would have been harder."

"Any time, Renard. You know that. I love group spells. They're better than sex and less messy. And, coming from me, that says a lot, eh?"

"Ah, Petunia, ever the stereotype. We should discuss your latest conquest over dinner sometime. Just, not tonight. I have a feeling I'll be working over the air mage. If the pure blood isn't with her, I doubt she'll give him up easily."

Petunia nodded at him before disappearing. Bethany figured that she teleported away back to headquarters, but there was no indication of the spell, no hint that was what she did. Seeing as how they were in the middle of a field, Petunia could have teleported anywhere in the world and it would have been impossible for anyone to track her. Anyone, that is, other than a blood mage.

"Come, come," Renard said. He raised his arms, holding them out as if he were inviting the team to a group hug. "Let's do ride along so we're not held up by your ineptitudes."

"Needing coordinates to teleport to isn't an ineptitude," Igloo said through gritted teeth.

"Not already knowing them is," Renard said.

Arms still raised, he waved his hands forward, trying to draw them to him. When that didn't work immediately, he sent out a wave of air magic, pulling them into his arms. Bethany's feet left the ground almost immediately and she flew through the air to the blood mage. As soon as the group collided together, they were gone, teleporting away. They were suddenly surrounded by conversation, the sun blocked overhead. Renard let them go as quickly as he had grabbed them up, letting Dan double over to vomit away from him.

The merchant district was more of a grand bazaar, several tables set up in the open air under the remnants of an overpass. The highway that the overpass had belonged to was long ago overgrown, yet the overpass itself still remained. The main support beams had been replaced by crystal spires at some point, though the road overhead was still cement and asphalt. Enough sunlight came in through the open wall for people to see by, but the ever-burning torches above were still lit, bathing the area.

Bethany recognized the place immediately. She had brought Ardith there plenty of times over the years, getting resources for school projects. It was one of several similar places that had sprung up since The Arrival, a place for craftsmen to sell off their wares to those mages that work with enchantments. Some of the best items in the world came out of places just like that. Although, it was sometimes hard to tell just by looking at it.

There were more merchants under that roof than there were places for them to sell at. The tables were all bunched together, sometimes overlapping and overflowing onto one another. The merchants weren't licensed, so most of the people there were pure bloods, scavengers, people just trying to sell whatever they could find in order to afford food. The open air from the missing wall kept a decent breeze flowing through, though the smell still piled up over time. The three merchants right in front of them were all in desperate need of baths. When they noticed the new arrivals, all three of them smiled at the group, showing off the fact that none of them had teeth left to their name. Any one of them would be grateful to be pulled into jail for a few years, giving them a stable diet and a roof over their heads.

"Are these them?" Bethany asked, pointing at the smiling pure bloods.

"Do they look like air mages to you?" Renard said. "No. Now shut up. We don't want to clue her in that we know she's here."

Bethany bristled at his tone, at the fact that he was ordering her around, despite the fact that she outranked him. She wanted to yell at him, to reinforce her authority, but she knew that any threat would be hollow, not even backed up by her boss, the new captain. As Renard led the way through the district, as he led the way on the hunt for her daughter, Bethany felt more powerless than ever.

None of them bothered looking at the merchants' wares as they passed. Most of the merchants near the front were the ones with the low quality goods. Those were the ones eager to sell their goods, usually at below market prices, so they could go out and collect more items to sell. They all had locations picked out in the trash dump from which they got their goods. Rumor had it that they fought, even killed, each other for those territories. However, no one knows for sure, as their bodies would have quickly been buried beneath the trash. Many of the merchants they passed had pieces of garbage lodged into their skin. None seemed to notice, as preoccupied as they were to hock their goods.

Once they got deeper into the merchant district, Bethany started to recognize some of the merchants she had gone to with Ardith. She remembered the ones that had the best goods, the best materials to work with. They had all been in the deeper sections of the district. Although, as they passed through that day, they were barely somewhere in the middle. It was starting to look like, even those known for their quality, were coming on hard times as the economy continued to decline. Even one of her favorite merchants had half of a beer bottle sticking out from beneath his shirt.

When they came up next to him, Renard pulled up short. Bethany's heart skipped a beat, her thoughts whirling with the implications. Was this it? Was this the person that he had tracked? Was Ardith not actually here? After a moment, though, Renard just took a long, deep breath of the air coming off of the man before continuing on. As Bethany passed him, he started to look paler, more worn out. The smell of blood soon drowned out the unpleasant smells that had always lingered in the place. It seemed that the injury around the beer bottle had reopened by some low powered spell of Renard's.

"Sorry," Bethany mumbled to him as they passed, not sure what else to do. Even if she could prove that Renard broke the law, the captain would never stand for it.

Deeper and deeper they went into the district, weaving between the rows as Renard stalked his prey. Bethany wasn't sure what he was tracking, if he actually knew exactly where the target of the spell was or if he was following the trail that they left behind. Usually, whenever she tracked someone, whenever a member of her team did, it was the latter. However, with how Renard bobbed and wove through the area, even backtracking a couple of times when he went too far down one row, he could have just as easily been tracking them through proximity alone.

They made their way, mostly in silence, towards the very heart of the district. As they approached the back of the structure, the place where the road came down to meet the ground itself, there was a VIP area blocked off with a long velvet rope. The rope had seen better days, having been used to block off the inner area for as long as Bethany could remember. The velvet was frayed in certain places, pulled away from the rope within. The stands that held it up, the generic pre-arrival stands made of metal, were all rusted and falling apart. It seemed to Bethany that it was getting to a point where they should invest in the magical versions that were going around. But she knew that the merchants that ran the district were too pure to stoop to that, and probably too poor to afford it. Even the ever-burning torches that lit the VIP section were only there as a matter of necessity, as no other light source worked without needing to constantly be replaced.

The VIP section was the area that Bethany always went to, that she always brought Ardith to. If her daughter was there, that would be the place to find her. All of her favorite merchants had once been within that most hallowed section. But they must have been demoted beyond it years ago to have fallen so far as the middle. None of the merchants that were in the VIP section then were the least bit familiar to Bethany, which, for some reason, just made her sad.

Renard walked forward, ducking under the velvet rope as he was too bullish as to stoop to use the entrance. One of the bouncers near the entrance moved to stop him, but Renard just stared the man down until he returned to his place. Bethany kept her eyes peeled, looking for any sign of Ardith. When she looked over at Greg, she saw that he was doing the same. She just had to hope that one of them would spot her before Renard did, though she wasn't sure what that would have accomplished.

As they got further into the VIP section, as they got closer to his quarry, Renard sped up. With just three more rows of tables to go, he was practically running through the lanes, making his way through the labyrinthine area as quickly as he could without running into anything. Those walking past his mad dash weren't so lucky, many ending up knocked down to the ground in his wake. At some point, he managed to get a row ahead of the others, and Bethany was left stuck too far away to stop him as he approached his target.

"Ah hah," he yelled, victorious at last, as he reached out his hand, hitting someone on the shoulder heavily. The crowd seemed to swell up, actively blocking Bethany's view of the person Renard had found. "I got you," he shouted. "You're under arrest."

Chapter Twenty-Three
The Broken Oath

Ardith

Ardith was kicking herself for having gotten sucked into TS's scheme. She still had no idea what his actual plan was, what he hoped to achieve. Even after having left him in the dump, she just couldn't get that thought out of her head. She just couldn't put it behind her, and she wasn't quite sure why.

Then again, she had never broken an oath before. Loopholes or no, it wasn't an easy thing to do, often costing the mage their magic. She didn't do it lightly.

After leaving TS behind in the junkyard, Ardith had gone to Merchant Row to help her forget about all of that. She wanted to forget that she had abandoned the man there, perhaps to die from the accumulating trash. That she had left him to his own devices, when those had already proven inadequate. It wasn't fair for him to have expected her to do everything for him, to drop everything in her life to help him flee from The Authority. And, yet, that was exactly what she did. It had been almost two days since TS dropped into her life and upended everything. It was time to get back to some semblance of normalcy.

When TS's coin purse exploded back at the junkyard, Ardith had managed to get one of the smaller pouches. The way that he had simply flicked one of them out at the black market, she figured that there was a thousand silver in it, just like the one he had paid the dealer there. It wasn't enough to get her out of debt, but it was enough to get her some supplies for her enchantment project. If she could just get the earrings to work, that one prototype would set her up for life.

The merchant district was as crowded as ever when Ardith arrived. The familiar sights and smells of the place were almost a comfort to her after the past couple of days. She lingered a little, taking it slowly as she made her way through the market. Although she had no intention of buying anything from the merchants close to the front, that was a trap for those less knowledgeable about the place, she actually spent some time looking at their wares. It was clear, even from a cursory glance, that none of it was worth buying. None would hold a spell, and many had already been enchanted at some point with minor effects that weren't meant to last. She saw one ring on a table that still let out a low light, the enchantment involved fading. Yet it was the only item on that table. The merchant seemed proud of his one item, perhaps rescued from the dump after days of searching. Ardith stayed there for a moment, watching the illumination spell ebb and flow like the waves in the ocean, before heading on, much to the disappointment of the merchant.

After about half an hour or so, Ardith started to get impatient, as she often did. She started making a more direct path towards the VIP section in the back, the only place worth buying anything from. Even there, one needed to be choosy about what to buy, what to get. That was a lesson that she learned often, even as recently as the morning before, when she tried to bind her enchantment to that set of earrings that were supposed to be ready to be enchanted. Since then, she had become convinced that the earrings had been created by a fire mage, making them completely useless to her. The residual fire magic would block any efforts she ever made and would be ingrained in every molecule of the gold.

As she approached the VIP section, she nodded a greeting towards the guard on duty. The man nodded his head back, giving her a light smile. She recognized Jerome almost immediately, the eternal flirt. On those few occasions where she would dawdle near the entrance, he would always hit on her, despite the fact that she had told him multiple times that she wasn't interested. She was pretty sure she even told him she was gay at one point, but that didn't deter him in the least. It had gotten to the point that she actively avoided the district when he was on duty, but she had lost track of the days while on the run with TS. She could have sworn it was Thursday already, but it must have only been Wednesday.

Jerome raised his finger as Ardith passed, making it seem like he was going to be at it again soon enough, but a commotion to Ardith's left quickly pulled him away from her. Ardith thanked her lucky stars as she continued onward through the district. She always hated the haphazard way the place had about it, but she understood the need for it. If the rows were nice and neat and all lined up, only those with the highest quality goods would ever get customers. With the rows a mess, the more impatient customers often buy closer to the front. It was the only trickle-down economy that ever made a lick of sense to Ardith, despite the fact that the rich still claimed that it worked.

Ardith had to go three further rows back to see the merchant that had sold her the earrings. The man had actually gone up in the world since Monday, when she was there last. A whole row further back. For some reason, that outraged her, infuriated her. Seeing that, all she could think about was giving that asshole a piece of her mind, even though it wasn't the reason why she had come. She was almost to his table, pushing her way through the crowd that always thickened the further in one went, when a voice came from behind her.

"Ah hah," came the voice. A heavy hand landed solidly on her shoulder, holding her in place. "I found you."

Ardith spun around at the words more than the hand. Her heart leapt into her throat as she was reminded that the Mage Authority might have been on the lookout for her as well as TS. But, when she recognized the face behind her, all she could do was smile.

"Dorth, you scared the hell out of me," Ardith said.

"I scared you?" Dorth asked. "I came back from scouting the dump, had three pure bloods throw things at me, only to find you gone. Sure, TS said you yelled at him and left, but I don't trust that guy anywhere near as far as I can throw him... Well, not even that far, 'cause I could totally throw him far. He's just a stupid pure blood. No offense," she said, when she noticed several of the merchants around her glaring at her.

"Yea, you really can't go off about pure bloods here," Ardith said. "It's rude. Plus, you know, I'd like to still be able to come back here. It'll be pretty hard to get more resources for my work if I'm banned from this place."

"Aren't there like a hundred places like this all over the world? The world is a big place; I find it hard to believe that there's only one of these."

"Yea, but you have to actually find them. It's not like you can just search some book or something for places like this. Ooh, wouldn't it be nice if there was?"

"Yea," said one of the merchants standing next to them. He was one of the older ones, missing his teeth with no replacements. Ardith was pretty sure it was the first time she had ever seen him in the VIP section. "And you could call it google."

"No, that's a stupid name. I'd call it something like... mage pages or something."

"Kids these days," the man scoffed. "Don't know your history."

"Can we go somewhere else?" Dorth asked. "This place is starting to give me the creeps."

"I want to tell this one guy off first, maybe try to get some free goods off of him in the process. If he didn't give me tainted earrings, I would have had my prototype and would never have had to take the job for TS."

"Sure, whatever," Dorth said, shrugging. "Maybe we could go to my place after? Get some real sleep for once? Or, you know, some other stuff? Wouldn't that be nice?"

"Yea, sure," Ardith said. But she wasn't paying much attention to her. Instead, she continued onward, leading the way deeper into the VIP section.

Before she got much further down the row, someone pushed her out of the way and into one of the tables. Ardith started to turn towards the pusher, her mouth already starting to form the curses, both verbal and magical, that she intended to sling at the man. She stopped cold, her magic fizzling all on its own, when she noticed the color of the man's coat. The man in the blood red coat continued to run down the aisle, pushing people aside in his mad rush through the crowd.

"On second thought, let's get the fuck out of here," Ardith said, all thoughts of telling off the merchant disappearing instantly.

"That's the spirit," Dorth said. "Let's get the fuck home so we can..."

"Dorth, come on. Something is going to go down here and I don't want anything to do with it. I've had enough drama and destruction for one day already."

Screams filled the space as the two girls fled the confrontation at the heart of the merchant district. Many people stopped to stare at the commotion that neither could see. Ardith wasn't sure if the blood mage was killing someone, but it wasn't her business. That was a job for her mom, but she couldn't risk calling her. If the Mage Authority showed up there, they could just as likely arrest her. Ardith was hoping to lay low for a few more days before reaching out to her family, and what few friends she had managed to keep over the years. The merchant district had seemed safe enough before, though with the blood mage killing people, the place would be crawling with Authority members before long.

It took Ardith longer to get out of the merchant district than it did for her to get to its core. People were scrambling all over as word of the blood mage spread. While many of them were heading for the center to see the blood bath firsthand, many more were scrambling to escape like Ardith and Dorth. The conflict between the two groups ended up causing a bit of a traffic jam, everyone trying to push past each other in the narrow space. Somewhere near the center of the district, close to the glowing ring she had looked at before, the tide turned in their favor and they managed to get through without any further difficulty.

As soon as people got clear of the overhang, they were all teleporting away. No one was even thinking of turning around to go back once the danger was done. Ardith was in full agreement, always opting for abandoning anywhere that was under attack. A few baubles weren't worth risking one's life. Nothing was worth risking one's life. However, as Dorth and Ardith came out from under the overhang, the teleportation blocks dropping away from them, Dorth teleported off like the rest of them but Ardith... didn't.

It wasn't like she wasn't trying. As soon as she felt the protections slide away from her, as soon as she knew she was free of them, she tried to teleport away. The only thought that came to her was of Dorth's apartment. The one they had picked out together soon before graduation. The one that they had originally planned on sharing before Ardith decided to try to go off on her own. Yet something was wrong. She felt her magic like always, it was there and ready to use, but the teleportation spell just wasn't coming to her. It felt like it was blocked somehow. Like there was something in the way between her and her magic, though she knew it was still there.

After about a minute of her constantly trying to teleport away, Dorth came back, a confused look on her face. "Are you alright?" she asked. "We were heading to my place, right?"

"Your place, right," Ardith said. She gritted her teeth and closed her eyes, trying one last desperate time to teleport away. "It's not working," she said.

"Here, let me," Dorth said.

She wrapped her arm around Ardith, pulling her close to her side, before teleporting the both of them away. Ardith actually liked the feel of Dorth teleporting her, never feeling the discomfort most people felt when another person teleports them. Still, she didn't like the fact that she couldn't do it herself, couldn't rely on herself to teleport anymore.

When they landed at Dorth's place, Ardith took a step away from her. Dorth must have noticed what she was planning, as she backed away from Ardith and the landing platform, giving her the space that she wanted. Ardith tried to teleport again, three times over the span of as many seconds, each failing her miserably.

"I don't understand it," Ardith shouted.

Her voice echoed around the room, drawing her attention away from her frustration and to the apartment they were in. It had been months since she had been there, and it had only been the once. It was a high-rise crystal apartment, giving her a beautiful view of the ocean on one side, the entire wall a large, crystal window. There was a long couch placed perfectly to look out over the view, and a tall pile of books next to it, all showing some wear from use. It was the apartment that Dorth's dad had bought, freeing her from using most of the expansive salary she must have been pulling as a journalist.

"I've never had problems with teleporting," Ardith said. "Other air spells, sure, always. I'm not really good at any element but my own. But, still, we're trained way too hard for way too long in The Academy for it to ever fail me. What's going on?"

"Well, what have you done differently recently?" Dorth asked, in that knowing tone that told her she already knew the answer. She sat down on the couch, moving another pile of books to open space next to her. Ardith tried to smile at the thought of just sitting there, looking out over the world, but her worries kept her from any other emotion. Still, as Dorth patted the couch next to her, she came around, sitting down on the comfortable couch, letting Dorth drape her arm around her and pull her close.

"It's the stupid oath, isn't it," she said, already knowing the answer. "Even with using Carissa's name, it still mattered."

"Yea, I'm not that surprised," Dorth said.

"Well, then, why didn't you warn me against it?"

"Would you have listened if I had? No matter how many times the professors said it, none of the students paid much attention. It's not the words of the spell that matter."

"Oh, yea, I remember that one," Ardith said. "'It's not the words of the spell that matter. That's why the more powerful spells draw the words out of you, rather than require you saying the words. The words just convey the intent that is already there.'"

"Exactly. Right name or wrong name, you meant that oath when you made it. It still hit you like it would otherwise, and it still meant something to you and, deep down, to your affinity. The longer it's been since you've broken the oath, the worse off your magic will become, until you're no better than a pure blood."

"Great," Ardith said. "And, then, you'll dump me."

"Never," she said. Ardith could see her smile in the reflection on the crystal window. "You're not getting rid of me that easily. Even without your magic, you're no pure blood. You'd be... a rare talent, only without a rare talent."

"Even worse, Carissa would be right. She always said I was no better than a rare talent."

"Don't worry, I can take care of you. I'll make a kept woman out of you yet."

"Oh, ha ha. No, there has to be something I can do to fix this, some spell we just haven't figured out yet. Maybe that's what I should be working on, what I could make my fortune off of. The cure for a broken oath."

"Well, there is another way to fix it," Dorth said.

"What? How?" Ardith pushed away from Dorth, standing up and turning around to face her. "You know what I can do to fix this? Is it some new trick? Is it classified?"

"No," Dorth said, smiling broadly. "It's rather simple, all things considered. I'm surprised you haven't figured it out yourself yet."

"Oh, come on, Dorth, stop teasing me. What is it? What do I have to do?"

"Keep your oath, obviously."

"I think it's a little late for that. I already left TS alone in that dump to die."

"No, you left him in the dump with a linking book. He's not there anymore, obviously. He's not that dumb... Well, he is pretty dumb, but..."

"No, you're right, even worse. He's not in the dump anymore, so I have no idea where he is, where to find him. I can't actually help him deliver that stupid thing, so it's all for nothing."

"Yea, no, you're right," Dorth said. She nodded her agreement, but the smile never left her face. Ardith glared at her, wondering why she was enjoying this so much, her annoyance, her discomfort, her loss of her magic. Is it just because she thought it meant they would actually be together? There was still the matter of their fathers, even if she was going to give up trying to make it on her own. "It's too bad that TS doesn't have something of yours, something that is almost even designed to be tracked."

"What are you... My linking book," Ardith said.

Finally, it all made sense to her. The linking books had tracking spells built into them, in the off chance that one was lost. If a book fell into the wrong hands, into the hands of a powerful and ill-reputed mage, it was completely possible for them to break through the locks and use it to enter a person's home, past any safeguards that were in place. When unlocked, the linking books had the same signature as the owner.

"Right," Dorth said. "All we have to do is track down the linking book, meet back up with TS, and start helping him with his stupid quest. Once we do that, your magic should come back good as new."

"Should?"

"Well, you did break the oath already, just by abandoning him with the intent of not going back. We're in the grey from here on out. It's not like I'm an expert on magical oaths or anything. But I don't see why not."

"Great," Ardith said. "You know, you don't have to come with me. I wouldn't blame you if you wanted off the ride here. You have a life to get back to, maybe some people you want to get back to." Ardith looked around the room again, looking for signs of other people, signs of other relationships. Everything was spartan, as Dorth always liked to keep things. The place definitely needed some of Ardith's clutter to make it feel like home to her. Nothing there seemed to contradict what Dorth had already seemed to indicate, that she had been waiting for her, and still was.

"Not on your life," Dorth said. "Not on mine. Not even on TS's, but then it would make this whole thing rather moot for me."

"What? You're not here to keep me out of danger?"

"Well, there's always that, but, no. Like I said back at the air bar, whatever this is, it has the feeling of being something epic. I'm in it for the exclusive. And, you know, to keep you safe and convince you that we belong together."

"Oh, I have no doubt of that," Ardith said. "The trick would be to convince the world of that."

"Screw the world," Dorth said. "And anyone that thinks we don't belong together."

"I'd rather just screw you," Ardith said, smiling at her play on words, and the thoughts they elicited.

Chapter Twenty-Four
Innocent Bystander

Bethany

"I got you," Renard shouted. "You're under arrest."

"I'm what now?" the man asked. He turned around, rising from his crouched position to stand his full, almost seven feet of height. It was clear that, whoever this person was, he wasn't the air mage they had supposedly been after. Renard's bluster faded almost instantly when he saw the man. His hand fell off the man's shoulder more because of the height difference than anything else.

"Um, you're, um," Renard said.

Bethany was still two rows over, but the crowd started to thin out around the two men, giving her a better view of the confrontation. She hopped up on the table right next to her, jumping off of it over to the next row over, sliding back down to the ground right beside Renard and the man that stood accused by him. Under normal circumstances, the maneuver would have been greatly frowned upon, perhaps even grounds for her to be banned from the merchant district. But under those circumstances they would probably have understood.

As Bethany landed next to Renard, he looked over to her, an unvoiced but quite desperate cry for help plain on his face. He took another step away from the behemoth who advanced on him, filling the space that he had just vacated.

Renard clung to the hat he was wearing, using it as a shield, and perhaps a little of a security blanket, against the raging man. The man actually looked down at the hat, at the Authority symbol mounted on the band, but he didn't back down from his anger.

"That's fake," he said, his voice a booming bass, resonating in Bethany's chest. "There are no blood mages in the Mage Authority. You're a fake. I'll break you in half."

"He's no fake, George," Bethany said, just remembering the man's name from the last few times that she had come in there. "He's a new recruit, a test program."

"I'd say this test failed completely," George said. "Blood mages have no right being in The Authority. Half the incidents that happen are because of them."

"Actually, I don't have the crime stats in front of me right now, but last I heard it was more like ten percent. Half the incidents were from enchanted items and creatures."

"Still, they're just a crummy mess and the lot of them should have been ousted with the death mages."

"No arguments here," Bethany said. "In the meantime, he is a member of The Authority... for now."

"I'm also a blood mage," Renard said, finally getting his spine back. He pulled his magic to him, using it to enhance his muscles and visibly grow a foot. This put the two of them on even footing. "You're lucky I don't just break you in half like a toothpick," he said, his voice noticeably lower than it was a moment ago.

"That's not helping, Renard," Bethany said. "Care to let me handle this?"

"No," Renard said. He swatted Bethany aside, slamming her into the table she had just jumped off of, as he came bearing down on George. George, to his credit, didn't back down, didn't back away from the raging blood mage. Instead, as Renard swung at the man, he stuck up a meaty hand, catching the swung fist in mid-air.

"Stop it, both of you," Bethany yelled. She pulled her magic to her, using it to create a wall of fire between the brawling men. The wall flared up, encircling both of them and blocking off the crowd from the confrontation. It was a delicate process, sending the firewall out like that, especially since Renard was the target. But her intent was clear and she threaded the needle perfectly.

However, it wasn't enough. Renard simply swatted at the flames, dispelling the entire effect and releasing both of the men from the cage. His anger flared as his eyes went between Bethany and George, turning almost red with rage. Bethany could feel the mana being pulled from the air, leaving behind a vacuum that was filled almost as quickly as it formed. With all that power at his disposal, Renard could have done almost anything. Yet, whatever it was that he was doing wasn't so quickly discerned.

George coughed, one small cough at first, but then several heavier ones in rapid succession. His hand went to his mouth to stymie the coughing fit, but it did little to help. Spittle started to flow around his hand, red with blood, as the coughing fit brought him to his knees. It was clear that, whatever was happening inside the burly man, Renard was the cause of it.

"That's enough, Renard," Bethany shouted. She jumped between the two men, her arms wide in protection of George, but it didn't seem like the spell needed line of sight to continue. "He's a person of interest in our investigation, is he not? You're not supposed to kill him."

Renard was already swelling with power, more so with the blood flowing out of George's mouth. He was drunk on the power, already too far gone to stop. Bethany's words didn't even penetrate his ire, his fury, his rage, his bloodthirst. Renard took another step closer to George, not seeming to see Bethany there at all as he approached his source of power.

As focused as Renard was on taking his fill from George's blood, he didn't seem to notice when Greg came up behind him. Greg landed a glancing blow of his fist across the back of Renard's head, heavy, ladened down by Greg's own power, directed inward. Renard fell to the floor like a ton of bricks, right on top of Bethany. She hadn't been expecting the move, so she toppled over under Renard's dead weight. George was right behind her, though, and he recovered from the coughing quickly enough to catch the both of them. He eased Renard down to the floor with one hand, pulling Bethany out from the middle with the other.

"See?" George said. "No right being in the Mage Authority."

"Oh, Greg, what did you do?" Bethany said. Her eyes went wide as the whole situation finally clicked in her head. Greg had assaulted a fellow officer. No matter how much in the wrong Renard had been, no matter how much he shouldn't have been in the Mage Authority, it just wasn't done. There was no telling what would happen to Greg, given the current political climate at The Authority.

"Eh, he had it coming," Greg said, shrugging. For once, his levelheadedness was going to work against him. "You know what he would have written in his report, if he had actually killed the guy here. He would have pinned everything on him and made the killing look justified. He would have gotten away with it. That just didn't sit well with me."

"Doesn't sit well with me, either," George said. "Pin what on me, anyway?"

"Should we take him in for questioning?" Igloo asked. She and Dan finally managed to make it through the crowd to them. Igloo was out of breath, despite the fact that the close quarters of the district made it impossible for them to run anywhere. Dan, on the other hand, was eating a pretzel of all things. Bethany wasn't even sure where they sold pretzels in the district and was convinced that he had brought it with him.

"I think it would work out better if George just laid low for now. Once Renard wakes up, he's going to be furious, probably still want to arrest him. But we all know he's not the pure blood we saw, right?"

"Yea, sure," Dan said.

"Whatever you say, boss," Igloo said.

"Do we...," Greg said. "I mean, it would solve--"

"No, Greg," Bethany said. "We're not going to hide anything by shoving the blame on an innocent bystander. Once George answers our questions, he'll be free to go. And, you want to answer our questions, right George?"

"Um... yes? Wait, is this really happening? That blood mage wasn't just screwing with me? What did I do?"

"Probably nothing," Bethany said. She knelt down next to Renard, feeling around in his pockets until she found the piece of gold. He must have tucked it away in there before approaching George. Once it was free from the confines of Renard's coat, she showed it to George. It no longer looked like the partially bent earring that Renard had called it. Instead, it just looked like a pebble of gold bent in on itself. "Have you seen this before?"

"Seriously?" George asked. "It's a piece of gold. I can't even tell what it used to be. Probably. I sell dozens of things made of gold, maybe hundreds. I... Yea, I guess it could have been one of mine. Given how insistent that guy was about it, I imagine it was. What about it?"

"Do you know who you sold it to?"

"Yea, just let me check my logs," George said, sarcastically. "Hell, no, I don't know who I sold it to. Like I said, I sell hundreds of things made from gold. They come off of the auto-replicators just like everything else that's made these days. Nothing gets made from scratch anymore, not anything worth using anyway."

"Is there a reason why you would still be tracked as the owner of this particular piece? Shouldn't that change to the person who bought it?"

"Sure, if the person paid for it. Usually, anyway. Hell, you'd know better than me. You're the mage. I'm just a rare talent, trying to make it in a mage world."

"So, if someone stole it--"

"No, no, no, stolen is something different. That's a whole other story. Ownership goes to the robber. Had that happen quite a few times over the years. Possession is still nine tenths of the law, and I got stiffed more times than I can count. What you're wanting is..." He trailed off as a thought came to him. Snapping his fingers, he headed back over to his table, taking a book out from beneath it. George quickly flipped through the book before coming to a page near the end. Bethany couldn't see what was written on the page, but she had an unsettling feeling she knew exactly what he was about to say. "There are three mages that bought on credit this last week and still haven't paid me. One of those is the one you're looking for."

"Were any of those air mages?" Igloo asked. Bethany tried to suppress her smile at that question.

"No, no air mages. Air mages don't buy these. It's mostly water mages, though really, between you and me, they're crap for enchantments. At least the permanent kind. They'll hold a charge for a month or two, but most water mages want to get rich and famous with the next rain rod. But, well, who am I to deny them of my goods? Here, let me write down their names. You can track them down better than I can. Good luck and all, you know, trying to find whoever it is you're looking for." He scribbled the names out on a page of the book before tearing the whole page out, folding it in half, and handing it over to Bethany. "Now, do I really need to lay low? I have a business to run and all that."

"We just don't know him well enough to know for certain," Greg said. "He could wake up, not say anything against either one of us, and let it slide. Or, he could report me to our new bloodsucking boss, and come back here to arrest slash kill you again."

"Yea, I really don't want to be arrested slash killed."

"Well, maybe if these names pan out before he wakes up, it won't matter," Bethany said. There was no hope behind her words, as she knew the truth of everything. The names won't lead anywhere, not without leading them straight to her daughter. She flipped open the folded page, glancing down at the list to make sure of what she already knew was true.

Sure enough, the second name on the list was Ardith DeSalvo. Still, Bethany's heart stopped when she saw the name.

Chapter Twenty-Five
Homecoming

Eric

Eric's feet were killing him by the time the bunker was in sight. He had walked more in the past forty-eight hours than the entire thirty years prior. After he landed at U of C, he walked about three miles south, spending the time flipping through the linking book to find a location closer to the bunker. At first, the best he could find was the locked entry for the workshop where he had met Carissa, Ardith. Despite Ardith's warning, he tried to use the page, but nothing happened. The page remained solid, smooth under his fingers. There was no pulling at his gut or a loss of direction or a sense of vertigo like he always had when using the book or being teleported by a mage.

After the first hour or so of walking, he managed to find a page for an old sandwich shop in New Chicago. He didn't recognize the place in the picture, but the sign over the dilapidated storefront listed Lynwood as the city. From his original walk out of the bunker, he knew that would cut about ten or fifteen miles out of the trek and jumped at the chance. The sandwich shop itself was closed, permanently, but the landing platform still worked. He stumbled out of the shop and into the street. The neighborhood that the shop belonged to, built up over the decades prior to The Arrival, was falling apart like all the other parts of the old new city. It was mostly abandoned by the population that once called it home.

Halfway through the walk from Lynwood, it started to rain, and Eric started to laugh. In some ways, things were coming around full circle for Eric. Once again, he was in New Chicago and it was raining, only this time he was heading home instead of heading out. He no longer had the rain rod that had protected him from the rain during that first outing. Instead, he had the case that he had traded it for, had gone through hell for. Still, it wasn't enough, nowhere near what he needed to complete his mission, his quest.

No, he was a complete failure, and getting stuck in the rain felt appropriate to him. He was tired, dead on his feet, and at a loss for what to do. Nothing had worked like he had planned, like Michael had planned before the old man died. Eric was convinced that, had it been Michael that went out instead of him, the quest would have been over that first day. Everything would have been over that first day. It was Michael that should have gone on the quest, that should have been The Scientist, the last scientist.

And so, as he approached the front door of the bunker, the rain falling on his head, the case a solid, dead weight in his hand, he felt like he deserved everything that he had been put through and more. The rain wasn't nearly enough without the streets flooding again or lightning to strike him dead or hail to hit him on the head. Or, better yet, a mage that tracked him there, tracked him home, to compromise the already compromised bunker.

"There he is," came a call behind him.

Eric laughed again, immediately recognizing the voice, even over the sound of the rain around him. Of course, it would be them. Of course, he would have failed in that, too.

"What do you want, Ardith?" Eric asked. He didn't turn around to face the mage, her girlfriend undoubtedly in tow. However, he did continue walking, straight past the door to the bunker. While the door wasn't all that hidden, it didn't look like anything more than a pair of metal doors to an old storm cellar. Tornadoes weren't unknown to the region, and there were plenty of storm cellars around. In fact, the bunker had started out as just another one, before the owner went a little overboard.

"She needs your help, asshole," Dorth shouted at him as he continued to walk away from them.

"Asshole?" he asked. Eric turned to face the two impetulant girls. His hand clutched at the case, using its solidity as a shield against their words, against his own ire. "Asshole? You two lied to me this entire time. My life has been in danger every hour of the past two days. All I was trying to do was make this world better, this life better. But, no, you two had to pull me through an endless line of dangerous situations, that were only dangerous because of magic, because you are mages. I needed your help, not your... your..."

"Our what?" Ardith asked.

It was then that he actually noticed the two girls. Actually saw them where they were standing in the middle of the road. Like him, neither of them had thought to bring a rain rod for the weather. They must have been out in the rain for about as long as he had, as they were both completely drenched, soaked to the bone. Something was nagging at him, telling him that there was something wrong with that picture. It took him a few moments to realize that Ardith, as a water mage, and he was relatively certain she actually was a water mage, should have been immune to the rain. Water was her element, her affinity, and she should have been powered by the rain, not weakened by it.

"What... What's wrong with you?" he asked.

"What's wrong with me? What's wrong with you?" Ardith shouted.

"No, honey, he means," Dorth started to say. "The oath you made her make, the breaking of it still hit her, despite her thinking that it wouldn't. She's as powerless as you are."

"How did you even find me?" Eric asked. "Well, yes, I know you're mages, but--"

"We tracked the book," Dorth said. "It took what was left of her power to do it, but we managed to get the relative vicinity. Then I tracked you the rest of the way. You walk really fast, by the way."

"Where are you even going?" Ardith asked. "Off to ruin some other mage's life?"

"I ruined... No, I'm going home. My quest is over, a failure, like me. I'm done."

"Oh, no you don't," Dorth said. "You need to finish this quest of yours so Ardith can get her magic back."

"But... I thought..."

"It's Dorth's idea," Ardith said. "I'm not that hopeful. Still, I don't think I could live with myself if I lost my magic without even trying to get it back. So, what's the plan? Where do we go from here?"

"Well... For starters, we should probably get out of the rain. I guess the real question is, can I trust you?"

"Can you trust us?" Ardith asked. "Seriously? When have we ever given you any reason not to trust us?"

"Oh, I don't know, Carissa," Eric said, pointedly.

"Okay, that was your mistake, your assumption. I just didn't correct you on it."

"Well, there's a big difference between being trustworthy and not being untrustworthy. You could have been playing along this entire time, for the sole purpose of finding out exactly where this place was."

"Fine," Dorth said. She took a step closer to Eric, walking away from Ardith who almost looked like she needed her girlfriend there for support. Looking Eric straight in the eyes, Dorth raised her right hand and took in a deep breath. "I, Dorth Geller, promise never to reveal what you are about to entrust to us, nor let Ardith DeSalvo reveal it in my presence or knowingly let her do it outside of my presence."

A shiver seemed to roll up her spine, though Eric wasn't sure if it was the cold from the rain or the magic of the promise.

"Dorth, no," Ardith said. "Now we're both tied to him."

"Good," Dorth said. "Now can you trust us?"

Eric thought on that for a few moments. It had seemed to work on Ardith, taking her magic down when she broke her own oath, though it hadn't stopped her from doing it. But they were right. Other than pretending to be this Carissa person, whom he had never met anyway, they had at least seemed to be genuinely trying to help him.

"Fine," he said. "Follow me."

Eric retraced his steps up the street, walking past the two drenched women. He stopped at the sidewalk that led up to the main house, looking up and down the street for several moments before walking up the path. The cement was broken in several places, the grass almost overrunning the path as it grew wildly. No one had maintained the lawn, and it grew up several feet to come to their shoulders. The entire neighborhood had gone downhill, much like most of the pure blood areas of the world. Even with being able to teleport wherever people wanted, they just all seemed to tend to clump together in the new crystal cities.

The front door to the house stood crooked, held up by only the bottom hinge. The entire weight of the door stretched the metal that was already compromised by the magic flowing through the air. Eric did his best to step around the door, not wanting to touch it lest that be the proverbial straw that broke the metal hinge. The hardwood floor of the main level of the house creaked under his feet, reminding him of the noises that storms always sent down to the bunker below him. Eric stopped in the middle of the main hallway, looking around at the house that he had only seen four times in his life, yet still felt like home to him. He took in a deep breath, inhaling the familiar scents of the place, the musky aroma that always perverted the airflow of the bunker.

The door slammed to the floor behind him, causing Eric to jump in fright. Ardith was standing in the doorway, shying away from where the door had stood. It was obvious she had come a little too close to where it had been hanging, accidentally bumping into the door and causing it to fall. Dorth was just shaking her head at her girlfriend, already having gotten past the door without incident.

"Sorry," Ardith said. "Was that important?"

"Not really," Eric said with a sigh. "It's all just one big facade anyway, something to hide the truth beneath our feet."

"Wait, it's in the basement?" Dorth asked. She looked down at the wood floors beneath her, as if she was able to see through the very floor to the bunker below. Given the fact that she was still as powerful of a mage as she always was, Eric had no doubt that she might very well be able to do just that.

"What is?" Ardith asked.

"The hole he's been living in these past thirty years."

"It's not a hole," Eric said. "It's a bunker. And, yes, it's beneath us, but not the basement. I think there's a crawl space down there, between this floor and the bunker, just for further disguise. The man who built the place, Billy, he was a bit of a paranoid guy. He always thought that the government was out to get him for some reason. Anyway, it worked to our advantage more than it did him. Billy died soon after The Arrival. Heart attack, of all things."

"But, wait, I... I don't get it," Ardith said. "If you've lived in a hole in the ground this whole time, how did you hear about Carissa? How did you know about the oath? How did you even make contact with that black market guy?"

"Moreover, why did you ever leave?" Dorth asked.

"You know, maybe it's better that you came after all," Eric said. "Maybe, if you see this place, if you can understand what's at stake, you'll actually understand my quest. What I'm planning on doing and why. Come on. Let me show you."

Eric led the way through the rest of the house. The hallway was narrow, causing their footsteps to echo around them as they headed deeper. At the back of the house was what was left of the kitchen, which showed a similar level of disrepair as the rest of the house. The oven had fallen apart at some point, the inner workings of it splayed out across the kitchen, a mound of rusted pieces that crossed their path. Eric just stepped over the pile, using his long legs to his advantage, while Dorth and Ardith helped each other over one at a time.

The back door to the house had fallen down years ago, laid down across the back steps. Eric walked down the wooden door, using it as a ramp rather than trying to step around it. The backyard wasn't nearly as untouched as the front yard had been. There was a clear path from the back door, through the tall grass. Eric continued down the path, his hands unconsciously reaching out to run against the tall grass to either side of it. At the end of the path was the door to the storm cellar, or, at least, what used to be the storm cellar. That was where he stopped, turning around to face the two women. Ardith came up short when she noticed this, causing Dorth, who was walking behind her, to bump into her.

"What you're about to see, well, let's just say you've never seen anything like this in all of your life. You've probably heard about some of it, read about some of it, but seeing it is something completely different. Whatever you do, don't touch anything unless I tell you that you can. You might break something. Nothing in here was designed to work for thirty years straight. It's something of a miracle that we've managed to have it all still work for as long as we have."

"That's stupid," Dorth said. "How can we not touch anything? Are we allowed to touch the floor? The doors?"

"The floor, yes. Doors, no. Some of them lead to private residences, most of which are no longer occupied. Some lead to areas that have collapsed. Those, definitely don't open.

This whole thing is a bit, well, tenuous at this point. That's the problem. That's why I left."

"It's a storm cellar," Ardith said. "We still have those, though the crystal buildings aren't bothered by things like weather."

"It's not just a storm cellar," Eric said. To demonstrate, he pulled open the doors to the storm cellar, heading down the stairs into the dark.

At the base of the stairs was another door, this one of solid metal. The door had been replaced several times over the years, which was why it was only showing the slightest bit of rust from exposure to the elements. Eric pulled the lever on the wall that was next to the door, holding it in place for a few moments. The indicator above the lever slowly changed from red to green, the dial mechanism behind it chugging along as it struggled to work in the mana enriched environment. Once it showed green, Eric spun the large wheel that was mounted in the center of the door, releasing the airtight locks that were in place. With a pop and a loud hiss, the door pulled open on the hinges, which whined a little as he did so.

"This is called an airlock," Eric explained as he walked inside. "This is what kept what's inside here working for thirty years, despite the world that's out there. Come on, it's perfectly safe."

"Says the man that lived in a hole in the ground for the past thirty years," Ardith said. Still, she followed him inside, pulling Dorth in after her. The two women were holding hands, though Eric wasn't sure if that was mutual support or just out of habit.

"Yea," Eric said. "This hole. Trust me, it's fine. Close the door."

"Oh, can we touch this door?" Dorth asked. Despite her snarky tone, she pulled the door closed behind them, even spinning the wheel at its center to seal off the airlock from the outside air.

Eric turned around to face the inner door. There was another lever next to this door as well, but the dial had broken years ago and no one had bothered to fix it. He pulled the lever, counting off the seconds as the air inside the airlock was cycled out, with fresh air from the reserves being forced in to replace it. Unfortunately, he lost count long about twenty.

A pounding, blistering headache started up somewhere around the base of Eric's neck, making its way up and down his spine. Eric hadn't had many headaches over the years, but it was like he had saved them all up for this one hell of a migraine. He couldn't think, couldn't hear, couldn't speak beyond screaming from the pain of it. His screams echoed around the narrow room, sounding more like three people screaming rather than just him. He wasn't sure what it was, what was causing it, where it came from, or even how long it lasted because he blacked out from the pain of it.

Chapter Twenty-Six
Obstructing Justice

Bethany

"This is bad, Bethany," Dan said. "Very bad. How could you not tell us?"

They were back at the office. All four of them were huddled in Bethany's cubicle with the sound dampeners ups so that the blood mages wouldn't hear them. Renard was in the conference room that he had used earlier, still knocked out from Greg's blow. No one wanted to bring him to the light mages at the hospital and have to explain his injuries. It was only a matter of time before he woke up and came knocking.

It seemed like the blood mages had doubled again in their absence. There were red coats everywhere. A few of the old Authority members had quit in protest over the move, but from the look of things they had just been replaced by more blood mages. At the rate they were going, the Mage Authority was going to be an extension of the blood guild by the end of the month, and all law and order would be out the window. Under different circumstances, Bethany would have tried to do something about it. As it were, though, she didn't have a leg to stand on.

"How could I not tell you about the 'air mage' that we were supposed to be tracking, because of a loose relation to a pure blood that had nothing to do with the wrongful death but is going to get it pinned on him anyway? Gee, maybe because I didn't want her to get arrested."

"I'm not talking about The Authority or the captain. Certainly not these blood suckers around here. I'm talking about us. Igloo, Greg, and me. Don't you trust us better than that?"

"It wasn't about trust; it was about not getting you in trouble. And, well, a little about chain of custody. If you guys didn't know about Ardith, then the investigation wouldn't have been tainted by you. I was going to document what little I had been involved in with that branch of the investigation, but then it all got dumped on the pure blood and the blood mages started showing up."

"Like the cockroaches they are," Igloo said.

"Please, no mixed metaphors," Dan said. "They're mosquitoes, obviously. I mean, the blood."

"I thought they were leeches," Greg said.

"Guys, can we not?" Bethany said.

"Why?" Dan asked. "They can't hear us."

"I think she meant to focus on the matter at hand," Greg said. "What are we going to do? How are we going to save Ardith?"

"Can we even do that at this point?" Dan asked. "I think it's a little late for getting her out of trouble. She's not a little kid anymore, and she got herself into this trouble all by herself."

"She's my little kid," Bethany said. "She'll always be my little kid."

"Whatever. I just meant she's an adult. Helping someone on the run was an adult move. A stupid one, but an adult one. There's not much we can do to save her at this point short of..."

"Short of what?" Igloo asked.

"That's your element, Dan," Bethany said, assuming she already knew what he was about to say.

"Or Greg's," Dan said. "He could have the paper absorb the ink."

"I'd leave a gap there," Greg said. "It would be noticeable. You could actually move the ink around."

"What are you guys talking about?" Igloo asked.

"They're suggesting that I alter the list of names, taking Ardith's name off of it. We'll end up investigating the other two, which will obviously come up with nothing, and Renard will write it off as another dead end."

"Hopefully," Bethany said.

"Wouldn't that be, I don't know, obstruction of justice or something?" Igloo asked.

"Yes," Dan said. "That's exactly what it would be. Obstruction of justice."

"Only if we get caught," Greg said. The three of them looked over at the burly man like his hair was on fire. "What?" he asked, shrugging his shoulders and bumping into the doorway of the overcrowded cubicle in the process.

"I had actually been working on a plan that would get everyone, including Ardith, out of the trouble we're in," Bethany said. She pulled open the bottom drawer of her filing cabinet, reaching in to pull out the papers she had gotten earlier. It was looking less and less likely that she would be able to outsource this part of her plan. "These are the logs for the blood guild from that night. I already have the logs from the bar. If we can find his signature in here, the blood mage, the actual culprit, we'll be able to track him to his next spot. Hopefully, from there, we can get a name, something to put on an actual warrant. If we can arrest him, get the charges to stick, then this pure blood guy is only going down for the black market stuff. And, since there's no evidence of that, nothing beyond the witness testimony of the ice tower, he might plead down to a slap on the wrist or something. That would get Ardith out of trouble and, by extension, me."

"There are a lot of ifs in that plan of yours," Dan said. "Not to mention, the whole thing is crazy. Didn't the captain, both captains, tell you to drop that part of the investigation? No one is going to listen to it. We don't have any evidence that a blood mage did it. We'd need an actual confession to get him for the crime, and what kind of idiot would confess to something like that?"

"Well, he is a blood mage," Igloo said.

"Exactly," Dan said. "A blood mage. For all we know, he's here, in this very office, pretending to be an officer of the law that he has been constantly flipping off his whole life."

"Well, not his whole life," Greg said. "I imagine there were some years that he was an innocent baby. Even blood mages start there, don't they? They're not born evil; they're just drawn that way."

"Whatever," Dan said. "The whole lot of them is just pure evil, whether they start out that way in life or not. I'll bet they're even behind the disappearances lately."

"You mean the other Authority members?" Igloo asked. "They all quit. We know this. We saw three of them walking out when we got here."

"No, I mean these." Dan stuck his head up above the cubicle, outside the sound dampening field. He reached over the cube walls to the next cube over, the one opposite from the hallway. When he came back, he had five posters in his hand. He tossed them down on the desk, where their ingrained magic splayed them out so each was readable. The five posters depicted five void mages, all saying that they were missing. "Half the void mages in the world have come up missing, probably dead. At the same time, they're taking over the Mage Authority. Coincidence? I don't think so. No, I think this whole thing is just one big conspiracy to take over the world."

"Paranoid," Igloo sang.

"How much you wanna bet that the quorum is next. Your husband, Bethany. He's on the quorum. He's next."

"That's nonsense, Dan," Bethany said. "The blood mages don't pay any attention to the quorum as it is. The blood guild master never showed up to this last one, just sending some representative in his place. That was the one that got me the logs."

"Then the logs are a trap, a trick, a lie. We should get rid of them before the whole blood guild comes down on us."

"Calm down, Dan," Greg said. "Quiet down. We don't want anyone hearing us."

"Yea, shush," Igloo said.

"Sorry," Dan said. He peeked out above the walls of the cubicle, looking around for any eavesdroppers that were about. "We can't let them know we're on to them."

"Dan, there's no big conspiracy to take over the world," Bethany said. "And what would using the logs do that would land us in a trap? Think before you start spinning your paranoid conspiracies."

"It's not paranoia if they're really out to get you," Dan said. "It's hyper awareness. And being right."

"Look, we're not settling anything this way," Bethany said. "We need to start thinking clearly, get ahead of this blood mage. If there is a conspiracy, and that's a big if, it's just the blood guild trying to hide a murderer."

"And, seeing as how they're blood mages, they're pretty much all murderers," Dan said.

"Not all of them," Bethany said. "Just... Okay, probably most of them. They get power from blood, not death. They're not the death guild. Let's not try to start Mage War 2 here."

"Actually, I heard our little tiff with the death guild was the second such war," Dan said. "Something about another mage war that happened before The Arrival."

"How could there have been a mage war before there were mages?" Bethany asked. "Fine, Mage War 3, happy? Anyway, we're not trying to start it, so it doesn't matter. We need to be smart, to be prepared for what they have planned next. Igloo, think you can go through this log and find the signature of the blood mage in question?"

"Um... How am I doing that again?" she asked.

"Check the logs against the list from the bar. There was only one that left there to head for the blood guild, so start with that entry and track it through here. Once you have the signature, find out where they went next."

"Better yet, compare it to the landing platform here," Dan said. "If they're one of the blood mages walking around here, we need to know it. Even if we can't get a name."

"Actually, that's... That's not a bad idea," Bethany said, hesitantly. "Here, use my badge when you pull the logs from the landing platform. That will give you the list of names along with the signatures. If you can get a match between all the logs, we'll know who we're looking for, where they headed after the blood guild, and if they're working with anyone."

"Wait, how would I know if they're working with anyone?" Igloo asked.

"Look for people teleporting away at the same time as the blood mage in question," Greg said. "Those would be their allies. Even with their swelling numbers, there's not enough of them for that to be a coincidence."

"And what will we be doing while she's delving into the logs?" Dan asked. "Please say 'kill Renard'."

"We're not killing anyone," Bethany said. "Not yet, anyway. Not unless they try to kill us first. We're cops, remember. We're the Mage Authority, the last line of defense for justice, and all that. Let's not try to break any more laws than we have to."

"Oh, you mean like obstruction of justice and aiding and abetting a fugitive?" Greg asked.

"We're only aiding and abetting a fugitive who is only a fugitive for aiding and abetting," Igloo said. "Doesn't that make it like the second degree or something? Much less of a crime."

"Ah, Igloo logic," Greg said. "I'll miss that when we're all in mage prison."

"We're not going to prison," Bethany said. "If it comes down to it, if everything falls down around us, I'll take the heat. I'll say that you were just working under my orders and didn't know what we were really doing. And, of course, what we're really doing right now is our jobs. We're not going to do anything to impede this investigation."

"Wait, what?" Greg asked. "But..."

"Yea, that makes no sense," Dan said. "How can we help Ardith if we don't, you know, help Ardith?"

"We're not going to impede the investigation, but we're also not going to help it. We're on a slowdown right now, in protest against the blood mages being integrated into The Authority in the way that they have. If they wanted in, they should have gone through proper channels, started with a pilot program with someone that people could actually trust."

"No such thing as a trustworthy blood mage," Dan said.

"In either case, this happened way too fast to overcome the mountains of distrust that is weighed against them. It's no wonder so many people have already quit, but that's the wrong way to go about it. That only gives them what they want."

"So, wait, we're not going to impede the investigation, but we're going to help Ardith by protesting the invasion of the Mage Authority?" Greg asked. "That's..."

"Stupid? Redundant? A waste of our limited time?" Bethany said.

"I was going to say genius, but after all that, I'd call it more of a stroke of madness. Or, well, maybe just a stroke. Do you smell toast?"

"What's toast?" Igloo asked.

"Oh, now, come on," Bethany said. "That is still around. Sliced bread cooked over a fire to a brown complexion."

"Oh, that," Igloo said. "Yea, we just always called it fire bread."

"Alright, look, just get the logs from the landing platform, find a dark corner to settle into, and get to work. If we can get a name for that blood mage, maybe we can take it to the commander and he'll call off the witch hunt."

"I thought we were hunting for a pure blood, not a witch," Igloo said. "Why would we hunt for a witch? Witches are just misinformed light mages living alone in the woods... or something."

"Igloo?"

"Yea?"

"Go away."

"Yes, boss." Igloo gave her a little salute before picking up the pile of papers that constituted the logs. Bethany's badge slipped a little as she tried to hold everything in one hand, but she managed to square everything away and head off to do her work.

"That really scares me a little, you know," Greg said, watching her go.

"What does?" Bethany asked.

"That our entire future is in the hands of... her?" Dan asked.

"Not our entire future, just mine. Seriously, no one is going down for this but me. You all have plausible deniability. None of you knew anything until, what, half an hour ago?"

"Hey, I have no doubt you'll jump on that grenade for us," Greg said.

"What's a grenade?" Dan asked. He only had his usual slight smile, so it wasn't clear if he was kidding or not.

"Gee, I don't know, Igloo," Greg said. "As I was saying, there's no way anyone is going to buy that we knew nothing of this. If we don't get the blood mage, like seriously get them, catch them red handed--"

"Which isn't hard," Dan said. "They're born with blood on their hands."

"Seriously, will you shut the hell up," Greg said.

"Well, someone needs to do the commentary."

"No, they really don't," Bethany said. "I'd cast a silence spell on you, but my affinity would be blocked just trying."

"I'd do it, but that's air magic," Greg said. "The one time I actually wish Igloo was here."

"Look, I get it," Bethany said. "This whole thing is rather iffy. If we can't get the blood mage, or we get him but can't get him to confess and can't get enough evidence to convict, it's still just down to this pure blood. Even if we can, the pure blood is still on the run from the law and Ardith is still helping him do it. We'll need to bring that to a proper close if Ardith is ever going to have a normal life again."

"And that means getting in the way of Renard's attempts to find her," Greg said.

"No, quite the opposite," Bethany said, as an idea played out in her head. "If he never finds the pure blood, he'll be like a dog with a bone. No turning him away from her, ever. No, he needs to find the pure blood, find him without finding her. As long as the two of them aren't found together, then the identity of this 'air mage', as she's always been reported, can go undocumented."

"That's assuming the pure blood doesn't blab," Dan said.

"And that she's not still with him," Greg said.

"It's been over forty-eight hours since the two of them first encountered each other. She knows he's being hunted by The Authority now. She's not going to still be helping him. Even if she helped him with an actual task, an assignment, or whatever you want to call it, she should be done with it by now, right?"

"I think it might be a good idea to send her another fire letter," Greg said. "Make sure she distances herself from the pure blood before we find her."

"The problem with that is that we won't be tracking the pure blood," Dan said. "I'm betting the next thing Renard does is try to track down Ardith from her stuff in the meeting room. He'll find her, not him."

"Either way, they can't be together right now," Greg said.

"Right," Bethany said. "Right."

Bethany pulled open the top drawer to her filing cabinet, pulling out a clean piece of paper. She didn't keep fire paper on hand, as the spell that the enchanted paper would perform was well within her capabilities. Her quill wasn't in its usual spot, though, so she couldn't write out the message. Despite her words of caution against the prejudices of her team, her immediate reaction was that one of the new blood mages had taken it. With a quick shrug, she popped up past her sound dampening spell to borrow a quill from one of her neighbors.

The arguments and screams of the office had only gotten worse while the group was ducked beneath the sound dampening spell. Several fist fights had broken out around the office as the different factions bumped heads. No one was throwing magic around just yet, but Bethany was getting the feeling that it was only a matter of time. Her plans of a slowdown started to seem like too little, too late to settle this raging argument that might very well cause the downfall of the entirety of the Mage Authority. When she ducked back down behind the protection of the sound dampening spell, she could still hear the fighting going on all around her.

"What's up?" Greg asked, obviously noticing that she was shaken.

"Oh, nothing. Just the whole world ending around us."

"Is that all?" Dan asked. He peeked out above the cube himself, only to come back seconds later. "Yea, that's about what it was before."

"Maybe this is what they wanted all along," Greg said. "Something to keep us busy while they... well, do whatever it is they're doing right now."

"And my investigation was just a coincidence?" Bethany asked.

"No, an impetus," Dan said. "They were doing this already; you just gave them an excuse to do it sooner. That's why they only have five of the void mages instead of all ten."

"Dan, all the missing void mages are old men," Greg pointed out. "They could have just got lost coming home from the store. It's only made national news because they're void mages. If it were five old pure bloods, no one would even care."

"In either case, we might want to start setting up shop somewhere else," Dan said. "If this place falls to the blood mages, from within or without, we're going to need to establish some semblance of law and order again. What happens to the world if the Mage Authority is no longer neutral, no longer legal, no longer defending those that need defending?"

"We need to find a new place to work out of anyway," Bethany said. "Somewhere away from the conflict. If people are going to be fighting over the future of The Authority, and I mean literally fighting, the rest of us need a safe, quiet place to do the actual work."

"Says the woman actively going against said work," Greg said.

"I'm not actively doing anything," Bethany said. She folded up the now finished note, holding it between her right index and middle fingers for a moment as she sent her magic through it. The note lit up quickly, going up in a flare of fire and a puff of smoke. "I'm just sending a note," she said.

A few seconds after she sent the note away, another flash of fire popped up over her desk. A fire letter flitted down, hovering in the air above the heated air for a moment before landing on the desk. Bethany froze, staring at the note for a moment, recognizing the writing on the folded-up piece of paper as her own.

"What just happened?" Dan asked.

"Return to sender?" Greg asked. "What could that mean?"

"It either means she's dead," Bethany said, "or somewhere that magic can't reach."

"That doesn't exist," Dan said. "There's nowhere on Earth that magic doesn't touch."

"Hey," Greg shouted. He moved forward, further into the cube, turning around in the process to face the doorway.

It took Bethany a moment to realize what was going on. Renard's face flitted around the doorway, peeking into the cubicle from the hall. Greg's large form blocked his view of the desk from there, but she quickly slipped the folded note into a pocket of her coat in any case. The last thing she needed was Renard finding out that she was trying to contact a fugitive.

"Conspiring against me in here?" Renard asked. There was a broad smile on his face, which either meant he was joking or that he actually thought he caught them red handed.

"We're actually discussing the case," Greg said. "Enjoy your nap?"

"We'll discuss my unscheduled unconsciousness later," he said. "In the meantime, I've tracked the officemate."

"The what now?" Dan asked.

"The officemate of Carissa Von Strucker, the missing water mage, the one we haven't been able to get a name on. Half the items that were collected were hers, so I was easily able to track them to her. I have a location on her. If the lot of you are coming, now would be the time."

"Um, sure," Bethany said. "Why are we tracking her, though?"

"Because the first tracking was a dead end. This Carissa person was already interviewed and had an alibi. That just leaves the officemate as a potential lead on the pure blood or the air mage. If she is the air mage, we have her. If not, she'll know who it is. Now, are you coming or not?"

"I wouldn't miss this for the world," Bethany said. "Igloo, on the other hand, is a little busy. She won't be joining us."

"Which one is Igloo again?" Renard asked.

Chapter Twenty-Seven
Hole Sweet Hole

Ardith

Ardith gradually came back to consciousness. The light above her was different somehow, like something out of a dream. It didn't flicker, like from a torch, and it was stronger than the sunlight had been through the storm that must have still been raging outside. The entire inside of her eyelids was red, and it was that redness that drew her to the surface.

The first thing she saw when she opened her eyes was the gun pointed at her face. Ardith knew what a gun was, though she had never seen one in person before. She had seen pictures of them growing up, depictions of how guns used to work, how dangerous they were, and still are. Guns were one of those items of the technological world that fell into the grey area. They could very much work in the more magical world, but they were more likely to blow up in the person's face. However, with how close this gun was, it was just as likely to kill Ardith, whether or not it worked.

"So, you're up," came a scratchy voice from behind the gun. Ardith managed to pull her eyes from the gun up to its holder. She was an old woman, probably in her seventies or eighties, easily old enough to be Ardith's grandmother. Yet, despite her age, she was still solid. The gun in her hands didn't waver the least bit. "I just want you to know that this is my home. You are a guest in my home. I expect you to act as such. Do we understand each other?"

"Um... yes?" Ardith said. "Yes, I, uh, I got you."

"Good." She pulled the gun away from Ardith's face, as if her words were sufficient to alleviate her concern over the mage.

"Where's, uh..."

"Your girlfriend is over there," she said, pointing off to Ardith's left. "We have our pick of beds at this point, but they all suck for sharing."

Ardith looked around her. She was in a small room. The door was right behind the old woman. To her right was a solid, cement wall, showing no signs of wear, though it needed a fresh coat of paint. The twin sized bed was practically built into the wall, with the cement blocks coming out to frame it at the head and foot. There was barely enough space to the right of her for the three current occupants of the room to all be standing up together. The place reminded her of the old dorms at The Academy, which no one ever used as living quarters but often used as hiding places and for scavenger hunts.

Dorth was lying down on a bed to her left, an echo of the one she was lying in. At first, the old woman was blocking her view of Dorth. But the woman backed out of the room as Ardith shifted on the bed, trying to sit up. Dorth still seemed out of it, though Ardith saw her chest rise up and down slowly with her breath. Whatever had knocked them out must have hit Dorth stronger than it hit Ardith.

It was the light source above her head that captured her attention the most. The light was too bright to look directly at, but it seemed to have been built into the low ceiling. It was long, rectangular, and a bright white that she didn't think she had ever seen before. Whatever this place was, their magic was like nothing she had ever heard of. Instantly, she thought of all the things, all the enchantments, the enchanted items, that she might find there. Whatever that place was, TS had seemed to have brought her to a gold mine.

"Where's TS?" Ardith asked, remembering that he had been there when she passed out.

"Who?" the woman asked.

"TS. The Scientist."

"Oh, him," she said, humor plain in her voice. "Don't worry about him. He's in the cafeteria. That boy can eat even when he hasn't gone two days without a decent meal."

"Wait, how long was I out?"

"A couple of hours. It hits people differently. I'm surprised it hit him at all; it usually only affects mages and the like."

"What does? What happened?"

"What? You mean you don't know what this place is?" the old woman asked. "He didn't explain to you why this place is so important? What we have in here?"

"Well, no, why? What is this place?"

"This is the last refuge of a lost era," the old woman said. She gestured around her, as if that small room were the perfect example of what she was talking about. "The era of science, the era when things worked the way they were supposed to, the era of electricity and machines, of thought and reason, where myths and legends were nothing but. This is the last place on Earth that has never been touched by magic, and I intend to keep it that way."

"What?" Ardith asked. "That's... That's impossible." She reached for her magic automatically, before remembering that she had been sealed off from it even before coming to that place. The woman's words could be one hundred percent accurate, but she would have no way of knowing until Dorth woke up. "But, why did I pass out then?"

"Because you're not used to it, not used to having no mana in your system. When the pure air was pumped into that airlock, the mana in your system tried to expand into the new space. It's like... Well, what do you know about vacuums?"

"But, wait, the mana coming out of my body made me pass out?"

"No, your body not having the mana made you pass out, dear. Your body was so used to it, it didn't know how to function without it. The low grade of that is just a headache, but, well, it's been theorized that, should the change be drastic enough, it could, well..."

"Kill? This could kill someone? Why didn't TS warn me? Why didn't he say anything?"

"Oh, don't blame him, dear. He meant no harm. He probably figured you were going to come after him anyway."

Suddenly, everything started to make sense to Ardith. Why TS seemed to know absolutely nothing about the modern world. Why he didn't have a linking book or anything other than that old rain rod. He grew up there, or at least spent much of his adult life there, away from the magical world, away from magic entirely. This world, the one preserved in this small bunker, would probably seem just as foreign to Ardith as her world had to him.

Ardith stood up, taking the half step needed to reach over to Dorth. She nestled her ear against Dorth's chest, listening to her breathe for a moment, just to reassure herself that she was alright. That she would wake up on her own without needing help. Dorth's breathing was shallow but steady, reminding Ardith of how her breathing always sounded whenever the two of them were sleeping in the same bed. Ardith kissed Dorth lightly on the lips, half expecting the kiss to wake her from the deep sleep she had been stricken with.

"Where's TS?" Ardith asked. "How long are we going to be stuck in here for?"

"Well, you'll be stuck in here at least as long as it takes for that one to wake up," the woman said. "As I said, this hits people differently. She might wake up in a few minutes, a few hours, I've never heard it take longer than a day to recover. Trust me, dearie, I want you out of here as much as you want out. As for where he is, well, I'll show you to him. We should probably get some food in you anyway. You're all skin and bones. We need to get some decent meat on you."

The old woman backed out of the room and started down the hall. Ardith scrambled to go after her, pausing at the door for just a moment to look back at her sleeping girlfriend before heading into the hall. The woman was already at the end of the long hall before she came out, making her run past several doors to catch up with her. Most of the doors, on both sides of the hall, were open, showing similar rooms to the one she woke up in. Behind her, the hallway stretched out into the distance, only to end at a large, metal door that must have been where they came in. The lights above her head were all the same as the one in the room, all the electrical lights shining down brightly from above, brighter than the sun. She ended up shielding her eyes against that brightness, once again trying to dip into her magic to protect her sensitive eyes, only to be reminded that her magic was no longer available to her.

Around the corner, the hallway split off in both directions. The old woman pointed off to her left before heading that way, but Ardith paused at the intersection for a moment. To the right, the hallway extended even longer than it had from the entrance. She could make out several wide doorways on either side of the hall, leading into large spaces that she couldn't quite make out. To the left were similar doorways, so Ardith figured it was just an echo of what she would be seeing over there.

Ardith followed the old woman down the hall. At the first wide doorway, which she figured was about as wide as four or five regular doors, the hallway practically spilled out into a decent sized eating room. The cafeteria had several long tables, reminiscent of her days in elementary school, before going off to The Academy. Against the far wall was what looked like a kitchen, rather than having the serving dishes and sneeze guarded food stations she was more used to. TS was sitting alone in the middle of the room, in the middle of a long table, rather than at the end like Ardith would have done.

Seeing him alone like that made her realize just how quiet the place had been as they made their way through it. The dorm rooms all looked the same, but they were also all empty. There were only three or four doors that were closed, but she couldn't say for certain that even they were occupied. Other than the four of them, TS, the old woman, Dorth, and Ardith, she hadn't seen even a sign of a single other person in that entire complex.

"How... How many people live here?" she asked, suspecting the answer.

"In the early days, long about when The Arrival happened, we numbered almost a hundred. Now, we're just down to the two of us. It's been a rather lonely couple of days, with him out in the world, you can imagine. You know, it's funny that he called himself The Scientist with you. I mean, yea, in a way, I guess he could very well be the only scientist that's out there now. The last scientist, if you will. The only scientist that will possibly ever exist again."

"What happened to everyone else?"

"Same thing that happens to everyone. Old age, mostly. A few accidents. Michael was the last to go, just this last week. Heart attack. It's kind of hard to get medical attention around here, so once it's your time, all that's left is to bury the body."

"And most of them are buried right behind you," TS called from his table. He got up and, after taking his plate back to the kitchen, came over to the two women. As he did so, Ardith turned around to see what he was referring to.

Across the hall from the cafeteria, through a similarly large door, was a large field. The field was so huge, she could only just make out the far wall in the distance. With the harsh electric lights beaming down from above, it almost seemed like it was outside, but Ardith knew better. The grass grew tall, though brown, and looked like it was blowing in a wind that couldn't exist.

"That's our last wheat field," TS said. "We had two others, down the other hall, and another five on a lower level, but the dirt wasn't meant to grow only wheat and we stripped the nutrients. Unfortunately, we were rather limited in the seeds available. It's not like we could just bring anything in from the outside, not without decontaminating it of magic first. We had some chickens too, even a cow at one point, but it's all gone now. If our population wasn't dying off, we'd all be dead by now." He laughed a little at his morbid joke.

"And this is what you're trying so hard to protect?"

"This? No, this is just what's in place to keep us alive. What we're protecting, that's down below."

"Wait, just how big is this place? Was this here before The Arrival? What? How? Who would put something like this together?"

"Well, long story short, the person who made this place owned the house upstairs, plus the five neighboring it. Together, they made up about an acre of land, give or take. Then there are six floors, the top two dedicated to living quarters and agriculture, like you see here. It's the bottom four that really matter, though."

"I... Well, I didn't actually count how many rooms were back there, but I don't see this holding a hundred people," Ardith said.

"Oh, that, yea," TS said, hesitantly. "Mom likes to say there were a hundred people here, because of the guests below. I mean, yea, there's room for a hundred and twenty, but--"

"Mom?" Ardith asked. "Guests?"

"There were ten rooms along that hallway, for twenty people, plus similar hallways on either side of this floor. The floor below has a similar setup, without the cafeteria. So, yes, we can house a hundred and twenty, though we never had more than forty really. The other sixty are on the sixth floor, but we can check that out later. No, what you'll really want to see is on the third floor. Come on. I'll show you."

None of this made any sense to Ardith, though she imagined that was due to them not telling her everything that was going on there. Even being in the building that he had always been so secretive about, TS was still keeping things from her, including his real name. She noticed that neither he, nor his mother, if that really was who the old woman was, had ever said his name since she woke up there.

TS led the way further down the hall, heading for another metal door at the end of it. Right before they came to the metal door, Ardith noticed the hall branching off, back towards her left. That must have been the other residential hallway that TS had mentioned earlier, though the lights were no longer working down there. The entire hallway from that point on was pitch black, leaving her imagination to run wild.

The metal door dinged while Ardith was distracted, opening up to reveal a small metal box. Ardith figured this was another airlock, a second layer of defense against the magical world outside, though she couldn't imagine why one would be needed. Or, perhaps, they were heading back outside. Despite the fact that she no longer had a headache from the loss of her magic, her body still ached for it, yearned for that power that was no longer at her fingertips. She no longer had any interest in what was below them. She wanted nothing more than to head back outside and bathe in the mana above.

TS and his mother headed into the metal box, turning around to look at her. After a few seconds, Ardith stepped inside, hoping that she would be outside soon enough. When she got inside, though, they didn't turn back around, didn't face the other side of the box. Instead, TS reached out past Ardith, who shied away from his reaching arm. Something clicked behind her and the doors closed, trapping the three of them inside.

When the box started to move, Ardith really started to freak out. It wasn't moving fast, though it shook and clanked as it lowered itself into the ground. They had claimed that the place didn't have any magic, but she couldn't come up with another explanation for the moving box as they descended further down into the complex. After a while, which felt like a small eternity to Ardith, the box stopped moving and, with another ding, the doors opened back up. Immediately, Ardith jumped out of the box, hoping never to have to go inside of it again.

"What was that?" she asked, staring at the box like it was about to swallow her whole.

"It's an elevator," TS said. "You've never heard of an elevator?"

"I've... I guess I've heard of them. I just never thought I'd actually see one. They cleared all the old ones out ages ago, too dangerous to keep them in place in the old buildings. Too many people falling to their deaths. That thing is a deathtrap."

"Not really, not when it's working properly. This one broke down a few times over the years, but they're easy enough to fix. Elevators have been around for a couple of centuries by now. It's the other one that you need to worry about."

"Other one? Other elevator?" Ardith asked. She turned around, feeling like the other elevator was about to gobble her up at a moment's notice. Instead of seeing the other elevator, though, what she saw took her breath away.

The elevator had opened up to a single room, running the entire length of the complex. She could see the other metal door in the distance, the other elevator. But what captured her attention was the wall of stars. Ardith knew they were still inside, still underground, and stars weren't supposed to be embedded into a wall. She also knew that they didn't actually flicker like that, blinking on and off in seemingly random patterns. There was a low buzzing coming off of the wall of stars, filling the silence.

"What... is... that?" she asked.

"It's a computer," TS said. "Well, technically, it's a data farm, but that's really just a big computer with a lot of data space in it."

"None of that made a lick of sense to me," Ardith said. "Try that again, maybe with less sciencey stuff to it?"

"Um, okay," TS said. "Think of a book."

"Any book in particular?"

"Nope, just any book. Your favorite book, if you'd like."

"Alright," she said. She thought of her favorite book, The Lone Mage, which always made her think of Dorth. "And?"

"Now imagine that there was one of those books for everyone in the world."

"There probably are. It's a very popular book."

"Now imagine that each of those books are completely different from each other."

"Then why was I imagining that everyone had the same book?" Ardith asked.

"And that each of those pages in the different books was another book," TS said, ignoring her question. "All of those books, and then more, are held within this one big box."

"Wait, so this star wall thing has books in it?"

"You're confusing the girl," the old woman said. "It's not just books, though, yes, there are books, just not like... Okay, imagine--"

"Alright, enough with the imagining things crap. What exactly is this thing?"

"It's a repository," TS said. "Everything ever written by anyone, anywhere, ever, that was documented is in here."

"So, a book repository? They have that in London now."

"Not just books," the old woman said. "We're talking about all of the internet here."

"What's the internet?"

"She's not getting it," the old woman said to TS.

"Alright, um... do they have plays these days?"

"Sure, plays, they're all over. Why?"

"Well, back before The Arrival there were plays constantly, in everyone's living room. It was called television."

"I've heard of television. I'm not a complete moron."

"Well, every television show, every movie, every play, every book, everything ever made that was stored digitally, electronically, everything that was supposedly lost during The Arrival, that's here, in this box. The entirety of human history, not penned to paper before The Arrival, is stored, preserved, here."

"Oh," Ardith said.

"Yea, and that's not all," TS said.

The old woman placed a staying hand on TS's arm. "Maybe let's not tell her about the guests right away," she said. "They have had some issues in the past."

"Well, I somehow doubt that Ardith specifically had any--"

"Still, let's just keep it there. This, this thing here, that's enough of a reason to keep magic away from this room, right?"

"Well, sure," Ardith said, as the two of them looked at her. "I mean, if there was some way to take that stuff out of here, some way for people to experience it again out in the real world, that would be awesome. But, it's just... well without being able to do that, you're pretty much just saving it all for posterity. I mean, yea, it would be a loss if it just went away, but the world already thinks it's lost and we got over it. I still don't see what all of this has to do with your little quest, though. How does delivering a briefcase solve anything with this? Is it some way to get this material out there in the world again? Were you trying to deliver it here to help preserve this thing?"

"Ardith, what are the two main things we know about magic versus science?" TS asked.

"Magic always wins?" Ardith asked more than said.

"That actually pretty much sums up both points," the old woman said, smiling.

"Magic destroys anything electronic or mechanical," TS said, ticking the points off on his fingers. "And mana decays metals."

"Other than gold and silver and some copper," Ardith said. "Though copper kind of just decays all on its own most of the time anyway."

"If the mana makes its way through the airlock upstairs, or through the metal shell that's around this place, it'll seep into the complex. It'll get down here to this machine and destroy it, along with everything that's stored in it. The only way to stop that from happening, the only way to preserve all of the digital history of mankind, is to stop magic."

"Stop magic? How are you going to stop magic? It's... well, it's magic. It's eternal. Apophis is constantly pumping it out, bathing the earth in it. The only way to stop magic would be to..."

"Yes," TS said. "My quest is to destroy Apophis."

Chapter Twenty-Eight
Successful Tracking

Bethany

Renard was furious. He kept insisting that his tracking spell had worked, that the target, that Carissa's workshop mate, that Ardith, was in the area. Bethany stood there, on the side of the road, watching the blood mage pace up and down the area, desperately trying to pick up the trail again. She held her breath through most of that time, desperately hoping that the man never figures out the relationship between her and his quarry.

Dan and Greg stood on the opposite side of the road from Bethany, watching the two of them with a remote look that somehow bothered Bethany. She felt like they should be holding a tub of popcorn, passing it back and forth as they mindlessly shoveled the food into their gaping mouths. They seemed so removed from the fire raging within her that they might as well have not even been there.

The whole time she stood there, though, she couldn't help but have a sinking feeling of deja vu. She couldn't quite place it, the feeling, the very real sense that she had been there before. What was worse, that feeling only intensified, only amplified, the feeling that they really were close to where Ardith was hiding.

"I mean, I just don't get it," Renard said. He stamped his feet like a petulant child, directing Bethany's attention to the ground beneath their feet. That seemed important to her as her memories struggled to come to the surface.

"Maybe your magic is on the fritz," Greg suggested, only to get a death glare from Renard.

"She was here, somewhere around here, then she just... disappeared."

"You mean she teleported away?" Bethany asked. "You know, us 'lesser' mages tend to have a problem with that, too. Especially when there are no landing platforms in the area."

"No, if they teleported away from here, I never would have come here. I would have sensed where they were when they landed. Even now, the trail leads here and nowhere else. I just... I don't get it."

"How old is the trail?" Dan asked. "Could they still be here?"

"More like how accurate is the tracking," Greg said. "I mean, being able to track someone anywhere in the world, that can't be that accurate, can it?"

"Initially, yes, it's not that accurate," Renard said. Bethany was taken aback by the fact that he was actually addressing the question reasonably, despite him tending to be unreasonable. "But the closer I get to the target, the more accurate the tracking becomes. That's why I could detect where that one merchant was in the sea of filth down in the merchant district." That was more like it. "I couldn't know for certain where he was in there until I was actually down there. This... This is like the opposite. I think I had a better understanding of where she was when I was back at The Authority."

"Well, maybe we should go back," Greg suggested. "Maybe you got it wrong. Maybe you're looking on the small scale too soon and they teleported away as we got here or something. That could happen, right?"

"I guess," Renard said. "But... I mean, it's more like she's just no longer there. No longer exists. It's like magic has somehow lost track of where she was."

Bethany had an unsettling feeling when he said that, an echo of her own issues when trying to send Ardith the fire letter. If the letter couldn't find her and Renard's magic couldn't find her, could something have really happened to her? Could she be dead? Could she have done another strange teleport and it went so horribly wrong that it didn't even register as a splinching? Without landing platforms nearby, would it even be detected if it happened?

Then, something else played across her mind, some sleeping memory from decades ago, something that she had tried to forget for so many years, but just couldn't quite manage it. Suddenly, she knew exactly what had happened to Ardith, she just wasn't sure how it happened.

Standing there, her eyes having gone wide, Bethany struggled to focus on Renard as he continued to pace. She tried her best not to look behind her to the house they had stopped in front of. It had been a long time since she had been there last, long enough for the house to have changed quite a bit with the aging of time. But that month was far too memorable for her to have forgotten exactly where she was. Relief would have come from the knowledge that her daughter was alright. But the fact that the blood mage was so close to Ardith meant that it might not be the case for much longer.

"In other words, it's another dead end?" Greg asked. "Wow, so glad they stuck a blood mage on our team. We're getting so much more done with your help."

"Oh, shut it, earth mage," Renard spat.

Renard flipped his fingers at Greg, moving them in a pinching motion. Greg let out a squeak of discomfort and annoyance before being silenced. Bethany stared over at him, surprised to see his lips puckered out as if something was pressing on them. She figured that was exactly the effect that Renard's spell had had.

"Now, let me think. She's here, but not. She's no longer trackable by magic, meaning she's... She's blocked my tracking somehow. Are we sure this is just an air mage?"

"Uh, aren't we looking for a water mage right now?" Dan asked, raising his hand as if in school. "This is the workshop mate of Carissa, who is known to be a water mage, right? This is supposed to lead to someone who can point us in the direction of the air mage, isn't it?"

"Water mage," he said, pensively. "Yes, I imagine that might actually make a little bit of sense. Water. Okay, then where would she be hiding? She can't be holding it in place, not without accessing magic, so there has to be some container. Is it underground? In one of these houses? A bathtub, maybe? But, then, how would she have cleared away her trail? Or... or did she? You, earth mage, you can track her, yes?"

Greg let out a few grunts of annoyance, his voice muffled with his lips forced together. Renard snapped his fingers in his direction, freeing his lips from the spell. Greg took several deep breaths, his face turning red, his normally mild temper flaring up further than Bethany had ever seen it go. He looked desperately over at Bethany, at a loss for what to do, before turning back to Renard.

"Yes," Greg said, thoroughly defeated. "Yes, I can track her. If she came this way at all."

"Well, then, get to it," Renard said, snapping again. Greg and Dan jumped back a step at the snap, but neither seemed affected by any spells thrown their way. "We don't have all day."

Greg watched Bethany as he came out to the middle of the road. He was clearly hoping that she had some idea, some plan that would save Ardith from the mad mage they were stuck with. Bethany was racking her brain, trying to come up with something, anything. But all she could think of was that this man was going to kill her baby. The best thing, the only thing, she could come up with was the slim hope that he would go into the complex beneath their feet and that it would work exactly like it had the last time she was there.

She was thanking her lucky stars that she had never reported that part of her encounter. Not that there weren't plenty of other events that went into her report. It was a rather eventful mission. A smile made it across her face when she remembered some of it. Greg had been with her that day as well, though they had gotten separated before she had come there.

With a deep breath and one last glance towards Bethany, Greg started to cast his tracking spell. Bethany could feel the power of the spell, though it wasn't as strong as the last time he had used it. She knew that he was trying to hold back, trying to help Ardith escape. But she knew that it was a moot point. Ardith was too close, the trail too new, for the spell not to direct them exactly where she had gone. The only way for them to save her would be to lie, and she figured he would have some way of detecting that if they tried.

"It's... It's that way," Greg said. At first, he pointed further down the road, but Renard's glare never left him, never wavered, and his finger turned towards the house. "That way," he said, again. "Into the house."

"You three are going in first," Renard said. He pointed a finger at them, though Bethany wasn't sure if that was an accusatory finger or if it was loaded. "I don't want to 'accidentally' fall into some trap. I don't trust any of you lesser mages."

"You don't trust us?" Dan said. "He doesn't trust us? Wow, how things have changed. When have we--"

"Shut it, water," Renard spat. "I've had just about enough of the lot of you. Why the captain doesn't just rid us of you all, I'll never understand."

"Because if he actively gets rid of the old guard, instead of just making it so unbearable for us to work there that we all quit, he'll be blamed and all his little plans will come to nothing," Bethany said.

"What's so unbearable about working at The Authority now?" Renard asked.

"Well, you're there," Dan said.

"Your breath," Greg said, at the same time.

"Something about working with the very people we should be arresting just doesn't sit well with most of us," Bethany said. Renard's eyes went wide for a moment before returning to their normal glare. Bethany wasn't sure what that was about, but it probably wasn't good.

"Go," Renard said, again, pushing Dan towards the door to the house. He looked like he wanted to push Greg as well, but the burly man would only push back twice as hard.

Greg led the way into the house, Renard hot on his tail. As Bethany came in, she couldn't help but look at the floorboards, imagining that she could see the cellar through the non-existent gaps between them. Despite the rest of the house falling down around them, the hardwood floors seemed to have held up rather well. Although, they still creaked as the group walked through the house. Dan took up the rear, keeping much more quiet than his usual self.

Bethany bumped into Renard when Greg and he stopped short in the middle of the kitchen. Renard turned around to glare at her for just a second before turning his ire back towards Greg. He clenched his fists as if he were about to actually hit the earth mage.

"Why--" he started to say.

"The trail ends here," Greg lied. Even Bethany could tell the lie in his voice; she knew Renard would be able to as well.

"Greg," Bethany cautioned.

"Liar," Renard spat, venom dripping from the words. "The trail doesn't just end here. It can't. I know it can't because she's not here."

"Who's tracking the girl here?" Greg asked. He hadn't turned around to face Renard, still looking out the back door in the direction Bethany knew the trail would lead. She sent him her silent thanks, knowing full well that the sentiment wouldn't help.

"That's irrelevant," Renard said. "I know you're lying. I can tell."

"Well, if you want to hunt down this innocent girl, why don't you do it yourself?" he shouted.

"Fine," Renard said. He reached out his hand to Greg, reached out his magic, his power, to him. Greg let out a grunt of startlement as his feet were lifted off the floor. Renard swung his arm out to the side, flinging Greg into the wall in the process. "I'll do it myself."

"Greg," Bethany shouted. She went over to the earth mage, who had fallen in a crumpled ball against the wall on top of the remnants of the stove. Her hand went to his neck, trying to see if he was still breathing, still had a pulse.

"Ow," Greg said.

Bethany's relief at her friend's continued life was short-lived as she felt the stirrings of magic flowing out behind her. Renard wasn't as sophisticated at earth magic as he was at blood magic, but he would get the job done just fine. He seemed to glow, to almost float, with the excess power flowing through him as he took over from Greg's tracking. Bethany looked between Renard and Greg, at a loss for which to stick with.

"Go," Dan said. He came up next to Bethany, sitting on the metal pile next to Greg. "I'll watch over him. Go."

"Call for reinforcements," Bethany said. "But from another division, one not already tainted by these blood mages."

"Already did. No one is coming. Something is going on at The Authority. We've been recalled."

"Why didn't it come in through my badge?" she asked. She reached to her badge, feeling around in the spot it usually was, only to be reminded that she lent it to Igloo before they left. "Just get him help," she said.

"What about you, and..."

"Don't worry about us. He's the one you need to be concerned about. Try to meet up with Igloo, work it from that angle. I... I gotta..."

"Go, go, go," Dan said, waving off her concern. "We'll be fine. Go save your daughter from that blood sucking leech."

Bethany ran after Renard, who was already out the back door. As she stepped out into the back yard, it was like she was stepping out into her past, into a memory long thought lost. She could almost see his face over near the old tree, which had grown far too tall and wide to be the same tree. The grass was as tall as she remembered it, but the path around to the side was much more noticeable.

The sound of wood slamming against wood snapped Bethany out of her reverie and told her exactly where she would find Renard. She ran around the corner of the house, down the heavily trodden path, to the entrance to the storm cellar. Renard had already opened the outer door as she came down the stairs. Bethany smiled, remembering the feeling of having the mana drawn out of you that first time. Once Renard was in the airlock, once the air was cycled through, he would be powerless. That would be her opportunity. That would be her chance to stop him.

It was almost poetic starting the new war here, exactly where she was when the last one ended.

However, suddenly, everything went wrong. Instead of closing the outer door, instead of cycling the air, Renard just went for the inner door. Of course, he would. His hands went to the wheel on the door, but it wouldn't move, wouldn't budge. Bethany ran down the stairs, racing for the door, desperate to close it before Renard got the inner one open. If he didn't cycle the air, she would have to. She knew what was at stake, and it wasn't just her daughter that she could lose.

Before she could get to the outer door to the airlock, though, Renard took a long step back from the inner door. He reached his hands over his head, pulling all the spare mana from the air. Bethany felt it, felt the vacuum, felt the loss, as he pulled everything available into his hands, right before throwing it at the door.

"No," Bethany shouted, but it was too late. The damage was already done.

The inner door to the airlock blew in, opening the pathway inside the bunker. Though the mana in the area had been momentarily drained, it flowed freely through the open cellar door, through the wooden house above their heads, through the very dirt around them. Mana flowed out from Bethany herself, only to be filled once more from the world around her. The vacuum of the total absence of mana inside the bunker had to be filled. For magic, much like nature, abhorred a vacuum.

Renard stood in the doorway to the bunker. His bluster was expended, quickly replaced with a stunned expression as he looked between the sky behind him, with Bethany standing in the way, and inside of the bunker. Sparks lit up as each of the overhead lights blew out, the light bulbs, the sockets, the entire system. It was like fireworks were lit off inside of a building, and just as dangerous. When the sparks ended, the entire area was bathed in darkness, the only source of light being from the open door behind them.

Bethany walked forward, her ability to see in the dark snapping on instantly. However, the air was also filled with smoke from the shorted-out lights and other scientific equipment that must have been fed throughout the bunker. She could just make out five forms in the main hallway, with Renard being the closest of them. Beyond that, she couldn't make out much of anything. She lifted her fist, putting just a little magic into it, and opened her hand, conjuring a fireball into it to light the hall.

Renard, now standing next to Bethany, flicked his eyes all around, obviously not having expected so many people in there. Bethany, on the other hand, had been expecting a lot more. The last time she had been there, the bunker was cramped, filled to the brim with people. She looked around at the four huddled forms that were standing in the middle of the hallway.

Bethany almost laughed when she noticed the gun in the old woman's hands. She knew that would no longer work reliably, not once mana had invaded their space. However, standing right next to her was Ardith, her eyes wide as she stared at her. It took her a couple of seconds to recognize Ardith's friend Dorth, but once she did her eyes locked on the fourth individual.

And her chin practically hit the floor.

"Eric?" she asked, her heart stopping.

Chapter Twenty-Nine
Knock Knock

Eric

They had just gotten back from the tour of the lower level. Ardith had been quiet the entire trip back to the top floor, barely saying a word since Eric sprung his plan on her. He was worried, closely watching the girl, wondering if she was about to turn on him. With his mother's gun at the ready behind him, and her locked off from her magic, he wasn't too worried that the small girl would get the better of them. But it was only a matter of time before Ardith headed back out into the world, back out to her magic, and the front door to the bunker wasn't as secure as he would have liked.

Dorth was standing in the middle of the hall, obviously having woken up while they were away. Her head ticked around, as if she were desperately looking for something. Her hands flipped every which way, waving through the air like she was trying to catch a fly. It was clear from the look of sheer panic on her face that she wasn't taking being blocked off from her magic well.

"Hey, hey," Ardith said. She headed over to Dorth, pulling her into a deep hug. Normally, Dorth would lean into the hug, but she kept to her seemingly random jerking movements, desperately trying to reach something that wasn't there. "It's okay, it's okay."

"It's gone, Ardi," Dorth said. "I can't... I can't..."

"It's just some weird feature of this place. It's not you. Your magic is fine. Just relax. Once we get out of here, you'll have it back."

"I can't... I can't..." she said again.

Eric stepped forward, his hand hovering in the air, unsure what to do, what to say to make things better for them. Before he could think of anything, though, there was a whoop, whoop, buzz pattern of sounds coming through the loudspeakers that only barely worked on a good day. Originally, the front door to the bunker had a proximity sensor, though that had died the instant that Apophis arrived. Since then, they had been trying to rig up something of a hybrid system. However, any system they managed to set up only worked half the time on a good day. When the alarm shut off as quickly as it started, Eric wasn't sure if it was just a squirrel or an army at their door.

They didn't have much time to think after that before the inner door to the airlock was blasted forward. Ardith and Dorth were too close, so Eric jumped forward, grabbing onto both of them and pulling them back away from the door. The metal door fell to the cement floor a good three feet away from where the girls had been standing, but the person who had destroyed the door was still standing in the airlock.

The lights above them shorted out in rapid succession, first one by one then all the rest together, as the mana from the outside flooded into what was once the pure insides of the bunker. Eric started cursing under his breath as the four of them were plunged into an impenetrable darkness like nothing he had known before. The bunker had only ever lost power twice in all the years he had been there, but the emergency lights had automatically snapped on. However, those lights too would have been just as destroyed as the rest of them.

Eric tried to make out the person standing in the airlock, tried to see if there were more with him. With only the four of them there, and only one fully functioning mage among them, he doubted they would be able to hold off a full-on invasion. He wasn't sure if that was the intent, or if this was the Mage Authority finally finding him, or even how they found him in the first place. Either way, he knew that he had brought doom down onto the bunker, onto what was stored within it, just by having come back there.

A light flashed out near the doorway, making Eric shield his eyes against it. He may not be able to see in the dark, but that didn't stop his eyes from trying. Before he could see again, a voice came to him from the light. A familiar voice, like something out of a dream, a long-forgotten memory.

"Eric?" it said.

Eric pulled his hand away from his eyes, staring directly into the light to try to see who it was that had spoken. There were two of them in the airlock, a man and a woman, though he wasn't sure which said his name. He didn't immediately recognize either of them, the expressions on both of them vastly different from each other. Eric struggled to remember the tone of the voice, trying to tell if the recognition on their part was a good thing or a bad thing.

"That's him," the man said, making it clear who had spoken before. It wasn't him. "That's the pure blood."

"What?" the woman asked. She stared at the man, startled by his words.

In the flickering light from the ball of fire in the woman's hand, it was hard to tell the colors of their coats, though they both looked alike. Not that it would have made much of a difference to Eric. Any mage would be able to rip through him and his mother easily enough. The only question was would Dorth, the only mage in the group that still had access to her powers, be able to stand up against both of them if it came to a fight. And, from the look on the man's face, he imagined that a fight was exactly what he had planned.

"You... are all under arrest," the man said. His eyes darted between each of the four of them, as if unsure how to handle any of them. However, his distress only lasted a few moments before he raised his hand at Eric, a finger pointed in his direction in an imitation of a gun. "Please resist," he said, a twinge of glee coming out through his voice.

"No," the woman said.

She pushed the man aside. Though she was smaller than him, she had taken him by surprise and he ended up toppling against the wall. Once the man was out of the doorway, she ran through, heading down the hallway towards them. Eric wasn't sure what to expect from the woman and so he dropped into a defensive crouch. He tried to remember something, anything, from the old fighting movies he used to watch. Eric's mother pumped the shotgun, making it clear that she was prepared to use it.

"Mom," Ardith called out. She rushed down the hall to greet the woman. Eric placed a staying hand on the shotgun, though he had a feeling they would need it soon enough. As Ardith and her mother embraced in the middle of the hallway, the man's face came back into view by the door.

"Mom?" he asked, rage filling his voice.

This was it, Eric thought. This was how his quest was going to end, in complete, total, and utter failure.

"Mom?" the man asked again. "You... You knew all along, didn't you. You knew that the mage we were chasing was your daughter. Oh, the captain is going to love this. He was just aching for a reason to sack you. You and your whole crew. They were probably in on it, too. You made an enemy of the wrong people, lassie."

A spark of recognition flickered in Eric's mind when he said that. "You," Eric said. "It... It was you. You were the one at the bar. You... You were the one that tried to help the water mage."

"What?" the woman asked.

"What?" the man asked.

"What?" Ardith asked.

"Yea, you're that red coated guy," Eric said. "Weren't you like Scottish or something, though?"

"Uh..." the man said, his voice dead, his expression cold.

"And I'm the one in trouble?" the woman asked. "I should have known it was you. I should have known the guild would know who you were and put you right in my path. You are not going to get away with this."

"Oh, am I not? Am I not? Really?" His voice seemed to go through a wide range of accents over those few words. "I'd say who would the captain believe, but he's in on the whole thing himself. It's only a matter of time before your precious Mage Authority will be made completely of the blood guild. Unfortunately, none of you will be around to see it. 'Cause you'll all be dead."

A lot of strange things happened all at once. The woman moved to position herself between the man and her daughter, shielding her from an oncoming onslaught that never came. The man jerked his fist back and forth several times, as if it were a high-powered shotgun with massive recoil. However, nothing actually came off of the man, no spells, no blasts, no words, nothing. At the same time, Eric was overcome with something akin to an adrenaline surge.

At first, that's what he thought it was. The fight was on, his life in danger and all that. It only made sense. But it kept building up from there, making him want to run down the hall screaming at the top of his lungs, charging at the enemy. His heart quickened, beating faster than he had ever felt, faster than it had any right to. And then the buzzing started, this low resonance at the base of his neck, working its way up and down his spine.

And, suddenly, he could see. It wasn't just the fireball still hovering over the woman's shoulder, which seemed to disappear just a few seconds later. He could see in the pitch blackness that the hallway had become, his eyes piercing through it better than headlights. It was like there was no darkness at all, like the hallway was open to the sky above or there were spotlights everywhere, chasing away the slightest shadow. More than that, he could feel the very air around him. It sung to him, a musical melody that he had never heard the like of before. Then, other sensations came to him as well, the heat of the people around him, the blood pumping through their veins. For a moment, a terrifying moment, Eric thought he was turning into a vampire, though the thought came from nowhere, with nothing to base it on.

"Not a pure blood after all," Ardith said, her eyes turned towards him. He wasn't sure what she saw, what she was seeing, how she was seeing, but it was something. Whatever was happening to him, she knew what it was.

"What... What is it?" he asked.

"Oh, god," the woman said. "Everyone down. Eric is having his awakening."

"His what?" the man asked.

"His what?" Eric's mom asked.

"My what?" Eric asked.

Immediately after saying that, there was an explosion that seemed to start from inside Eric. His chest seemed to burst forward as the rest of him was pushed back into the wall of the hall. The close quarters of the hallway seemed to channel the blast, sending it out both backwards and forward, out towards the man and back towards his mother. Ardith, Dorth, and the woman had all ducked, lying flat on the floor, just missing the brunt of the blast as it flowed out from him. He could see the blast as it flowed through the hallway, a distortion in the air like a sonic boom.

The entire complex shook under his feet. Eric wasn't sure if that was from the blast, if the complex was actually hit by it, or if he had lost all semblance of stability within himself and it was just him that was shaking. He figured it was probably the former when the ceiling started to come down, blocking his view of the exit and the mage that was still standing over there. The cave in started near the door, but then it was rumbling towards them, filling in and blocking off the hallway. Whoever the mysterious mage had been, he could no longer get to them. But, at the same time, it was likely they would never be able to get out again.

With the women pinned to the floor, their feet dangerously close to the approaching rubble, Eric reached out to them. He wasn't sure what he was trying to do, go to them to pull them up, jump over them to protect them from the debris. Neither happened, though. Instead, as the rocks fell towards them, they seemed to stop in mid-air, hovering over them as if there was some kind of protective barrier around them. The cave in continued, rolling up an invisible incline, only to stop right above their heads. Eric didn't move as the rumbling abated, worried that he had been doing something, and if he moved it would stop.

After a few moments of calm silence, the women all opened their eyes to look up at the rocks floating above their heads. Together, the three of them scrambled forward, heading back towards Eric and his mother. As soon as they were clear, something inside of Eric seemed to relax and the rocks fell to the ground where the women had been lying. The floor rumbled under the impact, but it settled back down quickly enough.

"Thanks," the woman said, patting him on the arm.

"How did you do that?" Ardith asked.

"I... I don't know."

"He's a void mage," Dorth said.

"A what?" Eric asked. He tried to remember back to the explanation of the affinities that they had given him the day before, but he couldn't remember void being on the list. Was that like null and?

"How can you tell?" Ardith asked.

"Oh, that whole thing, totally something my dad would do."

"Not to mention the fact that he blocked Renard's magic back there," the woman said.

"Who's Renard?" Eric said. "Who are you?"

"Oh, ouch," the woman said. "You mean to tell me that I had that little of an impact on your life? You completely changed mine."

"I'm sorry. I don't--"

"Well, it was a while ago. About, say, twenty-two years or so?"

Eric racked his brain, trying to think that far back. A lot of his life had been monotonous, repetitive tasks, trying to maintain the complex and learn as much science as he could. It didn't make for a very memorable life, but a good one nonetheless. His life was dedicated to something that went far beyond himself, far beyond his own desires, though he had wanted to learn as much as he could during his short time on this earth. Tracking the years was difficult enough, what with no seasons and an artificially created night and day. It all seemed to blur together, nothing really jumping out at him.

Then something clicked, a memory of the one time that something did happen, that something very much out of the ordinary came into being. A girl, bruised, broken, bleeding, stumbled onto their doorstep. He had no way of knowing how long ago that was, but if this was the same woman then it made sense.

And, with that realization came another.

"Wait, twenty-two years?" Eric asked. "And you're her mother? How... How old are..."

"Mom?" Ardith asked.

"Ardith, this is your father."

Chapter Thirty
About Twenty-Two Years Ago

Bethany

Bethany eyed the area as she limped her way through the deserted street. The confrontation with the death mage had left her drained and injured, unable to teleport to safety. Most of her team was taken out by that one mage, though she was relatively certain that Greg had managed to make it out alright. Bethany could feel the gaze of the death mage on her back, though she couldn't see him anywhere. She knew that this one liked to stalk his prey before he killed them.

When the rain started to pick up, Bethany was tempted to use the old bridge as shelter, not minding how poor shelter its crumbling form would provide. She was exhausted, incapable of taking another step on her injured leg. The blood had stopped seeping out of the long gash that ran her entire leg, from ankle to crotch, just barely missing the artery. Still, it hurt to put weight on it, and she feared it would open again if she stepped on it wrong. Death mage or not, she wasn't going to make it much further without rest.

Leaning heavily against the underside of the bridge, she tried to pull enough mana into her for a low level illusion spell. She hoped that, if she looked like nothing more than a pile of garbage, the death mage would just run past her, too intent on his hunt to notice his prey so close at hand. Her arm felt weak, stiff, as she tried to throw the dweomer over herself. The lack of mobility in the arm could just as easily have caused the spell to fail, if the mana had flown through her enough to cast it.

"Damn it," she swore silently. She threw her verbal curse into the darkness behind her, aiming for the death mage that still refused to show himself to her. She knew he was back there, knew that he knew exactly where she was. He was just playing with her. Or at least that's what she was convinced of.

"Who's there?" came a call from ahead of her, the exact opposite direction from where she had been expecting him to come from. The new spike of fear that shot through her barely registered over the general din that she had been experiencing since the ambush. "I know I heard something," the voice said. "Come out now, or I'll shoot."

This took Bethany aback. For one thing, the death mage, none of the death mages, were ones to make threats. They acted, killed without mercy, for every kill they witness, they caused, made them grow that much stronger. For another thing, the voice wasn't familiar in the least, wasn't the taunting voice that had followed her from the battlefield.

Bethany peaked out from around the edge of the bridge. There was little cover there, none save the corner of the bridge itself. The man standing in the middle of the street saw her as soon as she saw him. He raised the gun in his hands, pointing it straight at her, though he didn't fire. Even back then, barely eight years after The Arrival, guns were little more than collectors' items. But, every once in a while, one would get a lucky shot off and she wasn't in a position to risk it.

"Come on out," the man said, flicking the gun towards the open street.

The man was a little on the old side, with a long grisly beard that was almost completely grey. His long hair, sweeping out from a wide hat, was completely grey, though better kept than the beard. He wasn't wearing a guild coat, though she hadn't been expecting him to. No self-respecting mage, not even a rare talent, ever tried to use a gun. Still, the man's suit was crisp, well kept, and spoke of money that hadn't quite been depleted just yet. She banked on that meaning he would show mercy to a mage in need, one sporting the colors of the fire guild at least.

Bethany stumbled out from under the cover, going down hard on her bad leg. The smell of fresh blood billowed up to greet her, to surround her, as her tentative grip on consciousness slipped away from her. She could only hope that, should she die that day, she didn't wake up before it happened.

The smell of bacon greeted her as Bethany started to wake up, drew her out of her stupor. Bacon had been hard to come by, even before the war, with most pig farms having trouble finding a new balance, a new order, under the new way of how the world worked. So, the smell suggested that either she had died and gone to heaven or that she found herself somewhere where pigs were being raised. She wasn't quite sure which would have been preferable.

She slowly opened her eyes. The lights above her, reminiscent of an age that should have been dead, startled her and made her close her eyes again. Fluorescent lights? How could they possibly be working? Yet, their low hum, only audible for lack of other sounds in the room, was unmistakable. She covered her eyes, giving them more time to adjust to the light, the brightness that was no longer possible without the sun or a hell of a lot of magic.

"You're awake," someone said, drawing attention to the fact that she wasn't alone, wherever she was.

Bethany hadn't gotten much of a look at the room she was in, though she had expected to be alone. When his voice came, she jumped in fright, scurrying away from the sound. She still couldn't see, her eyes only just getting accustomed to the lights. When she moved, she realized that she was no longer wearing pants, though, thankfully, her shirt and underwear had remained in place. Her orange coat had been draped over her, though it had fallen off when she moved across the bed.

As the room came into focus, she desperately looked around her for some kind of escape. The room was small, smaller than the dorm room she had had at The Academy just a few months earlier. There was another bed across the way and a desk against the far wall. The door was right next to her, but he was sitting between her and it.

The man wasn't the one she had encountered outside. This one was younger, though it was hard to tell just how young. She was relatively certain that he was older than her, but not by much. Maybe late twenties, early thirties. His hands were up in front of him, trying to calm her or defend himself against her, it was hard for her to tell. His lips kept trying to flick up into a smile, though his eyes never showed one.

"I-I-I can't believe you're actually awake," he said, his voice a subtle tenor. "That is so cool. A real life mage. What's it like out there? Is there magic everywhere? Are there dragons? Does everyone have magic or just a few? Is it hard to cast spells? Do you have to drink mana potions to power up?" His questions gushed out of him like he was a child, incapable of containing his excitement.

Instead of answering the questions, Bethany asked one of her own. "Where are my pants?"

"Oh," the man said, his stream of questions instantly stopping. "Sorry. They're gone. Dr. Carruthers had to cut them off to get to your wound. That was a nasty cut. Was it caused by magic? Dr. Carruthers seemed to think that the wound was too sharp or too straight or too clean or whatever to be caused by a blade. Who would want to attack you?"

"Seriously?" she asked, stunned by that question. Where had these people been the past couple of years? Had they been hiding there from the war the entire time? "How do you not know about the war happening out there?"

"War? Seriously? Waged by mages? Or are there humans directing you?"

Bethany flinched at his choice of words, as if being a mage had somehow made her less of a human, not even a human. The term pure blood had been around much longer than magic. He had no excuse not to know it.

"It's not just mages," she said, answering the less offensive questions. "It's the whole world against the death mages. You should be out there too, not hiding out in... Where the hell are we? How do you have working lights? Electricity?"

"Oh, that," the man said, sounding crestfallen by the change in topic. "Long story short, we're in a bunker underground, protected from magic. There's even an airlock to get in and out of here. Nobody and nothing gets in or out, except for Elias. Fresh, clean air is too much of a commodity in this day and age to waste it on going outside."

"Waste it?" Bethany asked. As they had talked, she had gradually gotten over her initial reaction, her initial fear of the man, and had slowly moved back to the center of the bed. She pulled her coat back around her, hugging it to her for comfort, for warmth. "The world outside is important. It's the world. People live in it. It's not a waste to go out and join it. How can... Wait, have you been in here? This whole time? Since The Arrival?"

"The Arrival?" the man asked. "That's what they're calling it? Elias has been calling it the end of the world."

"The world's not over. I'm living proof of that."

"I'd say you should try to convince Elias of that, but that dude is stubborn as an ox. Wait, do oxen still exist?"

"As far as I know," Bethany said. "I don't go out in the wilderness much."

"That's a shame. What I wouldn't do to get some fresh air, some real fresh air, not polluted like in the cities or recycled like in here."

"The cities aren't that bad anymore, not since cars stopped working."

"Oh, I guess that makes sense," he said. "By the way, I don't think I caught your name."

"Nor I yours," Bethany said. "I'm Bethany. Bethany Young."

"Cool," he said. "I'm Eric Salt."

"I can't believe you have to go already," Eric said. He hugged Bethany close to his chest, the two of them looking out over the indoor grain field. The lights overhead were slowly dimming, marking the end of the day in an attempt to simulate the real world over their heads. Elias had designed the fields that way, insisting that it helped the grain grow faster.

"Already?" Bethany asked. "It's been almost a month. The war could be over outside and I'd never know." Bethany hated the idea of her leaving as much as Eric did, but her wound was healed up and she had a life of her own to get back to, out there in the real world. The light mages could have healed her quicker, more completely than the doctor in the bunker. But she wouldn't have been able to get to them without risking being spotted by the death mages that still hunted the area. Or, at least, according to Elias. Bethany still hadn't gone outside since she arrived there.

The two of them had gotten close while she was there. He was the youngest of the adults, with the few children that were roaming around all under ten, all having been born since The Arrival. The bunker was already crowded, with most people feeling like they were living on top of one another, and there was no room for expansion, so procreation had been stymied from the beginning. Still, there wasn't much else to do in the close quarters besides tending the fields and livestock and studying the sciences.

More than the closeness of their ages, though, Bethany rather liked Eric. Despite him being older than her, he was actually rather naive. He had an underdeveloped view of the world and practically idolized the idea of magic, despite the almost ghoulish nature of it sometimes. That duality drew Bethany in, despite her better judgement, despite the fact that she would be leaving.

"You don't have to leave, you know," Eric said, and not for the first time. "You could stay in my room. We could share. I'm sure that, if you helped out in the fields, Elias would let you stay."

"It's my world out there, Eric. I've enjoyed my time here, my time with... But, my magic. I've been hopeless without it. Even now, I reach for it unconsciously, itching at its absence. I've been a mage for more years than I wasn't one... well, more years than I can remember anyway. I'm not going back, not even for..." She didn't want to say it, refused to admit her feelings for him, his power over her. It had a magic all its own, one that she insisted on controlling, despite being cut off from her affinity.

"Well, maybe I'll come out with you," Eric said. "That's possible, right?"

"What would you do out there in the world?" she laughed. "You'd be a pure blood in a world of mages. There isn't much of a demand for scientists these days. Besides, we could never be... Relations between mages and pure bloods... It's frowned upon. We'd be freaks, outcasts, worse than pure bloods. They'd drive us out of town, out of the country, out of the world. And, we certainly could never come back here. Elias wouldn't have it. No, I must go, and you must stay here. You belong here. I belong out there."

"We belong together," Eric said, he begged. He already knew her answer, though, before she could voice it and quantify his impetuous interjection. "For tonight, at least."

Bethany held Eric's hand tightly, kissing it gently with her lips, before pulling away from his chest. She turned around, facing him with a knowing smile. They kissed, lightly at first, then hungrily, before making love in that strange, underground wheat field.

Chapter Thirty-One
The Failing Machines

Eric

"My father?" Ardith asked. "What? No. What... What about Dad?"

"Oh, honey, I met your dad soon after I was pregnant with you. He knows, of course he knows, and he's still your dad, he'll always be your dad, but... well..."

"Why didn't you ever tell me?" Eric asked.

"I didn't know until a month later. You made certain I wouldn't be able to find my way back here. I probably could have figured it out from my mad run towards it, but... Well, I wanted to follow your wishes."

"Screw him, why didn't you tell me?" Ardith asked. "I'm your daughter. I've lived with you for over twenty years. You couldn't have even mentioned a random tryst in the one place on Earth that magic never touched?"

"It wasn't a random tryst," the woman said. Eric still hadn't remembered her name, but he was certain it began with a B. He had always been terrible with names, even in the best of times, though it was hard to forget a name when there were only fifty people you ever saw. "We fell in love. It was just... well... short."

"I asked her to stay," Eric said, trying to remember the details. "I think. Or did I just think about asking you to stay."

"No, you asked. I said no. The war was still out there and I needed to get back to it. The death mages wanted to kill everyone, not just those that they knew about. Not just those they could find. Staying with you, staying here, it wouldn't have helped anyone."

"Uh, not to be a downer or anything, but can someone turn on a light?" Dorth asked. Eric and the woman, Bethany, he finally remembered, both looked at Dorth, neither having any trouble seeing her in the dark.

"Oh, sorry," Bethany said. "I sometimes forget not everyone can see in the dark." She lit her hand once more, pulling forth another fireball that hovered over her hand, lighting the area up.

"I guess that means this place is open to the mana outside now," Eric said, looking at the spinning ball of fire.

Ardith was looking away from them, facing the wall. At first, Eric thought she was just shielding her eyes against the light. But when a muted sniffle came from her, he knew the truth. Dorth headed over to her side, placing a reassuring arm across her shoulders.

"Mom," Eric shouted, when he noticed his mom was still lying on the ground. He ran to her side, worried that he had somehow killed her in all the confusion. It would be such a thing for him to do, killing off the last member of the bunker team. If the others had still been around, had seen him become the very thing they were hiding from, they would probably have kicked him out. In the spirit of that, in the memory of them, he had half a mind to kick himself out. And, if his mother was dead, there would be no one left behind to pick up the pieces of what remained of the bunker.

"Is Grandma alright?" Ardith asked. He was surprised to see her standing over him. Tears were still sliding down her cheeks, though they had mostly stopped. They had been replaced with a worried expression he had never seen on her before.

"Grandma?" Eric asked. He looked up over at Ardith, at his daughter, as it slowly dawned on him. "Oh, right, I guess... Yea, she's... She still has a pulse, she's breathing. Anything more than that I'd have to get her down to the med bay for."

"Which is where exactly?" she asked.

"It's down a level," he said. "And just as exposed to the air outside as here is. Damn it. That is not going to be helpful in the least. Nothing down there will be working anymore. We... We gotta get her some help."

"Well, if the bunker is exposed to the outside, we should be able to just teleport out of here," Bethany said. "I can take her on a ride along, bring her to the light mages. They'll be able to heal her easily enough."

"What about The Authority?" Ardith asked. "Won't they be looking for us? Won't they be looking for you?"

"What were you even doing with that guy?" Eric asked. "Shouldn't he be in a jail cell somewhere? I don't know about your magic laws, but it didn't seem like he helped that girl any. If anything, he probably made the whole thing worse, nearly killing half the people in that bar."

"We were supposed to be arresting him for it, but the higher ups decided to make him a member of The Authority instead. Long story."

"God, you mages..." Eric said.

"Uh, try we mages," Ardith said. "You're one of us now."

"Technically, he always was one," Dorth said. "We just didn't know about it."

"Yea, how exactly didn't you know you were a mage?" Ardith asked. "There are tests for that. Everyone gets examined in preschool."

"Not when I was in preschool," Eric said. "When The Arrival happened, I was... well... your age."

"Oh, ew," Ardith said. "That means when you and mom... Ew."

"It's only a ten year age difference," Bethany said. "Not that out of the ordinary. Besides, he was a bit... socially awkward when I met him."

"I think he still is," Dorth said.

"Wait," Ardith said. "Wait, wait, wait. You're my father."

"Uh, yea, I think we've gone over that already," Dorth said.

"No, he's my father," she said.

"Yea, I... Oh."

"And you already know that Dorth and I are together."

"Yea," Eric said.

"Wait, you're what?" Bethany asked. It was clear that this took her completely by surprise.

"Oh, um, yea. Mom, I'm in love with Dorth."

"And I say all power to you," Eric said. "I've never been all that hung up about those kinds of issues."

"But Dad is," Ardith said.

"Oh," Bethany said. "Yea... Yea, he is, isn't he."

"Sounds like a complete douche," Eric said.

Ardith squeaked with glee as she jumped forward, wrapping her arms around Eric and squeezing him tightly. "I don't even know what a douche is, but I am so glad you said that."

"Why... why didn't you..." Bethany said. "Yea, they don't make douches anymore. But, yea, why didn't you tell me at least?"

"I don't know," Ardith said, breaking the hug. "I just... I mean, with Dad being... well, Dad. I just figured I couldn't. That it wouldn't happen."

"Still might not," Dorth said. "We still have to get by that other impasse. My dad. If I tell him I'm marrying a woman, he'll probably pass a law making it illegal."

"Pass a law?" Eric asked. "Who exactly is your father? The president?"

"Yea," Dorth said, with a slight shrug.

"Okay, there's a lot going on here right now," Eric said. "Maybe let's try to take things one at a time. First, let's get Mom some help, alright? Think you'll be okay out there?"

"At worst, Renard went back to The Authority and reported me to the new captain as an accomplice to you two. That would make me about as wanted as you are. If I just take her to the light mages and get her the help she needs before teleporting away, they won't be able to tie her to me, to us. It should be fine."

"What about the wall of stars?" Ardith asked. "Is it dead?"

"The wall of... Oh, the data farm? I... I don't know," Eric said. He sighed deeply as he envisioned the server two floors beneath him. There was another level of fail safes between the top two floors and the servers, one that should have snapped on the moment that the front door was breached. But there was no telling if that was triggered at all. Or worse, how deep the blast had gone. If the floor had been compromised at all, the mana would have gotten in and fried the whole thing.

Thankfully, there was another level of fail safes between the data farm and the floors beneath it.

"Can you reinforce the bunker at all?" Bethany asked. "Now that you're a mage and all, and a void mage no less, you should be able to pull the mana out of the bunker as you seal it back up again. You won't be able to get back in, not with the airlock gone, but you'll protect anything else that's in there. For now, anyway."

"You say that like I can just wave a magic wand and have all my wishes come true. Magic doesn't work like that, does it?"

"Pfft, no," Ardith said. "But it is more of an art form than a science."

"From what my dad usually says, void magic is more about need than intention," Dorth said. "It'll take time for you to get a handle on your powers."

"Time that we don't have," Bethany said. "Just... Just do what you can about this place. If the lower levels were compromised, you might just need to give it up as a loss. With how mana works, that might be the case anyway. I'm surprised this place lasted this long. I'll bring your mother to the light mages. Where are we going to meet up afterwards?"

"How about the merchant district?" Ardith suggested.

"No, we already tracked you there. We can't go to either of our places either, for a similar reason."

"What about my place?" Dorth asked. "I doubt that blood mage noticed me, let alone recognized me. We can just go there."

"Why wouldn't he have recognized you?" Eric asked. "You're the first daughter."

"It doesn't work like that," Bethany said. "Not anymore. Not since TV ended."

"Yea, I've never really been in the spotlight," Dorth said. "No one even knew at school. No one but Ardi, anyway."

"What about tracking, though?" Bethany asked. "Have you been there since you escaped your workshop? We do need to talk about how you did that."

"Did what? I just teleported. Oh, crap, yea, I have been there since then. We were just there."

"No, but I teleported you," Dorth said. "It'll be my signature, not yours. My place it is. You take Ardi's grandmother to the light mages. I'll take these two to my place and set the safeguards to let you in. Oh, you need the address though. Um..."

She fumbled around in her pockets, looking for something, only to come up with a small piece of paper. Eric would have called it a business card, except it wasn't a card. Instead, it flexed and waved in her hand as if there were a light breeze flowing through the hallway. Eric didn't see what was written on it, but Bethany just glanced at it for a moment and stuck it in her pocket. Something seemed to flash in her eyes when she saw it, like the address was being engrained in her memory. He had wondered how that sort of thing worked with teleporting around everywhere.

"I'll meet you there," Bethany said.

Bethany positioned herself right next to Eric's mother, kneeling down next to her. With just a single hand on her arm, Bethany teleported them both away, taking the fireball with her. It took Eric a moment to realize that he couldn't see in the dark anymore, while he tried to let his eyes adjust to the lack of light again. Whatever power had been granted to him didn't seem to have taken.

"Uh..." Ardith said.

"Don't look at me, I don't know what to do," Eric said.

"I'm not looking at you," Ardith said. "Or, at least, I don't think I am. Dorth?"

"Hold on. I'm trying. I'm not a fire mage."

"Yea, how would that have worked?" Eric asked. "You two being together if she had been a fire mage."

"It's only when you take an aggressive stance against someone with the opposite affinity that it becomes an issue," Ardith explained. "Otherwise it would never come up. Dorth would have a fiery temper, though, if she were a fire mage."

Just as a light appeared off to the side, Ardith shuddered visibly. Eric wondered what she had been thinking of right then, but whatever it was must have disturbed her immensely. She and Dorth were standing next to each other, holding hands, though he was certain they hadn't been when the light went out. He smiled at the thought that they were able to find each other even in the dark.

"Did you want to check anything before we go?" Dorth asked. "We might not be able to get back here again. Like ever. Not if we want to keep this place a secret. Not that it is anymore, what with that blood sucker running off to blab to all his friends."

"Honestly, I'm a little too scared to touch anything at this point. There's not much I can do without risking making it that much worse. If the fail safes worked, everything downstairs is still in place. If they didn't, it's too late to do anything about it. Though, I guess... Well, you don't have your powers anymore, though. That would have been nice."

"What?" Ardith asked. "I can still do some things." She snapped her fingers a few times, as if she were trying to make a small spell work, but nothing happened. After a while, she got frustrated from her failed attempts and gave up. "Or, at least, I thought I could."

"I was thinking that, if you still had your powers, we could flood the upper levels. That would give some extra protection for the lower levels from the mana that's now flooding in here."

"I don't get it," Ardith said. "What does water have to do with mana? You talked about that before, in your plans to..." She glanced over at Dorth for a moment before looking back at him. "In your plans. What does any of that have to do with how tall the great tree grows?"

"The what, what, in the what now?" Eric said, taken aback by her saying. "It's... Well... What do you know about radiation?"

"Nothing. What is that? It sounds sciencey."

"Incredibly sciencey, but not the kind that mana works against. In fact, believe it or not, mana is just a different kind of radiation, one that we had never discovered before."

"Um... okay, I'll take your word for that."

"Anyway, water works well for protection from radiation, mostly because of its density. While I haven't been able to study mana much, mostly because of its properties, we are reasonably certain that it's a form of radiation, something akin to positron radiation but with different properties. If we had been able to study it more closely, we might have even been able to shield our electronics against it, have science and magic work side by side, maybe even augment each other. But, as magic was so... overwhelming, science pretty much, well..."

"Died?" Dorth supplied.

"More like it was exiled from Earth. It's still out there, among the stars, just not here."

"Well, if water will help, then we can try to get you some water," Ardith said.

"How? Without your magic, how are we going to fill this place? I imagine that would be a bit beyond what Dorth can manage."

"Probably," Dorth said. "I'm no slouch at water magic, but filling two floors of what is basically just an underground building seems a bit of a stretch. Especially since it's summoning water that needs to actually stay in here. We're better off trying to get a water mage to do it."

"But it shouldn't be beyond what you can manage," Ardith said. "How about your first magic lesson?"

Chapter Thirty-Two
Lessons

Eric

"Um... okay," Eric said, hesitantly.

"Don't worry. No one is going to get hurt on this one."

"If anything happens at all," Dorth said. When Ardith and Eric looked over at her in confusion, she shrugged at them. "What? Void magic is difficult to control, if it can be summoned at all. Dad sometimes has trouble turning the lights on, and those are enchanted to work on their own. We had to keep extra torches on hand because he kept draining them all instead of activating them. Mom had to turn them on most of the time, and she's a rare talent."

"What's her talent? Turning the lights on?" Ardith asked.

"Nope. Best I can figure it's eavesdropping on my dates, but that's not magical. I'd say she was a pure blood, but Dad would have divorced her if that were true."

"Can we focus?" Eric asked. "What am I doing here?"

"It's really simple," Ardith said. "Here, hold my hand."

Ardith reached out her hand to Eric, who gladly took it. For a moment, Eric stared at their hands, bound like that, father and daughter. He tried to see the similarities in the two hands, despite their difference in size. But he just ended up picturing all the things he must have missed out on when she was growing up. Did they still have bikes? Father daughter dances? First dates where he could threaten the date with bodily harm? Well, that last one had definitely sailed, but she seemed to have made at least a halfway decent choice in Dorth.

"Now, focus on my hand," Ardith said. "Focus on the magic that I still have in me, though dormant and blocked off at the moment."

"How? It's not like magic is something tangible. It's just a power, an effect."

"But it can still be sensed," Ardith said. "There's kind of a flavor to it, a taste. It's like..."

"Cotton candy," Dorth suggested.

"They still have that?" Eric asked. "I figured that would have been one of the first things to go with the loss of machines."

"It's easy enough to make with magic," Dorth said. "It's even fun, swirling the sugar around like a spider web, over and over and around the stick. Can we get some sugar when we're done here?"

"Sure, honey," Ardith said. "First things first, though, okay? Now... Um, TS, um, focus on my magic, the raw power flowing off of me and into you. Can you feel it?"

"I... How do I know if I feel it? There's your body heat, but I'm not feeling much else."

"Here," Dorth said, coming up next to him and taking his other hand. "You should be able to sense both of our powers, one from either side of you, but they should have a different sense to them, a different flavor. You should probably be getting something like bubble gum from me and blueberries from Ardi."

"Nope, sorry," Eric said, laughing a little at their attempts to explain what must have been simple to them. "All I'm feeling is the heat off your hands. Is this something I should be training to sense? Like, maybe have you casting magic at me for me to dodge or something?"

"What?" Ardith asked. "No, that's... That's combat training. We're not anywhere near that anyway, and most people don't opt for that branch of training. I mean, who goes into combat anyway?"

"Uh, we did, just a few minutes ago," Dorth said. "I think if we had taken that self-defense class, like I suggested, we would have been able to do more than just duck and cover."

"Hey, don't underestimate a good duck and cover," Eric said. "It got a lot of kids through the cold war."

"Anyway, just... just close your eyes," Ardith said. "Picture it, our hands in yours, the power flowing through them."

Eric closed his eyes, trying to picture it, but all he got was blackness. "Why exactly is the power flowing through our hands?" he asked. "Is this something you're doing? Can I learn that?"

"Actually, you already are," Dorth said. "This isn't something we're doing, or something we can even teach you. It's how void magic works. You just, normally, draw the energy out of everyone around you. That's why you could see in the dark, not because you're a void mage but because Mrs. DeSalvo is a fire mage. She has that capability normally, just as a part of her affinity, and you drew that out when your affinity was activated."

"I think that maybe this is something I just don't know how to do," Eric said. He dithered there for a moment, his eyes still closed, feeling very much like he was trying to learn how to make his eyebrows grow in a different color than gray. "When I did it before, it was just... instinct, I guess. I was defending myself. Once the blood mage left, once Bethany left, everything just stopped."

"Except it didn't," Dorth said. "It never will again. Once you have your awakening, that's it. Your affinity is active and there's no stopping it. There's just controlling it, so you don't have another awakening, so you don't hurt anyone else with your magic. Being a mage isn't a choice. It's something you're born to be. That's just something you're going to have to get used to."

"Maybe he's blocking it," Ardith suggested. "I mean, he's been a scientist his whole life, right? Magic kind of goes against everything you've ever learned."

"Well, not everything," Eric said. "I mean, yea, the shaping it through your will is a bit much to take in at times, but it's just a type of energy like anything else."

"No, she's right," Dorth said. "That's it. Magic isn't the energy. It's the effect of your will. Sometimes, it just comes down to wishing your way to the results. You're trying to come up with... Oh, what was that thing?"

"What thing?" Ardith asked.

"Oh, you know, that thing. That thing we don't use anymore. What's it called?"

"Oh, yea, that thing," Ardith said. "Um... Math."

"What? We still use math," Eric said. "Math is important."

"Yea, math," Dorth said. "Hated math. No use for it at all these days. Heck, even the credit system is all automated somewhere. It's not like anyone has to balance anything anymore. Credits come in, credits go out. Only thing you even need to count is silver, and we're not supposed to be using that anymore."

"Wait, really?" Eric said. This took him completely by surprise. "I've been using it constantly out there."

"Yea, we know," Ardith said. She smiled over at him, trying to soften the humor she obviously saw in it. "But, yea, it's kind of illegal these days. The black market still uses it 'cause no one can track it. Really, it's as worthless as cash in most circles."

"How come you were so eager to take it as payment, then?" Eric asked.

"We don't generally run in those circles," Dorth said. "Plus, you know, my dad's the president. He could probably just slip the value into her credit account without anyone noticing. Anyway, you can't think of the magic as energy. There's mana around you in the air, there's power, or ability, or whatever in us. You need to take the mana from the air, the ability from us, and your own will to shape it all together in a spell."

"And you actually expect me to be able to do that?" Eric asked. "You guys have been doing this your whole lives. I've only found out I was a mage like... ten minutes ago." He looked at his watch, forgetting that it had broken the moment that the door had been blown open. For a moment, he regretted putting it back on when he got home. But, then, he realized it would have been exposed to the mana anyway, left back in his desk.

"That's the thing, though," Dorth said. "You don't need to practice like we did. You don't need to use your own talent. You draw from us, from our talent, our experience. Everything, all of that, is at your fingertips. You're a void mage."

"What even is a void mage, though?" Eric said. "I don't think you ever really explained it. I mean, earth, air, fire, water, I get those. They're the basic elements, though not the real elements, not the ones we use in science. Light and darkness even make sense, life and death and all that stuff."

"Actually, it's more like creation and destruction," Ardith said. "Death is something completely different. Death is its own affinity."

"Blood and death feed off of those things to power their affinities," Dorth said. "Blood is flowing through them, and everything dies a little bit every day, so those are always the most powerful."

"But what about void? What is void? I mean, I know what it is in math, in science, but I don't get how that translates to anything."

"Well, what is it in math?" Ardith asked. "I don't think I've ever heard of that."

"It's a lack of something, an emptiness. How can you base an affinity on a lack of something? Isn't that like saying I don't have an affinity at all?"

"More like you don't have power yourself," Dorth said. "You sort of borrow it from other people, because you lack it yourself."

"That's... It sounds more like a siphon, a vacuum of some kind. I don't have it so I draw it from other people. Is that it?"

"Yes, exactly," Dorth said. "That's exactly it. Dad draws power from everyone, everything. Most of the time he blocks it, but it just sort of happens all on its own. It's almost instinctive at times."

"Which means, yea, it basically goes against everything I've ever learned over the years."

"Well, then you just have to unlearn what you have learned," Ardith said. "Forget everything you know or you think you know and just feel it, Dad. Feel your way to the power in my hands."

Eric smiled, looking down at her hand still in his. The heat coming off of it seemed to take on a different tone as he practically floated there on the spot. She had called him Dad. Not TS, not The Scientist, not the pure blood, not even Eric. Dad. Suddenly, it felt like he could do anything. Something seemed to go through him, maybe a little bit of pride, of love, of something he couldn't quite put a name to. Whatever it was, it seemed to go away just as quickly as it had come, leaving behind nothing but a small amount of emptiness.

"I missed so much of your life, didn't I," Eric said. He squeezed her hand a little, trying to extend his comfort, his love to her. "I'm sorry about that."

"It's okay," she said, her words almost drowned out by an odd creaking sound from above their heads. Eric figured it was just the earth resettling above their heads, what with the gaping hole in the ceiling just on the other side of the debris. "You're here now, right? And you're not going anywhere."

"Not without you," he said. He squeezed her hand again, smiling dumbly over at her, at his daughter.

"What was that?" Dorth asked.

"Probably just the earth settling over our heads," Eric said. "The house and all that weight finding a new equilibrium with the reduced support beneath it."

"No, I mean... Didn't you feel that, Ardi? I think he actually did it."

"I didn't feel anything," Ardith said.

"If I did anything then where's the water?" Eric asked, motioning around at the unchanged hallway. Another groaning sound came from above and the pile of debris shifted beneath it. A single rock fell down all the way from the top of the pile to the bottom, bouncing several times along the way, to come to rest at Ardith's foot. Once it did, the groaning stopped again. "Uh, we might be in bigger trouble than I was thinking."

"What are you talking about?" Ardith asked. She was looking up at the ceiling of the hall as if she could see through the very stone and the dirt above it, all the way to the sky.

"The entire ceiling might be compromised. Forget flooding this place, let's just get out of here."

"That might be a good idea," Ardith said. "Dorth?"

"Not just yet," Dorth said.

"We don't have time to train him more here. We should get out of here before the roof falls down."

"Yea, no, I agree, but the problem is what happens when we're teleporting away. We should... Can we get down a floor? That should be more stable, right?"

"What are you talking about?" Eric asked. "This place is coming down around us. I'd like to not be here when that happens."

"Except if we teleport away right here, the displaced air might just make things worse. And, if the ceiling collapses from it before we're fully away, we'll be crushed just as easily as if we stayed here. Plus, what kind of protections did the bunker have against people teleporting into it?"

"None," Eric said. "We didn't feel the need to protect the bunker against people trying to teleport into a space they didn't know was there. Secrecy was the only protection we ever used. Now that's gone, and we should be too."

The groaning intensified. This time, it was accompanied by the sound of rock hitting rock as the ceiling splintered further. A fissure started to form directly over their heads, though it wasn't wide enough to see through just yet. Eric didn't plan on being there when it was. He held onto Ardith's hand tighter, holding her close to his side.

"Fine, teleporting away, down the stairs, doesn't really matter. We just need to move." Eric led the way further down the hall, heading for the little used stairwell opposite from the elevator. They didn't get far, though, before the groaning seemed to drop an octave and a completely different sound came from the far side of the hallway.

Eric was frozen in place, staring behind him at what looked like the walls moving towards them. With Dorth right next to him, the small light that she had conjured when Bethany left didn't make it anywhere near as far away as the oncoming wall. They didn't have to wait long for it to catch up, though, as the wall continued to rush towards them. When it played with the edges of the light, Eric knew instantly what it was, though he was kicking himself that he hadn't figured it out sooner. Instead of a wall of debris or of dirt, it was water. Pure water. Magically created water. His water.

"Ah, shit," he said.

Those were the only words he got off before the world around him suddenly disappeared. He wasn't sure what happened, how it had happened, if the water had claimed him and Ardith, his daughter. It didn't feel like it, though. He wasn't cold, he wasn't wet. The ground was no longer beneath him and all sense of gravity, of up and down were gone. It didn't feel like he was teleporting, though. The feeling of the hook in his gut wasn't there. Instead, he felt free, like he was flying, soaring through a dark cloudy night over the ocean, with nothing within view all around him.

Pain suddenly interrupted his euphoria and he screamed loudly. His face impacted something hard, knocking him over to his left, but his foot didn't want to move. Something snapped loudly and more pain rushed through him. There was light somewhere, but he couldn't tell where it was coming from, why it was there. The pain was more important, more present, and distracted him from asking questions he didn't have answers to.

"Dad," Ardith called out to him. "Dad, are you alright? Why did you do that? Why did you teleport like that? That was stupid, Dad. You... You're not supposed to teleport without training. God, your foot. Can you move it?"

"My... My foot?" Eric asked. He tried to look down at his foot but he couldn't see much. He tried to feel where his foot was, but there was only pain. Was his foot still there? Was it still attached? Did he still have a foot to move?

"Just... Just relax. Lie still. You shouldn't move it. It's stuck in the beam."

"What's stuck in the beam?" Eric asked. "My foot... Is my foot...?"

"Yea, I think it's just a couple of toes. You should be fine without them. It might just take some getting used to. That's why you're not supposed to teleport into areas you don't know. Where are we? What is this place?"

"Place?" Eric asked. He tried to look around them, tried to figure out where they were, what happened, how they got there. All he knew was the pain and the bright light in the distance, seeming to come closer.

"Dad, you have to get up," Ardith said. "Someone's coming. You have to get up. We need to get out of here."

"No," Eric said. He knew there was no moving his foot. Whatever had happened to it, he wasn't going to be crawling, let alone walking, away from there. "You go on without me. Teleport away while you can."

"I can't," she said. "My magic is still blocked. I don't have my linking book. You had it. What did you do with it? Where is it?"

"What?" Eric asked. His mind was slow to move around the pain. He reached for his coat pockets, where he last had the book, but he couldn't find it in them. He must have left it behind in the bunker, probably drowned and destroyed by the water that had filled the place. "I don't have it. Where's... Where's Dorth?"

"I... I don't know," Ardith said. The pain in those three words almost distracted him from his own.

Almost.

"Well, well, well," came a raspy voice from the direction of the light. "What have we got here? Looks like a couple of infiltrators."

"They're mages," came another voice, this one a higher pitch, but just as raspy. "Kill 'em."

"Yea," came the first voice. "Looks like we'll do just that."

Eric looked up at the two of them as they stepped out of the shadows to stand in front of Ardith and him. There were actually three, but the third hadn't said anything and was hanging back behind the other two. The pain in his foot made it hard to focus, but the guns in their hands helped to anchor him. Ardith's hand was still in his and all he wanted to do was teleport away, to bring her back to safety, but nothing was happening. He had no idea what he did the first time, how he had teleported them out of there, and no idea how to do it again.

"I'm sorry, Dad," Ardith said.

"Oh, honey, you have nothing to be sorry for." Eric winced as he accidentally moved his foot. "I'm the one that got us killed."

Chapter Thirty-Three
Escape

Ardith

Ardith closed her eyes, shying away from the people with guns. She would have wanted to shy away from them anyway. They stunk bad enough to bring water to her eyes. Her father, her real father, the one that actually understands her, loves her, cares about her happiness, was lying injured next to her and she couldn't do anything to save them. If only she hadn't betrayed him, rebelled against him, then she could have teleported them both out before the guns went off. Even the water that was dripping off of the both of them, water they had brought with them from the bunker, wasn't enough to restore her magic. Then again, wasn't she meant to rebel against her father?

As a loud clicking sound came from one of the guns, she flinched, turning into TS. Ardith had never heard a gun fired, had only read about them in some of the old books they had them read in school. So, when she was still breathing, when nothing hurt, she opened her eyes. She looked between the gun wielding people and her father, looking for some signs that he had been shot. Nothing seemed wrong with him, though, other than the broken ankle and the foot that was still stuck within the cement pillar that they had landed next to.

"What?" she asked.

"Damn stupid piece of crap," said the male gun holder. "I told you we should have brought the shotgun. That one at least works half the time."

"Brian," the woman said. "Go back to the camp and grab the shotgun."

"Yes, mom," said the third one. Brian turned around, running back to the light in the distance.

"Please," TS said, his voice still filled with pain, his eyes barely open. "Please. Just kill me. Don't hurt my daughter. Please."

"Daughter, huh?" the woman said. "Well, you should have known better than to bring another mage into this world. If there's one thing we don't need right now is another mage." She spat on the ground, not too far away from Ardith, the spittle bouncing onto her shoe. "Just as soon as we get our shotgun, we'll be putting the both of you out of your miseries."

"Wait," Ardith said, as an idea came upon her. "I-I'm not a mage."

"Yea, right," the woman said. She spat again, though this time it just dangled in front of her, hitting her on the neck. "We're not stupid. We know very well what that blue coat means. You're a water mage. If you weren't, they would have killed you for wearing that."

"Okay, okay. I was a mage. I'm not anymore."

"That's not something you can undo. It's something you're born to, like evil. The devil claimed you from the start. Only thing to do is to send you back to him."

"Oh, please," TS said with a huff. "You don't actually--ugh." He groaned in pain, his hands automatically going to his injured ankle.

"Don't you go telling me what I think," the woman said. She pointed the gun back at TS, shaking it at him emphatically. "You don't know me. You don't know what I've been through."

"Just like you don't know me," Ardith said. "I was a mage, born to it like you said, but then I broke an oath. There's no going back after that. So, I'm not a mage anymore."

"Okay, okay, you mighta. I got no way of knowing. But, he sure as hell still a mage. And there's no way in hell that I'm taking the word of a mage."

"Here, mom," Brian called out.

Brian was running back to the group, the shotgun carried awkwardly across his arms like he was afraid of it. She snatched up the shotgun before Brian had made it all the way back, flipping the smaller gun over to him afterwards. Brian tried to catch the gun, but it tumbled from his hands, hitting the cement hard. Ardith flinched away from the gun again, expecting it to go off on its own.

"Now," the woman said. She flipped the shotgun around in a weird way, using the weight of the gun to pull on the lever that was beneath it. The gun clicked several times in the process, causing Ardith to flinch at each one. "Let's put this matter to a close, shall we?"

"No, Brandy," the man said. He had been surprisingly quiet the entire time, standing next to the woman as if he were just an innocent bystander, despite his own gun in his hands. "Perhaps we can let them go. That one looks like he's about to keel over anyway. And her? Well, if she's no longer a mage, shouldn't we just let her suffer with that? See what it's like for the other ninety percent of the world? That seems like it would be so much worse than killing them."

"If we don't kill them, they'll just bring The Authority down on us," Brandy said. She eyed the man, though the gun was still pointed straight at the two of them.

"No, we won't," TS grunted. "They're looking for us, not you."

"Who says they ain't lookin' for us?" the man said. "We could be wanted felons."

"We are wanted felons," TS said.

"Dad, hush," Ardith said. She wiped some sweat off of TS's forehead. "Don't listen to him. He's injured. He doesn't know what he's saying."

"Uh huh," Brandy said, obviously not believing her.

"Fine," the man said. "If you're going to shoot them, then shoot them. I'm going back to the fire. It's getting cold out here and I'm hungry. That rabbit should be done by now."

"No," Brandy said. She reached out, grabbing onto the man's arm before he could get far. "That rabbit is for the boy. He hasn't eaten in days. You want him to starve?"

"It's alright, Mom," Brian said. "Dad can have some of it. I'm not that hungry."

"Besides, if you're going to kill them, maybe the rabbit will just be the appetizer."

"Ew," Brandy said.

"Oh, hush. No sense in perfectly good meat going to waste. Kill 'em, don't kill 'em. I don't really care."

"Why, why, why would you want to eat us?" Ardith asked. The idea rolled around inside her head, making her want to vomit. How could someone even think of eating another person?

"Well, it's not like we have much of a choice on the food available to us," the man said. "That's what happens when the entire economy collapses overnight. Of course, you mages wouldn't know that, living up there in your crystal towers, not even bothering to look down at those you left behind in the mud."

"I-I wasn't even born then," Ardith said. "Are you seriously blaming me for The Arrival? Blaming us?"

"Who said anything about blame," Brandy said. "We're just hungry. We're hungry, and you're not. It's the way the world works."

"It's the way the world always worked," TS said, grunting through the pain. "The rich get richer-ugh..."

"And the poor get dead," the man said.

"Enough of this," Brandy said. Without any further warning, she pulled the trigger on them. The gun didn't make a sound, though, didn't even move in her hands. Brandy pulled it back, the barrel rising into the air so she could stare at it. "Dang it," she said.

As she turned the gun around in her hands, bringing the barrel around towards her face so she could look down it, the gun went off. The loud bang resonated around the area, drawing attention to the fact that they were in some kind of an enclosed space. Despite the darkness and the cement pillar next to her, Ardith hadn't known if they were under an overcast night sky or somewhere underground. The echo suggested the latter.

Brandy jumped away from the gun, losing her grip on it in the process. The bullet wasn't anywhere close to her, whizzing off into the darkness faster than anything Ardith had seen, or not seen. The echo hid any other sounds that it might have made as it traveled through the dead space. The gun tumbled through the air, the handle hitting the cement ground hard. Another blast went off, this time inside the gun itself as another bullet exploded without being fired by the gun. Bits of the gun exploded out from the whole, narrowly missing Ardith's face as it sailed past the two of them.

"Dang it," Brandy shouted again. "Stupid guns."

"Maybe the rebellion will have to wait until the mages make better weapons for us to use against them," Brian said. The smile on his face made it clear that his words were meant to be a joke. But from his parents' demeanor, it might not have been that far from the truth.

"Look, we didn't mean to intrude," TS said. "We would have left by now, but, well, I don't know how."

"And I can't," Ardith said, trying to emphasize their hopelessness in the eyes of their would-be killers. "On the run from the law. Perhaps just as destitute as you fine people. More so, perhaps."

"Well--" TS started to say.

"Shh," Ardith hissed.

"Now, now, now, little lady, let the man talk," Brandy said. She pointed at Ardith, using her hand in place of the guns that she was no longer holding. "What was that you were going to say?"

"Actually, I was thinking I could pay you not to kill us," TS said. "I have some money stashed away, somewhere you won't find if you kill us. We'd want some kind of-ugh-guarantee that you're not going to kill us though."

"How much are we talking about here?" the man asked. He used his own, unused pistol to scratch the side of his forehead. "Credits?"

"Silver," TS said. "I'd say a thousand ought to cover our lives."

"Dad," Ardith whined.

"Oh, don't worry. There will be plenty left for you."

"That wasn't what I was worried about. These people are killers. What's to stop them from killing us anyway?"

"Killer is as killer does," TS said, a saying that confused Ardith to no end. "Besides, I already said we'd need some kind of--"

"Take the gun," the man said, holding his gun out to them. "None of them work half the time anyway. The other half of the time, well, you've seen what happens."

"Simon," Brandy scolded.

"Brandy, it's silver. We weren't really going to hurt them anyway."

"Speak for yourself. I wanted them dead. Still do. They're going to bring the law down on us one way or another. At least if they're dead we can get out of here without them followin' us."

"We won't follow," TS said.

"We can't follow," Ardith said. "Look at his ankle."

"Why?" TS asked. "What's wrong with my--ugh." He had looked down at his ankle, seeing the blood as it continued to pour out of him. The flow was slow enough that he wouldn't black out from blood loss, but that might change if he tried to move it. Besides, his toes were still stuck within the pillar and would need to be extracted if there was any chance at saving the foot.

"We'd need a mage, a real mage, to come save him. Please, let me... Let me send a signal to my mom. She's probably worried about us already. She won't know where we are."

"That's a good thing," Brandy said. "She's a mage like you, isn't she, only one that can actually do magic. See? What did I tell you, Simon? They're going to bring the law down on us."

"No, she's--" Ardith's words of denial were broken off by a flash of fire above their heads. She recognized the fire letter immediately, even before it materialized, though the flames continued to expand much further than usual for a normal sized sheet of fire paper. Before the flames had burned out, two more popped up into existence right next to the first. All hope that her mother was trying to send word fled from her mind as the three large sheets rained down on the group, falling on the damp ground next to them.

Ardith stared down at the sheet that landed right next to her. Ardith stared up from the paper at herself, the word Wanted printed in big, bold, red letters across her forehead. The background was yellow, though as she was watching the wanted poster, another flash of fire flitted across the page and the background switched to blue. They knew; whoever had sent the poster knew who she was, knew that she was a water mage, knew that she was out of the bunker, knew that she was still alive.

The other two posters, falling to either side of hers, were of her two parents. Her mom's badge was depicted next to her face, complete with the badge number that Ardith had memorized when she was younger. This was to show that she was a member of The Authority, despite being a fugitive. TS's poster didn't show any background, just the blank off white that came from the generic fire paper.

"Oh, that's not good," Ardith said.

"What... Why are there posters on the ground?" TS asked. "Were they there when we got here?"

"They-they don't send these out for just anyone, Dad. We're... God, we're really wanted right now."

"Damn," Brian said. "What did you guys do? Kidnap the president?"

"No, we didn't do anything," Ardith said. "I don't understand this. We didn't do anything. Why are we so wanted? There are real criminals out there, and they're putting all this on us? Why?"

"Well, I did buy something on the black market," TS said, raising his hand. He over balanced as he did that, though, and ended up falling backwards onto the cement, bumping his head in the process. "Ow."

"Yea, that stupid briefcase that you keep losing," Ardith said.

"I don't keep... Crap, it's in the bunker."

"Which is now flooded with magical water. Whatever was in that briefcase is probably destroyed by now."

"The case needed to be airtight, not just watertight. Trust me, it still works."

"And will somehow..." She broke off when she remembered that they had an audience. "But, yea, I don't... I just don't understand it. At least Dorth isn't on here... yet."

"Well, maybe your mother can shed some light on this," TS said. "I have a feeling she'd have a better handle on the politics of it all. She's a..."

"A cop," Brandy said, pointing down at the badge in the corner of Bethany's poster. She smiled a knowing smile, like she was somehow vindicated by the posters. "Maybe this will work out for us after all. Call her."

"Wait, what?" Ardith asked. "I'm... I'm sorry, you actually want me to call my cop mother?"

"A cop fugitive? Yea, that's something we could use right about now. If she's as wanted as all that, it's not like she can turn us in for a lighter sentence. The opposite is much more likely to happen. Besides, she'd be able to tell us if something were going to happen, right?"

"Um... sure... well... I hadn't exactly figured out how to contact her. It's not like I carry fire paper around with me. Unless, I mean, you guys wouldn't happen to have any?"

"Ha, do we look like we're rich enough to afford fire paper? We can't even use regular postage anymore, thanks to the latest increase in costs there. If you can't even call your mom, what good are you?"

"Brandy, stop," Simon said. "Go get the doc."

"Why don't you send Brian to do it?"

"I can--"

"No, Brian, I want Brandy to. The doc likes her and I'd like to talk to our new guests without her watching over my shoulder."

"Guests?" Brandy asked.

"Guests?" Ardith asked.

"Yes, guests. If we're not going to kill them and they can't leave, what else are they? I'm just going to go over the rules, like no magic in here, no cops, obviously, and you'll have to carry your own weight."

"That's not going to be a problem," TS said, though his voice was weak, barely loud enough for Ardith to hear him when she was sitting right next to him. "I'm used to..."

"Without magic," Simon said again. "We have enough trouble with the mages coming through the area above us."

"What?" Ardith asked. "Wait, where... Where are we, exactly? Is this some kind of old tunnel or something?"

"Ha," Brandy laughed.

"No, dear," Simon said. "This is New York City."

"Or what's left of it," Brian added.

Chapter Thirty-Four
Hiding Out

Ardith

The doc wasn't much of one, not even by the old standards. The old man was barely a medical professional, with shaky hands that could hardly hold a knife. Still, he directed Brian and Ardith in the delicate work of cutting TS's foot out of the pillar. In the end, he only lost one toe, though the doc was worried about him losing the foot if the break healed wrong.

The entire time they worked, Brian was eyeing her in that way that young boys often did. Ardith knew she was attractive, though she never put much weight behind that growing up. She didn't want to be attractive. She wanted to be good, to be able to handle herself and be able to take care of herself. Besides, she really wasn't into guys.

"Why do you call your dad TS?" the doc asked.

The doc was putting the finishing touches on the bandages holding his foot in place. TS was lying on a cot in the corner of a small, enclosed space. Ardith wasn't quite sure where they were, even in relation to the rest of the complex. The entire place was dark, save a few fires that seemed almost haphazardly placed around the area. There was a small one in the opposite corner, barely giving enough light in the small area to see by. Three other cots were in the space, each one occupied by someone, though it was difficult to tell if any of them were there for medical attention or if that was just where they bunked down.

"I didn't really notice that I did," Ardith said. "I... I had only just started calling him Dad. He... I didn't know he was my dad until a few hours ago."

"But why TS? I'm sorry, it's probably none of my business. I just thought..."

"It stands for The Scientist, if you can believe that. He was being all secretive when we first met, not telling me his real name. Actually, I still don't know his real name. Mom said it earlier, but I didn't catch what it was."

"Scientist? Like a real scientist?" the doc asked. "I thought he was a mage."

"No, I... Well, he's... sort of both I guess. He's been... He was studying the old sciences for a while. I'm not sure why or whatever," she lied.

Something told Ardith that it wouldn't be a good idea to tell these people about the bunker. Whether or not it survived the flooding, whether or not the lower levels remained intact, a stockpile of scientific devices, a data farm, wasn't exactly something you told to a bunch of poor people living under a...

"Wait, where exactly are we? How is this New York City? Shouldn't we be able to see the stars? Or light of some kind other than those fires?"

"Well, technically this would be old New York City, the city of old, the remnants of what the city was before the mages got to it. Sorry, no offense. It's just, well, they built the new city right on top of the old, not even bothering to worry about people that were still living here. There's a whole nexus of crystal towers above our heads right now, blocking out much of the stars. During the day, we get maybe enough light to see our hands in front of our eyes. Little more than that."

"Why don't you guys just move?" Ardith asked. "Seems like there are better places out there for pure bloods."

"You would think, wouldn't you," Brian said. "Of course, you would. You've lived up there in those towers your whole life. You don't know what it's like for us pure bloods."

"I've been to pure blood neighborhoods before," Ardith said. "I was in one last night, in fact. It looked normal enough, for pure bloods. People walking around, looking very busy, probably heading home from work the only way that's open to them. Walking."

"And where exactly is this glorious place you speak of?" the doc asked. "It must have been a rather affluent neighborhood to have all that."

"Not really. Honestly, the place was rather disgusting. Not as bad as... Well, it looked like a city. I don't know, I think it was in Panama or something. I... Honestly, I don't spend much time worrying about where I am. Teleportation doesn't work like that, really. It doesn't pay attention to borders or anything. It's all coordinates, altitude, where you're going, what direction, how far, all that stuff."

"Panama, huh? You're not talking about Panama City, are you?"

"Maybe," Ardith said, shrugging.

"Panama City is one of the richest pure blood neighborhoods there is. All the rich people, what we used to call the one percent back in my day, the ones that had enough surplus wealth in gold and silver and gems, items worth trading once all those ones and zeros went to dust. They all sold off their wealth for credits and went to retire in Panama City, pretending their world didn't go to shit."

"Doc," Brian scolded.

"Well, there's no better word for it. The world went to shit. Sure, it's fine for you folk, the new one percent, or the ten percent I'd guess you'd call yourselves. Those lucky enough to have the ability to use magic. The rest of us? Those that weren't rich before this all happened, but weren't exactly poor either. All of us had a sudden wakeup call. So many people died of starvation that first year alone, just because the food could no longer get around from place to place. Linking books hadn't been invented yet, so we were stuck in places like this. And places like this just got paved over by the crystal towers. Even if we wanted to leave here, it would be on foot, and all the bridges were broken by your towers, all the tunnels caved in. We're as stuck here as we are in our station in life. Still think the world hasn't gone to shit?"

"Except... I mean, what about climate change, the growing divide between classes, between ideologies?"

"And you don't think that's still around? Sure, climate change may have been fixed. I'm not sure about that. We don't get out much. But magic has been so much more of a disaster than climate change ever was. If it was only a certain kind of person, the right kind of person, the kind that would use it for good, the betterment of mankind, maybe, just maybe, magic would have been a good thing to come to the world."

"But, then, with its impact on science, probably not," Brian said. His words seemed flat, over-rehearsed, like they didn't belong to him. Brian was younger than Ardith was, so he wouldn't have remembered what it was like before any more than she could. Surrounded by some of the pure bloods that got hit the hardest by the change, it was no surprise that he would be a little bitter in all of that.

"Well, maybe if you actually got out there, weren't just stuck down here, you'd see how amazing everything is."

"Everything was already amazing; it was just in the way you saw the world. Besides, it's not like the mages are going to go around handing out linking books to us."

"Really? Why not. They're not that expensive. A couple hundred credits a piece, last I heard."

"It might as well be a couple hundred thousand. We're not getting that kind of money and they aren't giving it out to all of us. There's billions of us, that's billions with a b, little missy. Mages aren't about to spend billions of credits on us, just to let us get around easier. Besides, that money would be better spent on food, better housing, stuff we could actually use. Magic might as well just go away for all I care about it."

"Yea," Brian cheered.

Ardith looked down at her father. He had fallen asleep from the pain at some point while they were moving him from the pillar. His brow was furrowed, an echo of the one Ardith would often get when she was trying to concentrate. Even in sleep, he seemed determined, motivated, hell bent on getting his quest done. Now that Ardith knew what that quest was, she wasn't sure if she wanted to help him anymore. It wasn't like her magic would come back if he did. If he succeeded, no one would ever have magic again. And, yet, if these people knew, if they had known what his quest was, they would have celebrated, tried to help him in any way they could, given anything, everything they had to do it. Even if it meant their lives.

And if The Authority knew about it, about where they were, it might very well mean their lives.

The three posters were folded up and stowed in a deep pocket of her coat, along with a few remnants of failed experiments long forgotten and a couple of her address cards. The only people that had seen the posters were Brian and his parents, and she intended to keep it that way. Most of the people there were keeping to themselves, but that would change quickly enough if they knew. She just had to find some way to get out of there, to get word to her mom and Dorth and get a one-way ticket out of the city.

"Anyway, he should be fine," the doc said. He patted TS's injured foot lightly. TS jerked in his sleep from the pain, but he didn't wake up. "You mages are made of some strong stuff, otherwise we would have taken our world back a long time ago."

"Yea," Ardith said, smiling at the boast.

The doc headed off to one of the other people in the room, leaning over them like he had TS. There weren't any noticeable injuries on the other person, but that didn't mean they didn't need his help as much as her father had. It seemed archaic to her to leave her father in the care of this man, but it wasn't like she had many choices. Her grandmother was hopefully well on the mend with the light mages, but TS wouldn't have that option. They were already hunting him to the ends of the earth, and that was before they knew what he was after.

"So, your dad's a scientist?" Brian asked.

Ardith jumped a little at his words, forgetting for a moment that the boy was even there. "Yea," she said, shrugging. "At least, that's what he keeps telling me."

"Cool. Maybe he could help with... things."

"Things? Is that code for something specific?"

"What? No, no. I'm not. No, there's nothing to tell."

"Oh, relax, Brian. It's not like we have anyone to tell your secrets to. Besides, you guys have already been so nice to us."

"We pointed guns at you. Tried to shoot you."

"Yea, and then you helped me get my father out of that pillar. You didn't have to do that. You could have just left us there to die."

"Dad said you would have made too much noise if we did," Brian said. "Would have brought The Authority down on us. Nobody wants that."

"Well, The Authority does know you're here, right?" Ardith asked. "I mean, they checked before building the towers, right?"

"I... I'm not supposed..." He looked over at the doc, but the old man seemed oblivious to their conversation, oblivious to his discomfort.

"Anyway, I guess it doesn't matter," Ardith said. "You're here. There's no way for you guys to get out, according to the doc at least. Seems like you guys are as trapped here as we are."

"Yea, you can say that again," Brian said. He rolled his eyes. "I'm like the youngest kid here, too."

"What? How is that possible? You're like almost my age."

"I'm fifteen, actually," he said. "I just look older. Dad says it's the hard living. Nobody is making babies these days. Food is too scarce already."

"How... How many people are down here?"

Brian shrugged. "A couple hundred, I think. Like the doc said, most died of hunger. Those that could leave, did, early on. I don't know why my mom and dad didn't. They never told me. But I think it's because of the trains."

"The trains?" Ardith asked. She wanted to ask what a train was; she thought she remembered something about them from books, but they never actually explained what they were or what they did. It was something about transportation or something like that. All she knew was that they were much slower than teleportation. She had quickly lost interest in the idea after that.

"Oops," Brian said.

"Don't worry. I won't tell." She winked conspicuously at him, smiling a little.

"Well, the trains used to run on and off the island all the time. People used them more than they used the bridges or tunnels. I think Dad use to run them himself. He thinks he can get them running again, take us all out of here and back to the world that was."

"Brian, that's... That's never going to happen. The world that was doesn't exist anymore. Even if it did... There's no way your dad can get an old machine to work. Not while... Not while magic rules this world."

"I know," Brian said. "I know. Mom keeps telling him that, but he doesn't give up on it. Maybe, once your dad gets better, he could help."

"Sure," Ardith said, smiling. "Sure, Brian. I'm sure he could help."

"What about your mom?" Brian asked. "She's a..." He trailed off, looking behind him at the other people in the room, before turning back to Ardith. He mouthed the word cop, which Ardith could barely see in the low light. "What's that like?"

"I don't know," Ardith said, shrugging. "She's always been one, for as long as I could remember. I don't really have anything to compare it to. It's fine, I guess. Not like in the old days, at least from what I've read. It's a whole lot less dangerous."

"Really? Dad always says magic makes everything more dangerous."

"No, that can't..." Ardith trailed off as she remembered everything that she had been through those past few days. She had mostly been blaming her father for it. But looking back she realized that most of it was caused by magic. Or at least escalated by it. Now that she didn't have her magic anymore, now that she was less than a rare talent, she was in the same boat as those people there. Would she really be that better off than them? Even if she was able to clear up her legal problems, which were seeming less and less likely, would she ever find any sense of normalcy again?

"See?" he asked, obviously taking her silence as his victory. "Trust me. Once Dad gets the machines working again, there is going to be a reckoning like the world has never seen before. The mages will fall, at least the ones on the wrong side of the war. Maybe you and your family will help out, eh?"

"TS probably would," Ardith said, nodding. "If he makes it."

"Oh, he'll be fine," the doc said. He was suddenly over in the far corner, tending to yet another patient, but the close quarters made it impossible for them not to be overheard. "It's just the foot I'd be worried about. Not much you can do about it, though, so you might want to just get some rest. I'll wake you up if we need you."

"Sleep?" Ardith asked. She wasn't sure when the last time she slept was, other than the few hours that she was passed out in the bunker. "That-that might be a good idea. Where can I... Is there a cot free somewhere?"

"Probably not," Brian said. "Usually when people die, they die in their cots. The doc always makes us burn the cots with the bodies."

"It's only sanitary," the doc said.

"Plus, when wood gets scarce, they're the first things to go. I've been on the floor most nights. It's not that bad."

"The floor?" Ardith looked down at the cement floor beneath her with a level of disgust she usually saved for rare talents... or Carissa. It was marbled in rather conspicuous shades of red, yellow, and brown. She didn't even want to be sitting on it, let alone lying on it. "Maybe somewhere outside?"

"I think you'll be hard pressed to find a more sanitary piece of ground than my clinic," the doc said. "Every time the scavengers come back with bleach, at least some of it ends up on this floor. You could eat off of it... Well, if you had food. Then again, don't."

"Yea, I don't think that's a good idea," Ardith said, turning her nose up at the thought. She had to admit, though, compared to eating off it, lying down on the floor didn't seem so bad. Absentmindedly, she reached for her affinity, meaning to wash the floor clean with a blast of water. Her loss hit her all over again when she realized that she couldn't, that the part of her that once was able to do that was no longer there. It was like a hole in her very heart, one that could never be filled. It reminded her of when her gran died when she was six. It was like someone had died, like a part of her had died.

"Anyway, if you're going to bunk down in here, I should probably get going," Brian said. "Mom and Dad are probably wondering where I am right now as it is. It's gotta be after midnight."

"It's barely nine," the doc said. "But, yes, you should move along now."

"I'll see you tomorrow, yea?" Brian asked.

"Sure," Ardith said. "I guess." If she didn't manage to find a way to send a message to her mother.

Brian gave a short nod before getting up from the floor. Ardith stretched out her legs, filling in the space that he had been in. Instead of lying straight down on the floor, she scooched over so that she was leaning against the wall. The wall seemed considerably less soiled than the floor, and that would keep her hair away from much of it. Her coat, spread out over her like a blanket, could protect her from most of the rest of it.

She barely closed her eyes, barely dozed off, when she heard her name being called.

"Ardith," Brian shouted. "I think you're going to want to come see this."

"You're going to want to come see this cliché," the doc muttered.

"Oh, what now?" Ardith asked.

Slowly, she managed to shake away the growing fatigue as she pushed herself back up onto her feet. The small room only had the one door, leading out to a large building that was mostly in ruins. The one hall led out to a large entryway, with a grand marble staircase leading down from a higher floor. The railing that must have once been on the staircase was long gone, probably melted down for the raw metal. The place had a feel to it that suggested that someone had been trying too hard to make it look more grandiose than it was.

Brian was standing by the far wall, or what was left of it. There was a frame that must have once held glass windows. There would have been enough to satisfy what TS had planned to do with it, except they were all long gone. Out beyond that was the road, the main part of the city, which she hadn't seen much of as she came through there. However, as she looked out into the night past Brian, she could see quite a lot of it. The torchlight coming from the mob made it seem like day.

"Um, hi," Ardith said, waving at the crowd.

"Bring them out," someone called from the crowd.

"Yea," the crowd called.

"Bring them out," another voice called, garnering the same response. The chant was repeated several times as Ardith stared out at the crowd. As few people as Brian had said lived there, they all seemed assembled at their doorstep.

Ardith wanted to ask Brian who they meant, wanted to go over to him to get a better look at the crowd. But before she moved an inch, a flash of brown caught her eye. Someone in the crowd was pumping their fist in the air, clasping a poster in that hand. Most of the poster was crumpled up, blocking out much of it, but enough was visible for Ardith to know exactly what it was. Of course, she shouldn't have been surprised that The Authority had sent more than one set of the wanted posters into Old New York.

"Crap," Ardith said, lengthening the word so that it was stretched over several syllables. "How do they know we're in here?"

"We don't get many visitors," Brian said. "Word travels fast."

"Crap," Ardith said, again.

Chapter Thirty-Five
Mob Mentality

Ardith

Ardith left the front of the building, the mob still calling for her surrender. As she came back through the hallway, she laughed a little as an errant thought passed through her head. The Authority wanted them captured for some reason, though she had no idea what it was. However, the one reason why they should have wanted them dead was definitely not it. TS was working to take away magic, but no one knew that besides her. On the other hand, the mob outside would have wanted that exact thing, yet they were just as determined to see the two of them turned over to The Authority. She wondered for a moment, just a moment, if they should confide in these people about their quest.

"What's going on?" the doc asked.

"We need to wake up TS," Ardith said. She came over next to her father, giving him a light jab with her foot in an attempt to wake him. He didn't move, didn't so much as grunt, from her kick. "We need to get out of here."

"He's out cold. That's a good thing. He needs rest to recover from the injury. If he's going to at all. I've never been teleported inside solid rock, not even partially, but I imagine it hurts a lot."

"Not as much as an angry mob pulling us apart limb from limb. We need to get out of here before they come in."

"I'm not sure why they haven't," Brian said. Ardith jumped at his voice, half expecting him to be accompanied by the crowd outside. "The windows were blown out ages ago. Nothing is stopping them from coming in here."

"They wouldn't dare," the doc said. "They know that they'll never get medical treatment again if they do. Not if they encroach on my territory. They won't come in here, not for a few hours at least. However, you're also not getting out of here. That's another reason why you should just let your father sleep."

"No, you don't understand, he's the only one of us who has... I mean, he doesn't know how to use it, but he still has it. We need to teleport out of here, or at least reach someone who can teleport us out of here. My mom or my girlfriend or... Hell, I'd even go for my father at this point."

"Your father?" the doc asked, confused.

"Your girlfriend?" Brian asked, disappointed.

"My... My stepdad, I guess you could call him. The one that raised me. TS... I only just met him."

"Well, I wouldn't know how to reach anyone outside this place, but I'm no mage. Maybe your father would have some idea on it, but, well, you said he doesn't really know how to use his powers just yet?"

"No, but I do. I just have to figure out some way to get him to understand. Well enough to actually do it, at least. God, if we only had just a scrap of..." She trailed off as she thought of something that might actually help. Something that she had that she might, just might, be able to use to send a message.

Ardith pulled out the pile of posters. With the mob outside knowing that they were all wanted, she didn't bother with secrecy or subtlety, tossing the three posters across TS's sleeping body. Normally, when a fire paper was sent off, the magic that was ingrained in the paper itself would be used up. However, with the posters, there had to be some low level power still within it. Otherwise, they wouldn't be able to update the posters for when the fugitives were inevitably caught.

She froze in place for a moment, her hand hovering over her own face, as that thought played out in her head. In all the years, growing up in the same house as her mother, she never once heard of a fugitive surviving on the run for more than a few hours once the posters had been sent out. Greg, one of her mother's coworkers, often had a pool going for how long the fugitives could stay out there without being caught. He, no doubt, would be doing a similar thing for her own case. No one ever bothered betting on anything more than twenty-four hours, because no one had ever made it that long. What made her think she would be the exception to that? It's not like she was some master criminal.

"You okay?" Brian asked. His words shook her from her fear, allowing her to turn back to the posters and the matter at hand.

The problem with the posters, though, was that the background of the portraits ran to the edge of the posters. Every inch of the paper was being used with the original message. There wasn't any way to redirect just part of the paper to her mother. But then she remembered, she noticed, that her father's poster didn't have a background. Either they didn't know he was a mage or simply didn't know what his affinity was. Then again, she wasn't quite sure what color belonged to the void mages. They've never even used their guild hall; it was blank and empty, built more out of symmetry than anything else.

Ardith tore the smallest shred of the paper along the edge of the poster, trying to stay as far away from the original message and the dweomer that still stayed on it. She had to hope that enough of the base paper still had the original spell worked in it to send one last message. Once that was done, she looked around for a quill, fumbling around in her pockets though she already knew that she didn't have one.

"Damn," she said. "Got any quills in this place?"

"No," the doc said. "We don't really have much to write these days, so we don't bother with that stuff. Besides, we're not likely to find one around here. All we have is what we can scrounge from good old New York City. The real one, the old one, the one that existed before all of that stuff upstairs."

"God, I need something, anything to write with. I mean, Mom had this way of writing on these things with just a dry quill, but I never quite figured out that part. Besides, I'd still need a quill. Something. Anything. Heck, I'd write in my own blood right now if it means we can get out of here already."

"Oh, actually, now that you say that, I might have something you could use." The doc held up a finger towards Ardith as he headed over to the cabinet that stood next to the fire. He fumbled around inside for a moment before coming out with something. It was long, thin, and pointy, with some kind of tube attached to it. Ardith had never seen anything like it before. "Be careful," the doc said. "It's dirty. Maybe you might not want to stick yourself with it, but it should work to hold the blood. A bit awkward to write with, though, I'd imagine."

"What the hell is that?" Ardith asked, staring at the thing, half expecting it to bite her even from across the room.

"What? You've never seen a needle before? Don't they still vaccinate kids these days?"

"Vaccinate?" Ardith asked, playing the unfamiliar word around in her mouth. "Nope, sorry. Doesn't ring a bell."

"Well, this area here can hold a liquid, coming out through the needle here. You can pull back on this plunger to pull the liquid in, push it to squirt it out. If you're careful, you could probably get enough blood in the needle to write your message. But, well, with a paper that small, you shouldn't need much ink anyway."

"So, I just stab it in?" Ardith asked. She came over to the doc, holding her hand out for the needle.

The doc pulled the needle away from her, holding it close to his chest like it was somehow precious. "What? No. I just said it was dirty. Are you insane?"

"Uh, okay, can we clean it then? We don't have a lot of time. That mob outside isn't going to be patient for much longer."

"Just... Unfortunately, I don't have a scalpel to let you use to cut yourself. We would need to get the blood flowing first, then use the needle to pull the blood, after it's outside of you, and clean the wound fully after that. Science may not be with us anymore, but I somehow doubt diseases have just disappeared from the world."

"Ugh, biology," Ardith grunted. "The only ology that still ologies. Fine, do we have something sharp I can cut myself with?"

"It's too bad your dad's wound isn't still bleeding," Brian said. "There was plenty of blood on the floor where we picked him up from."

"That wouldn't... He wouldn't... Doc? Can we somehow restart the blood flow? Just a little?"

"That's not a good idea," the doc said. He went a little pale around the face at the very idea of that. "His injuries were already pretty extensive. It might cost him the foot."

"You already said he might lose the foot if we don't get him proper help. Now, if we can't get him out of here, he'll lose a lot more than just a foot. We need to get my mom here, fast, and there's little else in options right now."

"Fine, fine, fine," the doc said. He finally passed Ardith the needle before heading back over to TS's side. "But let me do it. That way at least I can help reduce the risk of it all."

Ardith watched from over his shoulder as the doc gradually unwrapped TS's ankle. The ankle didn't look good, still not quite reattached to the rest of his leg. It seemed to her that he should have been further along in the mend by then. The doc left the supports around the ankle in place, and some of the bandage that was still holding them there. His head blocked her view as he examined the injury. She figured he was trying to see why he wasn't healing faster, but he didn't say anything. With a quick, targeted dab of his finger, a small squirt of blood shot out of TS's ankle. Ardith moved to catch the squirt with the needle, but it went by too fast and ended before she even saw what he was doing.

"Here," the doc said. He stood up, his hand cupped awkwardly. Inside the cupped hand was a small pool of blood. "Make sure not to stab me while you get the blood in the needle."

"Umm... sure," she said, looking between the small pool of blood and TS's mangled ankle. She quickly stuck the needle in the small pool, being extra careful not to stick it in too far. There wasn't much blood to pull, but it seemed to fill more of the needle than she expected.

"Great," he said. "Now get your note done while I redo these dressings. Then I'll have to wash my hands very thoroughly, using resources that didn't come easily to us."

"Don't worry," Ardith said without looking at him. "Once this whole thing is over, we'll make sure your people get the resources they need, maybe even get everyone out of here... Well, maybe not the mob. That's just rude, calling people out like that and all."

While the doc started to tend to her father again, Ardith took the small scrap of paper over to the cabinet. It was too tall for her to use the top of it, but the side was a better, smoother surface than anywhere else in the room. The doc was right about how awkward writing with it was. After several false starts, where she wasted over half the paper she managed to rescue, she was able to get in the words "under NYC" on the last bit of paper before she ran out of both. She just had to hope that would be enough to let them track her down.

"Now to just get this to send," she said to herself.

Ardith held the small scrap of fire paper in her hand, blowing on it softly as she thought of her mother. She tried to put a little bit of her own power into it, figuring that would help things along. That only reminded her once more that she no longer had access to it. Unfortunately, it quickly became clear that the paper didn't have enough power in it either. It shimmered a little along the edges, but stayed in her hand.

"Damn it," Ardith yelled. The patient that was lying next to her jumped in his bed, almost falling out of it in the process. "Sorry. Sorry."

"It's not working?" the doc asked. "Anything I can do to help things along?"

"No. What? No, there's nothing... Now I really need him awake... Or... or do I?"

Ardith came over to her father, standing next to his head. He seemed so lost, so innocent, just lying there, oblivious to the crowd outside calling for his surrender, his arrest, his possible death. There was no way The Authority wouldn't have him executed for trying to do what he was trying to do, for purchasing whatever it was in that briefcase that could destroy Apophis. And yet, as he slept, he was the only chance they had of getting out of there.

She flipped over his hand, holding it closely to her. His hand was clenched from the pain, even in sleep refusing to let it get the better of him. It took some doing to open the hand, to lay it flat out in hers. Once that was done, she carefully placed the sheet of paper in his hand, hoping that he wouldn't try to close it again and crush the paper. With every ounce of her will, she poked and prodded at the place within herself where her power once was, still was, though blocked off from her. She pushed at it, willed it into TS's hand and, through it, into the small piece of paper that possessed all their hopes. Then, once she was relatively certain that some power had flown through them, even though she could no longer feel it, she blew on the paper once more.

At first, nothing happened and Ardith started to fear, started to dread that it wasn't enough. That she wasn't enough. That she would never be enough again. Forget being with Dorth, she wasn't good for anything, not without her powers. Then, the paper started to flicker again, the same level of shimmering as before, just a flicker along the edges. But, this time, it grew, it continued to flow inward, like little threads, the veins in a leaf. Finally, with one last blow of air from her lips, the small piece of paper lit up, consuming itself in a fire high, tall, powerful. And, then, it was gone.

"That's it," she said. "It's away."

As soon as she said those words, there was a loud bang from outside the door. The screams from the crowd, which had just barely been audible to her in that back room, suddenly got louder. Obviously, the crowd had lost its patience. They no longer cared about the sanctity of the doc's workroom. They were not taking no for an answer.

"They're coming," Brian said. He slammed the door, putting his back against it to brace it for the coming attack. "We're going to die in here aren't we?"

"You're not," Ardith said. "Not if you get away from the door. You shouldn't try to draw their attention. There's still a way for you to get out of this alive."

"If I get away from the door, they're going to come in."

"They're going to get in anyway. It's only a matter of time. Once they do, you run, get away from us. There's no sense in you going down with us."

"That's funny," the doc said. He was holding one of the posters that Ardith had left on the bed, though she couldn't see which one. "This doesn't say what you did. It also doesn't say whether or not they want you alive."

"I don't really think the angry mob outside cares much about that," Ardith said. "We're mages. They're pure bloods. They'd want our heads just over that."

"What about us?" Brian asked, pointing between himself and the doc. As he did, something hit the door hard, pushing him away from it. He quickly got back into place, putting his legs against the nearby cot for better support.

"Oh, please, your mom tried to shoot us, twice. It wasn't her fault the gun didn't go off."

"But, I didn't," Brian said, his words falling short.

"You got the second gun," Ardith accused. "If we hadn't met before the posters came, you'd probably be out there with the rest of them. Dorth was right."

"What was I right about?" Dorth's voice seemed to come out of nowhere as the air suddenly pushed past her. Ardith turned, staring, smiling, at her girlfriend standing over by the cabinet. Her mom arrived right after it, just barely avoiding splinching herself on the patient that Ardith had disturbed earlier.

"Oops," she said. "Sorry. Wow, this place is small."

"What, how?" Ardith asked, surprised they had gotten there so fast.

"We were already upstairs," Dorth said, pointing up at the ceiling. "That city is a madhouse right now. The entire blood guild is out looking for you guys. You're like public enemies one, two, and three for some reason."

"You mean you don't know either?" Ardith asked.

"Oh, your mom tried to explain it to me, but none of it made sense. Something about office politics."

"The blood guild is trying to take over The Authority," Bethany said, simply.

"See? She just keeps saying things like that. How does them wanting to take over the place mean they have to have you guys arrested?"

"Because of the one in the bunker," Bethany said. "Renard was the one at the bar, the one actually responsible for that death. If he's arrested, it'll threaten the blood guild's plan to take over The Authority."

"Oh, I don't care," Ardith said, waving off her mom's words. She charged forward, grabbing Dorth up in a huge hug, kissing her square on the lips. But something was wrong, and not just the crowd actively trying to break down the door. Something was off with Dorth. She could feel it in the kiss.

When Ardith pulled away, she tried to look her girlfriend in the eyes. "What's wrong?" she asked.

The door banged loudly from the crowd outside trying to break in. "Okay," Bethany said. "That's enough of that." She threw her hand at the door, sending just the smallest amount of power through the air to it. The door let off a crunching, grinding sound as the wood darkened, swelling outward from the wall as it did so. With a hiss, Brian jumped away from the door, shaking his arm.

"That's hot," Brian said.

"Yea, try growing up with her," Ardith said. "She has some funny ways of grounding people."

"Hey, I only used that fire cage once," Bethany said. "And I dropped it before you could burn yourself on it."

"My mother, folks. Super mom."

A weird sound suddenly came out of Dorth at that comment, somewhere between a laugh and a sob. Whatever it was, the sobs won out, as Dorth started to weep openly. Quickly, she placed her face in her hands, trying to hide the tears from the group as she turned around to face the corner.

"Hey," Ardith said. She came over to wrap her arms around her girlfriend, holding her close to her chest. "Hey, what's wrong?"

"My dad's missing," Dorth said, her voice barely above a whisper.

Chapter Thirty-Six
Power Vacuum

Ardith

"Your dad?" Ardith asked. She wanted to say that was a good thing. She wanted to celebrate that maybe, just maybe, the last obstacle in their way was finally gone. However, it was still Dorth's father. No matter what, Dorth still cared about him.

"They're all gone," Bethany said. "All the void mages. Every single one of them is missing. It was them. It had to be them."

"Them, who?" the doc asked. Bethany glanced over at him for a moment, seeming to not have noticed that he was there before. Still, he didn't seem to warrant any consideration to her as her words spilled out of her.

"Dan was actually right for a change. The blood mages kidnapped, or... Well, they've taken the void mages. Without them, I... I don't know what we're going to do. I mean, with the void mages gone, with the death mages gone or on the run, that just leaves..."

"The blood mages," Ardith said. "They're now the most powerful group of mages out there."

"And it's looking like they're already trying to take over. The Mage Authority was just the start, and even that they haven't quite managed to subjugate just yet. But, without the void mages, it's only a matter of time. Without the void mages, we're completely at their whim."

"What about dad?" Ardith asked.

"I haven't been able to reach him, not while on the run like this. There's not much information we've been able to find out. But with the blood guild out en masse in the city above, hunting the three of us down, it was easy enough to figure things out. There was only one batch of the missing persons posters with all ten void mages on it before those were stopped at the source. It's all the three of us now, everywhere, on every wall above. Air alerts, fire letters, you name it. If I know your father, he'll be hunkered down in the guild, trying to keep people calm."

"No, not... Not dad, TS," Ardith said, pointing back to the sleeping form of her father. "He's a void mage. He could help, if he could figure out how to use his powers."

"The last void mage," Bethany said. It seemed like that hadn't quite clicked with her while they were gone. "That might have gone into why they're pulling out all the stops to catch him. I was thinking it was about bearing witness against Renard, but, yes, you're right. He's a void mage. He could stop them."

"No," Dorth said. She pulled away from Ardith, no longer needing the support. Her eyes were red, though dry, and her sad expression was replaced by one of determination. "No, there's only one of him. He can't take on the entire blood guild. My dad couldn't even take them on, and I doubt they sent the whole group to grab him. I don't... I don't want you to lose your father like I did."

"We don't know he's dead," Bethany said.

"Yes, we do," Dorth said. "Yes, we do. There's no reason for them not to have killed him. He's gone, I know it. I... I feel it."

"On the bright side, at least we can be together," Ardith said, finally voicing her hope. "Not that I would have wanted it to happen this way."

"Yea, I know," Dorth said. "Maybe after we're done being hunted, though, yea?"

"Where are we?" Bethany asked, finally looking around at the clinic.

"It's a pure blood neighborhood beneath New York," Ardith said. "They were here before the construction and ended up being trapped down here."

"Well, that was rather inconsiderate of us. And the people outside clamoring to get in here?"

"Those would be the pure bloods. They got the wanted posters. We should get out of here before they manage to break down the doors."

"We can't," Bethany said, shrugging. "If we leave here, the blood mages will be on us in an instant. If they even knew this place was still down here, they'd be here already. Without that note, I wouldn't have been able to find you. I kept trying to track you guys, but all I was getting was 'around here somewhere'. Tracking isn't exactly a science, you know. Nothing is. Anyway, without actual tracks to go on, all I could do was look around here. Wait, what's wrong with Eric? Is he alright? Why is he asleep at a time like this?"

"He's not as bad off as he looks," Ardith said. She headed over to stand next to her father, gently placing her hand in his. His hand was still open on the edge of the bed, as if still holding the slip of fire paper. "He just teleported into a pillar. Lost a toe and has a broken ankle. If we can just get him to a light mage, he'll be fine. Of course, we can't do that, can we? Anyway, the doc helped him out."

"The doc?" Bethany asked. "As in a doctor? Like a real, medical doctor? I didn't think those still existed."

"Hey, don't look at me," the doc said, his hands up in surrender. "I just know some first aid and found some medical books a while back. I learned what I could. Mostly it's just scrapes and bruises, a few broken bones here and there. Anything more serious, well, there wasn't much I could do without the right meds anyway."

"Great," Bethany said. "So, we're basically surrounded, blood mages above, pure bloods down here, both ready to tear us up if we leave this room. The only one that has any hope of defeating the blood mages is injured to the point of unconsciousness. We could take the pure bloods, or at least some of them, but we'd probably need to kill them to do it. And, if we do manage to get out of here, we'd still have to carry a very heavy man in the process. Does that about cover it?"

"That, and the fact that I don't have my magic," Ardith added.

"And, if we don't stop the blood mages, they'll take over the world," Dorth said. "But, hey, at least we can be together, right? There's a bright side to all of this?" Despite her words, a fresh load of tears started forming at the corner of her eyes as she sniffled loudly.

"What if you just teleport to another part of the old city?" the doc said. "The place is huge. You could just find somewhere to hide out, away from the pure bloods outside. If they didn't see you coming in here, they wouldn't have known where to look."

"Except we don't know the city," Ardith said. "If we just teleport around, we could end up inside of a wall, like Dad."

"Plus, if the pure bloods don't think we're in here anymore, they might head up to the surface," Bethany said. "If the blood guild knew about this old city, they'd be on us already. They have this way of tracking that just goes far beyond anything I've ever heard of. The only thing that would block it would be..."

"What?" Ardith asked. She was surprised to see a look of shock, of hope, pass across her mother's face. Whatever she was thinking, maybe it was a way out of all of this.

"What about the bunker?" she asked. "When you were in there, when you went inside, he couldn't track you anymore. He tracked you to the bunker, but you were outside at the time. If we could just teleport right inside, they wouldn't be able to track us."

"That wouldn't work," Ardith said. "We can't teleport into an area with no magic in it."

"Woah, wait, what?" the doc asked. "There's a place without magic? Can we come, too?"

"Yea, that would be cool," Brian said. "Like a preserved section of history or something."

"Besides, the bunker was damaged, remember? Oh, and, uh, we kind of flooded it, too."

"Right," Bethany said. "Damn."

"Maybe we can create a new bunker," Dorth suggested. "That was the point of the water, right? We find somewhere that we can use, flood it with water, then send the water off. And, tada, we have an all new bunker."

"Except we'd need somewhere that was airtight," Bethany said. "And we'd need some way to purify the air. Plus, you know, food, water, a lot of consideration goes into a bunker like that. Only the conspiracy nuts had places like that back in the day."

"Dad's a conspiracy nut?" Ardith asked.

"No, he's... I think it was his neighbor, or his uncle, or something. I don't really remember. It was a long time ago."

"Yea, Mom, I know." Ardith shuddered once more at the reminder of her conception. "What about your dad, Brian? You said he had some machines he was trying to get working again. Is there anything like this air purifier thing that Mom was talking about?"

"I don't think so," Brian said. "I think it's mostly trains. A generator or two to power them. Nothing like a puritier."

"Of course, if Dad were awake..." Ardith started. She looked over at her father's sleeping form, wondering if he'd make it, wondering if he'd ever wake up. The pain shouldn't have knocked him out for that long. He should have woken up by then. But, then again, he was a recently awakened void mage. There wasn't much any of them knew about that sort of thing. An awakening can take a lot out of some people. Plus, you know, he was old.

"What?" Bethany asked. "What would he say?"

"Nothing," she said, shaking her head. "It's stupid."

"You know," Dorth said. "He told you what his quest was, didn't he."

"I--"

TS suddenly sat bolt upright on the cot, gasping heavily for air. His eyes, open farther than they should have been able to, scanned the room slowly before locking on Ardith's. "They're here," he said, in a low, raspy voice.

"Oh, Bethany," came a voice from the hall. "Come out, come out, wherever you are."

"Oh, crap," Bethany said. "They are here. That's Renard."

"How could they know we're here?" Dorth asked. "They were completely clueless before."

"So were we," Bethany said.

"Those stupid pure bloods must have sent word," Ardith said. "Or the posters were bugged or something."

"Can they do that?" TS asked. He seemed surprised for some reason.

There was a loud bang as something slammed heavily into the door. TS jumped down from the cot. He stumbled at first, shaky on the injured leg, but he seemed much more stable as he slammed his hand heavily into the solid door. He stood there for a moment, as if his very presence would keep the door closed, though Bethany's spell still held.

"Dad," Ardith said. "Are you okay?" She came over to his side, moving to help him stand, though he no longer seemed to need it.

"I think I'm fine," he said. "Just... I'm a bit... It feels like adrenaline is coursing through my body right now, only, you know, not."

"It's the power," Dorth said. "You're draining the magic out of the blood mages outside."

"Even through the wall? How is that... I mean, I'm not even trying to."

"It doesn't matter," Dorth said. "That's how it works. They're aligned against you, so you're automatically pulling their magic from them. It's filling the void inside of you. Depending on how powerful you are, you'll pull the magic until..."

"Until I die?" TS asked.

"No," Bethany said. She looked around at the group, the nine of them, including the three injured people in the cots. "With no training in magic, you'll have another awakening. The explosion... It'll kill everyone in here."

"Oh, is that all?" TS said.

Chapter Thirty-Seven
Blood from Air

Bethany

"What are we going to do?" Brian asked.

"We?" Ardith asked. "You're just a kid. A pure blood kid. If that door could open, you could just run out there and they wouldn't do anything. Just stay out of our way and you'll be fine."

"Not that she's threatening you or anything," Bethany said.

"We need to get out of here," Eric said. His words were coming fast, close together, making it hard to understand them. "We can't be here. We need to get out of here."

"Where are we going to go?" Bethany asked. "With the blood mages in the city, it's not just a matter of finding a new place to lay low here. We'd need to find a new place that they don't know about, somewhere that they can't track us with that... weird tracking ability they have. There's nowhere on Earth that we can hide from them for long."

"Another obstacle in our path to be together," Dorth said. She and Ardith were huddled together in the corner, holding each other as their end drew near. Seeing them there like that reminded Bethany of her own husband, lost out there, hopefully safe at the guild hall.

"What about the guilds?" Bethany asked, as the idea popped into her head. "I mean, yea, together they won't stand a chance against the blood guild, but that would at least slow them down, yea? They're trying to keep some semblance of a cover in place, trying to do this coup bloodless, or as close to one as possible. They'd have to drop their facade to attack the guilds."

"Yea, and they will," Ardith said. "Filthy bloodsuckers. They'd go to any lengths to take over the world. There's only one way to stop them now." She looked rather pointedly at Eric when she said that.

"The briefcase," Eric said, hitting his palm against his forehead. "It's... It's still in the bunker."

"Which is flooded right now," Ardith said.

"That shouldn't stop you," Bethany said. "You're a water mage. You should be able to swim through there and rescue this... briefcase? Really? The fate of the world rests in a briefcase? What's in it?"

"That's... not important," Eric said. He took a few steps away from the door, not seeming the least bit pained by his ankle as he did so. "Even if we had the briefcase, we have no way of delivering it."

"Well, we have a fire mage now," Ardith said, pointing to Bethany. "We'd just need the raw material. And we're in the middle of an old city, one that must still have some windows out there, right?" She looked over at Brian, of all people. "You probably know this city better than anyone here. Are there windows still out there? Intact? Like on the buildings even?"

"Would someone please fill me in on whatever the hell is going on here?" Bethany asked. She felt completely at a loss as the rest of the group seemed to be talking in code.

"Dad, you'd better tell her. If she's going to help..."

"Help what?"

"Inside the briefcase, the one I bought from the black-market dealer at the bar--"

"The deal that started all of this?" Bethany asked.

"Yea, right. Inside that briefcase is a nuclear bomb."

"Oh..." Bethany said. Her face went white as she started to feel faint. The old stories she grew up with, the tales of the bombs that could destroy the world a hundred times over, came flooding back to her. At the time, there weren't many left, held in the firm death grip of a small handful of countries that refused to give up the power to destroy the world. Still, even then, there were enough horror stories to give a girl nightmares. "But, how? How would one of those work with magic in the world?"

"It might not even work in one without magic," Eric said. "I never got a chance to check it. The case could be filled with rocks for all I know. I meant to check it at the bunker, but we were interrupted. Anyway, I'd need to build an airtight space, a box or something that we can send up to the asteroid."

"You're... You're going to blow up Apophis?"

"What? Really? Cool!" Brian said.

"But we'd need something airtight," Eric said. "That's where the glass and you come in."

"So, let me get this straight. You want us to go out into the city, grab a bunch of panes of glass off the buildings, hoping we find enough that haven't been smashed by the group of pure bloods that have been living down here for thirty years with nothing to do but slowly starve to death, while a bunch of blood mages hunt us down, so we can make a glass box to send a bomb up to the asteroid to blow it up, thus removing all magic from the world?"

"Well, when you put it that way, yea, it can sound a little nuts," Eric said.

"A little nuts?" Bethany asked. "A little nuts?"

"Uh, guys, not to break up a family quarrel right now, but is there a reason why the blood mages haven't already broken down the door?" Brian asked. He pointed towards the door, which hadn't made any sound since the large bang earlier.

The group all turned to the door together, as if they could see through the wood and drywall, all that was protecting them from the blood mages in the hall. It didn't make much sense to Bethany. They knew they were in there. They knew exactly how to find them. Why hadn't they just broken down the door and blasted away.

"Because of Eric," she said, answering her own question. "They can't just come in here all out because of Eric."

"I can... I think I can feel them out there," Eric said.

"You can," Dorth said. "You should be able to feel them exactly, if you were trained enough."

"You mean like x-ray vision?" Brian asked. He seemed to think the whole thing was awesome, despite the fact that they were all about to die.

"They're not going to just wait out there all day, though, are they?" Eric asked.

"Actually... Um... They can," Dorth said. "They can just wait out there until we... well..."

"Until I have another awakening and everyone in here dies," Eric said. "But, I won't, will I? Not that I want the rest of you... I'm just saying, if you guys leave, if you get clear..."

"There's too many of them out there," Bethany said. "Thousands of them, probably all outside the door."

"There's not enough room out there," Ardith said. "Not with the pure bloods out there, too. It's a narrow hallway leading out to the front of the building. But, yea, I guess the front of the building is probably packed with all of them."

"There's just...," Eric started. "If we're going to do this, if we're really going to do this, if we're going to stop the blood guild, there's just too much for us to do right now to stick together. We can't do half of it with the blood guild breathing down our necks."

"What about you?" Bethany asked. "Your ankle?"

"What about my ankle?" Eric asked. He looked down at the offended ankle, noticing the blood on his pants almost instantly. His face blanched a paler white than it already was. Slowly, he tested out the ankle, lifting his other foot to put his full weight on the injured one, even hopping on it a few times. "Seems fine," he said, shrugging, as he put his other foot back down.

"Yea, as arrogant and self-righteous as my father is... was... Um... Void mages really are great, aren't they?" Dorth looked down at her hands for a moment, leaning into Ardith more than she already was, as she visibly tried not to cry.

"It must have been all the blood magic you're draining from the mages outside," Bethany said. "Some part of you just automatically healed your ankle, is all."

"Great, so now that we know I'm alright, we need to split up. Ardith, you and Dorth head back to the bunker, grab the briefcase. It should be in the room across the hall from where you woke up. Brian and Bethany, you head out into the city, find those windows."

"Uh, teleporting inside this place? I don't think so," Bethany said. She shuddered at the possibility of teleporting into the middle of a building.

"Err towards the middle of the street," he said. "Brian, do you know of anywhere that the windows are intact?"

"I... I don't think so," Brian said, as if he were trying to rain on their plans. "Wait, maybe uptown, near the northern part of the island. No one ever goes all the way up there because it's too far of a walk. Not enough lights and the torches don't last that long."

"Oh, we don't need lights," Bethany said. She held her hand up in a fist, lighting it up with a bright, blue fire.

"So cool," Brian said. "Why did we never get a mage before this?"

"Because they're dangerous," the doc said. "And, well, because none ever came down here."

"And, I'll stay here," Eric said. "I'm the one they're after, right?"

"We're all on those posters," Ardith said. "You, Mom, and I. They're not going to just let us go all over the world right now. Mom's right, there's too many of them outside. They'll just split up and take us out."

"If we split up, they'll come after us," Bethany said, nodding her agreement. "And without you to block their magic, they'll block ours. We won't be able to teleport back here."

"Well... What about linking books? God, we're so close to this. We're so close to getting what we need to end the threat of them once and for all."

"No, we're really not," Bethany said. "We're so close to them ending us once and for all."

"Eric, your hands," Dorth said. She pointed at the man's hands, drawing the attention of everyone in the room, even the three injured men in the cots.

Eric's hands were glowing. It was low at first, but as soon as his attention was drawn to them, they spiked up considerably. They were already brighter than the low fire in the corner, causing the room to be lit up like it was directly under the sun, rather than several floors below it. His hands seemed to flash, to pulse with an internal beat all his own.

"What's happening?" he asked.

"You have too much magic right now," Dorth said. "You need to burn some of it off."

"That's the trick to not blowing up constantly," Bethany said. "Controlling the level of magic that your body normally contains. The more you use it, the less power your body feels like it needs to keep stored. Just... I don't know, shoot a blast off somewhere."

"What? Where? I don't want to hurt anyone."

"Uh, yes you do," Ardith said. "Send the blast through the wall. Try to target the blood mages. If we can take a few of them out, you'll be drawing less magic."

"Plus, it'll mean there are fewer of them to hunt us down if we get out of here," Bethany said. "I'd hate to advocate for killing, but if we don't, we're going to have another war on our hands. This one will be worse than the last one."

"I don't know," Eric said. "The last one brought us Ardith."

They both looked over to their daughter, the product of their one interaction, which had happened in the middle of the war with the death guild. She had to admit, that was one good thing that had come from the war.

"Ha," Eric said. "That's what it's good for."

"Huh?" Bethany asked.

"Never mind. Just, blast away? How exactly?"

Bethany, Ardith, and Dorth all jumped to give him instructions for how to send a beam of energy through the door. Their voices all converged, drowning each other out in a jumble of sounds. Eric just nodded at them for a while, as if he were actually hearing all of their words together. Once their voices faded, their explanations completed, he nodded one last time before turning around to face the door.

Bethany took a few steps to the side. In the process, she bumped into the cot that Eric had been in and flopped down to sit on it. The smell of blood suddenly surrounded her, though she felt it was rather appropriate given what they were about to do. What Eric was about to do.

Eric's eyes were closed, his breathing steady, as he seemed to be following Bethany's instructions. Part of her wanted to hurry him up, to get him to strike out, no matter how accurately, just to offload some of his excess energies. There was no telling how long he could hold the energy within him. There was no telling how long the blood mages would wait for their plan to work.

Bethany watched with bated breath as Eric's eyes flicked open. He took a step back, turning his body so it was pointed at the door. His hands were cupped together, the glow escalating as his excess power centered there. With a deep breath, Eric threw his hands forward, extending his fingers out so that his palms would flash forward.

"Sadoken," Eric said, or something along those lines, as he pushed his hands through the air.

"What was that?" Bethany asked, when nothing came forth from him. There was no spell, no movement of the energies from him. Whatever he tried to do didn't seem to have any effect whatsoever.

"Yea, I know," Eric said. "Would have been so cool if that worked, though, right?" He turned around to look at the group in the room, though no one seemed to mirror his enthusiasm. "Yea, I know. Not the time. Still, it would have."

"Try again," Bethany said. "No jokes this time. This is serious."

"Don't you think I know how serious this is?" Eric asked. "These people... From what I've seen of them they have no respect for life."

"Well, yea, they're blood mages," Ardith said. "They gain their power from blood, flowing through their veins, spilling from other people's. They may not be the death guild, but they might as well be."

"No, I mean mages, like in general. It's like a bunch of kids finding God's toolbox and playing with them like toys. No one seems to understand just how dangerous this stuff is. This magic is. That's why so many people have been dying. That's why someone has to take the dangerous toys away."

"So, then, do it," Bethany said. "The people on the other side of that door are the ones stopping you. The only way to get through them is to use their power against them. Send those beams of light through the door."

"But, that's just it," Eric said. "Don't you see? It's not just the people that don't care what they're playing with. It's the people that know exactly what they're doing and they do it anyway. It's the people that use this dangerous tool to destroy, to kill. If I do this... If I do this, am I no better than they are?"

"Yes," Bethany said. "Because you're doing it to stop them."

"No," Ardith said. "You won't be." Everyone turned to her, surprised by her words. "Killing them won't make things better. It won't make you better than them. It'll make you alive and them dead. You're right. Of course, you're right. I've... I didn't know what I really had until it was gone, until it was being used against me, trying to kill me. But, Dad, I'm here. I need protecting, because I can't protect myself. The ends don't justify the means, but without the means, there would be no ends."

"Worse," Dorth said. "This would be our end. There's always going to be someone trying to kill for power. The only way to stop them is to become them."

"Whatever you decide," Bethany said. She placed her hand on his arm, feeling the familiar strength in it, the reminder of the one month they had together, all those years ago. "We're here. We're not going anywhere."

"And that might very well kill us all," the doc muttered.

"If your plan works, if we can destroy Apophis, no one will ever use magic to kill again," she said. "Isn't that enough?"

"No," Eric said, shaking his head. "But it's the best I'll ever be able to do. The lesser of two evils, eh?"

He turned back to face the door, extending his hands towards it, his fingers out. Bethany wasn't sure what he was trying to do, what form the spell would take if he managed to get one off at all. All humor was gone from his face, all peace. He was a man, a good man, going to war.

The light in his hands glowed brighter as they started to shake. Bethany wasn't sure if they shook from the power flowing through them, the adrenaline no doubt coursing through his veins, or from a conscious effort on his part. Whatever the cause, it seemed to aid in his building of the energy in his hands, the brightness within only gaining power.

Bethany closed her eyes, blocking out the brightness before it blinded her. When she did, she could sense the flow of energy down Eric's arms towards his hands. He was doing it, actually draining his reserves as he threw it all into one blast, one spell, one outcome that could very well tip the balance in the fight against these blood mages. If he could do this, if he could kill enough of them with one blast, only to build up for another, they could win the war that the blood mages had so foolishly started.

And, yet, the power continued to grow in his hands, radiating outward with the light of the sun. Even with her eyes closed, Bethany could see it, could see his hands glowing there. They were shaking more than before, so much so that there was no way he would be able to aim the beam coming off of them. Whoever was on the other side of the door would get the full brunt of the blast, but so would the door. They might be able to get one or two in the blast, but the path between the two sides would be clear as soon as he did.

She was about to say something, to stop him, to draw his attention to this fact, but it was too late. Before she could take a step towards him, she could feel the power being released, could see the light suddenly die. Instead of a single, wide beam like she was expecting, though, she noticed what looked like literally a million fireflies shooting out from his fingers. They flew off, taking the light with them, as they pushed their way through the door, the walls, even the ceiling and floor as they tried to escape the room. Bethany was able to open her eyes just in time to see the last of them fly off.

"What was that?" she asked.

But, then, the screams started coming. It was just one or two at first, but they quickly escalated, drowning out any other sound that might have come. So many of the fireflies must have hit their targets, though there seemed more of them than there could possibly have been blood mages in the building, in the city, in the entire world.

Eric stood there panting, seeming oblivious to the cries of pain as they slowly died off. His hands were resting on his thighs and he was doubled over, as if trying to regain his strength after running a marathon. The spell must have taken a lot out of him, draining all the reserves he had pulled from the other mages. Bethany could no longer sense the magic brimming within him, and his hands had stopped glowing. If anything, they seemed darker than the rest of the room around him.

Bethany was about to stand, about to go to Eric and help him back to the cot, when suddenly a bolt of light came flying through the wall from outside. The holes that Eric had punched in the wall helped its passing, and it came through without any preamble. To Bethany, the bolt of light was slow moving, though she wasn't sure if that was the truth or just her perception of it. She felt like everything was moving slowly, the world practically standing still around her, as her mind tried to grasp the simple fact that the blood mages had struck back. Hard.

"No," someone shouted, but Bethany wasn't sure who it was, couldn't tell if the voice was familiar or not.

The bolt of light lanced through the air, narrowly missing Bethany, completely missing Eric, whom she would have thought the intended target. Her head slowly turned as it passed her by, heading deeper into the room. Heading for her daughter.

But it wasn't her daughter who had cried out.

Bethany was paralyzed on the cot as the bolt of light lanced through the air, straight for her daughter, unable to move, unable to think as the worst thing she could possibly imagine was about to happen.

And, yet, it didn't.

Dorth must have seen what was about to happen. She must have figured out what it meant much faster than Bethany had. And, better yet, she was right next to Ardith when it happened. Her cry of denial seemed to echo in the room, distorted oddly by Bethany's impaired perception and the holes in the wall. Dorth pulled Ardith closer to her, turning both of them just so in order to put her back to the bolt of light. Bethany feared that it wouldn't be enough, that Dorth's sacrifice would only allow for them both to die together.

She never once thought about Dorth's death or what it would mean to her daughter.

Chapter Thirty-Eight
The Empty Purse

Ardith

"No," Ardith said. Her word was a denial. Of what happened. Of what it meant. Of the very reality that would have allowed such a thing to have taken place. They were meant to be together, meant to grow old together, if they never found a spell to prevent aging. Even if they did, she knew the two of them would head off into eternity together. An eternity wouldn't have been enough for Ardith to be with Dorth. She had wasted so much time apart from her, worried what their fathers would have thought of them being together. Neither had even tried explaining it, to anyone, least of all each other. They were just meant to be.

And, yet, as Dorth died in her arms, Ardith lived on.

She hadn't seen it, had barely felt the spell as it took away her love. The only woman she had ever loved in her life. The only person she would ever love. All she knew was that the spell was aimed at her, perhaps even intended for her. But it was Dorth that had taken it, had stopped it from hurting her. The shock of the spell entering Dorth may have saved her from the pain. The look on Dorth's face as she passed was a smile, looking up at Ardith's face as she looked down at her.

"No," Ardith said again, refusing to acknowledge it, refusing to believe that it was over. That Dorth's life was over.

That her life was over. That she would even be able to live on, to live in a world without her.

Without Dorth.

It was unthinkable.

"No," she said again, this time louder, screaming at the universe, screaming into the void, screaming her pain and her fury and her rage and her loss.

And, suddenly, as she let all of that out, as her voice rent the air around them, she felt it. It was like a click, the flicking of a switch, though she had never actually used one. Suddenly, her magic was back, her affinity was back.

But it was too late. She already knew it was too late. There was no point, no reason, no way that it would help at all, in any way.

Because Dorth was dead.

"No," she said, one last time, the word lost in the air between her lips and her own ears.

And, then, there were arms around her, trying to give her comfort, trying to bestow strength. They did neither. They only reminded her that Dorth would never hold her again. She tried to shrug them off, to pull away from those arms, but she no longer had the strength to. Instead, she turned her head, the tears that were already threatening to drown her falling on those shoulders, the familiar shoulders of her mother. How often had those arms held her, comforted her. And, yet, they weren't the ones she wanted, the ones she needed, the ones she longed for.

"I'm... I'm sorry," came TS's voice from behind her mother, unbidden, unhelping. It was his fault. If he hadn't come into her life, if he had just stayed in his bunker, Dorth would be alive. And, yet, her rage was lost to her, when it would have had a proper target, when it could have been directed at a cause of her misery, if not the main cause.

But the world wasn't done with her, wasn't done causing her pain. The wall crackled as another bolt of light lanced through the air, once more heading for her, once more trying to claim her life, as punishment for the deaths that her father had caused. Part of her wanted it. Part of her wanted to embrace it, the pain, the death, the darkness. Anything to see Dorth again, or to just let the pain of her loss end.

However, another part of her didn't. Another part of her wanted the blood mages to pay for what they did. And it was that part of her that had access to her power.

Suddenly, she was surrounded by darkness, surrounded by her affinity. Ardith wasn't quite sure where she was at first, except that there was water everywhere. With her affinity back, she had no trouble swimming there, not even needing air as the water around her helped her, embraced her as part of it. However, as she floated there, she suddenly realized that she wasn't alone. Her mother's arm was still around her, still holding her close, still trying to lend comfort, though the strength of that arm was quickly fading.

Ardith pulled the power out of the water around her, quickly shaping it into a spell of water breathing and casting it on her mother. Bubbles flickered all around her as the spell took effect, enveloping the two of them in a pocket of air. It wasn't exactly the effect she was going for, but it worked out just as well.

"Thanks," Bethany mumbled, her voice in Ardith's ear.

Light flickered into the space in front of them, Bethany's hand aglow in the small space of the air bubble. The light played out across the area, across the room that they were in. Ardith quickly recognized it, knew exactly where she was and why she was there. It was the room that Dorth and she had been brought to in the bunker, had been asleep in when the mana was sucked from their bodies. Dorth was there too, her lifeless body having landed on the bed that she had lain in just a few hours earlier. Her hair floated in the water, dancing through it like it had a life of its own. Ardith's tears floated through the air, passing through the air bubble to join its brethren below.

"Come on," Ardith said, reluctantly turning away from her love. "We need to get that briefcase before the blood mages follow us here."

"Are... Are you sure?" she asked. "Are you sure you want to leave her here?"

"She was my world, and my world is gone. It seems almost appropriate to bury her here, with the remnants of the world that came before it."

Bethany swept her arm out around them, shining the light around the room until she found the door. With the two of them floating together like that, the pocket of air had only formed around their heads, leaving their arms and legs to help them move through the water. It was awkward, the two of them swimming together like that, something they hadn't done since before Ardith could remember. Through her affinity, she could remember it from the water's point of view if she tried. What the world forgets, water always remembers.

The two of them swam through the door, which was still open from earlier. However, the door across the hall wasn't. As they came into the hall, their momentum propelled them straight into the door, lightly slamming into it. It took some doing to open the door, slowly moving into place at the door handle and trying to turn it. When the knob refused to turn at first, Bethany slammed her free hand against the door, trying to use her affinity to burn through it. Ardith could feel that power, could feel the intrusion into the sacred space of her affinity. It rebelled, threatening to pull the pocket of air from them.

"Mom," Ardith called out, her voice bubbling through the water. "Stop."

Ardith pushed back away from the door, pulling her mother with her, getting her away from the door. Bethany was slow to recognize the danger she was in, slower still to understand its cause. The air bubble dwindled to the point of only being around Bethany, leaving Ardith to rely on her affinity.

It felt good, the raw power behind her affinity coursing through her veins again. Ardith reveled in it, despite the cost of its return. She wanted to scream, to rebel, to cast it aside, to be rid of it and its constant reminder of what she had lost. But there was work to be done, and more lives could be lost before the day was through.

Ardith swam free of Bethany's arms, heading back to the door. Instead of struggling with the knob again, she delved deeper into the realm of her affinity, into her realm. The water around her was also all through the latch and the lock of the door. Once she felt that, once she attuned herself to that, it was a simple matter to push against it, against everything.

And everything was pushed away from her. Her mother drifted further down the hall, taking the light with her. The open door to the room that would be Dorth's final resting place opened further. The debris from the ceiling that had been floating through the water and covering the floor drifted further away, clearing the area and returning it to its former, though still waterlogged, glory. The sound of the door opening, distorted though it was, quickly reached her ears as the door was pushed free.

Bethany's light quickly left Ardith as she swam into the room. While she could no longer see what was in the room, she no longer needed to. She was in her element, attuned to it, surrounded by it. All she had to do was ask and the water directed her to it. The direction came in the form of slightly warmer water. It was imperceptible to those that didn't have a strong affinity for water but was as obvious as the sun at midday to her. She swam down, letting her affinity be her eyes for her, letting the water around her tell her where she needed to go. Her hand bumped against the case, knocking it off the table that it was on, but she managed to grab it before it fell far.

Ardith couldn't swim while carrying the case, so she let her affinity move her forward for her. When she had returned to her mother, the air pocket was about to pop all together. Bethany was taking several deep breaths, preparing for the moment that she would no longer be able to breathe at all. Ardith moved forward, heading for her mother as quickly as she could in the enclosed quarters of the hallway. Just as the bubble burst, Ardith slammed her hand on her mother's leg and the two of them teleported away again.

Water rained down around them, but they didn't fall with it. For some reason that Ardith couldn't understand, they floated there in the air, in the same positions they had been in the water, for several seconds after teleporting back. It was just long enough for both of them to get their legs under them before they fell back down to the earth, as gravity reclaimed its power over them.

"That was..."

"Did you get it?" Eric asked, drawing Ardith's attention back to the room around them. Not much had changed. Everything had changed. Still, she held up the briefcase, showing it off to the room.

"That was quick," Brian said. He gave her a somewhat sad smile, but he couldn't keep his eyes off the floor by the cabinet, the pool of blood that was the only sign that Dorth had been there.

"For all the good that'll do us," the doc said. "We should just give them what they want."

"They want the world, doc," Bethany said.

"You missed it," he said. "They sent in their demands."

"And I already said I'd surrender, if I thought they'd stop at me," Eric said. "They didn't tell us anything we didn't already know. They want me, my head on a pike. If... If it would save my daughter, I would. But it won't. They won't stop there. Like Bethany said, they want the world."

"So?" the doc asked. "It's not my world."

"It is now," Bethany said. "They know about you down here now. Do you really think they'll let you live in peace?"

"What makes you think they didn't already know about us?" the doc asked. "They knew enough to send those posters."

"Those go out based on population density," Bethany said. "They wanted them everywhere, so even you're... what, two hundred people down here? That warranted a couple of posters. Usually, they have it one every ten thousand, but when it came to us they were desperate."

"And that's why we're not surrendering," Eric said. "The longer we can hold out, the longer they're stuck down here and not up there ruling the world. Maybe if we delay them long enough, someone will figure out how to stop them."

"What about your idea?" Ardith asked, gesturing to the briefcase. "You wanted me to get this thing, didn't you?"

"That was... That was before. I'm sorry, Ardith, but without..."

"Oh," Ardith said, her heart breaking all over again. "Right. Without Dorth, there's no way to get it up there."

"Then... Then let's blow it up down here," the doc said. "If they're as terrible as you say, if we're better off dead than under their thumb, maybe it's better that way."

"I like your spirit," Eric said. "Really, I do, but..."

"But, without an airtight room, we can't risk opening the case," Ardith said. "If anything in the world would be affected by the mana in the air, it'll be what's in this case."

"So, we make the room," Bethany said. "I'll head uptown, grab what glass I can. It'll be a bit difficult teleporting it back here, though. Ardith can come along, teleport back when we're ready and bring you and the case with her. Once the blood mages detect that you're no longer in here, they'll give chase and come after you. While they're figuring it out, we'll get the bomb set up and blow them up. If the pure bloods are all clustered down here, they shouldn't have too much to worry about from the blast. Assuming it's not large enough to take out all of New York. Though, with that crystal ceiling, it'll make things interesting to say the least."

"And, if we're very, very lucky, we might even be able to teleport out before the bomb goes off," Brian said. He sounded hopeful of the plan, though he was the only one.

"You're not going," the doc said.

"What? Says who? You're not my father."

"No, but if I let you go, your father is going to kill me. Besides, they'll have enough trouble getting themselves out of there in time. They don't need you getting in their way."

"You just stick here with us, kid," Eric said. "We're the bait. Much more dangerous here."

"But... But I know where to look for the windows," Brian said. "It'll take too long for you to find them without me."

"No, you don't," Bethany said. "You already said you didn't, just that it was more likely that they were still intact uptown. That's enough for us to go on. Come on, Ardith. We're wasting time here. We need to get things in place if this is going to work."

"Right," Ardith said. She nodded her agreement, though she wasn't sure she cared what was happening, if their plan succeeded. If they killed the blood mages, then she'd have revenge on them for killing Dorth. If not, well, then she'd be joining her love soon enough. "Here." She passed the case over to Eric, figuring it was safer there than out in the city. "Don't lose it this time, alright? Our freedom kind of depends on it."

"I won't," Eric said. "I promise. Be careful out there, you two. If they come after you, just teleport back here. I'm not sure how well I'll be able to protect you guys from them, but it's better than being out in the open, surrounded by blood mages."

"No, it's much better hiding in a hole surrounded by blood mages," Ardith said. "Even if we do this, even if we manage to survive, those wanted posters are still out there. I don't think blowing up all the blood mages in the world is going to help things either, whether or not they were trying to take over the world. But, then again, at least we'll have that silver you promised me, right? It'll be enough to live off of while we're in hiding, right?"

"Silver?" Bethany asked. "That's what this was about for you? Honey, you know if you had money troubles, you could have come to us."

"Uh, yea, about that," Eric said. He pulled the purse out from behind his back, tossing it on the bed. Instead of making a heavy thump, with the coins shifting inside, the sack just collapsed in on itself, falling flat. "Between the costs of everything and dropping it a few times, and then bringing it into the bunker... I... It's been empty for a while now."

"Ha," Ardith gave a halfhearted bark of a laugh. "That... That just figures. I guess it's typical for my dad to come into my life and completely destroy it, eh?"

"Ardith," Bethany scolded.

"No," Ardith said. "Let's just go."

Ardith took one last look towards the puddle of blood, the not so subtle reminder of what she was fighting for, before taking her mother's hand. She no longer needed the help teleporting, no longer needed the support of her mother, but the tie to her would help them stick together as the two of them teleported away.

Chapter Thirty-Nine
The Box of Glass

Eric

Eric was getting anxious as he waited for word from the women. He wasn't sure if the buildup of energy within him was just the adrenaline from the threat of the blood mages, the magic pouring off of them, or the impatience he was feeling. Or, perhaps, they were all part of the same thing. Either way, he paced the small room, trying to burn off the extra energy. But all that did was make it worse.

"What could be taking them?" Eric asked. He wasn't sure how long they had been gone, with no time piece and no view of the sky. It could be morning already for all he knew, but it could have just as easily been midnight. "They could already be dead, couldn't they."

"Can you tell if the blood mages are still outside?" the doc asked. "If they're there--"

"Oh, they're out there alright. But, there's so many of them, it's impossible for me to tell if one or two broke off from the group. Hell, half the guild could be over there right now, killing them, and I would never know."

"Want me to go check?" Brian asked.

Brian seemed eager to be of some kind of help, though Eric didn't know how much help he could be. The boy had no magic, no training, no weapons. If he even stepped outside the room, the blood mages would take him down without batting an eye. And it wasn't like Eric would know how to teleport them off after the women, even if he knew they were in trouble. All he could do was wait it out.

"If they're not back in five minutes, you might need to go outside," the doc said. "They gave us an hour, right?"

"How can you tell?" Eric asked, having forgotten the deadline part of the ultimatum. It hadn't been like they were going to give in to it anyway, so he didn't pay much attention. "Without clocks on the wall, I have no sense of time."

"Hmm, I got used to it," the doc said, smiling. "I've gone thirty years without a clock, twenty without a reliable view of the sky. It makes one... adapt."

"Well--" Eric's words were interrupted by a shout from outside.

"What have you decided in there?" came the familiar voice of the mage that had given the ultimatum.

Eric was relatively certain that, whoever it was, wasn't the blood mage from the bar. He had no way of knowing if that man was still out there. No way of knowing if he had managed to take him down with the initial barrage of magic missiles. No way of knowing if he had managed to kill anyone with them. They were blood mages, and something told him they were quite capable of healing their critically injured. His strange senses of the mages outside, the flow of magic off of them, was probably subtle enough for him to tell the difference between each of the mages out there. But he had no training on how to use it, how to tell one signature from another. If he had the time, if he could focus on any one of them out there, he might have been able to figure it out.

Perhaps that was why they only gave him an hour.

"We're still thinking," Eric called out to them.

There wasn't anyone in the hallway anymore, so their low voices wouldn't carry to the blood mages. The wall was like so much Swiss cheese and they could see through it quite easily, even without his ability. If... when the blood mages attacked, they wouldn't be able to take them unawares. But, then again, they wouldn't have to. There were far too many of them, only one of Eric, and it wasn't even like he knew what he was doing.

He tried to send off another barrage of missiles, for the third time since the women left. Again, he felt something move within him, some flowing of power from what he had figured was his internal reserves. But whatever it was wouldn't go all the way to his hands. He wasn't sure if there was some mental block that he needed to overcome, a fear of causing more death and destruction like the first one had, or if he had strained himself the first time around. Was he supposed to stretch first? Had he eaten too recently, or not recently enough?

"Time's ticking, pure blood," came the voice that Eric knew all too well.

Eric cursed the empty air between him and the blood mage that had started it all, the man that had killed that poor girl in the bar. He could picture the man's broad smile, gloating at him from around the corner and down the hall. As he did so, something seemed to click into place. Eric could sense exactly where the man was, where he was standing, who was next to him. The blood mage was in the middle of the crowd outside, standing in the entryway of the building. He could even see the smile on the man's face, broad, gloating, exactly like he had pictured it.

He tried once again to send a barrage of missiles at the blood mages, extending his fingers towards that face, flexing and tensing his muscles, forcing the flow of energy down through his arms, ever closer to his fingers, through them, to the target. A grunt came out of him as a single missile popped out of his finger. The missile flew freely, swooping in and out, down and around, out through one of the holes in the wall and straight down the hallway. The smile that was plastered on the man's face quickly disappeared as the missile slammed right into his chest, dead center mass.

As the man fell, hitting the floor with a solid thump, the mages surrounding him moved out of the way, giving the corpse space to fall freely. A few of them, those closest to him and those around the edges, all seemed to flutter out of the way, rushing off out of the line of fire. Eric quickly lost track of them as they rejoined the general mass, the large blob that was their collective energies.

After a few moments of confusion among the blood mages, the blob seemed to shift, to shrink around the hole of the donut it had become. The hole seemed to get bigger, but he could tell that the rest of the group wasn't getting thicker, more dense. Eric wasn't sure what the cause of it was, not at first. He just knew that he could no longer sense the people that had been there, had been standing in the gap that the dead mage had caused. Instead, he felt something else coming from that gap. Not through the sense he had discovered before. Not from feeling their energies emanating off of them. Instead, it was like the air itself was singing to him, was projecting something in the general feel of it. He had no idea what it was, blaming it on his inexperience with this strange new ability that he had suddenly gotten.

Whatever the cause of the mages disappearing from his senses was, it didn't last. Soon enough, the center of the donut filled back up, the general blob returning to its original form before anything happened. Whatever the blood mages had done, they no longer seemed the least bit perturbed by his killing of one of their own. Of course, from what he had seen of the man, Eric was of the impression that he was an asshole, and figured the group knew they were better off.

Then again, maybe not.

"So, can we take that as a no?" the man asked. The dead man asked. The dead blood mage that Eric had just killed asked.

"What? How?" Eric asked. He was too stunned to whisper his question, so his voice carried across the distance between them.

"We're blood mages, moron," he said. "Death doesn't stop us. Did you really think you killed any of us? Our numbers only grow. Nothing can stop us."

"Not while we're together," said the other blood mage spokesman, the one that had given him the ultimatum. The ultimatum that was now up. "And together, we will take you," he said.

"Oh, god, they're coming," Brian said. Eric looked at the boy, surprised that he knew that, surprised that he would be able to tell something that even Eric was hard pressed to discern with his strange senses. However, it quickly became clear that he was just voicing his fears, not any knowledge that he had actually gotten from any outside source. "We need to get out of here while we still can."

"Go where?" the doc asked. "It's the only door."

"You know, in my day, there was a thing called a fire code," Eric muttered.

"I'm pretty sure I'm older than you, young man," the doc said. "And all the other exits were blocked up years ago from debris, from your mage city above. Don't blame us for your mess."

The blob stepped into the hallway and Eric instantly reacted. Their proximity was like a trigger. He threw out one of his hands, trying to send another barrage of magic missiles down the hallway. Only two missiles flitted out from his hand that time. They whizzed through the air, slamming into the front two mages in the mass that was coming for them en masse. None of the others seemed the least bit deterred by their death, probably knowing that their demise would be short lived.

"We need to get out of here, we need to get out of here, we need to get out of here," Brian chanted, a mantra, a verbal defense for what was to come.

"If I could teleport you two out of here, I would," Eric said. "If I could just get them to stop, to take me alone and leave my family out of this, I would. But I can't. Like they said, nothing will stop them now."

"Then you might as well call me nothing," Ardith said.

As preoccupied with the oncoming storm as he was, Eric hadn't noticed when she arrived. The wind flowed around him as it tried to accommodate the new mass in the room. When he turned around to face his daughter, the wind blew her hair around, making it seem like she was in a windstorm rather than inside of a building. While she wasn't entirely smiling, not with the loss she was still suffering, she did seem almost better than she had when Eric had last seen her.

Ardith reached out to Eric, holding her hand out palm up, inviting him to take it.

"Come on," she said. "Mom is waiting for us."

Eric stood there for a moment, looking between her and the hallway outside. He could still feel the mages coming for him, slowly making their way down the hallway, none seeming interested in being the next to take a missile. The shadows they threw down the hallway reached the first set of holes in the wall. Eric knew the owners of those shadows wouldn't be far behind. Without thinking, without looking at the five pure bloods they were leaving in the room to welcome the blood mages, Eric reached back behind him, back towards his daughter, and took her hand.

The moment his hand touched hers, they teleported away. The familiar sensation of a hook in his stomach, pulling him along behind her, hit like a freight train, reminding him of why he hated that method of travel. Yet, as his feet found the ground beneath him, he actually welcomed the nausea that followed it, the motion sickness that always came from teleporting, no matter who it was that was doing it. That familiar sense told him that, no matter how much Eric changed, no matter how powerful he became, or didn't, he was the same person that had set out on this quest almost three days earlier.

"They're not going to be far behind," Ardith said, getting to business quickly enough. "Where's the... Damn it, dad."

Before Eric could ask what she was asking about, Ardith teleported away again, leaving him there in the middle of the street. Next to him was a large, glass box, easily ten feet tall and six to a side. The front of the box was missing, though another pane of glass was leaning against it. The edges of the top of the box were still glowing as the glass gradually cooled.

"Sorry it took so long," Bethany said. She was standing next to the box, her hands extended as if preparing to catch the last pane if it fell. "It was a bitch getting the panes off the building. Plus, you know, they're heavy as hell. We're mages, not bodybuilders."

Ardith teleported back to Eric's side, slamming the briefcase into his stomach in a single fluid motion. "Seriously, if your head wasn't attached..."

"Sorry," Eric said, clutching the briefcase to his chest. "I was a little preoccupied with the oncoming blood mages."

"What about Brian and the doc?" Bethany asked. "Are they going to be alright?"

"Who cares?" Ardith asked. "They're just pure bloods. There's plenty of them out there."

"Now, Ardith, that's not nice," Bethany scolded her daughter. "They helped us, didn't they? They didn't have to. I'd hate to think that the blood mages would punish them just for doing so."

"It's too late to worry about that now," Eric said. He walked forward, still clutching the case to his chest, to examine their hasty work. Eric hated the thought of using something so untested for the task at hand, to risk their one chance at removing the risk of the blood mages on this, but they didn't have much of a choice.

The edges of the box had cooled enough that their welds could be examined. There was no way of testing how watertight it would be without actually filling it with the water, but they would have to save that for when it was sealed up. Eric walked inside, testing how close the quarters were. While the place was just a little bigger than an old phone booth, which he had once seen in a museum when he was young, it seemed like he would have enough room to do the work necessary. He even propped up the case against the wall, using his stomach to pin it against there so he would have use of both hands. There were still a few inches behind him, allowing him plenty of room to maneuver within there.

"Yes, this will do nicely," Eric said.

"Oh, good," Bethany said. "Ardith seemed to think we should have gone with something smaller."

"It's just the case we need to protect from the mana," Ardith said. "Why do we need all that room? But it worked out anyway, 'cause the windows were that size already."

"We need the extra room... I need the extra room, because I have to be in here when I set the bomb."

"But... I mean... You know..." Ardith stuttered as she gradually realized what he was saying. "But... You can't teleport out of there, not after we've drained the place of mana. Or, were you thinking we'd drain the mana then you'd set the bomb and close it again, then we'd open the box and you'd step out?"

"We're not going to have that kind of time," Bethany said. "They should be tracking us even now. I've seen them at work, tracking you. We should already get things moving."

"Once you seal me in, you'll need to fill the entire box with water. Don't worry about me, I can hold my breath long enough to do what needs to be done."

"But... No," Ardith yelled. "No. I only just got to know you, and I didn't even do that all that well. Dad, you can't just leave me like this."

"It's always been the plan, Ardith. I've always known this was a suicide mission. The bomb needs to go off. It needs to go off at the right point, and not too soon or too late. I'm not even sure if the bomb has a timer or if it's just a push to blow kind of one. Heck, I'm not even sure if this really is a bomb. It could be a stupid iPhone 30. I won't know until I open the case, and I can't do that until the mana has been washed out of this box."

"How long will you have?" Bethany asked. "I mean, it's not like the bunker. The mana will seep through the glass, won't it?"

"Yes, eventually. It depends on how porous the glass is. I'd say it'll take at least a few minutes, maybe as much as an hour. If I was still going to Apophis, that might have been an issue, but we lost our air mage."

"No," Ardith said again. She ran over to Eric, wrapping her arms tightly around him, refusing to let go. "You can't just leave me. I can't lose you too."

"Now, now, Ardith," Eric said, patting her on the back. "You still have a father. While I have never met the man, and haven't really heard anything that I like, I'm still grateful for him. He was there for you when I wasn't. When I couldn't be. You've grown into a fine young woman, one I could be proud of. He must have done something right, no matter how much he got wrong. We're all just humans, doing the best we can. Now, come on. We need to get everything in place before we're surrounded again. Without the protection of that building, we'd be sitting ducks, and they're already all out of patience."

Slowly, Ardith backed away from her father. Tears were spilling down her face as she was faced with yet another loss. It broke Eric's heart to see that, to know that he was the cause of it, but it couldn't be helped. There were only the three of them there, and he was the only one that knew how to work the bomb, knew how to fix it if need be, knew how to build it from spare parts if that was all that was left. Heck, he could build the bomb from an iPhone 30, if he had enough nuclear material to work with.

"You take care of our daughter," he said to Bethany, smiling at her. "Make sure she knows she's loved."

"I will," Bethany said. Eric couldn't be sure, but he thought he saw a tear starting to form at the corner of her eye too. It could just as easily have been a trick of the light.

"Alright, seal me in. Once the seal is done, fill it with water. I'll signal when it's safe to drain the water. If my theory is correct, it'll take all the mana with it and it'll be safe to open the case."

"Right," Ardith said, nodding. "Wait, theory?"

"I've never been able to test it," Eric said, shrugging. "I've never met a water mage before."

"Come on," Bethany said, pulling the last pane of glass away from the side of the box. "Help me put this in position."

Eric leaned against the far side of the box, holding the case against his chest again, giving the two women all the room that he could to finish making the box. Ardith held the pane of glass in place as Bethany focused on her magic, melting the glass into one piece. The pane of glass didn't line up exactly with the rest of the box, leaning a little to the left. But it covered the entire wall, leaving no gaps for water or air to get through. The box didn't look perfect when they were done, but it didn't need to. Besides, they were going to be blowing it up soon enough. As the pane was melted into place, the excess bent away and fell off, forming a more perfect, less lopsided finished product.

Before the edges could cool, Ardith placed her hands against the wall of the glass as Bethany stepped out of the way. Ardith scrunched up her nose as she started to concentrate on her powers, letting the water flow into the box. It was weird, watching the box fill up, especially from the inside, as there was no real inlet of water. Even so, Eric had expected it to come in like it was coming out of a spout. Instead, it just sort of drifted up from the floor, as if he were gradually falling into the water rather than the water rising up to meet him.

The water was cold. Eric wasn't expecting that. He wasn't sure what he was expecting. The heat from the melted glass barely made a dent in it before even that went away. Eric shivered visibly in the water, his arms automatically going across his chest to protect his core against it. He tried rubbing the feeling back into his arms that had already gone numb. The briefcase, once again forgotten, fell to the bottom of the tank, hitting him on his foot when it bounced against the floor before settling.

When the water rose up past his shoulders, Eric started to take several rapid deep breaths, trying to prepare for the time that he would be completely submerged. The water needed to be in place inside the box, filling it completely, for long enough that all the mana would be absorbed by it. While he had no way of knowing just how long that would be, he originally calculated that it would take five minutes in a box twice as big as the one he was in. In preparing for that day, he had trained himself to hold his breath for seven minutes. Yet, without a watch, with no indicator for time, that would be the only marker for when it was time to drain the box. As his head went under the water, he had to hope that would be long enough, and that the water would be drained quickly enough that he didn't drown in the process.

Eric hated having his eyes open underwater, but there was no avoiding it this time, this last time. He had to watch for the arrival of the blood mages. Had to make sure that his family would be alright. Had to be ready to signal them when the time was right, when his air was starting to fail him. The two of them were standing next to the box. Ardith's hand was still on the side, though she was no longer concentrating on her magic, no longer pumping water into the box. Bethany was looking concerned, her furrowed brow so much like her daughter's, their daughter's. It reminded him of that one month they had been together, all those years ago. He smiled at her, trying to reassure her that he was alright, that he was fine with this being his death. As long as they managed to get away before the blood mages arrived.

But they didn't, they couldn't, because the blood mages were suddenly there. Front and center, Eric recognized the smiling face of the man from the bar. Renard. He cursed the name silently in his head, reminding himself not to waste any of his precious oxygen. The rest of the guild arrived soon after, each teleporting into the street in a large mob heading their way. All they were lacking were the torches and pitchforks. And, yet, these people were the monsters, rather than the innocent townsfolk trying to repel it.

Almost immediately, Eric could feel the power, the magic, flowing off of them again. He worried, feared, that the water wasn't doing what it needed to, wasn't pulling the mana from inside the box. It took him a moment to remember that he was still floating in that water, that the mana would still be surrounding him, just in a different form. His blood quickened, his adrenaline peeked, as his reserves were already overflowing with the energy that he could barely figure out how to use. This time, though, he couldn't even try to offload it at the mages, not without destroying the box he was in. Instead, he just tried to concentrate on using it to heat up the water. If there was too much mana built up within himself, no amount of water, no amount of time, would drain it from the box.

"Well, well, well, what do we have here?" Renard said. His wide smile made the words sound like he was already laughing at them, though it was clear he had no idea what they were doing, what they were planning. If he had, if any of them had, they would have done anything they could to stop them.

"It's not going to work," Ardith muttered to herself. Eric couldn't hear her, the water blocking out her words. But he could read them on her lips. He knew the despair that was already settling in around her. "But..." She looked up at him, looked right into his eyes, and Eric was surprised to find hope in them.

"I think these two have trapped our prey," said another of the blood mages. Despite how his voice was distorted by the water, Eric was pretty sure this was the other mage that had spoken before, the guild's spokesman. "How considerate of them. Are you hoping for some kind of leniency?"

"Not particularly, captain," Bethany spat at him. "We just thought we'd have a little fun before we died. Care to try next?"

This seemed to take the man by surprise, that she wouldn't cower at their very presence. That she would talk back to him in that way. Whatever the relationship between the two of them was, he obviously wasn't expecting resistance.

Ardith slammed her hand against the glass three times, claiming Eric's attention back from their oncoming doom. "It's now or never, Dad," Ardith called to him through the glass and water.

"Dad?" the captain said, sounding surprised. "Am... Am I to believe that this man, rather than your husband... Oh, that's rich. That's rich indeed. This certainly makes the whole case that much easier to close, doesn't it? Long lost father, and the old lover covering it all up. I mean, we don't even have to kill them anymore, do we?" He turned around to the mob behind him, as if expecting them all to back down, to turn from their killing ways. "But I guess we're going to anyway. Can't have you spinning any conspiracy theories in jail, now can we? I had enough of those from the rest of your team."

"What did you do to my team?" Bethany called out to him.

As she engaged in a screaming match with the captain, Eric tapped lightly on the glass, nodding to Ardith. She seemed relieved as she started turning inward again, using her affinity for water to pull it all out of the tank. It was slow at first, slower than putting it in to begin with. Eric tried to swim upwards into the bubble of air above before it was large enough for him to draw in. Once the air hit his lungs, the rest of the water seemed to disappear almost all at once, leaving him wet and gasping for air.

"Oh, god, the water," he said to himself, realizing that even with the water gone, his clothes were still soaked in it, still holding water that would contain mana. Even one drop of mana could be too much for the bomb, could short it out just as easily.

"Don't worry, Dad," Ardith said. She placed her other hand on the glass and leaned away from the box, as if she were trying to pull the water out physically. Eric was suddenly getting very thirsty as the air around him dried out. He half expected the box to fill up with steam, but even that disappeared quickly enough. When Ardith finally opened her eyes, all the water was gone.

And, more importantly, so was the feeling of power flowing off of the blood mages.

Eric smiled as he looked out at the blood mages that were surrounding him and his family. He knew they had no chance against the blood mages, not without his help. But he also knew they could take care of themselves, once the blood mages were gone. And that was the plan, wasn't it?

Quickly, he knelt down in the small box, trying to get the case set just right so he could work with it. The latches gave a satisfying click as they easily flipped open at his touch. He held his breath before flipping the case open, hoping against hope that the black market dealer hadn't cheated him, that the bomb he had been expecting was indeed inside. He wasn't disappointed.

As soon as the case was open, the timer on the bomb started ticking down from three minutes. Eric hadn't been expecting this, hadn't been expecting that the bomb would automatically start up. He looked out at Ardith and Bethany, wondering how to signal them that they should run without warning the blood mages. Ardith's eyes locked on his, noticed his panic, but she was still smiling.

"Don't worry, Dad," she said again. "I got this. A little present from my dying love."

Ardith reached out her arms, as if she were going to hug the box to her. But her hands were held palm up. The box shook a little at first before lifting up off of the ground. Eric looked down at her, surprised, amazed. He knew that she had trouble with elements other than her own, and this would most decidedly be air magic she was using. The box was rising slowly, too slowly for him to get up to the asteroid in three minutes, but he trusted her, trusted that she knew what she was doing.

"Ardith?" Bethany asked, finally noticing the two of them behind her. "What are you doing?"

"Finishing the quest. I think when Dorth died, she gifted me her affinity. That's how I got my magic back."

"Is... Is that even possible?" the captain asked, similarly stunned by what she was saying. He looked around at the rest of the guild hungrily, as if he wanted to drain each and every one of them for their magic.

"Goodbye, Dad," Ardith said, her last words to him, before she teleported the box, Eric and the bomb included, away from the city.

Chapter Forty
The Last Scientist

Eric

Eric's nausea and vertigo didn't disappear when he came out of the teleport. Instead, they only got worse as he continued to rise into the air. The city below him, the crystalline city of New York, quickly dropped out of sight. He had no way of knowing how quickly he was going, how fast he was rising up into the sky, but he was pretty sure it was faster than when the box was first lifting off the ground. The cloud layer came and went in just a few seconds, their fluffy whiteness dropping below him, leaving behind a dampness on the glass that was quickly swept away by the passing air.

He eyed the timer on the bomb, sitting on the floor beneath him. Barely a minute had passed since he opened the case, though he had no way of knowing how soon he would arrive at his final destination. All that time spent out in the world, wishing he had some way of marking the time. And now that he did, it was counting down to his death. As long as he managed to take Apophis out with him, as long as his mission, his quest, was complete, it would be a good death.

Eric sat back into the corner of the box, bringing the case forward between his legs so that he could watch the readout count down his last few seconds. Above him was Apophis. As night seemed to settle around him, it shined down like a spotlight, a lit up and all too tempting target for his vengeance. So many people had died since its arrival. From the loss of science. From the uncontrollable nature of magic. From the misuse of magic by people who had no right to have it in the first place. His intent clear, his focus locked on his target, with no control over the box he was in or the trajectory it went on or the timing on the bomb next to him. All that was left to Eric, the last scientist, was to wait. Wait for his death, wait for his end, wait for his victory.

With a laugh, at his situation, at his victim, at his nemesis, Eric reached into a pocket of his poorly dyed coat, pulling out the old harmonica he had found at the junkyard. He had never gotten around to washing it, to cleaning it of all the diseases that must have been festering within it. But, with his death already upon him, he doubted that a cold would do him in sooner. He blew through it, experimentally, but his dry lips and tongue made it difficult. Licking his lips did little to moisten them, but after a few tries his tongue started to work properly again. He managed to find a few of the notes he was looking for, managing to get out a simple song as he sailed through space.

Up and up he went, his propulsion slowly switching from the spell to pure momentum. While the energy, the radiation, the mana flowed out from Apophis, it was only when it was mixed with the air of Earth that it could be used to cast spells, only by the will of those few born with the gene to be a mage. Still, it was far too late for Apophis, too late to keep it from its fate. As the box approached the asteroid above him, Eric could swear that he saw a cavern that looked like a mouth, screaming in denial of that fate, long after it was sealed.

It was the last thing that Eric saw before the timer reached zero.

Many people around North America and some of Europe saw the explosion in the sky, though none knew what it meant. None, except of course, for Bethany and Ardith.

The ramifications of that explosion were slow to come to pass. Magic didn't disappear instantly; it lingered on the earth, slowly becoming a limited resource. Spellwork became restricted, taxed, and eventually rationed off by the quorum as they desperately tried to find a new source of mana. The damage was already done, though, even without the mages who continued to do their spells, thumbing their noses at the establishment.

What mana wasn't used by the mages soon enough dissipated into the ether, into space, into the crevices of the world that drew in such energies. With the cities built around the use of magic, the loss of it was devastating. Many people ended up getting stuck in the crystal buildings, too slow to evacuate when the call came through. The old cities, the ones built on the principles of science, had already been worn away by the decay that mana caused in the metals that they were built with. That just left the rural areas, the farmland that had long since been abandoned to the automated golems that had been harvesting the food. Those behemoths too gradually died off, leaving their lifeless husks to rot in the fields they once tended.

Panama City, after having replaced all their metal frames with crystal ones, had mostly made it out intact. The rich pure bloods who had claimed the city as their home managed to get a few more good years out of the good life before their reserves of wealth dwindled as the mana had. Without the nostalgic mages to bring in outside funds, outside goods and foods, the city needed to be abandoned, just as the rest of the cities were. However, most of the inhabitants refused to leave. People say that their spirits still haunt that city, waiting for their old wealth to return to them, the one lost when all the ones and zeros disappeared.

No one claimed the treasure trove of knowledge that was stored beneath the waters of a certain bunker south of Chicago. The damage caused by the arrival of Renard had little impact on the lower levels, save a small crack in the wall that had stayed airtight, despite running all the way down the seven stories. The water on the top floors gradually worked its way through that crack, eating its way all the way down to the cryotanks in the basement. That clean, pure, mana free water triggered an alert in the systems, waking their occupants from their long slumber.

None of the old machines ever came back online. No one knew how to fix them or how to make them anew. Even the knowledge of farming was lost to the ages, relying on the magical processes that were put in place to feed and clothe the world. Those that had survived the loss of magic were soon on their own, left to try to restore an old world that they no longer knew, no longer understood.

Fortunately, or perhaps unfortunately, someone soon came along to help them figure it out.

For magic wasn't the only thing that Apophis had brought to the world of man.

###

About the Author

Cassandra Morphy is a Business Data Analyst, working with numbers by day, but words by night. She grew up escaping the world, into the other realities of books, TV shows, and movies, and now she writes about those same worlds. Her only hope in life is to reach one person with her work, the way so many others had reached her. As a TV addict and avid movie goer, her entire life is just one big research project, focused on generating innovative ideas for worlds that don't exist anywhere other than in her sick, twisted mind.

Other books by this author

Please visit your favorite ebook retailer to discover other books by Cassandra Morphy:

Crowbarland Chronicles
In Time for Prom
The Awakening
Demons Force
Angels Innocence
Crowbarland Prep
Light Through the Windows
Last Scientist
Missing Mars

The Delnadian Invasion
Alien Fireworks
Alien Life
Alien Death
Alien War

Desparian Legacies
The Prophecy
Mountain Princess

Doors of Despair
The Mind's Door
The Door in the Sky
Gates of the Inferno
Heaven's Door
Door to Victory

No One Can Hear You
Travel
Train
Thrive
Fly
Spy